The Knife Thrower's Wife

SHEILA McGRAW

2020 White Bird Publications, LLC

Cover by Sheila McGraw

Published in the United States
by White Bird Publications, LLC, Texas
www.whitebirdpublications.com

ISBN 978-1-63363-477-0
eBook ISBN 978-1-63363-478-7
Library of Congress Control Number: 2020943245

PRINTED IN THE UNITED STATES OF AMERICA

To all the spouses who realized they were their family's "javelin-catcher" and took action to change the status quo.

Acknowledgment

I couldn't have done it without you!

A heartfelt thank you to everyone who took the time to read, critique, edit, make suggestions, or discuss my manuscript. An extra special thank you to Brantly Minor, for his wit, insight, and his unending forbearance and belief in this project. Plus, a mountain of thank yous to editor and friend, Joelle Yudin, the first to lay eyes on this book. And many thanks to all my writer and artist friends, and good buddies. Because of the risk of leaving someone out, I'm not naming names—you know who you are. I've treasured your input, comments, support, and (wink, wink) your many "likes" on social media.

Thank you to my sons James, Max, and Graham for their good-humored patience.

A giant thank you to White Bird Publications for giving ***The Knife Thrower's Wife*** a nest in which to hatch and take wing. Thank you to White Bird's team, including your skillful editors, and others, who work behind the scenes to turn words and art into a darn good read. And thank you especially to Evelyn Byrne-Kusch for taking a chance on me.

The Knife Thrower's Wife

White Bird
Publications

CHAPTER ONE

As my daughter, Sarah, would say, "WTF?"

Last night I was sick as a dog, and something else…not hallucinating exactly, but a vivid and lingering nightmare. My hideous illness—food poisoning maybe—had me in the bathroom most of the night, on my knees zorking, then lying on the cool tile floor, shaky and unfocused.

At least the physical nastiness seems to be over—but my bizarre fever-dream—there was heart-pounding, claustrophobic fear. A sliver of it comes back, and I'm immersed in the stifling dreamscape.

August in Texas, and I'm on an old, roofless stage edged by moth-eaten velvet curtains, spread-eagled and manacled to a plywood board like the female version of da Vinci's Vitruvian Man. *I wear a merry-widow, stilettos, and fishnets, a getup worthy of the cover of a vintage, hard-boiled detective novel, and most certainly not my style. Downstage are papier-mâché comedy and tragedy masks, their expressions more Edvard Munch's* The Scream *than court-jester.*

I go back to sleep and spend the morning in bed recovering, then haul myself, still drained, to the sofa. I polish off the afternoon by binge-watching a TV reality series about detectives solving cold cases. Austin is away on a business trip, and I text him, *How goes your trip?*

He calls instead of texting. “The trip’s okay, getting lots of work done. But darlin’, Monday is your birthday. We’ll do the usual; okay?”

“Aw, you remembered.” I smile.

“Of course I remembered.”

I’m not sure how to address his statement because he’s forgotten my birthday several times. To ease the stress, I came up with *the usual*, which is dinner at a nice restaurant and sometimes a token piece of costume or crafted jewelry. I err on the side of gracious. “Looking forward to it. I should mention, though; I was pretty sick last night.”

“You want to cancel?”

“No. Not a chance. It’s only Thursday. By Monday, I’ll be fine.”

“Okay, I’ll be back late Sunday. Love you.” *Love you* is the equivalent of goodbye for Austin, and he hangs up. I notice he didn’t ask about my illness.

Hearing Austin’s voice brings on the recollection of more of my nightmare. He was in the dream.

The sound of a gathering crowd penetrates the drapes, and Austin, tall and handsome in a tux, stands in the wings. Thank God, I think. He will get me the hell off this ridiculous contraption. As I wait, sweat stings the welts on my wrists and ankles raw from leather ties that tighten when I struggle, like the Chinese finger-traps we played with as kids. My exposed flesh is broiling, although mercifully, the sun is edging lower, soon to set. Daggers materialize on a table, along with a faded banner touting The World’s Greatest Knife Thrower, which sends tiny, hairy centipede feet of fear whispering up my spine. On the horizon, inky clouds drop lightning bolts. One-Mississippi, two-Mississippi. At seventeen-Mississippi thunder rumbles—seventeen miles out.

What a weird dream. I shiver and turn back to the TV. This ten-day trip is one of Austin's longest. Usually, they are two or three days. I give up on the TV and slide between the sheets early, around nine.

I wake later than my usual spontaneous time of seven, and amazingly, I'm well—as if I were never sick. I pull laundry from the dryer, fold and put it away, then change the bed. Ahhh, nothing like clean, fresh bedding after being sweaty, sickly, and smelly.

I fall back onto the bed and roll on my side, prop my head with a pillow, and notice, as I have a hundred times or more, a watermark on one of the drapes from rain through the window. The stain is something I've meant to fix, but there's no point when the entire master suite needs overhauling. The room's taupe color scheme, worn carpet, and drapes with old-style valances, is tired and dated. We bought this house when I was pregnant with the twins—their 25th birthday was last month—and the kitchen is the only room we've renovated.

I note the stained curtain again and reproach myself that new drapes would be a good start. However, installing new drapes only to later have the place swarming with painters and guys who create plaster dust would be silly. I suppose I could go the do-it-yourself route, hauling out drop sheets, paint trays, and rollers. However, the challenge of getting Austin to agree on paint color choices, expense, and so on, fills me with dread. Maybe I still don't have my strength back, or at least not enough to support an enthusiasm for rehabbing.

For some reason, the rain mark, maybe its shabbiness, brings on more of the nightmare. In it, I finally get to view our location.

The curtain slowly opens to reveal a scruffy nomadic carnival set in a drought-blasted farmer's field. Into the distance, the seared earth has split like God's craquelure, while closer in, the ground is being pulverized by boots and sandals. Dust devils whirl the loosened grime up into the crowd, where it settles in sweaty wrinkles and creases, reminding me of the crosshatched shading of dry-point etchings.

"Enough," I say aloud. I put the nightmare out of my mind as Beav, our longhaired tabby, hops up and head-butts me. Ten years ago, the twins scooped the kitten from a neighbor's litter and brought him home. They named him Beaver, thoroughly delighted with their naughty pun.

Showered and dressed in my uniform of jeans and T-shirt, I head to the kitchen and note the atmosphere is muggy and a bit musty. Damn. Fiddling with the thermostat is for naught. I call the AC guy.

When I step outside to run errands, the weather is drizzly and surprisingly chilly for spring in Houston, and I retreat indoors for an umbrella and coat. As I open the hall closet, a sliver of red winks from the breast pocket of Austin's jacket. A jewelry box. Like a kid who finds the Christmas stash, I guiltily take the box and open the hinged top. Inside is a gold Cartier wristwatch rimmed with diamonds. Holy shit! I snap the lid shut and shove it back into the pocket then take a step back like there's a tarantula in the box instead of an expensive timepiece. My feet seem stuck to the floor, and my fingertips stray to my lips.

My birthday gift, but far too expensive; I'd guess twenty grand or more. Besides, whatever fantasies I entertain of redecorating, repairs on the house and cars have gone untouched, and our monthly expenses are killing us. Hell, I have guilt pangs over buying art supplies for my work. Austin works partly on commission, and maybe he made a great sale and is about to score a windfall, but he wouldn't keep that under wraps. He would have bragged. And while he usually buys items that suit me, the watch is far too blingy. I snort laughter as I visualize wearing gold and diamonds, working with pastels or acrylic paints, or digging in the garden.

My fingers creep back to the red box, and I open it again. Something is attached—a pendant in the shape of a tiny gold motorcycle, the sort of jewelry that girls collect for charm bracelets. Austin loves his Harley, but riding isn't something we do together. Would he like to? Perhaps I should tag along on his out-of-town trips. In any case, the watch is way over the top. Somehow, I'll have to talk him into returning it to the store.

Heading to my car, there's an odd sound like a whimpering baby, which upon investigation is coming from the pool's pump, no doubt an expensive sound to fix. Damn. As I drive to the store, a segment of the nightmare returns, and I get a look at our audience.

They stand shoulder to shoulder. Their tanned and sweaty faces remind me of crates of brown eggs beaded with condensation from being left out of the fridge. Smirking men size me up while the scrub-faced women shriek at Austin, who is basking in their adoration. Carnival noise—screams, calliope music, and laughter—clash in my ears, go blunt, and drift away, as sound can do outdoors. I desperately hope the storm will arrive fast enough to cancel this ludicrous show.

There is a foul smell. From my elevated position, I can see that what was once a pond has become a dry dip in the field. There are bleached cattle bones and a dead longhorn. The creature's head is at an unnatural angle, with one horn jammed into the ground. A wake of vultures rips at the carrion.

After visiting the liquor and grocery stores, I return and unpack the bags, then head to my studio, where a disturbing tableau awaits me. Stuck in the wall is my biggest butcher's knife, and the merry-widow from my dream hangs by a shoulder strap looped over the blade. Blood spatter is drawn in scarlet oil pastel, as if sprayed from a chest wound. My castoff fishnet stockings lie flaccid on the hardwood resembling shed snakes' skins, next to stiletto-heeled shoes, one tipped on its side. This is my handiwork. A chill runs through me; my sleepwalking is back.

How did I do this? Surely, I wasn't sleepwalking and throwing knives. I yank the blade from the drywall and stab the sheetrock a few inches from the first jab. Surprisingly, with almost no effort, it sinks into the drywall and stays put. Ah, so this tableau was conceptual, an art installation using some elements from the dream. No violence intended. Strangely, I'm inspired. A scene from the nightmare might make an interesting subject for a painting.

I scrub the pastel with mineral spirits, leaving a pink stain, and I hide the knife gouges and the pastel's lingering mark by blue-tacking one of my old illustrations over them. I gather the items, which are Halloween relics from long ago, and put them in the box labeled *costumes*, at the back of my bedroom closet where they belong.

As I return to my studio-office, I stop in my tracks as the rest of my nightmare comes barreling in.

Austin abruptly turns and throws two knives that stab the board on either side of my neck. The impact reverberates, shaking me to my bones. The crowd cheers. My husband. Really, who is this guy? Evidently, he is no longer a middle-class suburban husband, salesman, and dad of grown twins.

A shiny red apple appears in his hand, and he strides to me and places the apple on my head, his expression menacing. I think, "You're doing the wrong trick. The apple trick is for a bow and arrow, not knives!"

The audience is eerily quiet, and I sense seething bloodlust. Austin balances the dagger by its blade, pirouettes, lets it fly, and halves of the apple fall at my feet. The blade's quivering stops. I am relieved, but then there is intense pain. Blood runs into my eyes, tinting the landscape red.

Finally, lightning cracks open the clouds to release their burden, and the rain thins my blood to a watery pink. Petrichor and the electric-burn smell of ozone displace the greasy, sugary midway smell, and stink of rotting cow. The crowd goes mad, cheering the knife thrower and the downpour. And Austin displays a self-satisfied grin, a grin I would typically dutifully return, but this time I don't. I shout over the thunder and the cascading rain, "For an NRA card-carrying crack shot, your aim stinks ... or did you deliberately hurt me?"

Chapter Two

Trix calls, and I picture her in her downtown loft, lighting a Gauloise cigarette. “Hey, girlfriend.”

“Hey, to you too, Trix.” Trix and I met in college nearly three decades back. I studied commercial art while she studied fine art and art history. Her appearance hasn’t changed much since then and runs to Goth catwalk-model—thin, pale, and intense. As an artist’s model, she’s an Egon Schiele subject. The fated expressionist painter would have drawn her in black Conté with a splat of orange watercolor on her short, vertical hair, lots of reckless eyeliner, and a burgundy smear on her lips. Trix is a single, chain-smoking, successful gallery painter. Her demeanor is edgy and sophisticated. We are different, but we truly click.

“Your birthday’s next week,” Trix says in her smooth contralto, with a lilt suggesting irony. “Doing anything to commemorate the egregious and relentless passage of time?”

“Going out with Austin for our standard dinner date, but—”

"But what?"

"I don't know what to think. I just found a ridiculously expensive watch in a jewelry box in Austin's jacket. Sometimes he buys me jewelry, but nothing so crazy-lavish."

"Sounds to me like he's trying to pay you off."

"For what?"

Trix grunts. "For his dickheadedness. He's got a guilty conscience."

"Whoa. Austin can be a pain in the butt, impossible, stubborn, but a dickhead?"

"Actually, shiny-balls-syndrome might be the diagnosis."

I blurt laughter. "Shiny balls…what? His balls are shiny?"

"I saw it on a trivia show. When turkeys get unruly, the farmer distracts them with baubles. For some reason, they can't take their eyes off the objects, and they calm down. Austin will distract you with the bling, and you'll forget his chronic douchebaggery."

"Surely, Austin wouldn't be that calculating."

"Julia, he's a guy and a salesman. Utilizing shiny balls is an instinctive behavior for his type. When I think of you as a couple, I can believe the saying that opposites attract because you're nice, and Austin…well, not so much."

"Now I feel guilty. Let's not bash Austin, okay?"

"Hey, my opinion is not only based on what you've told me, but also what I've seen."

Trix is referring to a time near the beginning of our relationship when Austin got physical, and I had bruises. Ever since then, through the years, my mission has been to avoid provocation. I found relief in my role of rationalizing that I was calming the waters, keeping the peace. But a painful thought creeps in, that maybe I've surrendered my power, or worse, I was manipulated into giving up my power and even my autonomy.

Changing the subject, I say, "Well… I had a crazy

nightmare, and I sleepwalked."

"What? Do tell!"

I relate the dream and add, "The carnival in the dream was in a farmer's field in Hill Country, where we visited some friends when we were first married. There was a drought. Cattle bones were all over the place, and there was a dead cow, sort of dried up. What a stink."

"Did you sleepwalk outdoors?"

"No, thank God, but in my studio, the merry-widow was hanging from a butcher knife stuck in the wall, with red pastel for blood. I couldn't get all the pastel off, so I covered the stain with an old drawing. Clearly, I roamed outside the bedroom."

"Why hide it? It's cool." I detect her smile through the phone.

"Mmmm-no. Too embarrassing."

"The merry-widow and fishnets…you've got the body for it, Julia."

"Yeah, right," I say skeptically.

"You told me about your sleepwalking as a kid and the awful dog episode."

"I felt terrible. Still do. It was horrifying waking up in the street in the middle of the night. There was so much blood. I barfed up my spaghetti dinner." I can feel my face darkening with horror and embarrassment at the memory.

"I know…even I can't eat spaghetti around you."

"And speaking of being sick, I had a rough night, spent in the bathroom. Ugh. I'm okay now, but the illness was probably what caused the dream."

"What made you sick?"

"I'm not sure. I drank some wine that might have been old."

"Ha! That's a first, an illness from wine that's not a hangover."

"Yeah, strange. Not like any hangover I've ever had. More like what I'd expect from a napalm and kryptonite cocktail. In any case, I haven't sleepwalked in decades, and

I hope it's a one-time thing. But the dream was so real; I can still visualize the whole thing so clearly. I'm considering painting a scene. A dreamscape."

"Now, you're talking! Remember way back, when you painted for fun? You have a ton of talent. Life's too short. Carpe fucking Diem, honeybun." Her lighter flicks.

"Finding time might be tough. I'm pretty busy. But I'll maybe give it a shot, okay?"

"And welcome Austin home in the outfit from the dream, and it probably won't be knives he'll throw at you if you get my drift."

"Might be a good idea. These days I can't seem to get within ten dick-lengths of him."

She laughs. "I gotta run. Next week, if you can get into the city, I'll buy you a birthday lunch."

"Thanks!"

I concentrate on bookkeeping for an hour until a cheerful "Hellooo!" signals the arrival of next-door-neighbor Lucy, letting herself in the back door. As usual, she's carrying baked goods, this time chocolate cookies. In our subdivision, Lucy is my closest friend and coffee buddy, and as the saying goes, 'she isn't ashamed to eat,' a trait that has altered her appearance over the years from svelte to zaftig. Lucy is a gorgeous, radiant, spongecake Renoir model. Her fleshy body spills from low-cut, gauzy clothes, and unruly, wavy auburn hair cascades over her shoulders.

She hikes her bottom onto a stool at the breakfast bar. "Eat," she insists, pushing the cookies toward me, then asks, "How are your kids?"

"They're fine. I'm a bit concerned about their slothfulness, though. Yours?" I pour coffee into two mugs and slide one across to Lucy.

"The same. Lazy brats." She laughs. "Did Sarah get more tattoos? I saw her the other day, and she's the illustrated girl."

"Don't think so..." I bite into the cookie. "Remember how perfect they were when they were little?"

"Yep." She jabs the air with her cookie to emphasize her words. "We bent over backward to keep them from getting scarred or messed up, and then they go out and get some pretty bad art etched into their skin."

I lean forward with my elbows on the counter and smile devilishly. "You sayin' you think leopard spots and black roses dripping blood are bad art?"

"Yep." Lucy pauses. "The kids have changed. They're not tough, exactly, more like they're jaded."

"Remember how we were, trying to squander our youth and innocence, get rid of our vulnerability? They're like we were, and they're still tender and lovable under that grown-up scaly veneer." I break off a piece of cookie and nibble.

"They're like M&Ms, crunchy on the outside, soft and sweet on the inside," Lucy smirks and starts on another cookie.

"The twins were five when Austin's mom died, and they fell apart. I wonder if they'd still react like that now."

"What do you mean, 'fell apart?'"

"When his mom died, both Bryan and Sarah insisted on sleeping in my bed. They'd go to sleep crying and wake up crying. During the day, they'd cling to me like those toy koala bears with the Velcro arms. Their grief lasted months. It was bittersweet."

"That's heartbreaking." Lucy makes a sad pout as she pours cream into her coffee.

"When they were little, we did so much together; crafts, baking, splashing in the pool, sports, watching Sesame Street. Where the hell did I find the time?" I chuckle.

"How's Austin?"

"Traveling on business pretty continually."

Lucy raises her eyebrows. "That's never changed. He was even away when his mom died."

"True." I nod. "He nearly missed her funeral."

"Are your twins making any headway toward moving out?"

"Not really." I sigh. "But, just wondering…if we allow

moochers to mooch, can they be called moochers?"

"No kidding, Julia. But it might be because they're part of the snowflake generation. The era of trophies-for-everyone."

"Willie Nelson could have a new song, Mama, don't let your babies grow up to be snowflakes."

"No shit. Especially in Texas. They're liable to melt." Lucy smiles. "The app your twins are inventing. What does it do?"

"Something to do with finding local, live music, which means they're out a lot at night, talking to the kids who go clubbing."

"Right. I want their job. I don't understand our kids. I was aching to leave home. Maybe our kids need to be warehoused longer than we did."

In our community, boomerang children are an epidemic. Like my twins, Bryan and Sarah, the others left for college, graduated, worked a year or so, and then returned like echoes. They inhabit their childhood bedrooms and partake of parental perks while flexing their youthful arrogance, scorning our electronic ignorance, our ideals, and taste. Apparently, the sentiment, *You can't go home again*, doesn't apply to some generations. Lucy finishes a cookie and starts another, then pats the countertop. "Can you give me the name of your kitchen guy? I'm going to remodel."

"Sure. I'll email the info to you." Rehabbed three years ago, the kitchen renovation transformed the builder's grade cabinets and appliances into a chef's paradise, with stone countertops, high-end appliances, all the perks. And thrifty me, I saved the old cabinets for the garage and my mini-greenhouse potting shed.

"I love your kitchen. I can hardly wait."

"My fantasy was gourmet meals and parties of all kinds, but none materialized." As if the parties should have somehow magically happened.

Lucy notices, and says, "Don't say stuff like that. Parties ain't rocket science. Just invite some people over. So, what else is new?" I relate my nightmare, and she grins. "Well, that's how relationships work. Our job is to be our man's support system, and we better look cute while we do it."

"Surely, there's more equality in our relationships than that."

"Forget equality. I'll tell you what feminism got us." She smiles thinly. "Give men science, and they fly to the moon. Give women science, and we get boob jobs, Botox, and in-vitro fertilization."

I lean my forearms on the counter. "Or maybe, give men science and women end up with boob jobs and all that." We snicker. "On my run the other day, I saw the guy at the end of the block puttering in his yard."

Lucy starts on another cookie. "Yeah, Paul. Downsized."

"Damn. Hope he finds something."

"Nah, he won't. He's too old. The big firms are all hiring kids because they're cheaper and computer literate. And the longer he's on the market, well, he'll be forced into early retirement. Hope he's put aside some cash." She guffaws. "So far we're safe, but if Earl got fired, I'd have to kill him and collect the life insurance."

"Whoa! Drastic." Glancing at the clock, "Hey, I have to get to work, okay?"

"No problem," she says and lets herself out. At my drafting table, I watch her stroll home. She turns and smiles, and with my cell phone, I snap a photo of her holding her platter, her house in the background. Lucy, queen of suburbia, so sure of her life. Is her view overly simplistic?

I spend the day working on an illustration of grapes for a raisin package. At this point in my career, I'm capable of painting a scene from my dream, time permitting, of course. Will Austin be upset if I portray him as the knife thrower? Maybe he'll like the depiction. However, there's barely time for my household basics and work, but what the hell, perhaps I'll give it a shot. Carpe fucking Diem, indeed.

Chapter Three

Saturday, just as the young, fit pool guy arrives, Lucy appears bearing peach cobbler. I show Pool-guy the pump, which is now sounding a death rattle. The pool came with the house and was once the center of our social life for cocktail parties, barbecues—celebrations of all kinds. Over the years, it has fallen into disuse but still requires constant upkeep.

Pool-guy has a natural manly grace, unaffectedly sexy. Lucy pulls two barstools to the kitchen window, loads plates of pastry, and places mugs of coffee on the windowsill. We sit and watch him work. He's about the same age as my kids, and I suddenly fiercely wish the twins had jobs like this, to demonstrate initiative and a work ethic, to have their own money and perhaps conjure some dreams and goals for their future.

Lucy winks at me, "I saw him check you out."

"Yeah, right." I pause eating cobbler and sipping coffee. "So, is this how it happens?"

"Sure, why not?" She chuckles. "First, you offer him lemonade."

"Wearing?"

"A tiny bikini with a sheer cover-up. The cover-up shows you're not desperate."

"Or too slutty." I cringe but smile self-consciously.

She dishes more pastry onto her plate. "Make small talk, flirt a little," she demonstrates with a hair-toss and a corny come-hither pose.

I snort, "That's so, um, Mrs. Robinson," and after a pause, "Wait. Have you ever...?"

"Never!" She appears scandalized, but her color goes Pepto pink, and she adds, "Okay. Just a couple of times." My jaw drops, but unfazed, she continues, "There was a cute plumber…" She trails off, lost in a memory.

"What? Please continue."

She's slightly startled, being brought back to the present. "It started as retaliation for Earl screwing the babysitter. After that, it was pretty easy."

My hand strays to my mouth in disbelief. "Babysitter? Not little Mandy from around the corner—pigtails?"

"She's the one. They were having sex in Earl's SUV at the grocery store parking lot when a security guard caught them and ratted them out to her parents. She tried to say it was rape, but she was nineteen, plus there was no alcohol or drugs involved, and Earl got the store's security video. There was Mandy, on top, bouncing away. No coercion there. Our only two rules are condoms, of course, and full disclosure. No secrets. Otherwise, we do what we want with whomever we want. Anyway, later. I've got a Neighborhood Watch meeting in an hour." She hops off the stool and picks up her platter.

I walk Lucy out, and the pool-hottie calls me over. Unidentifiable parts are spread on the pool deck as if a child dismantled an old-fashioned mechanical clock to see why it ticks. "Are you sure you can put it back together?"

"This thing is an antique." There's a hint of disdain in

the remark, what I assess as youthful superiority. "I can fix it, but it'll be temporary." He hands me his quote.

"Yes, the pool and equipment came with the house." I hate how apologetic I sound, and I pretend to concentrate on his quote. "Your price is about what I expected," I say, hoping I appear boss-like.

As I head to my studio to write a check, he follows me inside and asks to use the restroom. I point him in the right direction. Why did he enter the house when he knows there's a bathroom next to the outdoor shower? Is it a ploy on his part? Or has my conversation with Lucy about sex with visiting workers influenced my thoughts?

If I invite him to stay a while longer, for a beer. Yes, of course, alcohol to break down inhibitions, but how do you go from having drinks to romping in the bedroom? There could be a touch, bump up against each other, or come right out and say something like *You're so hot*. The porny plot embarrasses me. Someday I'll have to ask Lucy how she managed her encounters. He loiters at the studio door, and we make eye contact. If I want to take this further, this is the moment. Instead, I hand him the check, and in a motherly tone, remind him to take all his tools.

I head upstairs to look in on Sarah and Bryan. Her bedroom smells of body odor, morning breath, and whatever she's off-gassing through her pores: alcohol, weed, junk food, or something else unhealthily pungent. Black cloth Sarah draped over the blinds makes for near-impenetrable darkness. My eyes adjust, and I make out her pale form against black sheets. She's wearing a bra and thong panties. While away at college, she acquired tattoo-sleeves and vignettes on her torso. Now, in the dim, only her tattoo-free skin is visible, and disturbingly, the inked portions appear cut away.

"Sarah, get up and clean this pigsty, okay? Your room reeks of dirty clothes and rotting food," I say assertively, and flick the light switch without success.

"Nooooo. Go awaaay."

"Did you take the bulb out of the fixture?"

She giggles. "Like, duh."

"Your room's a friggin' petri dish with new and disgusting life forms evolving as we speak."

"What*ever*. Go away, ugly old woman!"

"Sarah, please don't talk to me like that, okay?"

She mimics me in a high-pitched and begging voice. "Oh Saaarah, pleeease don't talk to me like thaaat. Okaaay?"

Down the hall, Bryan's room is marginally cleaner. "Bryan, please get up and clean your room." Bryan doesn't have tattoos and piercings, so he is perceived as an approachable, clean-cut kid.

No answer. My jaw is tight, and my hands are fists. I sigh, shake out my fingers, and decide to talk to Austin about our sloths whenever I catch him in a good mood. Maybe I can convince him the kids need to find employment and start being more independent. How do other people motivate their kids? Perhaps my fault is, as Trix has said, that I'm nice. Too nice. Codependent-nice, dysfunctional-nice, enabling-nice, ridiculously-nice.

Both educated in IT, the twins lived independently for a year, then had their app-brainwave and requested they move in to free them from jobs and financial constraints and allow them to concentrate on product development. If we are being conned as I suspect, as smoke-and-mirrors tricks go, they've cooked up a good cover since we can't know if they are on the brink of a hugely successful invention, or not. I leave them to their languor.

The balance of Saturday and Sunday are eaten alive by housework. Not that I mind upkeep, which I view as protecting our investment.

Sunday evening I watch a movie called *Hidden Figures*, a true story about three black women who are mathematical geniuses working at NASA. The film shows their struggles with segregation and the white male hierarchy. NASA is only a ten-minute drive and I hope if Lucy has seen the movie, NASA's proximity might hit home and help her recognize the perils of embracing conformity.

Austin arrives home and comes to bed after midnight, which briefly stirs me, and I shift over to spoon against his solid form. His presence is comforting.

I haul myself out of bed Monday morning and slip into panties and my favorite kimono. I bought the kimono in Chinatown decades ago, and I've worn and washed it to near transparency. At Austin's office door, I observe him. He stands to gather his things and says, "Happy birthday, honey." But he doesn't look my way.

I cross the room and hug him. He stiffens, and it's like embracing a mannequin. I kiss his neck. "Looking forward to dinner. It's been *eons* since we've spent real time together."

He pulls away, frowns, and wags a finger at me, "Now Julia, I told you a million-billion times, don't exaggerate." A silly admonishment we say to the twins. I chuckle, although I'd prefer to justify my statement, however, the last thing I want is an argument.

He stares at my forehead, and puzzled, I reach up and touch my hairline tentatively. "What?"

"Nothing. Just, you've got a lot of gray roots." I wilt, and he kisses me with a loud smack and laughs.

I follow Austin as he leaves the house. The pool pump is purring, no more whimpering baby sounds, but the shower still dribbles, and I turn the handle hard. He glances around and says, "Garden's looking like shit."

I'm not sure what is bothering him, given it's spring and expected that while some shrubs are blooming, many plants are just starting, but I acquiesce, "I'll get to the gardening soon."

Lucy's husband, Earl, ambles over to chat with Austin. Earl is tall and reasonably attractive in spite of his dad-bod with a beer belly, a hawkish face with close-together, deep-set eyes and a beaky nose.

In the morning's dewy light, Austin and Earl are striking, two businessmen wearing expensive, dark, tailored suits that contrast with crisp white collars and cuffs. Their hair is freshly clipped. Their teeth are healthy and gleaming. Their ties are silk, their shiny briefcases are Italian leather, and they stand next to Austin's lustrous black-and-chrome beast of an SUV. The background is tree-lined and verdant. The scene has the polished trappings of a gorgeously photographed car advertisement, and I watch a moment and contemplate our incredible life. The bounty of what we have is staggering in so many ways.

Recalling his and Lucy's extra-marital dalliances, I picture Earl having sex with the babysitter, and I blush. Earl gazes over, and I give him a quick smile and enter the garage. In the dusty cache buried since college, there's a cardboard box marked ART, which contains paints and brushes.

Laughter and the words *Astros* and *season's tickets* drift in from the driveway. Silence descends, Austin's SUV starts with a roar, and he drives away without saying goodbye. Another token of affection lost over time; I suppose. I stack some boxes, shift some tools, and a hedge trimmer—I really need to sort out this junk—and reach down to shove a plastic container of old clothing out of the way.

When I straighten up, a tall dusty mirror at the back of the garage shows Earl also staring into the mirror. My kimono's sash has come undone, and the front has parted, exposing my breasts. I hastily close and tie my robe, and I watch his confused expression, no doubt trying to decide if my boob-flash was deliberate, and an invitation. He puts his briefcase down and carefully comes several steps closer, moving as if he's trying not to startle his prey. Stacks of boxes surround me, and he blocks the only open path. I'm trapped, but while I'm not encouraging him, I'm also not rebuffing.

He edges closer until he's a few inches from me, and his scent and body heat bring on an intense wave of lust, born of deprivation—not only a lack of sex but of touch, attention, attraction, desire. His gaze is enthralled, his color high, and we lock eyes. I break eye contact but find myself ogling the bulge in his pants, an unashamed declaration of his intent.

Is sex about to happen, and am I in favor? No. Yes. No. And the thought puckers my nipples into pebbles, visible bumps in the thin silk. He reaches out and brushes my upper arm with his fingertips, and his touch snaps me out of the reverie. I pull away, and he's suddenly back in his proper context, as Lucy's husband, good old Earl, the guy next door. My face grows hot, and I cinch my robe tighter. "Shit! Earl! I didn't know my robe had opened. I thought you'd left…"

"You're so beautiful, Julia," he says as he leaves, smiling, striding backward, watching me as he crosses the wide lawn. "Shit," I say again aloud, crossing my arms. I'm not overly troubled about Earl viewing my breasts because I can rationalize the wardrobe-malfunction as a genuine accident, but I had a moment of intense temptation. Or was I simply going along with a man who let me know what he wants and expects, as is my habit? Hopefully, I'm not that submissive, and my reaction was the result of many months without nookie.

He called me *beautiful.* Is he sincere, or is *beautiful* something men say to get into our pants? Staring into the mirror again, I glance around to make sure no one is watching, and tentatively open my robe for a look-see at what mesmerized Earl. I've always thought of my build as average. Sure my figure has some curves, and I guess gravity hasn't exerted too much of a toll, and my skin is clear, but that doesn't add up to beautiful. However, it also doesn't equal homely.

My phone rings. "What do you think about what Lucy told you?" Earl asks. "Our options, since I have permission?"

"I'm sorry, Earl, neighborly sex is way outside my comfort zone."

"Oh well." A sigh. "If you ever change your mind, I'm right next door..."

"You'll be the first to know, Earl."

I pause a moment, shake my head, chuckle, and gather my dusty folding easel, a canvas wrapped in now-brittle plastic, brushes, petrified oil paints, a small table, and a piece of glass for a palette. Dropping the dried tubes of paint in the garbage, I take the rest to the house.

Lucy calls, and I debate answering, but I cave and pick up. She says, "Earl says he's got the hots for you."

"Shit Lucy, I'd never—"

Laughing, "It's okay. Living next to a hot chick like you, I'd be a doofus not to notice him staring at you every chance he gets. But today was a step up because he saw your titties."

"I'm sorry, Lucy." First Earl says I'm beautiful, and now I'm a hot chick? These people are delusional.

"Don't be sorry. Men!" She laughs and hangs up, but I wonder if she's genuine. How weird if she's dishonest, after telling me about their so-called *arrangement*. The last thing I want is complications with neighbors.

Where to set up my painting area? I settle on a portion of the screened porch outside my studio, dust off the art equipment, and unwrap the canvas. The brushes are extra-crispy, clogged with dried paint, and I dump them. I'm on a new adventure, and my spirits rise.

CHAPTER FOUR

I dress in yoga spandex and go for a run to boost serotonin and knock down some mental cobwebs. Spring has pirouetted into season on ballerina-toes with her tutu splendidly aflutter, bringing butterflies flapping onto gardenia and wisteria, translucent pale foliage unfurling, and flocks of migrating robins dotting the lawns with their heads tipped, peering into wormholes. I jog.

Not to be rude, but our subdivision is toilet-shaped. The bowl portion is full of twisting roads, and in the morning, most of the residents are flushed through the single point of egress to schools, daycare facilities, and the vortex of Houston's corporate collection system. Now, at the height of the afternoon rush hour, there is the usual clog of returning SUVs. I wave to the gatehouse guard and start back.

As a freelance illustrator, along with a handful of stay-at-home moms and retirees, I don't leave during the day. I've worked at home in solitary concentration nearly all my adult life. If forced to work in an office-honeycomb buzzing with water-cooler drones, the interruptions, politics, and personalities, structured and scheduled breaks, my cubicle would double as a padded cell, my business suit a straitjacket. Like clockwork, the Smiths' barking dogs charge their fence then drop back.

Our suburb's roads are asphalt edged by concrete sidewalks. Each of these *swankiendas*, or *McMansions* if you prefer, has a severely trimmed, predictable square of lawn bordered by dependable shrubs, each separated from the next by ten inches of mulch, and clipped into tortured shapes that bring to mind Jell-O molds. Paid help who tend the uniform patches of interior and exterior real estate arrive and leave. This life with maids and landscapers is a far cry from our beginnings.

My knife-thrower dream's timeframe is from before we moved to this place. For me, those early days were a time of persistent happiness and excitement for our future. Like most young couples getting established, we had financial challenges. Art college spat me out two years before Austin graduated. We got by on my paycheck from a magazine, where, using hot melted wax on a roller, I stuck typeset columns of text onto blue-lined pages. I can still smell that wax. Paste-up is now a job as obsolete as elevator-operators or bowling alley pinsetters. Those were the days, as Trix mentioned, when I painted for fun in my off-hours.

Our rented one-bedroom garage apartment was in downtown Houston's funky student area. It was drafty in the winter and roasting in the summer, and our ineffective window-shaker air conditioner was no match for the Texas heat, which invited sweaty sex on every surface. Despite our lack of money, we needed nothing more than a burger shack, our old Ford pickup, jeans, T-shirts, and good friends. Parties were a snap, just beer, chips, and music.

I turn the corner a block from home and downsized-Dave emerges from his triple garage and begins shaking fertilizer or some other chemical—fire-ant killer perhaps—

onto his lawn from a large plastic container. His next-door neighbor is home for lunch, still wearing his tie, his briefcase lying on the grass; he plays catch with his son. Mayberry is what everyone aspires to here. We were no different. When Austin earned his business degree, he began interviewing. He didn't graduate in the top half, and Houston had a glut of business grads, but he was determined. During the first year of his job hunt, he worked part-time in construction. Back then, a vacation was a road trip, ours for the price of gas, and my sleepwalking dream was, as I told Trix, based on one of our forays to visit friends in Hill Country.

On our trip, driving west, the irrigated, green sprawl of Houston became farms gone brown from drought. At our friends' place, we smoked weed, drank beer, burped, and never once thought about our waistlines. A roasting one-ten in the shade and no one cared. Behind the weathered rent-house, the men shot snakes, while indoors, the women, barefoot and wearing cutoffs and bikini tops, prepared food. We laughed till we were mute and laughed some more. With dusk approaching, we went to the dream's setting, a traveling carnival set up in a nearby farmer's field.

God only knows, if those hucksters hadn't rolled in all swarthy, sweltering, and offering the farmer cash for the privilege of shilling and scamming the locals, the only thing sprouting on that parched land would've been For Sale signs. The carnival generated local excitement despite its third-rate rusted rides, and faded and shabby gaming huts, tents, and clown suits. Main attractions like the knife thrower got a rickety outdoor stage. We played games and gawked at sideshows of gypsies, fortune-tellers, and freaks. And our youthful optimism and enjoyment of all things creepy, quirky, weird, and ironic, converted the carnival to hip entertainment. Off the midway were the victims of dehydration and famine, the dead vegetation, bare and bleached bones, and the stench of the dead longhorn. Rain clouds rolled in at sunset, and we'd dashed for our truck in the downpour.

After eighteen months of applying for jobs, Austin was hired and found his place, his career, and he's been with the same distributor of oil and gas drilling equipment ever since. His starting salary was respectable, and I quit my job to freelance. Fortunately, I was busy from the start, and our combined incomes allowed us to purchase the house, start our family, and eventually put some savings aside. Austin's bonuses bought extras like his pursuit of hobbies and sports trips. Lately, his bumps in pay have been few, which puzzles me, given Houston's current oil boom.

Why did I dream of our long-ago trip? Was it because back then we were a team? He has always been a man of few words and not terribly affectionate or passionate, but we were best friends building our life together. However, those memories aren't our current state. Lately, intimacy and communication have been limited, if not downright scarce. My God, when did our bliss end? I want that connectedness back.

Back home, I turn toward the house, and the turquoise water of the pool catches the corner of my eye, hatching a memory of the Caribbean sea in the same glorious color, and then the flash of déjà vu is gone, but not before the snippet brings anxiety. I stop and stare, trying to bring the thought back, to no avail. I give up and head indoors.

I work until five, and then turn my attention to grooming for my birthday dinner. Hopefully, I'll even get a birthday boink. My birthday dinner demands the whole nine—starting with a box of hair color for the gray roots, although there really aren't very many. Besides, they're not very visible since I am blonde-ish. I follow with a leisurely bath, evening makeup, hair in an updo, sexy undies in sheer nude trimmed in black lace, and lace-top stay-up stockings. On go my low-cut LBD, heels, and gold jewelry.

I deliberately leave off my watch for the new one, and text Austin that I'm ready. There's no response, and I kill time studying my drawing of grapes. The kids emerge from their rooms, and there are sounds of them pillaging the fridge.

Bryan sticks his head around my studio door and says, "Why're you all dressed up?"

"It's my birthday. Your dad is taking me to dinner."

"Oops." He grins guiltily. "Happy B-day. We're goin' out."

"Okay. Have fun."

I text Austin again and watch an episode of a crime show in which a man kills his wife and claims she fell down the stairs. A hunger spasm catches my attention, and I notice it's after eight. Maybe something's happened to Austin. But also, if he lost track of time and hasn't left the office yet, by the time he gets home and we leave, the restaurant will be well into the last sitting, and we might not get a table. I recheck my cell phone. Still no response—what the…? Then I check the landline, which shows he called, probably when I was dressing.

I phone his cell, and he picks up. "Hey, it's getting late. Are you on your way?"

"Didn't you pick up my message?" He asks, sounding put out.

"No. There've been no messages."

"I called the landline."

"Why? We always text if it's important. What was your message?"

He exhales impatiently. "I have to work tonight. All right?"

"Well, yes, of course...just disappointed. I got dressed up, and I was looking forward to a date night with you."

"You're acting like I stood you up, but you're the one who didn't check messages."

A taut wire of anger quivers through me. I carefully modulate my voice. "Can't you get away now? We could still get there in time for dessert."

"Not going to happen. Uh…happy birthday. Love you."

"Yeah…thanks. Really? Austin…" the phone is dead.

At the bedroom door, I kick my shoes off with more

force than intended. One flies across the room onto Austin's bedside table, sending books, reading glasses, a bowl of spare change, and his alarm clock crashing to the floor. The other shoe lands on his pillow. Woohoo! I viciously yank my dress over my head, wad it up, hurl it across the room, and then do the same with my bra. The dress lands appropriately, covering our wedding photo framed in heavy silver atop the dresser, and my bra lies in the middle of the floor, the lacy cups like two joined happy faces. My stockings fly like streamers, crumpling into small mounds on the hardwood.

I stomp to the bathroom, wipe off my makeup, remove my jewelry, and mess up my hair with both hands. I've never behaved in this manner. Throwing things, including tantrums, is Austin's specialty, not mine, although I must admit, it's quite therapeutic, even calming. I shrug into my robe, which reminds me of my close encounter with Earl, and I blush again. Phew.

In the kitchen, I pile a bagel, smoked salmon, and crackers on a plate with a chopped hardboiled egg, cream cheese, and capers, and grab the bottle of champagne I've held in abeyance for a special occasion. As I untwist the wire cage, before I'm ready, the champagne cork explodes from the bottle and smashes the bulb in a pendant light above the breakfast bar. Champagne sprays over the counter-top. I start giggling then can't stop laughing until I'm breathless. Screw the mess and broken glass. Swigging from the bottle, I take my food to the living room.

I eat and drink while I watch a movie called *Big Eyes*, the story of a female artist whose husband takes the credit and the cash for her work. "Asshole," I mutter, then louder, "Dickhead!"

After the movie, despite the champagne in my system, I snap back to normal and clean up broken glass and sprayed bubbly, then in the bedroom, I tidy my clothes and shoes and put Austin's nightstand in order. He arrives after two. At his office door, I have a pang of guilt considering he's been toiling into the wee hours while I've been guzzling champers and watching TV. "Hey, handsome."

"Hey. Why are you awake?" He looks me over and says, "I thought you said you got dressed up."

"Well…" I want to say *you must be joking*, but I don't.

He hands me the red jewelry box. "Here." There's impatience in his gesture. I've got butterflies. I'm tipsy and not sure I can pull off being surprised. I open the attached card and read aloud, "Happy birthday from Austin, Bryan, and Sarah."

"Open it." He says with a hand gesture indicating he's on edge.

I ready myself and pry open the top, and my surprised expression is authentic because inside is a three-strand amethyst necklace, not the extravagant watch. "It's beautiful! Thank you." I'm relieved.

"You're welcome. Glad you like it. Happy birthday, darlin'."

I ask, "Can we talk awhile? Please?"

Austin takes a deep breath, "No. I don't want to talk. I'm tired, and I need to check email. Besides, you're going to pinch my head off for not taking you out tonight."

I open and close my mouth. "I won't. I promise. Please?"

"Julia, stop being so fucking needy and high maintenance." His gift-giving duty fulfilled; he turns away to concentrate on his monitor. Is working late a lot and perhaps being tired justification for being constantly cranky and abrupt?

And wow. High maintenance. Needy. Am I? I've always considered myself easy-going and undemanding. Yikes. What if my self-awareness is that far off reality? As I lie in bed, Austin's murmur reaches me. No doubt he's dictating a memo or something else super-duper important—even my thoughts are sarcastic. I put my wakefulness to use, visualizing the painting I'll create from my nightmare, and fall asleep before he joins me.

CHAPTER FIVE

Austin sleeps late and rushes out of the house. The weather is perfect for gardening, and I head for the greenhouse, adjacent to the kitchen, which doubles as a potting shed and herb garden. After planting some seedlings, I bring in some basil and a bulb of garlic for lasagna. Our house. I have a love-hate relationship with this pile of sheetrock, tile, and stucco.

The house is a V-shaped, 5000-square-foot structure, and an inefficient and ornery tyrant that devours our most precious resources—energy, time, and money. At the center are the kitchen, dining, and living rooms. One wing has three bedrooms separated by the laundry room and a bathroom. Those bedrooms have become a guest room, my studio, and Austin's home office. On the other arm of the V, a long hallway passes the living areas and ends at our master bedroom. Upstairs are the kids' bedrooms, a bathroom, and a communal open space.

There aren't many windows on the front of the house,

but on the back, banks of French doors let in plenty of light and give access to the screened porch, what our realtor called the lanai. At first, we joked about the word, but in the end, lanai became familiar and stuck. The lanai runs the full length of the main floor overlooking the gardens, the pool, and the continuous lawns, which are uninterrupted by fences or hedges, a pretension of the homeowners' association, whose rulebook mandates a sweeping vista, a park-like setting. The no-fences rule, while attractive, puts everyone in view of their neighbors. Any carelessness with the window coverings and one's most intimate moments are on display. I'm careful to keep private things private, but it occurs to me that Earl, given his oversized libido, could be peeping in our windows after dark, and I shiver.

In the shower, the sudden lust I experienced at Earl's ogling keeps coming to mind like an oily residue I can't wash away. I visualize completing the scenario and become aroused again. Of all the men in the world that I could choose to boff, having Earl on the shortlist is weird. But…he wants me, obviously admires me, and is clearly turned on by me.

I dress in jeans and an old T-shirt, check on the twins who are as usual sleeping off last night's inebriation, then get to work. I try to access email, but the internet is down. I try again, then reboot with no luck. Damn. I set up a hotspot with my phone. An email requests a quote for a drawing of little kids playing with a toy robot. I've quoted this client on other jobs, and they have a habit of grinding me down, so I nearly double my usual rate. Heh heh.

The grapes illustration is on my drafting board, but the blank canvas is a tease with so much potential, I'm seduced into shunning the grapes. The first task is deciding on the subject matter of the painting. In commercial work, art directors sketch a composition and specify the style, but now this is all on me. Whatever shows up on my canvas is mine alone. My inclination as an illustrator is to create appealing impressions. The carnival setting, and our young love at the time, suggest the mood be fun and happy, which is all wrong.

The dream comes flooding back in all its contradictions: my expectation of safety while Austin throws knives at me; the happy and sad theatrical masks; the arid landscape, the ugly crowd, and the rain.

The sentiments of comedy-tragedy masks, clowns, and mimes have always seemed maudlin, emotionally manipulative; however, while those symbols may be stale, the emotions are universal. There must be a fresh way to represent those moods. To me, they aren't separate, they're layered, like Russian nesting dolls, or strata of sediment. Heartbreak can exist under a blanket of happiness; a kernel of joy can dwell within despair, waiting to break out. My small revelation, but an essential one is, what I leave out is as important as what I include.

Then there's the issue of painting my image, my self-portrait if you will. My appearance was youthful, with the years removed like the shell of a hard-boiled egg, peeled to expose a smoother and glossier, springier version. Such a self-portrait could be criticized by viewers as vain. At the end of the dream, I'd seen red through the blood, signifying anger. Anger, why exactly?

My analysis brings waves of prickly discomfort and insecurity; that my thoughts are shallow and trite, I'm not equipped, not well educated enough, for such introspection. My preference is to abandon the canvas, to clear my mind and get back to a simplistic reality. But if I genuinely want to paint—and I do—this thought process is necessary, perhaps even crucial, for the finished piece to be not merely pretty or nice, but meaningful.

I change the viewpoint from standing backstage looking out, to visualizing the scene through the eyes of an audience member. Austin has thrown the knife that split the apple and cut me, while above the stage, the clouds roil. I start sketching with charcoal and become caught in a new feverish vitality. I'm blending and smudging with my hands, working the sky black, creating distance and threat through perspective and value.

Stepping back, I inspect the sketch. Sarah's door closes upstairs, then silence. The twins' request to move back home came through Austin. In hindsight, we would have been smart to impose a time limit. Among other inconveniences, the kids' presence has helped erode our intimacy. Exclamations of *Ew, get a room! No PDA! Gross!* brought on by any touching or kissing has taken us back to the quiet calculating behavior of parents engaging in coitus near sleeping children. Also on hold is my hope of unloading this millstone of a property, downsizing, moving into the city to enjoy nightlife and the arts.

I start drawing Austin in his tux. He has just thrown the knife, his arm and body extended, and in line. Over the years, I've let my introspective and creative side go dormant. There's always been a small voice admonishing: *You're an illustrator who idealizes commercial goods, not a fine artist.* I don't doubt my ability, but I've been on a different trajectory, of earning a paycheck the only way I knew how. But, if I turn my role on its head, is the reality something else, something unpleasant? While I've been proudly laboring to be the ever-present support system, has my family been taking advantage and using me? Has my role of dedication and duty—and my family's response—become codependent and dysfunctional, to use the popular psychology-buzzwords?

I'm suddenly wary. Lately, my ever-present positive beliefs collide with uneasy negativity. Are these thoughts destructive or simply realistic? Over and over, I find myself reining my instincts in, boxing them up to be filed away and considered later, or preferably, never. After drawing for an hour, my inner small-but-perpetually-pestering voice says, *Get back to your real work.*

I wash charcoal from my hands, change out of my smeared clothes, and into snug skinny black jeans and a wrap top accentuating "the girls" with an eye to enticing Austin's attention. At my drafting table, I block in color on the illustration of grapes.

The AC guy arrives, and an hour later announces he's fixed the problem, proven by chilled air blasting from vents. Like monetary karma, I write him a check for almost the same amount I'll charge for the grapes job.

For lunch, I make a turkey and avocado sandwich. Bryan and Sarah saunter in, both in pajamas. Bryan says, "There's no interwebs."

"I rebooted the Wi-Fi without luck," I answer. "I'm sure it's temporary and will be back on soon."

"Like, did you forget to pay the fuckin' bill?" Sarah says.

"Watch your tone, okay girlie? I have the power of disconnection. Wi-Fi usually comes back on in a while."

"Doubt that's happening," Bryan says, perusing the fridge's contents.

The fridge door starts chiming, and he slumps when I push it closed. "All right, I'll call the cable company." I dial and make my way through the prompts for an appointment on Saturday.

He droops in disgust. "Saturday. Fuck."

"Language." I admonish.

He frowns and says, "Well, it's pretty fucky trying to work on an app without any internet."

"Ohhh, you were working on your app all morning, in bed?" Bryan shoots me a disparaging look, and I give him an exaggerated, wide-eyed grin.

Sarah adds, "So lame. Saturday's the soonest they can come?"

"They said a tech could be here in an hour, but I insisted they wait till Saturday." I smile.

"Wow, sarcasm. Haha, Mom," Sarah says mirthlessly, sounding a lot like Austin.

"If you can get them to show up sooner, go ahead, okay?" I head back to my studio, where I abandon the grapes again and continue sketching on the canvas.

Unexpectedly, Austin arrives home early evening, which is rare these days, and I'm happy we can have a date night. I go to his office door. "Hey hon, I'm glad you didn't have to work late. How about if we go for dinner, just you and me, okay?"

Austin says, "The kids are coming too."

"Austin, please, I'd rather just the two of us go. Please?"

"No. They're coming." He glances my way, "Can't you wear something half decent?"

I'm puzzled. "Are we going someplace special?" Maybe this will be my belated birthday dinner.

He grunts and goes to the bedroom to change out of his suit. My optimistic internal dialogue convinces me it's an opportunity to sit down and eat as a family, to communicate. I remove my jeans and don a floral-patterned dress and heels.

Going to the car, I notice Austin's clothes are new and far more casual than what I'm wearing, tighter than his usual style, and manufactured to appear worn, the careful distressing an obvious affectation. The gold chain he wore when we first met gleams between his second and third shirt button. They were in style back then, but these days, I'm fairly sure the only men who wear gold chains are rappers, pimps, and maybe some hipster types. He's morphing from Marlboro man to lounge lizard.

"Where are we going?"

He doesn't answer, but a few minutes later, he pulls up in front of our local Tex Mex restaurant. What the hell? Compared to the other patrons, many in T-shirts, shorts, and flip flops, I'm dressed to attend a wedding. We take a booth. The kids sit in texting posture, heads down. Sarah has pinned her hair up and displays new tattoos of purple leopard spots in a semicircle under her left ear. As always, I wonder where she got the money. Was it from Austin, or someone else, and if so, whom? The waiter brings tortilla chips, queso, and salsa, and the kids absently dip and munch, eyes still on their devices.

Austin's phone rings, and he says, "I gotta take this. It's Marcy." He goes to the restaurant's entrance. Marcy Forsyth is his boss. She joined the company ten years ago, and I know her from business functions and the occasional phone call when she's trying to track Austin's whereabouts.

An attempt at small talk with the kids elicits grunts in response. "Well, isn't this pleasant." I observe, opening the menu.

A waiter takes orders for drinks, and Austin returns. I ask, "How is Marcy these days?"

"Okay."

"What did Earl want to talk about this morning?" I'm nervous at my mention of Earl and hope I'm not blushing. Would Austin confront Earl if he knew what happened? I'm sure he would blame me for not keeping my robe closed. Society tends to hold men blameless if titillated. A hundred years ago, a sexy ankle peeking from a long skirt was risqué. Today, it's a yoga-pants camel-toe or tube-top-cleavage, not to mention women who are helplessly incapacitated by drugs or alcohol. Apparently, according to some, men can't help themselves. I don't consider Earl's interest to be sexually over-the-line because I enjoyed the thrill; however, if I told Trix about the incident, I'm confident she'd have a different opinion.

Austin says, "Earl wants to get some guys together to buy a block of seats for the Astros this season, so I said I'd pitch in."

"Ha! A pun." The twins chuckle. So, they are paying attention.

"What?" Austin asks, confused.

"*Pitch in* for baseball tickets." Austin rolls his eyes, and I add, "Lucy and Earl are planning to renovate their kitchen. She asked for our contractor's number."

"Big waste of money," he says curtly.

Surprising myself, I ask, "Unlike season's tickets?" The twins glance at us, and Austin gives me a *screw-you* stare. His phone signals a text, which he reads, then puts the phone face down on the table, an action I'm supposed to ignore. I'm not sure why I break the rule, but I ask, "Who texted you?"

He says, "Nobody."

"Reminds me of the song, *Nobody*, by Sylvia. About how *nobody* keeps calling her boyfriend." I sing a few bars, but Austin ignores me. Indignant, I want to demand to read the text, but I hesitate, and the moment is defused by the waiter bringing margaritas. I order fajitas for four.

Austin's phone rings, and again, he leaves. He finishes talking, then stands for a while manipulating the phone before returning, and I debate whether to address the issue. Finally, I say, "Here." I place my phone on the table. "Go ahead and scroll my texts and calls. You know my password. Check it any time you like." Sarah and Bryan glance up, intently this time. I'm acting out of character, and they're wary.

Austin shoves my phone back to me a bit too forcefully, and it falls off the table onto the seat, then to the floor. "Austin?" He makes no attempt to pick it up, so I duck down below the tabletop where grime darkens the places the furniture meets the floor. There are crumbs and something, maybe a silverfish or small roach, scurries by. I pick up my icky phone with two fingertips, add antibacterial gel to some serviettes and wipe it down, then rub the gel onto my hands. The tension in the air fairly crackles.

"What the hell, Dad?" Bryan says.

"Yeah, Dad," Sarah adds, "you're being an asshole."

"Watch your mouth, girl," Austin snaps.

Bryan says, "She needs a mirror to watch her mouth," and they both laugh.

Sarah leans forward, squinty-eyed, "I mean it, Dad, you're being a total asshole. I heard you tell mom to get dressed up, and then you brought us to this crappy restaurant. Like, why?"

Austin, red-faced with anger, says, "Restroom," excusing himself. As he crosses the restaurant, I watch his love handles strain his shirt, and another version of him emerges, of a puffed-up underachiever trying to fake confidence but coming off as desperate. Shocked by my thoughts, I wonder if losing respect is the first symptom of falling out of love. Sarah follows my gaze and makes a *what the hell?* grimace, and she giggles.

Returning, Austin says he must confirm Marcy's meeting, and he leaves again. The kids continue their electronic absentia, and when Austin returns, he sits gazing into the middle distance, distractedly folding and unfolding his napkin. The food arrives, which has the effect of lifting the kids' heads. Austin's phone rings again, and as he leaves the table, I ask, "Can you please take the call here?" as I touch his arm.

He yanks his arm away as if scalded, stands up, and bends level with my face. "Don't ever fucking do that again!" He purposefully strides away with his phone to his ear.

Tears sting, and I blink them away. The twins are watching me intently, and I try to soothe, "Don't worry. He's okay. He's a bit stressed. I shouldn't have asked."

"Dad's such a dickhead," Bryan says.

"Yeah, a world-class dickhead," says Sarah. "It's not like you slapped him or even grabbed him." There it is again. Trix declared Austin a dickhead, and now the twins.

Bryan says, "Like, why is he always on his phone? So rude, man."

I pointedly stare wide-eyed at their phones and raise my eyebrows. Bryan and Sarah look at each other, and we all laugh. We are still laughing when Austin returns and asks crossly, "What?"

"Nothing," Sarah says, then pretending to notice his outfit for the first time, she exclaims, "Dad! What are you wearing?"

Austin appears bewildered. "What's the matter?"

"Jesus, what *isn't* the matter? You're dressed like a sleazebag gigolo."

Her comment gets Bryan's attention. He examines Austin, and then he and Sarah glance at each other and crack up again. Bryan says, "What's with the gold chain?"

"You don't like it?" Austin asks.

Sarah answers, "I'd like it better in a pawn shop window."

Are they teasing him in retaliation for his outburst? They laugh again, and I stifle the urge to join them. I have a pang of guilt about ganging up on Austin. Plus, keeping a straight face is self-preservation since I have a good idea of how his temper might rear up later, in private. Back to my peace keeping role.

At home, Austin spends the evening in his office talking on the phone. I catch up on a TV series called *American Greed* about people who have dcfrauded vast sums of money. At eleven, I put art materials away, fold laundry, feed the cat, and at his office door, I wave to him. He's still on the phone and reciprocates with a wave, and I go to bed. Sometime in the night, Austin slips into bed. I stir and go back to sleep.

CHAPTER SIX

The knife thrower nightmare has recurred, waking me before five, and while I'm quite sure I didn't sleepwalk, I wander the house in my now tightly-cinched robe—no more flashing the neighbors—looking for evidence I roamed in the night. Relieved to find none, I get to work, adding highlights to each of the grapes.

Near eight, there are sounds of Austin in the shower, then in the kitchen. He enters my studio, takes hold of the sides of my head, and plants kisses all over my face until I'm laughing. He smiles and says, "I probably have to work late. I'll let you know."

A job comes by email from a new client, an ad agency art director who found my page on Facebook. I'm probably the last person on the planet who doesn't have a show-everything-in-my-life Facebook page. Mine is business only; no friends, like my website—set up specifically to showcase my work for potential clients to view—social media as free advertising and promotion. The client wants a drawing of an ornate door with planters and a welcome mat for a condominium ad.

I pin watercolor board to the drafting table to start sketching, but restlessness overcomes me. With a rubber-band snap of impatience, I can't bear another moment of diligence, of repetitive jobs, of rendering images of happiness to buy at the store, of a paycheck compromising my ability. Screw it. I drive to the art supply store and purchase oil paints, mediums, solvents, and new brushes.

Back home, I squeeze grays, yellows, and red onto the palette and start the underpainting, establishing shapes and values on the canvas. Dipping my brush into the solvent, then into the near-black Payne's Gray, I swirl paint onto the clouds. The loaded brush swipes over the sketch seemingly of its own volition, working viscous pigment into the primed weave, and I'm transported to another time and place, with the freedom to try, fail, and try again.

I step back and assess the tension in the exaggerated perspectives and asymmetrical composition. The scene is dramatic and distressing, capturing the emotional texture of the dream. Maybe Austin is right; I am the queen of drama, but not in the way he means. I smile.

The underpainting is finished around midnight, and I fall into bed and deep sleep. Close to three, I wake to the sound of the kids, then Austin, arriving home. Shortly after, I sense Austin's nearness and reach for him, but he isn't in bed. I open my eyes. The room is very dark, but I make out his form standing close to my side of the bed. He has something in his hands, his cell phone perhaps, and clothes, no, maybe a pillow. I say, "Austin?" He quickly and quietly retreats and leaves the room. I go back to sleep.

Morning, I'm up and out for an early run, and Austin has slept in. I see him drive by. He doesn't notice me, and I view him as a stranger would. He's wearing a dark suit and tie and talking on his phone. Yup, he's a hunk all right, and I have a thrill, the lightning-in-a-bottle sensation, desire, pride—what everyone covets.

Upon returning home, I empty the pool filters of grass clippings. The water is warm, but even though the pump works, algae grows in a few spots. I set the pool vacuum meandering. For all its maintenance and expense, I can't recall the last time someone went swimming. Standing on the stone coping, staring into the depths of the water, the bouncing, sparkling light on the surface is hypnotic and the déjà vu sliver of memory that I had a few days ago starts to surface, but I can't tease it out completely.

I work on the pretty-door illustration. Midafternoon, as the kids are finally emerging from their dens, Austin texts: *Going camping for the weekend. Leave tonight.*

I respond: *U don't have ur camping stuff. It's here.*

Austin: *I'll stop by with Clayton and pick stuff up.*

I respond: *OK. Who?*

Austin: *Clayton. Husband of a woman from work.*

After my dinner of heated leftovers at my drafting table, Austin arrives. A glance out the front window shows a hulking man waiting near a white van. I go to Austin's office, where he is collecting his gear, lean against the doorframe, and ask, "The biker dude outside with the shaved head and bandana…is he who you're going with?"

"Yeah, I'll be back Sunday late."

"Who is he again?"

"Clayton. I told you, he's the husband of a woman at work. Nice guy."

What I'm going to ask is loaded, and I cross my arms as if bracing myself. "Austin, what were you doing last night beside the bed?" Usually, I wouldn't address the subject for fear of poking a hornet's nest, but something single-minded is driving me.

"What?" He stops stuffing his duffle bag and straightens up, attentive.

"Last night, when you came into the bedroom."

"What are you talking about?" He knits his brow but

turns away.

So, he's going to play dumb. Or more to the point, he's playing like I'm the stupid or crazy one. "You were beside the bed, holding a pillow and something else, maybe your phone."

"Julia, for the love of God, get a grip. You're imagining things."

"No. I'm not. If the person wasn't you, who was in our bedroom?"

He shakes his head. "I gotta go." He turns away, then turns back, and smiling, bear-hugs me and pecks five kisses on my cheek. I head for the sofa and the television but change my mind. I clench fists against my temples. My God, I need to get out for a while. "Screw this."

I dial Trix. "Hey," she says.

"Hey… I'm feeling fucky. Cheer me up."

She audibly takes a drag on her cigarette. "Let me guess. You and Austin are fighting."

"Bingo. It's been more like a long fight that's lasted for weeks. Months. Years." I picture the cigarette in her thin fingers, bony from work, and a diet of nicotine, caffeine, red wine, and lettuce.

She exhales and says, "You need some syllogistic reasoning."

"Such as?"

"How about…people with penises are jerks. Men have penises; therefore, men are jerks."

I chuckle. "You're a hoot. Austin has a penis; hence…"

"Now you're getting the idea. Here's another. People who have argued are depressed. Depressed people need to get out and hit their local bar to cheer themselves up; ergo, you need to go out, be in a crowd, and grab a drink."

"Amen."

"I'm heading out to a dinner party," she says. "I'd invite you, but it's small and work-related. Hopefully, I'll land a humongous commission."

"Hope you do. Good luck."

Trix sips something and takes another drag. "For God's sake. Go out and get tipsy. Get out of that domestic-detention-unit you call a house. Seriously. Sorry, gotta run. Toodle-oo."

I pick up my car keys and purse. As I back out of the driveway, an odd sensation is percolating—anticipation, a foreign sense of adventure to be going out by myself. I'm aware of how nutty this sounds. After all, I haven't been tied up and kept in a dungeon. I'm not a hermit. I do function in society, but I can admit my social *self* needs a severe overhaul. I head to the Tex Mex restaurant again, but instead of taking a booth, which we do as a family, I sit at the bar and order a top-shelf margarita, rocks, salt. Couples and a few singles occupy the other stools. After nodding to them, I relax and enjoy the evening hubbub and people watching.

I can't remember the last time I was out on my own. In my ear, my mother's voice says, *And whose fault is that?* Mine. It's my fault. Granted, as a married woman, I've never felt entirely comfortable going out solo, even all the days and evenings Austin is away. Our lives operate like a teeter-totter. Whenever Austin takes off, I'm left sitting in the dust, immobilized, unlike Austin. But to be fair, Austin isn't out gallivanting around on his own, either. He always goes away with a buddy or a group.

After two margaritas, I drive home on back streets to avoid the neighborhood cops. At our subdivision, the gatehouse is empty; the gatekeeper is on his break. Rumor has it the night guard is schtupping Goldie, a middle-aged widow living on my street. His car is in her driveway, and I can't help smiling.

At home on TV, the hosts of a decorating show are cleverly repurposing objects, using an old door for a tabletop, and shutters for a room divider. I need to repurpose my vintage, threadbare marriage, recycle our relationship into something new, fresh, and stimulating. But how? The TV off, I head for bed.

The weekend, Austin away, is dedicated to gardening

and work.

Monday morning, I wake before dawn, and in my kimono, with coffee in hand, I open the French doors wide and work on the painting. Last night, Austin had barely arrived before the kids shook him down for cash. Then he worked in his office and came to bed after I was asleep. By eight o'clock I leave the painting and work at my drafting table. Austin enters my studio wearing only boxer shorts and carrying his mug with the slogan *Rum, more than a breakfast drink!* He stands at the open French doors, his back to me, and gazes at the yard.

"How was camping? Where did you go?"

"It was okay."

"Just okay? The guy you went with, is he a biker? It looked like he was wearing gang colors."

"His name is Clayton. What's with the third degree?"

"Just curious. Sorry." I notice he didn't answer either of my questions—a warning sign of bad temper ahead. I study him. Naturally, Austin is no longer as lean and chiseled as when we met. Time, like sun on a wax-museum figure, has softened his features and body, bleached his hair, and faded his complexion. While I'm realistic about his aging appearance, to me he's handsome and all things virile, with plenty of sex appeal. "Can we please spend some time together this evening?"

He says, "I have to attend a company party."

"Sounds like fun. Is there a possibility I can come? I haven't been to one of those parties in years."

"There's a reason you haven't been to the parties, Julia."

"Right. Spouses weren't invited."

"That's correct, Julia. Nothing's changed." The disdain in his voice is equivalent to him rolling his eyes.

I hesitate and try again. "Can you take a minute right now? It would be great if we could discuss some things, such as the twins' futures. And I'd love for us to spend more time together."

He sighs and says, "Here we go, Julia, the drama queen. The kids can stay as long as they want. We can afford it."

"I haven't checked our savings for a while, but I don't think we can afford it, unless we work until we drop dead."

"For the love of God, will you drop it?"

"Austin, can I please have a say in this? Sometimes I wonder if we're really doing the twins any favors by delaying their independence. There's a chance they're taking us for a ride, and they think it's clever, but we might actually be harming them."

"They're working on inventing the app." He takes a few steps toward the lanai and continues gazing at the yard.

"I'm starting to get a bit skeptical. How about I ask the twins to show us some evidence of progress?" I cringe at my insipid wording and pleading tone. No feathers ruffled today, thanks to good old milquetoast-y me.

"Take a fucking chill-pill, Julia."

I swallow a spike of anger because, not for lack of trying on my part, this is the first discussion we've had about the twins in nearly a year, and it occurs to me that it's about the same amount of time we haven't had sex. I'm not entirely successful in hiding my frustration, and ask, "Did you give the kids money last night?"

"Yeah," he says.

"And they earned it how? By breathing?"

"Very funny. They needed it for admission tonight, to a club. I suppose you wouldn't have given them any money."

"Correct. The saying '*Necessity is the mother of invention*' applies here, both literally and figuratively."

"What do you mean?"

He's genuinely puzzled, which surprises me, although Trix sometimes calls Austin 'meathead.' I pause a moment. "*Literally*—because if you stop giving them money, being broke is an incentive to get their invention finished and out on the market to capitalize on it as soon as possible.

Figuratively—because they might be more innovative about raising cash. They could start one of those crowd-funding web pages or something."

He says, "You need to clean the pool."

"Okay, but do you see what I'm saying about the twins?"

"There's algae on the bottom, so do it today."

His avoidance is so transparent, I chuckle. He's still standing with his back to me. Usually, when he changes the subject, I go along and drop whatever was contentious, but instead, I ask, "Are you trying to change the subject because you know I'm right?" After a while, ignored, I sigh and give in. "No one's been swimming in over a year and—"

He cuts me off. "Hardly the point."

"I'm aware. It's simply an observation, okay? The pump was making weird noises, but I got it fixed. The algae started before the pump was fixed. I've been vacuuming the pool, but it probably needs extra chemicals. I'll shock the water to kill the algae."

"It looks like shit. Get it cleaned today before more algae blooms."

To lighten the mood, I add, "Okay, already. Do you know what's weird? I'm the pool girl and the only non-swimmer." These days, sometimes he laughs at my observations. I can't anticipate which Austin I'll get.

He scolds, "It's not like you have to get in the water to clean the pool."

Ah, grouchy Austin. "I said I'd do it, okay?"

"And in case you haven't noticed, our shower needs caulking. Take care of it."

My jaw drops. "Don't talk to me like I'm an underling. I'm an equal financial contributor, and I take care of all the upkeep on this house." He doesn't answer and continues staring at the pool.

Frustration unhooks my mind from its safe zone. I leave my drafting table, sprint silently across the room, and give him a hard shove. Off-balance, he lurches forward, coffee splashing. He trips over the doorsill, plows across the lanai, knocking my canvas and easel flying, bashes headfirst into the window screen, ripping the mesh, and catapults into the rose garden. He's shrieking and flailing, trying to disentangle himself and his boxers, which hang on a thorny bush. He's naked, bloody, and drenched in coffee. Laughing, I call to him, "Maybe you should jump in the pool."

Of course, I don't shove him; that would be domestic violence. But it was a fun fantasy. What's happening to me? First, the sexy Earl urge, and now this. I've never had such wild thoughts before. I amble over beside him and follow his gaze. The hardscaping—terraced garden beds, patio, and coping around the pool—is a masterpiece, and spring perennials and annuals are in bloom, but all Austin sees is algae.

"Taking care of the house is *your job*. If you don't like it, get a divorce," he says belligerently.

"Austin… I don't want to fight. You know, you threaten divorce too frequently, and if you push me too often, I may get used to the idea, okay?"

"If you're so unhappy, you *should* get a divorce."

I think, "Do I have to do everything around here? Even take care of the divorce?" However, judging by Austin's shocked expression, I unintentionally said it aloud. Shit. I want to apologize, but sudden involuntary laughter bubbles up and escapes, and I clamp my hands over my mouth. Austin, resembling an enormous toddler in a snit, stomps out of my studio. The sight is humorously melodramatic.

Austin's cutting remarks might be the knives in the dream. Strange how they are tickling me now instead of hurting.

Chapter Seven

The queasy irritability hanging over us needs to be smoothed over before Austin leaves for work, and I go to our bedroom where he's choosing his clothes. He smells of a new aftershave. Draped over his arm is a yellow shirt and a luridly-colored tie I've never seen.

I recline and watch him. Times like this, both of us half-dressed, we would have had sex, a hot and passionate quickie. I go behind him and wrap my arms around his torso, my chin in the dip of his spine. Instead of turning and holding me as he would in the past, he freezes and says, "Cut it out, Julia. I have to get to work." He takes my wrists and drops my arms away from him.

I think facetiously, "Hey Austin, I can get plenty of dick, right next door," and instantly hope I didn't say it aloud as well, but Austin is still preening, so I guess my thought was internal. I step away and watch him a moment. I used to love watching him dress. However, his suit today is unlike his usual choices of black, midnight blue, or gray. This suit is beige with an orange undertone, and the yellow shirt washes out his complexion. I watch him knot his tie, and I want to ask him who the hell sold him his outfit. Maybe the same salesperson that sold him the tight shiny clothes he wore to the Tex-Mex restaurant, but I keep quiet.

"Let me know if I can come to the office party, okay?"

He exhales audibly and says over his shoulder as he leaves the bedroom, "Just clean the fucking pool." The musky aftershave hangs in the air, more like fumes than a fragrance, and wow, his suit is awful.

I say under my breath, "Fuck you very much, Austin."

Maybe his behavior is pushback or denial, a means of refusing to admit he needs some pills, some snake oil for his pajama snake. The backdoor slams and he's gone. Lately, I've been worried he's no longer attracted to me. No amount of flirting with the likes of Lucy's husband can compensate.

At times like this morning, his moods and temper have turned me off. But I still need the physical part of love. The sexual dilemma—horny, but you don't want to boink the available one.

Dressed and in the studio, another job has come by email from an ad agency, a regular client. Their campaign is for a furniture store, and this advertisement is for a dresser. They've updated the store's concept by abandoning their former murky black and white photos and endless "Sales" in favor of sketchy, contemporary illustrations, paired with witty taglines. This headline is *Time to Change Your Drawers*.

When I break for lunch, Sarah and Bryan enter the kitchen, still wearing their pajamas. They stare covetously at my salad, and Sarah asks, "What's to eat?"

I shake my head, refusing to dignify the inanity of her question, and she approaches and lays her head on my shoulder—something she did as a child—and I stroke her hair. Her hand creeps toward my salad, and I tickle her. "You little monster!" I laugh, and she kisses my cheek. "Hey twinsters, how's the app coming along?"

Bryan opens the fridge and stares inside, and Sarah says, "Okay, I guess." They glance at each other—the famed twins' ESP—and giggle.

"What's so funny, kiddos?"

Bryan shrugs, "I dunno, dude. Just, no one over thirty should be allowed to say app." They both giggle again.

"Ha, ha." I put my dishes into the dishwasher and intend to head to my studio, but looking outside reminds me. The pool. Damn. I set the vacuum in motion, shock the water with chlorine pucks, and whisper, "There you go, Austin, a clean pool. Happy now?"

Back in the kitchen, the twins continue perusing the contents of the fridge. "Back up," I demand, closing the door. "No matter how long you stare, the chicken isn't going to dance for you."

Sarah opens the fridge again, pulls a leg off the chicken, laughs, and says, "Now it really can't dance."

"Hey, I saw a bunch of shopping bags. What did you buy?" Bryan asks.

"Yeah, what did you buy?" Sarah mimics.

"Art supplies. I've started painting."

"Bummer. I thought you bought clothes. What do you mean *started painting*? You already paint."

"I've always wanted to do some fine art, maybe have a gallery show."

"Dad told me you're jealous of Trix. So, now you're going to copy her?" Sarah says smugly.

An unpleasant jolt of surprise slaps me. What the…? Sarah and Austin have discussed me behind my back. "Really, Sarah? What else did your dad have to say about my work and my friends?"

She catches my pissed-off inflection and turns away. Bryan says, "So, now you'll have a hobby."

Their words chill. I've also thought painting would be a hobby, that fine art is a higher discipline than illustration work, that I'm not worthy, and my commercial work is all I'm good for, to pay the bills. I respond, "First off, when you see what I've painted, you can judge whether I'm imitating Trix. Also, painting can be more than a hobby. I'd like fine art to evolve into a second career."

Sarah rips the chicken leg in half and gnaws on a piece. She says through a mouthful, "Like, you're too old. All the famous artists are in their twenties." She accidentally spits out a chunk of chicken and ignores the lump on the floor.

"First, don't talk with food in your mouth, and second, pick that up." She grabs a paper towel, flounces to the errant blob, and wipes it up. I raise my eyebrows. "But about your comment…in their twenties, huh? Right. You mean like you, and all your fame?"

Anger crosses Sarah's face. She turns away. "Pretty mean, Mom."

I catch myself about to roll my eyes. "Really? I'd like to see some progress on the app you are designing. Besides, don't dish it out if you can't take it, Sarah. And for the record, I'm not washed up. Not by a longshot."

Bryan says, "Yeah, Sarah, she acts way younger than our friends' parents."

Recovered now, Sarah chimes in, "Like Dylan's parents. They're so old; I bet they shit dust."

They laugh uncontrollably, and I can't help but join them, sputtering, "I'll take that as a compliment, I think."

Bryan says through his laughter, "They fart spiderwebs!" and we laugh until tears flow.

Trix calls, and I carry the phone to my studio. She says, "Sounds like a happy place over there. What are you up to?"

"My kids can certainly be funny. And I've started applying paint. My first canvas. So exciting."

"Great!" she exclaims. "And how are things with Austin?"

"Ugh. I can't figure him out."

"So, what's up? Trouble in paradise?" Her lighter snicks. "Your dream. I caught some stress."

"Not more stress than normal."

She exhales. "I don't know how you do it. First, there

was Austin's mom with all the feeding and ass-wiping."

"Funny, her death just came up in conversation with Lucy, and how attached the kids were. When she got sick, Sarah worked right alongside me like a little miniature nurse."

"Then she was finally supposed to go to Bingo Acres, and a week before check-in, she died."

"Shady Grove," I correct.

"Geritol Heights." She snickers.

"Something's off with Austin. He's always been moody, but lately, he's so unpredictable."

"You say moody; I say asshole."

"You're funny. A weird thing happened." I tell her about waking to find him beside the bed.

"What the fuck?" she blurts.

"He denies everything, and says I imagine things."

"This is scary stuff, man. You tell anyone about him standing over you with a pillow and they'd think he was about to smother you. But even blockheaded Austin should be aware he won't get away with suffocating or shooting you."

I shrug. "Maybe I do imagine some things, but I didn't imagine, or dream that he was beside the bed."

"There's another explanation. Saying you imagine things is gaslighting. Maybe Austin is trying to make out you're crazy, or he wants to make you go crazy."

"Sorry to be dramatic."

"Don't you dare dismiss it. This is serious. That is so *you* to say something important, and then chop it into confetti and toss it to the wind like it's meaningless. The threat you felt in your nightmare had to come from somewhere. The dream was vivid and memorable to the point you can paint scenes from it. Be careful."

"I will." We say goodbye.

As soon as I hang up, the landline rings. Austin's boss, Marcy, shrieks, "Jesus, woman! Where's your husband? He's impossible to pin down! We've got clients in a boardroom waitin' on him. When he gets here, I'm going to remind him who's the boss. In case he's forgotten, it's moi!"

Marcy is a Botero subject: plump, with sausage-casing-tight skin, the effect partly attributable to her stretchy clothes that run about two sizes too small. She favors stagy makeup and sculpted caramel-colored hair. Marcy's hands and feet are small and dainty, and she's nimble, as is her mind, and anyone who underestimates her ought to watch their back. Inside the pudge, she's Mensa smart and tough, with a big heart.

"Heavens, Marcy, he left here hours ago."

"I've been trying his cell, and he's not picking up, damn it! He needs to get his ass in here now and take care of business."

"Something must have delayed him. He was heading to the office. He said he had your company party tonight. Just keep trying his cell."

"Yeah, the party. So, are you coming? For ages now, there's always some lame excuse why you don't show up."

"Spouses are invited tonight?"

"Spouses are always invited. You must come!"

"You're sure it isn't for employees only?"

"Hell, no. Where'd you get that idea? Get your cute little butt to the Colombe d'Or tonight. I mean it! If you don't show up, I'll know you're snubbin' me."

Austin lied to me. A paralyzing chill begins in my scalp and runs down my body. "Marcy, I'll come to the party…but don't tell Austin. I want to surprise him."

"No problem. I won't blab."

"And, by the way, is he receiving a promotion?" I ask.

"Shit, no. Maybe I shouldn't be so blunt, but Austin only qualifies for a Worst Employee of the Month plaque. He hardly shows up anymore. Oh! He just walked in. Finally! Bye." She laughs and hangs up.

I consider Marcy's call for the better part of an hour, then I call Trix, relate my conversation, and add, "I can't believe he lied. Marcy must be mistaken."

"Because no man in history ever lied to a woman, right?" She laughs cynically.

"It's got to be a misunderstanding."

"There's one way to find out, Julia. Go to the party."

"It'll seem like I'm checking on him. I don't think I should. I'll just phone him and confirm I can attend."

"Julia! You *are* checking on him. He lied to you and if you call him he'll lie again. If you don't go tonight, I'll personally show up at your house, and tattoo *Welcome* on your forehead, doormat."

"You're right. I'll go. I'll go. I'll go."

"Show up an hour late and figure out what's what. If nothing's weird, then no harm done. If Austin's pissed, too bad. After all, his boss invited you." She adds, "I want you to think about this, though. Lies are like rats. If you see one, there are a hundred more you don't see. I'm home tonight, so after the party, give me the scoop." We hang up.

I set aside the grapes drawing and work on a quick job, a fashion illustration of a woman's profile in silhouette for use in generic ads and promotions. As the afternoon winds down, I lounge in a bubble bath then it's déjà vu, as I put on the same dress, makeup, stockings, gold jewelry, and platform pumps as I wore for my birthday non-event.

In the kitchen, Sarah is eating five-layer dip from a container. She's in pj's of harem pants and a tank top, its graphic reads, *Bite Me. I Taste Like Chick.* I'm dismayed by the tats on her arms and chest—the intense colors, black outlines, the large scale. "Hi, Sarah."

She asks, "Hey *ho*, got any 'tos?"

I'm aware her 'hey ho' doesn't mean 'hey there' that ho is the abbreviation of whore. "Are you asking for Doritos? Got the munchies, huh?" She puts the dip and her spoon on the breakfast bar. "Put the dip in the fridge. And Sarah, don't call anyone a *ho*, especially me, okay?"

"Okay, bitch. Is that better?" She saunters to the pantry, tears open a bag of tortilla chips, takes a bowl of tuna salad out of the fridge, removes its plastic cover, then moseys toward the kitchen door.

Cajoling, I say, "Sarah, don't leave any leftover tuna in your room, or it'll smell like the dumpster behind Skipper's Fish Shack, okay?"

She sniffs the air. "It's not tuna you smell. It's your nasty old-woman cooch." She laughs loudly, then deliberately bumps me as she passes.

I grab the back of her tank top, stopping her in half stride. Startled, she drops the chips and tuna salad. Chips scatter across the floor, and the bowl breaks spilling pinkish tuna goo in a heap on the tile. Her shocked surprise gives me the upper hand, and I seize her right wrist and twist her arm up behind her back, forcing her to her knees. Chips crunch underfoot with our every move. Still holding her wrist, I wind my fingers into her hair, push her head down, and rub her face in the tuna-and-oniony mush.

I shout in her ear, "I've had enough of your shit, you disrespectful, entitled, miserable excuse for a daughter!" I continue holding her face in the fishy muck. "Apologize right now!" She emits a strangled cry, and I add, "Apologize, or I'll put you over my knee and spank the snot out of you."

She cries out, "I'm sorry, mom! I'll be good, I promise."

But of course, I don't. I've only ever touched my kids in a loving manner, and I never believed in corporal punishment. To me, hitting sends the wrong message, teaching that violence is okay. Instead, I tell her, "Saying horrible things for shock value doesn't suit you, Sarah. You're better than that, so I want you to stop, okay? Plus, misogynist insults like that wouldn't be tolerated from a man, and coming from a woman I think it's even worse. It shows a stunning lack of loyalty to your gender."

She peers at me intently, and I notice she's moved beyond arm's reach, as if she knows she went too far. "Well, it's better than being like you, always saying *okay?* at the end of your sentences. When you do that, you're asking, begging, people to agree with you. Pretty pathetic." She turns and heads upstairs, food in hand.

"Sarah, you know I'm right, and I know you're deflecting," I call after her.

Is she right about my speech pattern? Am I always asking for…what? Permission, or for agreement, as she stated? If so, why can't I make a declarative sentence?

Chapter Eight

With necessities in a tiny evening bag, I check my outfit and makeup in the mirror and smooth my skirt over my hips. Driving to Houston, I have the same sensation of anticipation and fear as the other night when I ventured out solo, except it's more intense, because I'm checking on Austin and challenging his lie.

I arrive at the stone building an hour late, as Trix suggested. I valet park and insinuate myself into a gaggle of latecomers to drift through the entrance and the opulent lobby, and along a wide, carpeted hallway. I enter an anteroom set up for cocktails. Waiters circulate trays of martinis, pink cocktails, and wine, through clusters of salespeople, execs, assistants, and techies, some of whom are already well lubricated. The mood is of comfortable sophistication and reserved mischief. Adjacent is a ballroom with tables and chairs draped in white, a stage with musical instruments, and a dance floor.

Marcy's laugh catches my attention, and I follow the

sound. She wears a splashy-patterned, tight dress. If she sits on one of the tufted chintz sofas, she'll disappear. Her stiff hair is molded into a flip, her tiny mascara'd eyes sparkle, and her cheeks are clown-dots of fuchsia. She gives me a viselike hug, intercepts pink drinks, and hands me one, then toasts herself, shouting, "To promotions! Thank God, I got one!" and lets loose donkey-braying laughter.

"Congratulations, Marcy."

"Thanks, I finally crashed through the glass ceiling, darlin'!"

As a conversationalist, Marcy's good points—raucous, loud, opinionated, irreverent, and politically incorrect—are often her drawbacks. "Are you still Austin's boss?"

"Nope. He's under Bob's thumb now. Good thing, too. I'm so frustrated with him I might've gone and murdered him." She pretend-wipes her forehead. "Phew."

I catch a glimpse of Austin in the dining area. He's in a group of men. The others are in tasteful business wear that contrasts with Austin's bilious suit, yellow shirt, and gaudy tie. I take a small step out of his sightline. Marcy scrunches up her eyes, and they bore into me. "I'm tellin' ya, girl; you gotta kick Austin's butt. He's slipping badly."

A woman with white-blonde hair goes by, coyly wiggling her fingers at Marcy. Marcy openly sneers and turns aside, snubbing her. I ask, "Who is she?"

Marcy chuckles. "That bitch is Salem Kingston."

"Bitch? Really?"

"Really. That twat has quite a reputation. She'll screw anyone and screw anyone over."

Marcy can still shock me. "Is Salem her real name?"

Marcy squeals, "I know! What were her parents thinking? The witch trials, or the freakin' cigarettes? Salem *bitch* trials is more like it! But lucky me, I've been promoted out of her kennel." She laughs, full volume.

"Is she being promoted?"

"Hell, no! She plays hooky as much as Austin."

An attractive man in jeans, black T-shirt, and sportcoat, more casual than the firm's dress code of suit and tie, approaches and hands Marcy another drink. Marcy takes him by the arm, snuggles into him, and says, "This is Gage. He's my man." He smiles at her, prompting Marcy to screech like a banshee, punch my upper arm, slurp her drink, and shout, "These drinks are too small!"

Gage's heritage may be Nordic, his age close to my vintage. There's silver in his medium-dark hair, and he appears buff, but not a bulky weightlifter, more likely a runner. I picture him in an ad for Swiss chocolate, or as a model for the cover of a bodice-ripper novel about sexy Vikings ravishing lusty maidens.

Four women wearing nearly identical gray pantsuits arrive to congratulate Marcy on her promotion. She is in her element. We watch Marcy a moment, and Gage turns his gaze on me. I make brief eye contact, "They certainly go all out for these company parties."

He steps closer to hear me over Marcy, and nods. "I believe there's a dance band after dinner." His calm demeanor offsets Marcy's flamboyance. They are a well-balanced couple.

"Do you work for the company, Gage?"

"No. I'm a reporter for several Houston online and print publications. You?"

"Illustrator. Freelance. Mainly commercial work for advertising agencies."

"An artist. You enjoy your work?" His closeness has me flustered and a little breathless, animal attraction, pure and simple.

"Yes, I do enjoy my work. There's plenty of variety; I'm never bored."

A bulky man careens into me, knocking me off balance, and I stumble against Gage. He steadies me with a hand on the small of my back. Our faces are inches apart, and the contrast of five o'clock shadow against his skin is in hyper-focus, the scent of light aftershave, along with something pleasantly male—pheromones perhaps—collides with my libido. A shockwave of desire courses into my diaphragm. Breathless, I quickly step back. "Sorry," I mumble, and my face goes hot. Does he feel the attraction, too? Ever since I met Austin, all men have seemed genderless, gelded, so what gives?

"No need to be, I'm certainly not sorry," he says, smiling.

Is this flirting? A wave of shame smacks me. How embarrassing, flirting with Marcy's boyfriend within range of my spouse, and at a company party. My libido is off the chain—first Earl, and now Gage. I excuse myself and make my way to the restroom. I don't see Austin.

In the bathroom, inspecting my makeup, I start a monologue in my head. Screw this. Screw my passivity, my cajoling of Austin, tippy-toeing around his moods. Screw his abandonment of my needs and our marriage. Screw his rejection of my concerns. Screw his favoring his activities over me. Screw his absences. Screw his lies and screw his suggestion that I divorce him. I will find Austin, and we will check into a five-star downtown hotel, have some drinks at a bar, room service, and hot sex.

As I apply lipstick, the blonde woman, Salem, enters and stands next to me. We nod hello in the mirror. She's probably about ten or fifteen years younger than me.

She's striking but not beautiful; what some would call overdone. Tan too dark, makeup too thick, boob job too traffic-cone-ish. I expect she was seduced by the ruthless taskmaster *Pursuit-of-Youth* who counsels, 'if a little is good, a lot is better.' Before we know what's happened, we've gone from *oh baby* to *oh shit.*

But single women want to attract a guy, and sexy and superficial are effective. Then what? Hope the man will take the time to look under the hood, discover the real us, and fall in love? When we're finally coupled, we expect our ties—of history, family, a profound human connection—will hold tight. We expect security, a kind of insurance, solidarity that I hope Austin and I still possess.

It must be difficult being single, with the prevalence of dating sites that seem akin to catalog shopping for a mate. Then there are the expectations and terms your date brings with him to the table—perhaps he has kids, or health issues, or loses his job. Times have changed from women being labeled a bottle-blonde or disparaged as *gilding the lily*. Plus, there's a new acceptance of surgical, laser, and chemical enhancements, and in certain circles, women are expected to flaunt such augmentations; perhaps Salem's not trying to fool anyone. She applies lip gloss with her pinkie finger, then takes a vial of perfume from her clutch and sprays a cloud above her head and lets it settle over her. The label reads *Incredible Me*. She smiles again, displaying a glow-in-the-dark keyboard.

I glance down to put my lipstick into my bag and catch sight of Salem's left hand. A wedding band. So, not single after all. There's a flash under the halogen lights. Diamonds. My watch with the gold motorcycle charm attached. With a haughty little wave, she twitches her butt out the door as I stand stunned and immobile. And in her wake is the mist of her perfume, the same fragrance I've smelled in the night, trailing Austin.

No, this can't be. My brain has turned into my ceramic phrenology head with many outlined and labeled areas, including *Ego*, *Math*, *How to choose a ripe avocado,* and *The i-before-e rule*. However, there is a large blank section for this incident, this situation, and my confusion. And after several frozen moments of leaning stiff-armed on the vanity, my brain is still a blank. Nothing makes sense.

I test my ability to walk, but my legs have turned to jelly. I wait a while and finally leave the restroom. Austin stands in a circle of people, still unaware of my presence, and Salem is across the room from him. He watches her, and she returns his gaze. She waves, displaying the sparkling watch and points to it with her other hand like a TV game show presenter. He smiles proudly and nods, an animal that has marked his territory.

There must be an explanation. Those watches must be knock-offs, cheap copies in fake gold with cubic zirconia instead of diamonds. But how many have a gold charm of a Harley attached? My heart is pounding, my hands shaking, alerting me to the lies and denial in my reasoning, and I'm forced to give in to common sense and let comprehension fill the big empty spot in my brain.

Austin makes his way to Salem, and she greets him with a kiss. Their touch is natural, familiar, and I transition from denial to fierce fear, a foreboding that squeezes my heart into my throat, throttling me. Their magnetism is undeniable, and though I'm still attracted to Austin, his magnet has turned away from me and repelled him.

Salem whispers something. Austin scans the room and finally sees me, then in guilt, or surprise, or anger, he scowls and becomes the color of the pink drinks the waiters are serving. Austin speaks to Salem, and she smiles until he starts in my direction. She snatches his sleeve, but he breaks away, and Salem's smile warps into a pout. Ridiculously, I'm encouraged. He'll explain what's going on and we'll put an end to this nonsense. And I notice my belief parallels my thoughts in the dream that he would get me off the target and the stage, to safety.

Austin picks up something from a table. A dagger with a gleaming blade. This makes no sense. He can't be a knife thrower in this crowded place. Plus, I don't have on my proper outfit, and he's wearing his obnoxious suit instead of his tux, but he winds up and throws anyway. I watch the knife coming at me in slow motion. I'm rooted to the spot, and the impact knocks me staggering back as the blade stabs my breastbone and pierces my heart. All those books, poems, songs about heartache are correct; there is agony in my chest, unlike anything I've ever felt.

My dream was trying to warn me, and at my peril, in my denial and ignorance, I listened, but not hard enough because now I'm forced to admit, I didn't want to know.

There's a voice in my head—*Discretion is the better*

part of valor. You're above this. Walk away. Don't react. An aggressive group of hand-shakers delays Austin, and I start moving, briskly leave the ballroom, and stroll the long hallway. There will be no confrontation or discussion—not here, not now. I can't afford the humiliation of pretending civility while he lies to my face, to lose any more of my pride, and at that moment, my injury and my dignity merge. Together, injury and dignity make one tough-as-nails state of emotional bearing—the revenge served up cold, the British stiff upper lip, the comic relief of a self-deprecating joke.

Injury, Dignity, and I hold ourselves above public disgrace, and away from the combustible situation poised to singe my ego, immolate my entire life. In one package, I am Aphrodite, Princess Diana, Joan of Arc, Jackie Kennedy-Onassis, Queen Nefertiti, and every other tough, composed woman through history.

Although my purse is much too tiny, I pull a jack-in-the-box out of my bag. I place my husband's infidelity inside and crank the handle to give me up to twenty-four hours before the ugly truth will metaphorically explode. That's better, the awful surprise is boxed up, and I'm in control. I square my shoulders and start for the lobby.

Marcy and Gage stop me. Marcy says, "You okay, darlin'?"

I go close and say into her ear, "Marcy, please stall Austin until I leave."

"I'd love to! You go, girl!" she says happily, and she's off at a trot.

Gage accompanies me. I find the valet tag in my purse, and he asks, "Are you okay to drive? I could be your chauffeur."

At his kindness, tears haze my eyes, and I blink them back. I will not cry. "Thank you. I'm not going far. I'll be fine."

At the valet stand, I hand my tag to the attendant. I desperately want to make small talk but can't think of anything to say. The valet wheels my car around and holds the door open. Gage and I shake hands, and he lingers at the valet stand, watching me drive away.

As I exit, in my rearview mirror, Austin emerges and scrutinizes the parking lot as Gage enters the building. Austin takes out his phone. My phone rings, and I let the call go to voicemail. He calls twice more before I give in and pick up. His voice comes through the speakers.

He says in a loud whisper, "What the fuck are you doing here when I specifically told you not to show up. This party is a work event." I picture him, head ducked, cupping the phone, smiling and nodding to anyone who looks his way.

"You said the party was employees only. Then Marcy told me spouses are invited, so I decided to attend." My tone is meek. My conditioned obedience hasn't been banished.

"So instead of asking me, you called Marcy, who is—oh yeah—*my* fucking boss, in case you've forgotten. *My* boss, not *your* friend. But you went and called her behind my back. That's the trouble with you, Julia. Always sticking your nose where it doesn't belong."

Anger replaces the pain. I want to tell him I didn't call Marcy; Marcy called me and gave away that he'd lied, and if I had called him, he would have lied again. I want to say I don't need to justify where I go or who I see. But the tinkling tune from the jack-in-the-box reminds me to bide my time. Instead, I affirm, "I'm going to spend the night at Trix's."

"Great. Stay there. You two bitches deserve each other." He hangs up.

I drive ten minutes to Trix's building, park, and sit rerunning the evening, seeing Austin and Salem together, their kiss, their obvious connection. I hammer the steering wheel with my fists, but still manage to hold back tears.

Trix's building is brick and industrial, built in the 1930s and converted fifteen years ago to live-work lofts. The four-story structure's original freight elevator with wood-slatted gates lifts me to the top floor. The floors are concrete, and corridors are painted white.

Chapter Nine

Trix's door stands ajar. Unlike the undersized apartments in converted industrial buildings passed off as so-called lofts, Trix's space is authentic, an entire floor, with a wall of exposed brick, twelve-foot ceilings, skylights, and floor-to-ceiling metal-framed windows. Frosted glass delineates the bedroom and a sleek kitchen. Her sofa and chairs are oversized and low-slung with upholstery in natural linen, her dining furniture is constructed of steel and raw wood oiled and rubbed to a buttery patina. Blank canvases lean against walls awaiting their turn on her easel. There's a scent of oil paints, herbs, and French cigarettes.

This space is like an extension of Trix, and perfect for her. Austin has often accused me of wanting to be like Trix, but if her loft, her life, her work, is what Austin thinks I aspire to, he's wrong. While I chafe at the competitive domesticity of exurbia, living in Trix's loft would be like playacting, as artificial as wearing an itchy Parisian-artist's costume, a smock, and beret, with a big oval palette on my arm. Where I belong is an unanswered question.

Frankie and Trix are lounging, and melancholy jazz is playing—Diana Krall singing *The Night We Called It a Day*—goblets of red wine are on the coffee table. A stepladder stands before two nearly finished, six-by-eight-foot paintings, a diptych of ruby-red, enormous poppies. Even in the low lighting, it is obvious she has captured the plant's character in undulating fuzzy stems, and crêpe-paper-like petals unfurling from pods like the wings of butterflies leaving a chrysalis.

I examine the work. "Wow."

"Like it, Julia?" She inhales and blows smoke toward the rafters.

"Absolutely. It's wonderful, powerful. A commission?"

"Yup, some people in Dallas. They must have one big-ass house to hang this fucker."

Trix is wearing layered asymmetrical black gauze. If a garment is evenly proportioned when purchased, she'll take scissors to it and transform the piece to her liking. She sits with her feet tucked under her, taking on a likeness to twigs under a veil. Frankie appears boneless. I sink into a low chair and relate the scenarios from the party—of Salem up close in the bathroom, the shock of seeing the wristwatch, their kiss.

"That thing of the gift showing up on the wrong lover is classic. I watched a movie once with it in the plot," Frankie says as he lights a joint and hands it to me. "You poor bunny. At least you look fabulous."

"Thanks, Frankie."

Trix says, "Austin sure is old-school. These days, cheaters are more likely to be caught by crap on social media or their texts."

I inhale the scorching weed. Something I haven't done in decades, but I welcome the familiar burn in my throat. In a strangled doper's voice, "Something was off, but I kept shoving my doubts aside."

Trix says, "Denial."

"I've never wanted to be suspicious. Suspicion is like a shark. It'll eat you alive." I sip wine.

Trix leans forward to pick up her wine glass, silver bracelets clanking over her wrist. She says, "The shark analogy is dead on. I got jealous of a boyfriend once, and I started looking for proof of him cheating. I never found anything conclusive, but after a while, I became obsessed with finding something—I wanted to find something—and I constructed scenarios in my head and worked hard to dig up evidence to prove my theories." She lights a cigarette and exhales a column of smoke that smells not unpleasantly like a mix of molasses and horse barn. "In the end, I realized he wasn't cheating, but he left clues around and dropped hints to keep me off balance. After a while, his mind-fuckery was reason enough to break it off." She laughs. "Then I couldn't get rid of him. He wouldn't leave."

"I had one of those breakups," Frankie exhales and says, "It's like trying to throw away a garbage can."

"Exactly," Trix giggles. "So how gorgeous is this chick to deserve such an expensive trinket?"

"She's not extraordinary, but she plays up the sexy, although, to my eye, it's forced."

"Vulgar?" He asks.

"Not really. I'd say Salem is striking from a distance, but close up, not so much."

"Good from far, but far from good." Frankie gives me the side-eye with a smirk.

"Yep. And she's married."

"Younger?" Trix asks with eyebrows raised.

"I'd say about fifteen years younger than us." I sigh.

"Oh, *gurl*," Frankie drawls. "Straight men are so predictable. Austin definitely has a reservation at Hotel Hell."

"You need to think up some revenge." Trix declares. "Believe me. Payback is cleansing."

"I'm not the revenge type. Karma will probably take care of Austin."

Frankie smiles. "Time wounds all heels..."

"Good one," I gulp wine. "I hope you're right, but for now, I'm still in shock. I'm hurt and pissed, and I hope I can fix us."

Trix and Frankie stare at each other in disbelief. Frankie states, "Hon, sometimes things can be simple. You know he's cheating. Why hang in?"

"Call me a hopeless case, but it's too soon to give up."

Frankie snickers. "Talk about an optimist. You're the little girl in a room full of horseshit who starts digging because there's gotta be a pony somewhere."

"Hmm," I add wistfully. "The other day, I thought I was being Pollyanna-ish. Maybe it's a personality trait I've always had."

Frankie stands and stretches. "You need to beef up your survival instincts and figure out what you want. Do you really want Austin, even after being blindsided? And don't forget, Austin wasn't the only one who bought her the watch. You did too, along with whatever other extravagances. I gotta go. I have to get up early. I feel for you." He kisses our cheeks and lets himself out.

We sit quietly a while until Trix says, "There's something I have to tell you."

"Okay." I'm wary.

"You want to salvage your relationship, but... Austin hit on me, about eleven years ago. Actually, what happened was more like an attack. After, he sent me emails telling me to stay away from you. Later, he did the same thing to one of Frankie's female friends."

"He started tearing you down, right after the New Year's party..." I fight tears again. "What exactly happened?"

She hesitates. "Austin locked the door and cornered me in the bedroom where the coats were. He had me against a wall and stuffed someone's scarf in my mouth. He held my wrists. He's very strong. His other hand was fumbling to get his dick out when someone hammered on the door. He was drunk, but still."

I'm staring at her with my jaw unhinged. "Oh, Trix. My god." We hug, and then sit silently. Shock layered on shock. We listen to city sounds; the elevator chugs through the floors, there's a siren in the distance, faint traffic.

Finally, Trix says, "I've been happy not being around him."

I sip wine. "I wish I had known." Something else to add to the jack-in-the-box, or perhaps it's a Pandora's box, soon to be opened.

"I was worried if I told you, he'd lie and say I came onto him, or that it was consensual. But now you're at a crossroad, and you need all the facts." Her tone is resigned. "Promise me you won't let him talk his way out of his mess. You've been a mushroom for a long time."

"A mushroom?"

"Kept in the dark and fed shit," she says and laughs, but it's without humor.

I grimace and take a sip of wine. "I wonder if things would have been very different if I knew what Austin did eleven years ago."

"You would have been in a terrible spot. Husband versus friend."

"What if I'd left him then, or if we called the police?" I can't visualize Austin in handcuffs, and say, "Austin's a great manipulator. I see that now. Jesus, I am a mushroom. A mushroom of the first degree."

"A mega mushroom."

"A giant Portobello." We chuckle, and after a moment, I add, "Something's not right. At tonight's party, when Austin saw me there, he was angry and chewed me out for being at the party."

"But Austin has no idea you found the watch earlier, does he?" She grinds her cigarette out in a matte-black ashtray.

"No. He doesn't know I found the watch. So he believes I'm unaware of his cheating, and he thinks he's only in the doghouse for lying about staff spouses not being invited."

Trix smiles. "They both think you're clueless. Wow. Checkmate."

I finish my wine and put my glass aside. "That certainly gives me the upper hand. Now I think Salem deliberately followed me to the ladies room, then pointed me out to Austin."

"Of course, she did. She knows who you are. I'd put money on her stalking you on social media. Even though you limit your exposure, there are photos of you on my page and Lucy's and elsewhere. And tonight, there you were right in front of her, and she couldn't resist. I bet she felt clever putting the watch literally under your nose. Reckless overconfidence."

"Arrogance and hubris." I nod. "A very bitchy move and Salem isn't aware of the side effects of what she did. But I had to both find the watch and get Marcy's invitation to clue me in."

"Marcy's a dark horse. What's her angle?"

"Good question. Marcy was Austin's boss, but not anymore since she got promoted. Her dislike of Austin is obvious." I pour us more wine.

"Therefore, she took pleasure in getting you to the party to witness their tryst firsthand."

"No question. Marcy is wily enough to engineer the encounter. Plus, it's clear she loathes Austin and Salem." I pause a moment and remove my earrings and necklace. "What do you think Salem's deal is? Why Austin when there are single men available at work?"

"She might not want someone single, or the single guys don't want the drama of someone who's married. Stuff can happen when people are in each other's spacc day after day."

I nod again. "To me, Salem is a fairly attractive, married woman, who has probably had a couple of kids; body a bit lumpy, a few wrinkles, but trying to wring whatever she still can from her appearance. Maybe she got caught up in Austin's charisma and his appearance, and with gifts like the watch, well."

Trix says, "I got you something." She goes to her work area, returns, and hands me an odd gizmo, about four inches tall, with two legs, and an adjustable screw attachment.

"What the hell is this?" I ask, turning the gadget in my hands.

"A chastity belt for Austin," she says, and we both laugh. "Kidding. But after you told me about him standing over you with the pillow, I was scared. It's a doorstop to keep Austin out of your bedroom or studio, wherever you choose."

"This might be excessive. I just need to lock the bedroom door."

Trix snorts. "I bet your door has one of those lame locks that takes five seconds to pick with a screwdriver. I'm getting the impression his behavior has become more extreme, and you need to be careful."

I play with the gadget for a minute. "This is a thoughtful gift. Thank you very much. Although the chastity belt might be better." We giggle. "I can't believe I'm laughing." I place the doorstop on the coffee table. "I've been so dense. There were so many classic signs leading up to tonight: his absences, the lack of sex and affection, his criticism and spitefulness, his hiding of texts and phone calls, his new clothes. I couldn't see what was right in front of my face." Trix's face shows an inner turmoil. "What?"

"I don't want to hurt your feelings…"

"But?"

"But sometimes there's a lot you don't see, or you acknowledge things, but you still don't really, truly see them."

"Such as?"

"You don't see your incredible talent, your physical beauty, how hard you work, what you deserve in a relationship, and Austin's abusive behavior on all kinds of levels. You don't see why Sarah has taken on her tough-girl veneer and why Bryan lets Sarah dominate him. You don't see that there are four adults under your roof, but you are consistently the javelin catcher, and maybe your life isn't the American dream after all."

We sit in silence a while and drink wine. Trix goes into the bathroom, emerging with sleeping pills, and soon I'm slumbering dreamlessly.

Chapter Ten

Around five, I wake dehydrated and headachy. I dress, drink a bottle of water, and in the bathroom, I wipe off smeared eye makeup and pop two of Trix's aspirin. I leave a thank-you note on her coffeemaker, pick up the doorstop and my belongings, and let myself out.

Driving south away from Houston's core, the bright lights dim to darkness and thoroughfares widen, facilitating the ever-spreading development that is metastasizing into the countryside. Fields that grew food and sustained longhorns a few months ago are now bulldozed, and rows of crops have given way to lines of wood-framed skeletons, pale and strappy in the moonlight. Seemingly endless billboards for housing developments entice drivers with *Singles! Water view! Custom build! If you lived here, you'd be home now!* I can hardly complain, considering I live in exurbia, and we were early pioneers of the now-unstoppable, indelible, creeping stain on the landscape.

Will Austin be home when I arrive? Dread has me

trembling again. Trix's revelation that he was physical with her—there's no possible justification. Austin only stopped his assault because someone hammered on the door. It was a close call. I picture the scenario of Trix with a scarf jammed in her mouth. That alone indicates malice. Add Austin fumbling to get his erect penis out of his zipper, and I'm nauseated. I pull off the freeway and lean out my door, but there's only gagging and a few dry heaves, and I pull back onto the road.

More billboards advertise storefront medical procedures: *MRI Center*, *Lap Band*, *Plastic Surgery with No Downtime*. And lawyers: *We sue lawyers! Eighteen-wheeler Accident?* and *Fast, Painless Divorce!* The most flamboyant attorney is caricatured as a skydiver who advertises on television and billboards throughout the city. His tagline is, *Don't take a fall or a dive! Call attorney Otis Boudreaux and get a sky-high settlement!* Hopefully, we can somehow salvage the marriage, and I won't need an ambulance chaser like Boudreaux to do battle for me.

The sunrise is a thin pink line as I pull into a coffee shop near my subdivision. Instead of adding to the drive-through queue of idling cars, I go inside and order a concoction of sweet, creamy iced latte with whipped cream piled high, a decadent dessert somehow passing for breakfast fare. Facing my reflection in a window, wearing my cocktail dress, I could be viewed as a party girl or one-night-stand who didn't get home last night. I rerun the scene of Salem in the mirror, of her perfume, of her swinging her ass out the door. Am I imagining things now, Austin?

On the short drive home, the sunrise is full-blown and bounces glare off buildings and cars. Mercifully, the twins' and Austin's cars are gone, which is not unusual, given it's Thursday, a workday, and the kids often stay out twenty-four hours straight.

In the garage, my imagination slips its chain. What did Austin and Salem do, and where were they last night? Austin knew I was staying at Trix's.

Of course they ended up in a hotel, and had horny-monkey jungle sex on the floor, the bathroom counter, in the shower, all while knocking back champagne. This morning they're in their wrinkled evening clothes, hair askew, adorably hungover, drinking a hair-of-the-dog antidote of Bloody Marys, or mimosas. And they're eating; no, they're feeding each other eggs benedict, Parma ham, and fresh croissants. They're discussing what a dope I am, how I have no idea about their fabulous relationship. Fuck!

Was I a coward running away last night? Maybe I should have stayed, confronted them both, and demanded he go with me right then. But like my habit of asking permission, of softening any demand or request with *okay?* at the end of my sentences, aggressive behavior isn't in me, although aggression on my part has been prevalent in my recent weird daydreams. With the garage door closed for soundproofing, I scream until my throat is sore, which tranquilizes my anger and my imagination, but makes my headache worse.

Beaver streaks out the door as I enter the house. I strip and step into a scalding shower. How could he? The scope of such a simple question is colossal. How could he deceive me? How could he hazard everything? How could he not see the impending pain? How could he treat us, our union, so shabbily? How could he risk his children finding out? How could he pillory me before his peers?

And I start to bawl like a little kid, until I'm swollen, stuffed up, blotchy, and dehydrated from making snot and tears, and can't cry anymore. I towel off and go to bed, hoping for sleep, but his scent lingers in the sheets. I can't bear it, and head to the living room sofa.

Over and over, I run through what will happen when Austin gets home, but I can't imagine our script. Should we sit in the living room or at the dining table? Or stand in the kitchen? At the prospect of a showdown, by turns, my stomach is full of lead, then tingling with something writhing.

Tired of thinking, I tune into an episode of *Law and Order*. As the show progresses, clues pointing conclusively to a suspect unravel one by one, and nothing is as it seems, leaving the detectives wondering how they'd been so spectacularly deluded.

I go to my studio but, unable to concentrate, I wander the house. Panicky fear and doubt creep over me. I have no concrete proof because Austin and Salem weren't caught in flagrante delicto. And if erroneously accused, he would be put in the difficult position of trying to prove his innocence. Indicted, found guilty, and punished, he might as well commit the crime. My accusations could drive him to her, along with branding me as jealous or crazy.

Also, I'm the one who snooped and found the watch. Except, was I snooping since the box was pretty much in plain sight? Maybe the box was in plain sight because there is a good explanation for Salem wearing the watch. Otherwise, surely he would have hidden such incriminating evidence more carefully. I may be about to throw away our marriage with off-base allegations. The TV show with the misguided detectives has weakened my resolve. Losing Austin might mean losing everything, a bleak future. I may be erroneously jumping to conclusions.

I call Trix and tell her about my doubts. Straight to the point, she says, "Sounds like denial to me. A breakup is a loss, like a death. You have to go through similar stages: denial, anger, bargaining, depression, and finally, acceptance."

"Even though I'm mortified about everything, including what he did to you, I'm afraid of making a mistake. What if I'm wrong about him and Salem?"

"Julia, don't forget he lied to keep you away from the party, which should tell you he was hiding something." She says firmly, "As usual, your nature is to examine all sides and give him the benefit of the doubt. You'll even invent excuses for him to avoid a confrontation."

"I don't want to split up if we can make the marriage

work—if he gives us an honest shot. I'm terrified of divorce. The women I've known who have been through a breakup—the conflict, loneliness, the financial pressures—it's always so awful."

Trix says, "Seems to me you're already lonely and have financial pressures. Divorce is a big, stressful thing to go through, but people survive and come out the other side intact, sometimes even better off. Divorce no longer carries a stigma like the old days. Besides, could you stay with him knowing he's screwing that woman and lying to your face?"

"If he stops fooling around… I can't imagine life without him. I'm not ready to throw in the towel."

"Julia, back in the day, didn't you own a T-shirt with the slogan *A Woman Needs a Man Like a Fish Needs a Bicycle*? Honey, stay strong. He owes you answers to any questions you throw at him. Don't hold back."

"Of course, you're right, but I'm scared."

Trix says. "You can call me anytime, day or night."

"Thanks." We hang up. I'll confront Austin. We need to blow apart the bullshit and wash it away with a fire hose, a thorough cleansing. After, we'll see what remains. The jack-in-the-box music in my head is louder and beginning to slow to the eventual climax. I phone Austin. "Where are you? We need to talk, okay?" My *okay* makes me want to slap my obsequious self.

He's silent for a full minute, and I wait, refusing to fill the dead air. He says, "I'm at the office, and I'm planning to work late."

"No. You need to come home. Now." I nearly add, *okay?* but don't, and it feels unnatural. More silence follows, and he finally, reluctantly agrees.

I pat my puffy face with a cold, wet washcloth, then apply my usual mascara, blush, and lipstick. What does a woman wear to a confrontation when she still has a flake of hope? I choose jeans and a loose silk top, with no jewelry. The kids text they'll be out all night. Perfect.

Then I make dinner. Of course, I make food. A good

wife like me won't let my cheating husband go hungry while we have the most soul-destroying conversation of our lives. Besides, I need to kill time until he arrives.

Austin's arrival is standard. He stops into his home office, then saunters to the kitchen doorway. He's wearing slacks and a dress shirt, not his ugly suit from last night's party, so he must have come home last night and left for work before I arrived, or did he have a backup change of clothes in his car or office? He is so damned handsome; I can't imagine being without him. I remind myself he's not an ornament. He's supposed to be a full-fledged, loyal, and protective partner.

His expression becomes mixed; his brow furrowed, a slight smile on his lips, reflecting concern and something else, dread maybe, or hope. I've always viewed Austin as having nerves of steel, but perhaps there are fluttering moths in his gut and earwigs, fearwigs, crawling up his neck.

He rocks back and forth, hands in pockets, a posture begging scuffing a foot on the floor and saying something like, *Golly gee, ma'am.* He's different, weak and sheepish. I recognize his stance as one he adopts when he's messed up something trivial like breaking a dish or forgetting an appointment. His pose is his substitute for saying he's sorry, and I realize I've never heard him apologize. Why haven't I noticed that before now? Trix nailed it. Here's another example of something I didn't see even though it was in front of my face.

Maybe the aw-shucks pose isn't remorse, but embarrassment for his lie about spouses not being invited to the party. He might sense this is important since I've never demanded he come home before. He's about to find out he's a spider caught in his own web.

I dish out dinner, and he sets the dining table. Our innocent and automatic domestic habits, programmed through years of repetition, are from another life. A tear splashes on the countertop—a tear I'm not willing to part with—and I take a breath and remind myself what came before; how I've strived to live up to my responsibilities. Now I desperately hope I haven't been a fool, a clown, like the one in my imaginary jack-in-the-box. I tamp down my fear and misery and carry our plates to the dining table where we both take our customary seats, facing each other. He places his napkin on his lap, then pours merlot. I watch him closely as I sip wine.

I cut a small piece of meat, chew, and swallow. Eating is mechanical. We are silent as Austin looks at his plate and eats his meal as usual. His demeanor is self-satisfied as he waits me out, no doubt expecting a slap on the wrist for his fib.

I put my imaginary jack-in-the-box, stuffed with my rage and confusion, on the table, and the music slows, grinding down along with my patience, and I'm no longer curious what he has invented to placate me.

"Look at me." I hear my assertiveness. He eyes me warily and blinks. I lean forward to maintain eye contact. "I know you gave Salem an expensive Cartier watch."

The jangling music stops, and BAM! Austin flinches like I stuck a fork into an open wound, and the jack-in-the-box's top bursts open, and what spews from the box isn't a clown as I expected, but a thousand, rabid, screaming bats, a throng that's melting, coagulating into a revolting, viscous, black tar. And the stinking black pitch coats and smothers any affection I've retained or clung to, so I no longer care if he stays or leaves, loves me or doesn't love me.

I sit a moment and listen to be sure the shrieking of the bats isn't coming from me. It's not. I'm silent, still waiting, and the jack-in-the-box and the stifling swarm have vanished. Everything has changed. Now Austin is frozen in his seat, and I'm in control.

If he prepared a statement to justify his lie and charm his way out of the doghouse for his crapola about spouses being uninvited, I've stolen his moment.

But as I crest my wave of clarity, I teeter on the brink and plummet into a deep channel of resolve to save us. Surely, he and Salem are just friends, or their affair is emotional without physical intimacy. Maybe her husband bought the watch as a surprise and asked Austin to hold the box for him. Something, please God, anything but what I suspect. He must be wrongly accused, and we will settle this and keep going, keep our marriage intact, make everything right again. We will be stronger than before. *Come on, babe, give me a rock-solid reason you had the watch, and if you don't have a reason, lie to me. Save us. Make something up. You can come up with something convincing.*

Austin's eyebrows wiggle, something he does when he's thinking hard. I usually find his idiosyncrasies endearing, but now I see it as disconcerting evidence of immaturity, like moving one's lips while reading. Still, he stares at his plate.

Finally, he slaps his hand on the table, throws his napkin down, and shouts, "So, what is this? You're accusing me of fucking her? You're a real bitch—" He stands up.

I cut him off, "Sit the fuck down!" I demand, louder than him. I'm not surprised by his reaction. The table-slap is a threat, and deflection and belligerence are Austin's go-to tactics. I recall Austin and Salem's kiss, how he lied, that he attacked Trix. "Well, are you fucking her?"

"My god, Julia. You're ridiculous." His vague response means he's at a loss. Two pink spots appear in his cheeks, and he lowers himself into his chair. "Salem's had the watch a long time."

"Bullshit!" I shout.

From somewhere on high, a heap of steaming manure lands with a splat on the table between us. He reaches to take my hand, which puts his forearm on the stinking pile. His bluster didn't work, so this is his next stage of manipulation, to try to physically connect. I cringe away from his hand and the smell.

"Hell, Austin, that's the best you can do? The watch

was brand new. It was in a red box in your jacket pocket. I thought you'd bought the watch for me, for my birthday. Tell me the truth."

He goes pale. "Er..." The seconds tick in my mind like the clicking of a roller coaster climbing a long incline. At the peak, I will not allow myself to be drawn into a well of hope again. I shout, "Tell me the goddamn truth!"

He jumps, startled. "Okay," he says impatiently, huffing like a cat working on a hairball, as if he's about to cough up the story. Looking down, he again wiggles his eyebrows and nods, organizing his talking points. He says, "First, you are my wife, and I love you. I'd never put anyone above you."

I snort, "But you had Salem under you. Get on with it."

Caught flat-footed, he has no strategy. With the tables turned, the knife thrower's neck is under the guillotine's cutting edge. He is reduced to praying for a stay of execution, and I'm the executioner, sharpening the blade.

CHAPTER ELEVEN

He stares at his plate, then briefly covers his face with his hands and runs his fingers through his hair. "Everything we've shared means the world to me. You're the only woman I've ever truly loved." He inhales and continues. "What I did was wrong. No one was ever meant to get hurt. The lies and deception, the way I've treated you, it's been eating me up."

Wow. No cover-ups, no lies, no inventive excuses. And there is no going back to *before. Before* this painful ordeal. *Before,* when there was trust. *Before,* when there were only two people in our marriage.

Austin is indeed my dream's knife thrower, a man who appears diligent and caring to others while doing me damage. We're in a new reality with the choice of either joining forces, and fighting for our relationship, or to separate and battle each other.

"Did you meet her at work?"

He sips his wine, buying time. "It happened in stages. I

felt terrible as the situation escalated. Coming home each day to you, hiding things…well…"

"What? You want me to feel sorry for you?" I roll my eyes. "Just give me the unvarnished truth. The whole story..." I almost pin *okay?* onto the end of my demand but stifle the urge.

He sighs. "We met at a motorcycle show, started talking and emailing—"

"You met at a bike show?" So, this was the symbolism of the little motorcycle charm.

He shrugs, "Salem was a model."

I laugh hollowly. "She's no model. I work in advertising. Models are tall, slim, healthy, young, and naturally beautiful. Salem is none of those. With her looks, I'd expect her to work a stripper pole sooner than strut a catwalk, so don't insult my intelligence by trying to pass her off as something she's not."

"Okay, I'll call her a presenter." His face is pinched, resenting my critique of Salem's looks.

"Awww, he's loyal to his girlfriend," I say sarcastically. I've been to a few bike shows. The presenters' outfits are skimpy tube tops, Daisy Dukes, and knee-high boots, attire to attract the attention of the testosterone-challenged, aging males in need of a boost from the so-called models.

Austin never hid his longing to join the ranks of the RUB—Rich Urban Bikers—the legions of harmless, midlife-crisis-afflicted men advertising the caliber of their penis by donning display-armor of elaborate, shiny, noisy toys on wheels, unsuitable for transporting anything domestic. I visualize him flirting with Salem in her racy outfit as she hands out her moto-sexual pamphlets, and Austin swaggering, laying on his charisma and wit. But there's another side to bikers, a world of gangs, of insignias, of violence, drug dealing, and dangerous behavior, of pimping and sharing their women, which is probably Salem's world, more her ilk than the RUB.

A sudden insight strikes. "I get it! She's Eliza Doolittle,

and you're Henry Higgins. You thought you could polish her up and impress her. Right, Sugar Daddy?"

"Eliza, who?"

"Never mind." I shake my head.

He starts again. "As we got to know each other, we became friends. We emailed, then we met for lunch a few times. We talked a lot." He stops, possibly praying he's given me enough.

"Funny how over all that time of emailing and having lunch, you never mentioned this new *friend*." My face has clenched into an unfamiliar expression with forehead furrowed, eyes narrowed, teeth gritted, and mouth downturned. "Go on."

He sighs again. "Then, well…you know. It just happened."

I drop my cutlery on my plate, which makes more noise than I intend, and Austin glares at me. *The manure pile has increased in height, and I have to sit up straight to see him.* I hiss, "Don't act like you weren't aware of what was happening. The moment you decided to meet for lunch, and you kept your date a secret, you knew."

He says, "I should have resisted. It never should have happened. I love you."

"Do you mean you couldn't resist, or you could resist, but didn't?"

He shakes his head. "It won't matter what I say. I'll be the bad guy, no matter what."

"You are the bad guy! You betrayed me."

"You're right, you're right." The fake pacifist now.

I say, "Cut the crap, Austin."

He takes his dinner knife and cuts off about an eighth of the manure pile, scraping the crap off the table onto the floor. "There," he says. His cutting of the crap has given me clarity. He thinks half-truths and outright lies are acceptable.

A thought—that he bought his motorbike nearly three years ago—is like an anvil falling on me. The affair has been long-term, more than a fling. "You've been lying every single day for years!"

He's sheepish. "Yes, I lied, and I shouldn't have."

"Tell me the rest."

"Come on. Surely you don't want details."

"Yes, I do. Tell me the rest."

"As I said, it just happened."

"I've never understood the line '*It just happened.*' It never just happens to me. I've never been at the grocery store, and some guy's dick pops out of his pants, and suddenly his penis is in my vagina."

A flush has crept up his neck from inside his collar, and his gaze is unfocused. "What I mean is, I wasn't trolling dating sites to meet women online. We met, and there was chemistry."

"Where did you go for sex?"

He drinks his remaining wine and says, "The Paradise Motel on the highway."

"I drive past that hot-sheet dump all the time, going to my client's office. She put up with a by-the-hour joint like that? I'm amazed you didn't bring home a disease or bedbugs." I pause. "And speaking of such things, have you been tested for STDs?"

He shakes his head. "No. I haven't been tested," he says in a near whisper.

"You know, I used to think you were smart, but I'm having severe doubts now. And suddenly, I'm glad we haven't had sex for a year." I pause to regroup from the shock of what I'm hearing and sip my wine. After a while, I ask, "What was missing in our marriage? Why is sex better with her?"

He wilts. "You must be kidding." His tone is peevish, one he'd use for someone ahead of him at the express checkout with too many items.

I jump up, slapping my hands palms-down on the table, surprising myself. "Tell me right now, why is the sex better?"

Alarmed by my outburst, he cringes away, timid and shrunken. My respect and trust have fallen away to reveal Austin as the middle-aged, weak, balding, soft-around-the-middle, suburban dad he is. He's an average guy who ludicrously adopted the part-time persona of a Harley-riding, outlaw-wannabe with a mistress, chasing some mythical masculine ideal of a badass with a double life.

I suddenly comprehend that a large slice of his life is fantasy—yet another example of something obvious I hadn't noticed. There's Austin's arsenal of weapons to defend against a nonexistent enemy. There is his Harley and his biker leathers for dressing up and playing at being an outlaw, his survivalist-weekends for a pretend impending apocalypse, and his hunting and killing of animals to predictably discard the unpalatable flesh. There's his skydiving, a wasteful consumption of aviation fuel to make macramé patterns in the sky with his buddies—not exactly heroes dropping behind enemy lines to deliver food to starving orphans. All his he-man activities glorify an existence under the extreme conditions of war. But they have been acted out against the background of a cushy lifestyle and the creature comforts of the burbs.

He's always been an outdoorsman, but at one time, the hobbies were in moderation. More events and activities—excuses to get away, perhaps—were added when Salem came into his life. I'm not against hobbies, or a rich, inner fantasy life, but clearly, while he was fooling me, he was also fooling himself, playing at living on the edge when in fact, his excitement was, and is, a fragile, expensive coating on his mundane life.

Strangely, while the rest is make-believe, his affair is his real rebellion—but against what? Getting old, his wedding vows, his nine-to-five employment, his lack of teenager-like freedom, or the middle-of-the-road lifestyle to which he inexplicably clings? Or me? He couldn't have chosen an easier target since I've been oblivious, trusted him completely, wanted, needed to believe. Through it all, I was so lost in accepting responsibility, in self-blame, in my unquestioning acceptance, in giving him the benefit of the doubt, because each new bruise, slight, rejection or abandonment was like staring at one pixel of a photo, but I've stepped back to see the thousands making up *the big picture*, as the saying goes.

He shrugs and finally says, "The sex is okay."

I note his answer is in the present tense, and it's another compromise answer, admitting some but not much. I ask, "Good God, can't you be honest even now? Do you love her? Why did you keep the affair going?"

Austin frowns, shifts his posture, and looks away, squirming in the hot seat. He says haltingly, "No, I don't love her. I love you. I got addicted. It was exciting and different. Like a vacation, but of course, vacations end, and this one has ended in hell."

"Why is she working with you? I can't imagine how she'd be qualified to sell oil well drilling equipment. I mean, she was a bike girl, which is only a couple of steps removed from a cam girl, or an escort."

"Salem wasn't an escort!" Angry now.

"Don't you dare defend her."

He stares at the tabletop, tugs at his placemat, and sighs, "I convinced Marcy to hire Salem, that she would be good in sales. She wanted to get out of…"

"No. That's a lie. You hired her for convenience, so you two could legitimately have lunch, text or phone each other, suck back some happy hour drinks, and get laid wherever and whenever; in your offices, cars, motels. Quickies and nooners galore. As long as I stayed away from your office, and the office parties. Right?"

He shakes his head.

"Answer me."

"Right. You're right. We did."

"And the sporting trips—hunting, shooting, camping, whatever events? Was she there?"

"There were a few sporting trips she came on, and twice

her husband came, too. I'm friends with her husband. He trusted us, trusts us. And once, she brought her kids along."

"Unbelievable. All those times you were away, neglecting me, your family, your job, you were with her family, screwing another man's wife, right under his nose." I sit back in my chair. "Her poor schmuck husband. I guess you and Salem felt really clever, with your dirty little secret."

"He doesn't suspect anything." He examines me with a neutral expression.

"You're proud of yourself."

"No, not proud. I can't explain why really. I guess if Clayton doesn't suspect, then he isn't being hurt." He studies his plate, avoiding my gaze.

"Clayton, the guy you went camping with?" He nods. "You are unbelievable." I shake my head. The late nights Austin was supposedly working, every text, phone call, email, every trip out of town; I'll wonder if she was there, what they did together, if he spent money on her, if, if, if. "I want the watch. I paid for it."

"Okay… Julia, I want to get past this, and be how we were," he says quietly.

"You have to cut off all contact with her."

"C'mon Julia, we work in the same office."

In disbelief, "Are you kidding me? Fire her ass. If I find out you two are still in contact, I'll divorce you. There won't be any second chances."

"Okay," he says, nodding.

"I mean it, Austin. Get rid of her. No texts, no phone calls, emails…hell, no faxes, or carrier pigeon, no contact whatever. Are we clear?"

"Yes. We're clear," he says. "I'll do whatever you want."

"I may never get over what you did. We need couples therapy to find out how our relationship went off the rails and how to fix us. For now, you can sleep in the guest room. Now please get out of my sight." He picks up his plate and cutlery and goes to the kitchen. Something he's always done that I also never noticed, but now I see he's like a child who hasn't been taught to be considerate and offer to take anyone else's.

I leave the dinner wreckage on the table and take my wine to the lanai. Hundreds of bats are silhouetted against a full vampire moon, appropriate given how bloodless and hollow I am, with a grave emptiness and despair I've never experienced. Who is this man I married? What the hell else have he and Salem schemed?

Does he love her? I try to picture their disjointed fake get-togethers. With their homes off-limits, they were never in the other's actual environment. They tried to make a banquet out of leftovers, paltry crumbs, and sloppy seconds scrounged from their respective relationships.

CHAPTER TWELVE

I insist we both be tested for STDs, and fortunately, we're clean. I bask in several weeks of normalcy, which gradually becomes infused with restrained happiness. Evenings, Austin shows up for dinner, and we talk and joke about our history, the kids, our future. His belligerence is replaced by soft-spoken and patient helpfulness.

Two weeks in, we make love, and he starts sleeping in the master bedroom, which begets more lovemaking. My optimism soars, and I brag to Trix and Lucy about the solidity of our marriage and how wonderful Austin has been. There's skepticism in my friends' guarded congratulations, but I'm unfazed. The good times seem to have no end. I meet him at work, and we go for lunch. We watch movies and have a weekly date night. We go to Lake Charles for a romantic weekend.

Then, one morning, I pass Austin's office door and hear him on his phone. He says in a hushed tone, "I can't talk now. I'll call you when I'm at work and have some privacy."

My pulse quickens, thumping, and my first inclination is to backslide into the old me, to keep going and ignore what I know I saw and heard, to let sleeping dogs lie, leave well enough alone, all the clichés that counsel overlooking anything unpleasant, and to deny, deny, deny. And no wonder. Who wants a confrontation, to relive the betrayal and suspicion? I wrench aside the nearly overwhelming impulse to deny and negate the obvious, and I march into his office. "Who were you talking to?"

He inhales deeply, which has the dual effect of inflating him and displaying huffiness at my temerity to question him. He says, "One of the designers from the office. They're working on a patent, and they don't like anyone discussing plans on the phone or by text."

I dread what will happen next, how this will escalate, but I press on. "Austin, I'm not stupid. The company doesn't design or patent drilling equipment, they only sell the stuff." I hold out my hand, palm up, the universal sign of *give it to me*. He sighs, hesitates, and finally puts his phone in my hand. I go to recent calls. Most recent is someone named Melas. "My God, Austin, Salem spelled backward?" I hit *Settings* and block her number.

"Hey," he says indignantly, "I don't want to see her or talk to her. I didn't call her. She called me."

I laugh derisively. "Once again, you insult my intelligence. I heard what you said. You're going to call Salem back when you have privacy." Color creeps into his cheeks, indicating there could there be a molecule of conscience in him somewhere. "You're still seeing her."

"No, I'm not seeing her. I did what you asked, and the company gave her notice."

"Then why did you try to hide her number under an alias, and promise to return her call? Now we're back to square one with you sleeping in the guest room." I told him there would be no second chances, but here I am, giving in to hope.

He rolls his eyes. "Whatever. Fuck. I promise you; I'll

never see or talk to Salem again."

I leave his office and go to my studio. Austin leaves for work, and I sit at my desk, staring into space.

Trix calls, and I say, "A question. Sarah said I always put *okay?* at the ends of my sentences. For example, I don't just say *I'm going to make dinner*. Instead, I say *I'm going to make dinner, okay?* Do I really do that?"

"Well, yes. I've heard you do it. Women grow up learning to soften anything we say that's direct or confrontational."

"Damn. I'm going to stop, okay?" I laugh at myself.

"You're not as bad as the women who laugh after every statement, or as punctuation, diminishing everything they say as trivial. So…how are things going with Austin?" I relate the latest transgression, and Trix says, "Wow. He's behaving like a toddler testing his limits. His consequences should be more serious than banishing him to the guest room."

"I agree, but what consequences? Just thinking about revenge makes me break out in a cold sweat."

"There are plenty of ways to punish him. On YouTube, a woman wrapped her cheating husband's entire car in the wide plastic wrap that movers use." We both laugh. "Besides, how many times will he treat you like shit before you give up? What kind of proof do you need? You can't watch him every minute."

"Maybe I need to hire a private eye to follow him, but that would cost a fortune."

"A GPS tracker on his car would be cheaper. But Julia, what's the point considering he has proven nothing has changed? In my opinion, he's a lost cause." She sighs.

"A GPS tracker, of course. Perfect!"

"Did you even hear what I said about his continued cheating? Whichever way you spy on him; he's not going to change. Your situation will just turn into a game of cat and mouse. You need to see a lawyer to get your ducks lined up. Right away."

"Sorry, I'm aware my optimism is frustrating, but I keep hoping there is a way."

"Julia. Please. Consult a lawyer to see where you stand financially."

"Okay. I will. Now, where do I find a tracker?"

At the gadget store, having never stalked anyone, the idea of monitoring Austin is both alarming and thrilling. Maybe this thrill is what Austin feels when he's being naughty and might get caught. A person could get hooked on this tingle, the secrecy, the risk.

A fleeting urge to consult him about my purchase is evidence I've always run every decision past him first, for his blessing. He's become my boss, or perhaps my parent. How dreadfully co-dependent. Or do I want him to agree to my surveillance? The point being, if he's not hiding anything, his whereabouts should be open to scrutiny. At least my survival instinct and my mistrust are nixing that stupid idea. Back home, with batteries charged and the GPS app downloaded, I need an opportunity to attach it to his car.

The next morning, I take the GPS outside, rattle garbage cans to appear busy, and bending to pick up some litter, I attach the widget inside his wheel well. Movement catches my eye. Austin is in the lanai watching me. Shit. I assumed he'd be in the shower. Goosebumps race along my arms. What did he see? Nothing, I tell myself.

"What are you doing?" he calls to me.

"Waste management, probably a possum." I hold my hands away from my body as if there's smelly trash residue on them. In the house, I make a show of washing up at the kitchen sink.

I spend the next few weeks tracking him. The map for the tracker reminds me of the old Pac Man game, with progressive lit-up dots following his route. He's always where he is supposed to be. I show up at his work unexpectedly sometimes. At dinner, we talk, laugh, and resume a seemingly contented marital existence. My suspicion and cynicism are ebbing, replaced by a seed of trust that begins to germinate, sprout, and grow.

Then on a Tuesday morning, Austin is at my studio door. Something about him is off. He stands sidelong to me and makes only furtive eye contact. He's wearing a new silky tangerine shirt, and tight, bleached jeans that appear designed to accentuate his package. I force down a giggle. "You're wearing jeans to work?"

He says, "I've got a business trip. I don't want to mess up my suit on the plane. Anyway, three days. My flight's at ten this morning."

"Where are you going?"

"Charlotte, North Carolina. Gotta run," he says, turns his head to blow me a kiss, and rolls his carry-on out to his car.

Suspicion makes concentrating on work impossible. I obsessively picture Austin with Salem, my mind chugging like a top-load washer, chug, chug, back and forth, between wary distrust and dread. Is he taking her with him to North Carolina? Chug, chug. Are they having breakfast together? Chug, chug. Are they having sex right now? Chug. I wait to track his car until shortly after ten, when he said his flight would take off, to make sure he's on the plane.

I click the tracker app. Austin's car should be at one of two possible airports. The GPS has one dot flashing, indicating his vehicle is stationary. He's parked at an off-site garage at the midtown airport. Good. He's where he should be, but the chugging suspicion-dread cycle continues. Knowing he's on the plane is helpful but doesn't account for whether they are together. Now what?

Trix once said she checked up on a boyfriend on Facebook after he was caught screwing around. She said, unlike some other social media sites, the stalker's prey can't tell who views their page. Although I don't particularly care if Austin or Salem knows I peeked, at this moment, I prefer stealth.

Because my page is business only, I'm inexperienced in all things Facebookish, but how hard can it be, given every twelve-year-old has a page? For a moment, engaging in even more stalking behavior brings queasy shame, like a morality virus—but this is survival, and I'm out of options. And the tingle of excitement returns.

Trix believes *other women* are, by circumstance, insecure, which drives them to claim their illicit man by posting and tagging pictures of him. The name of the photographer isn't needed, just the name of my person of interest. In Facebook's search bar, I type *Austin Green.* A drop-down list appears. I click on *Pictures* and photos materialize, the most recent post this morning, a restaurant table selfie of Salem with Austin in his distinctive orange shirt.

The rat bastard.

Her caption says, *Another hard day at the office. Business (wink, wink) breakfast with Austin Green.* I right-click and hit Properties. The photo was snapped this morning at 8:40. In the picture, he's looking away, and he may not be aware she shot the photo. I slap my desk and direct muffled inhuman noises laced with cursing at the screen.

I recognize the *Hilton* logo on glasses of wine. Wow, day drinking at the Hilton. Clicking on Salem's name takes me to her Facebook page. Her page setting is public, open to anyone who cares to see. The top shot is the breakfast picture. She has several albums of photos, mainly selfies.

"Well, well," I say aloud. "You're certainly selfie-absorbed, but not very selfie-aware, Salem." I scroll her timeline.

She's a prolific poster, sometimes hour by hour, and I start to see random expensive hotel rooms, not the no-tell motel called the Paradise, that Austin claimed they frequented. According to the photos, except for the few weeks when he was behaving, Austin shared those rooms with her. Damn. If I'd been mistrustful and done this ages ago, I could have saved myself a lot of grief.

The dread-suspicion-cycle starts chugging away again, back and forth, but picks up speed and becomes an off-center and wobbling spin cycle as love and caring skirts closer to hate and revenge.

I refresh Salem's Facebook page, and a new photo appears, posted a minute ago. The subject matter is a selfie of her reflection in a floor-to-ceiling mirror. She poses provocatively the way teens do, back arched, stomach sucked in, breasts and butt stuck out, a smiley pout. Her outfit consists of skin-tight capris, a low-cut top, and platform-soled sandals with heels tall enough for a possum to scooch under. Austin isn't in the picture, but his faded jeans and tangerine shirt are hanging on a chair.

Through the window are several recognizable Houston buildings. North Carolina, my ass. Salem's postings smack of recklessness since her husband could so easily catch them. I type Clayton Kingston into the search bar, but he doesn't have a page. Funny how Salem keeps thwarting Austin's crafty setups, first at the party, now on Facebook.

I text him, *Where are you?*

He responds, *Just landed in Charlotte, NC. Why?*

Once upon a time, one called our traveling-spouse's hotel room to speak with them, which confirmed their location. Nowadays, a cell phone is the cheater's best friend. I don't text back because, as my mom liked to say, *You've got one mouth and two ears—use them accordingly*, and over the years, I've mastered the art of keeping my mouth shut and my ears open to consider my options. Let him think I'm still a mega-mushroom while I plan my next move.

To confirm my intel, I dial the downtown Hilton. The front desk puts me through to their room, and Salem answers the phone, and I hear her voice the first time. She has a breathy Marilyn Monroe affectation. In the background, Austin asks, "Who is it?" I hang up.

If Austin is in downtown Houston, why is his car at the

airport? Maybe they left his vehicle there and drove hers to the hotel. On Google Maps, I enter the GPS coordinates from the tracker. The map zooms in and drops a pointer on the parking structure's dumpster.

I'm chilled. Did Austin find the tracker, drive to the airport, toss the GPS into the dumpster, and then drive to the Hilton? Does he suspect me, or does he think Salem's husband is responsible? If he suspects me, as Trix had predicted, he's playing a twisted game of cat and mouse, and I better make damn sure I'm the cat.

Like a fist to the throat, rage strikes by surprise. Another calculated betrayal. I want to scream, but I hold back. Screaming's not my style, but confrontation might be.

I dress in a tight, sexy red and black superhero bodysuit with over-the-knee boots. My makeup is extreme, hair flowing, my long trench coat swirls like a cape. I jump in my car, stomp on the gas, fishtail out of the driveway, and burn rubber to the Hilton. Charging into the restaurant, I practically fly, running over chairs and tables, scooping and throwing Austin and Salem's cocktails in their faces, followed by plates of saucy pasta and bowls of Caesar salad and lobster bisque. They shriek and shout, flailing.

Austin grabs his phone, and I deftly kick it out of his hand. The phone spins through the air and takes out a bottle behind the bar, which has a domino effect on the many-tiered display creating an avalanche of shattering and crashing glass. Catlike, in slow motion, I leap down as they both jump out of their seats to grab at me, but in a Hollywood-film-worthy acrobatic stunt, I twist away and grab her hair while I extend my leg behind me in an arabesque, hoofing him in the nuts. He doubles over, holding his crotch, while I spin her around, screaming, and let go for centrifugal force to take her headlong into a huge aquarium, which explodes, sending water, glass shards, and tropical fish spewing...

Austin's ringtone ends my reverie. I don't pick up. After a few minutes of running through my fantasy again, I consider what to do. Confronting them would be satisfying, but my usual placid persona notwithstanding, I might lose my shizzle, and I'd be the one arrested for disturbing the peace, or assault, or murder. Murder. Grainy surveillance footage on crime shows would feature me leaving the hotel, hauling luggage full of body parts, and leaking a trail of blood.

Screw this. No. I'd prefer to outsmart rather than outgun the deceptive duo. I call Marcy, and ask without preamble, "Do you know where Austin and Salem are?"

Marcy says, "She's in Dallas at a convention, and Austin's in North Carolina. Why?"

I make the sound of a buzzer. "Wrong!" I laugh. "They're both here in Houston, at the Hilton. Check out her Facebook."

"Dickhead! Bitch! If I were still their boss, I'd fire them both. I'm going to rat them out."

I chuckle. "Marcy, please don't let Austin know I tipped you off. I'm working on my own comeuppance, and while revenge may be a dish best served cold, payback is even better as a surprise."

"No problem! I'll take all the credit for finding them!" She hangs up, laughing.

Chapter Thirteen

Austin, honey, you love saying I imagine things—well, imagine this—consequences are coming to get you. In Austin's home office, I boot up his computer. He once told me the laptop's factory password was *password*. He wasn't sure if *password* was the stupidest or the smartest password, ever. I type *password*, hold my breath, and his home page opens. Austin's simplemindedness, another thing in front of my face the whole time, but I never noticed.

You'd think a cheating husband like Austin would have his phone and laptop and all his accounts protected with creative and brain-twisting passwords he'd need to enter every time. You'd expect him to have a secret email account. You'd think he'd have any number of safeguards. Not Austin. What an ego. I quickly find out he's opted for his search engine to remember and automatically fill all his bank, credit card, and email passwords, among others. Ha!

The balance in his personal bank account is nearly six thousand dollars, which I wire into my private account.

Amazing what you can do online these days. I click on his credit card, the one he uses for personal items and trips. His balance owing is two grand, and his pending charges show, as suspected, that he checked into the Hilton this morning. I click on Customer Service, report the card stolen, and instruct the bank not to send a replacement.

I want to see where he and Salem have been staying over the last year, so I open a filing cabinet drawer and pull out a folder of business-related papers. I flip through the contents, consider refiling them, but change my mind, and toss the documents into the air, repeating the process file after file. I can be blatant too, Austin. Sheets of paper flutter festively around me. I continue through Austin's entire filing cabinet, and then start on his desk.

Finally, I get to his file of receipts. I dump them on his desk and spread them out. There are itemized bills for luxury hotels: The Four Seasons, Hilton, Westin, The Houstonian. There are bills for room service, bar tabs, and lavish restaurant meals, which means a lot of my hard-earned cash, went down the toilet at these ritzy locations. There are spa treatments, couple's massages, waxing, facials, hair salon appointments.

I've been such a trusting idiot, diligently, obliviously working, unknowingly supporting his deceit, all the while playing the role of retro housewife, polishing the commode till it sparkled like a fucking diamond.

Back at the computer, I wire nearly four thousand dollars from our joint account into mine and close the account. I check our joint credit card, which is supposed to be used to pay trades for work on the house. There are purchases from Neiman Marcus and other stores, including the Hilton's boutique. All are pending and haven't been charged to our card yet. I report the card stolen and tell Customer Service not to send a replacement.

Next, a biggie. What if Austin has no phone for business, for research, for personal use? I consider the consequences a moment, namely his anger, but at least he won't be able to phone and shout at me. Haha. I access Austin's mobile account and disconnect his cell phone, then cancel the landline, which is my leash. It lets him know I'm at home when all the while he's out roaming.

I search for *car repossession*. Something called voluntary repossession surfaces, where a person who has fallen on hard times can hand over their car by calling the leasing company. I dial the dealership that holds Austin's lease. An earnest young man takes my call, and I sadly confess, "I'm so embarrassed and humiliated to have to do this, but please, I hope you can help, *sniff*. We can't even afford to put gas in the car. Please send someone soon because my husband is very depressed and said he's going to get inside the vehicle and set the vehicle..." choked up now, "on fire!"

"What?" His anxiety is evident.

"These are dire circumstances. My husband is suicidal," I say despondently. *Sniff.*

"Yes, ma'am."

A despairing sigh, "I don't want to be pushy or sound unfair, but since your dealership is aware of the gravity of the situation, there could be liability on your part if you don't act quickly. The vehicle is at the downtown Hilton in the parking garage."

"No problem, ma'am." He doesn't question how someone who can't afford a fill-up is staying at the Hilton, and says spiritedly, "I've got the access keys in the office, and I'll go in person, right now."

I indulge in a minute of satisfaction, surveying the blizzard of paper that resembles the aftermath of a tornado's collision with a post office, and say aloud, "Austin, you need to do some filing," and chuckling, I leave his office. In my studio, on my computer, I change my passwords for banking, email, purchasing, and so forth to names of impressionist and expressionist artists, far beyond Austin's imagination or knowledge. I also lock down my phone with a new passcode. Yep, I'm a fast learner.

A text arrives from an unknown phone number. The text reads: *This is Austin. My phone, bank account, and credit cards aren't working. Wire me $3000 to pay for hotel and food.*

Borrowing his bimbo's phone, how embarrassing for Mr. Sugar-Daddy. The notion of big, tough Mr. Important, using her sparkly pink phone has me laughing until my cheeks hurt. He texts me again, and again, and again. Finally, I reply: *Whose phone is this?*

Of course, he can't answer, and I say under my breath, "Careful, Austin, you're going to use up all of Salem's data capacity and you have no money to buy her more."

At some point soon, without me having to say a word, they'll realize I'm the perpetrator. I'm curious what the fallout will be; probably another blow-up from Austin, lots of chest-thumping and grunting. He's not in a position to do much else.

Agitated and short on concentration, the antidote is gardening and sweat therapy. I step outside, and the late afternoon sauna-like heat is an assault. Glass sullied by poop from the bats roosting above the greenhouse distracts me, and I wash it with a mop on an extendable pole until the glass gleams and reflects the yard. In the greenhouse, I organize garden tools and pots and wipe down surfaces. I'm on a roll, weeding beds, and spreading the cedar mulch that was dumped on the driveway this morning. The mulch pile distributed, I'm sweaty, dehydrated, and fatigued, but satisfied. The revenge and exertion have worked off some of my anger.

The yard is an oasis. The plantings are as artful as an artist's composition and palette, and I fetch my big digital Nikon—my camera of choice to archive accurate reproductions of my art. I check battery levels and slip in a new card, then photograph this anomaly, an English garden cultivated despite the Texas heat and drought alternating with waterfall-like rain. The pool is a luminous opal, rimmed by flagstone, lush greenery, layers of color and texture.

Maybe the garden has been a substitute for painting all these years.

I set the camera in the lanai and shower outdoors. The dripping faucet has become a trickle. I turn the handle hard, towel off, scoop my clothes, and the camera, and enter the chill of the house.

In my studio, I remove the memory card from the camera and sit for a minute, until my earlier anger and sad thoughts interject. In a bitter instant, the obvious strikes me that all of my labors are entirely pointless—yet another obvious dynamic I've ignored. We don't entertain, and neither the kids nor Austin care about the landscaping. Strange how Austin has resisted downsizing when the yard was so meaningless to him. Ugh. Sick of thinking about him, I drop the camera's card into a box of miscellany on my desk. The shots can be viewed later.

Midafternoon, Marcy texts me: *Austin and Salem's new boss, Bob, sent both of them to Buffalo to do some selling because there are so many oil wells in Buffalo... NOT! He booked them into two separate crappy hot-sheet motels across town from each other and told them he'll be phoning them at all hours of the night on the hotel's line and they better pick up, or their asses will be spanked big-time.*

Me: LOL. Love it!

Marcy: *Plus, it's still colder up there than a cast-iron commode on the north side of a glacier...in a snowstorm. Hope they packed some thermal undies.*

Me: Suffer baby, suffer.

Marcy: *Austin called on Salem's phone and requested an advance on his pay. Bob wired it, and he got his phone back on. They'll be back early tomorrow morning.*

The revenge was helpful but doesn't cancel the pain of his deception, and I'm weepy. Finally, with no tears left to cry, exhausted, I pour chardonnay and drink until the bottle is empty. I watch a show about lottery winners spending their money, then take another bottle to the lanai and stretch out.

I wake in the lanai with a skull-cracking headache. There are two empty wine bottles at my feet. Austin is facing me, arms out at his sides, fists clenched, making himself more imposing. A showdown. His color is unhealthily high, and he shouts, "You bitch! You pulled some fucked-up shit, messing with my bank accounts and credit cards, they took my vehicle, and you had my fucking phone disconnected. Then you threw paperwork all over my office? What the fuck is the matter with you? I couldn't even Uber home, for fuck sake, and had to take a cab. Luckily I had some cash in my pocket."

"Jesus, chill. You're going to stroke out." His mention of having his car repossessed makes me hold back a smile. "What are you talking about? As usual, Austin, you're imagining things."

He appears confused. Tentatively, I slowly stand, picking up the empty bottles. My brains have somehow become disengaged and slippery, like raw oysters in a balloon, and with every tip or nod of my head, they slide and crash into my skull, causing a gong-like throbbing. He approaches until we're nose to nose, and shouts, "Don't lie to me." a mist of spit reaches me.

"Austin, back off." I cautiously straighten up, frozen, hoping the pounding subsides. He doesn't move. "I'm serious, Austin. Get out of my face. I'm liable to puke on you." He quickly sidesteps, and then follows me as I shuffle to the kitchen. At the door of his office, I stop. Drifts of paper cover the floor and furniture. "How strange. I wonder how that happened." I sound genuinely baffled, even to myself.

Doubt again crosses his face, and he says, "You really didn't do this?"

"Of course not."

He eyeballs his office again, then regroups. "Don't fucking lie to me," he shouts.

"That's rich. Because you've never lied to me, right?"

"You bitch. You better clean this up."

"Ha." I continue along the hallway. "Or what? You'll cheat on me? You'll spend our money on another woman? Where is the truth when I want it, huh? How does it feel for someone you trust to tell you that what you see with your own eyes is just your imagination?"

"Fucking bitch," he shouts, punching a fist-sized hole in the wall. I flinch, which starts the painful brain-crashing action again.

Punching of walls was a frequent occurrence in the beginning, but the number of incidents diminished over time. Austin got control of his rage, or as Trix pointed out, more accurately, he gained control of me. I'm aware the wall is a substitute for my head, but aside from a few altercations when we were new, I've trusted he wouldn't harm me if I didn't provoke him. However, given his recent behavior, I now think Austin is capable, provoked or not. He shakes and massages his fist.

"I hope that really hurt. If you punch anything else, I'll call the police."

Sarah clomps into the kitchen, agitated, with sleep creases on her cheek. "What's going on?" She notices the damage and asks Austin, incredulously, "Did you punch the wall?"

I'm surprised the noise woke her. Does she have buried recall from her toddler days of raised voices, the breaking of objects, of him hitting me, of me crying? Sounds of danger stay with us as warnings. He opens and closes his hand, trying to get under control. I say sympathetically, "Your dad had a meltdown, but he's better now."

She stands hands on hips, torso angled forward. "You're acting like some trashy reality show."

"I was pissed."

"Whatever…anger management, Dad. Get a grip. You know what mom taught me a long time ago?" Austin shakes his head, and she continues, "She taught me to say, 'Please daddy, don't hurt me. I'm just a little girl.'"

I gasp. Memories crowd in. The twins as toddlers, Sarah pulling Bryan to hide behind my legs as Austin slams doors and hurls objects. The twins at age six, running into Sarah's room, where she pulls Bryan into the closet with her to hide, as I block access to their door. At age seven, Austin grabs Sarah's arm and slaps her face, and she retaliates, hitting him, as I desperately pull her out of his grasp, leave the house with the kids, drive away and stay in a hotel. Why the hell did I bring them back to live here?

It's what Trix was talking about when she referred to Sarah's aggressive demeanor in her list of things I've ignored.

"If you hurt mom or Bryan, I'll fucking kill you." She states fiercely, pauses a minute, then goes back to her room.

I say calmly, "Get out."

"What?"

"You heard me. Get out. Pack your shit and get out."

"I can't. I've got nowhere to go."

"Go stay with your girlfriend, you know, the one you weren't supposed to be seeing anymore. Where you stay isn't my problem." My head is pounding, and the idea of arguing is turning my stomach.

"But—"

"No discussion. Pack up and leave."

"This is my house too. You can't make me leave. I'll stay in the guest room."

I walk away without answering. I'm aware Austin is within his rights to stay, although if he punches anything else, I will call the police. In the master bath, I swipe two pain pills Austin has left from a prescription for a torn ligament, and drink two large glasses of water. In bed, I zone out and drift on an opiate cloud into sleep.

I sleep until midafternoon, shower, and dress in a long, breezy, comfortable beach dress. Austin has left the house, thank god. I head to my drafting table, where I call my family lawyer for a referral to a divorce attorney. Reconciliation is impossible. Thoughts of Austin's affair and our impending divorce buzz like my head is a wasps' nest. Maybe a wasp nest portrait is a good subject for a painting. I draw a thumbnail sketch.

Suddenly I'm fully resigned. We'll divorce, and the kids will need to find their independence. I break for a bowl of chicken soup. Sarah and Bryan emerge from their rooms, pajama-clad, shuffling into the kitchen, looking like disoriented, catatonic, mental-ward patients. "What's to eat?" Sarah asks inanely as she takes chicken, lettuce, mayo, and bread from the fridge.

The phone rings with Marcy's caller ID, and I take the phone to my studio. "Hey, Marcy."

She says, "Have I got news for you, darlin'. First of all, did you know about a porno of Austin and Salem that circulated? I don't want to upset you by blabbing if you don't already know. Oh, well, guess that made a lot of sense—not." She laughs raucously. "This morning, there was a huge shemozzle. A porno of them went to everyone's email, and I mean everyone, including the corner-office penguins. Unbelievable. If he could talk his way out of this disaster, he could sell salt to snails. And we both know he's not that good." She takes a deep breath. "So, here's the deal. They're getting shit-canned outta here today."

My breathing stops. "Oh. Wow. I appreciate you telling me. Thanks, Marcy. Wait, wasn't Salem let go a while ago?"

She says, "Nope."

Another lie. "Who sent their sex video to everyone?"

"Gee, I don't know, but who cares?" She brays laughter. "Gotta go."

I'm left standing, staring at the dead phone. Austin was fired. What the hell? Have his bosses been waiting for a legitimate reason to kick him to the curb? I'd always thought his coworkers viewed him as steady, smart, and upstanding, but now he's a lying, self-indulgent, two-timing husband, slacker, and midlife-crisis cliché.

Three hours pass before Austin pulls into the driveway. I give him some time to settle then saunter to his office door where the drifts of paperwork and receipts still littering the floor are impressive. "Go the hell away." He doesn't look up. "Leave me alone." I can smell alcohol, and his words are slightly slurred.

"I know you got fired and why."

"Yeah, right, drama queen. It's got nothing to do with you," he says.

"Not true, now your smutty tape is out there for all to see, and everyone can either judge or feel sorry for me."

"Let me guess; you've been talking to that fat cow, Marcy, and you believe everything she says. Only Marcy and one other guy saw the video, and he's keeping quiet."

"Bullshit. Marcy said everyone in the office got it. You've fucked up over and over, and you're still lying. One way or another, you're going to pay."

He laughs. "You sound like some shitty actress in a B-movie."

"Ha! Are you trying to *shame* me? Good luck. How are you going to pay your share of the expenses on this property and pay me back what you spent on Salem?"

He doesn't answer. I go to my studio and wring my hands, then run them through my hair. The sheet of glass that's my palette beckons, and I squeeze mounds of black, white, yellow ochre, blue, and red, and start painting detail.

There are sounds of Austin moving through the house, popping a beer in the kitchen, then the TV blares in the living room. After all that has happened, having him in the house makes me antsy. Around midnight fatigue grips me, and I lock my bedroom door using Trix's doorstop and collapse in bed to sleep dreamlessly.

CHAPTER FOURTEEN

I wake before five and take coffee to my studio. Setting aside the knife-thrower painting to allow the last layer of paint to dry, I start work on the canvas of Lucy, queen of suburbia. I let the white of the canvas glow through the paint, brightening angled sunlight. Her house casts an almost black shadow, and in the distance is an approaching, towering tsunami.

The melodrama tickles me. My statement on the suburbs, the myth of perfection, of living in peace, and confidence, without fear, living invincibly. That the burbs are stable, a rock, but just lift that rock and see what slithers out. There's always impending heartache or doom around the corner. In Lucy's painting, she is simply a stand-in for any of us.

At eight, the sun is high and hot, and I stop painting and go to my drafting table. The grapes job is due today. I assess the illustration, add a few areas of the dusty appearance characteristic of grapes, a curling tendril, and scumble more highlights. I pronounce the job deliverable. Shortly after nine, there are noises from Austin in his guestroom quarters. He leaves without talking, and I'm relieved.

Lucy arrives with pecan tarts, and we sit poolside. I sigh, "Well… I recently found out Austin's been getting his rocks off with a woman at work." I shake my head. "With your situation with Earl and my single friends who have friends-with-benefits situations going, I'm starting to wonder if I'm sexually backward, like some sort of Victorian schoolmarm."

She slowly shakes her head. "I was devastated when Earl had his first one. I'm not sure how we stayed the course, except to say everything is a negotiation."

Lucy wants to know how I'm coping, and I bring her up to date with generalities about Austin's inability to let go of Salem, but I don't mention his firing. After a while, I announce I need to get back to work, and she heads home.

My call display shows Trix. "Are you painting?" she asks.

"Yes, but I got distracted because Austin got fired."

"Yoiks! What happened?"

"It's more like what hasn't happened. If you're up for lunch, I'll tell you the whole nasty story."

"Works for me."

"Great. I'll deliver my job and see you after." We sign off. I type up an invoice to deliver with the job and change into business attire. As I walk past Austin's office I notice he has picked up all the paper and receipts that were on the floor and stacked them on his desk. I leave without waking the twins. I'm thinking about Austin being jobless and our status quo as I drive past Paul pruning his shrubs.

Sometimes our lifestyle is as mysterious to me as Saturn or Pluto. Like Paul down the block, poor old Pluto, downsized from his job at Solar System Inc. Downsized. It's the latest polite euphemism for fired, laid off, or as the Brits call it, made-redundant. Termination is the employee's worst fear, employment's scarlet letter, and humiliating fodder for scandalmongers. In this enclave, gossip is the highest social currency, and Austin's unemployment, his affair, and our divorce will be a tongue-wag trifecta.

At the ad agency's low-rise headquarters, art-director Dave is in all black, jeans, T-shirt, and leather vest, his long hair in a topknot. The grapes illustration meets with his approval. Dried apricots are the subject of the next package in the series. Every new assignment is validation—that I'm still current, still relevant, our household expenses are met.

Next stop, Trix's. As I drive, I contemplate Lucy and Earl's open marriage—could I live like them? I visualize Austin leaving the house to meet Salem for a hook-up, a booty-call, a friends-with-benefits rendezvous, and somehow I have entirely accepted their liaisons. I would wave a cheery bye-bye at the door. Later he arrives home, smelling of sex and of her in all manner of ways. The thought sickens me. How does Lucy cope? Evidently, I'm still unsuccessfully trying to find a compromise to allow us to stay married. I should probably see a therapist, figure out what's the matter with me.

Trix answers the door wearing a paint-smeared loose smock over her clothes. I step into the scent of paint, solvents, and Gitanes cigarette smoke—earthy and herbal with a hint of tannery. The olfactory essence of Trix's particular genius.

Juggling her cigarette, she removes her over-shirt, revealing a sleeveless, long, black wrap-dress, asymmetrical of course, that contrasts with her pale skin and exposes her coat-hanger collarbones and slim arms. She hangs the smock on her easel and says, "The buyers are coming to give the piece their blessing—all part of the song and dance. They gotta visit the artist's garret; see how the other half lives." She smiles wryly and slips a large sterling cuff onto a birdlike wrist, and adds hammered silver earrings.

At a patio table at Empire Bistro, we order pasta with gulf shrimp to share. Trix flicks her lighter and inhales. I pull silverware from the wide-mouth jar on the table and relate my discovery of Austin and Salem's tryst at the Hilton and cutting off his financial lifelines, phone, and car.

She grins. "Bet Austin was pissed."

"Definitely. He punched a hole in the wall. Something he hasn't done in a long time."

"Damn. Are you okay?"

"What really got me was that Sarah remembered me teaching her to tell Austin not to hurt her because she was just a little girl."

"Wow. Sad. Sarah's not the only one who hasn't forgotten the bad old days. Your face was…practically unrecognizable."

"He hasn't hit me since," I wheedle. "Shit. Look at me, deflecting. Am I defending him?"

"Yes, you are. Besides, Austin stopped hitting you because your strategy was to back down, not because he's changed. I'll never forgive him."

"This morning, he got fired because a sex video circulated." I relate Marcy's phone call. "I told him to pack up and leave, but he won't, and I have no leverage to evict him."

Trix stares at me over her sunglasses and says, "I don't like the sound of this. Make use of the doorstop. Or stay with me. The most dangerous time for a woman is when you're breaking up." The food arrives, and we twirl fettuccini onto forks.

"I hear you. I used the doorstop last night." I pause. "Enough about Austin. I'm so sick of him… Anyway, I started painting, but there are bills to pay. I realized that we made the mistake over time, of jacking up our lifestyle. And now he's jobless, so…"

"Like hot frogs."

"First, I was a mushroom, and now I'm a frog?" I smile.

"Supposedly, if you toss a frog into hot water, he'll hop out, but if you put a frog in cold water and gradually turn up the heat, froggy won't notice, and he'll just sit there, and die. Lots of people, single or married, don't notice expenses getting unmanageable as they escalate."

"So true."

We pay and leave. Window shopping, Trix stops at a vintage clothing shop, points, and says, "There's just the T-shirt for Austin to wear around the house." The shirt's slogan is *The Floggings Will Stop When Morale Improves.*

"Ha! I love that."

At my car, we hug, and Trix says, "Watch your back, and call me anytime, day or night."

Back home, Austin arrives and stops at the door to my studio. He says, "Going to a shooting meet. We're leaving now."

"Why aren't you job hunting? You still have obligations."

Austin sneers, "Fuck you."

I flip him the bird, something I've never done before. He turns and heads to his office as Clayton lumbers down the hall. The upside of this trip will be his guaranteed absence for a few days. Austin has some brass *cohones* befriending the cuckold. There's the clatter of weapons and ammo being packed, more conversation, and laughter.

I tip my head back and stare at the ceiling. Surely Austin is aware that inviting Clayton into our house, to trade guns, is risky. I close my eyes and whisper, "Right, Austin, what could possibly go wrong? How would the mass shooting go down, and how can I protect myself and the kids?" I close my eyes.

Clayton's voice shouts, "Motherfucker!" and there's a deafening crack. A guttural cry. A loud thud. More shots. The doorframe splinters. A window shatters. Terror takes over as I grab my phone, drop to the floor, and crawl into the recesses of my storage closet. Through the folding door's louvers, I can see the floor. Black biker boots with chains clank and thump toward me—Clayton is carrying a substantial revolver. I'm trembling, and I freeze and hold my breath. He scans the room then lumbers away. There's another gunshot, which I assume is the head-shot, the coup de grâce for Austin, then heavy steps leaving the house.

I need to rein in my imagination. That one scared me. I leave my drafting chair and pace the studio, raking my hands through my hair. If Clayton murdered Austin, would my problems be solved? These wild fantasy scenarios must be related to the nightmares or originate from the same portal in my brain. Or maybe, understandably perhaps, the stress is getting to me.

Austin and Clayton leave in Clayton's van. The twins nuke chili for lunch, all the while trading fart and sex jokes, and they depart, early for them. The house is dim, chilled, and hushed; the only sounds are the hum of the refrigerator and the AC. This home is too big and expensive for me alone. Austin and I will divorce, and I'll sell this heap of sticks and stucco. What to buy? A townhouse, a quaint cottage in the countryside, a sleek condo in the city? I pull up real estate listings on my computer and surf a while. I check my email as an ad for insurance runs down the side of the monitor and reminds me I haven't had any statements in months from Michele, our finance goddess. There's still time to call before they close. I ask, "Are we supposed to be picking up statements online now?"

She says, "Sorry, Julia. You don't get statements since you signed over control of the accounts to Austin."

"No, no, no. I would never do that. The accounts are in both our names. Why didn't you call me?"

She says, "Believe me, woman to woman; I wanted to call you. I'm emailing you the document that gives him control, signed by both of you. According to confidentiality regulations, once you signed, I simply could not talk to you."

I open the email attachment. "I remember this. Austin brought these documents to me for my signature and said it was to renew our life insurance. He flipped up the bottom edges of the other papers for me to sign. I can't believe he did this."

She says, “I’m so sorry. I tried to reach Austin to get permission to call you, but he never returned my calls, or he would call after hours, obviously avoiding me. This document wasn’t passing the smell test, and I was hoping you’d phone me. I even went to my supervisor, and they confirmed since I had your signature on the form, confidentiality rules dictated I absolutely could not notify you.” She pauses a moment. “I want you to look at your accounts.”

I open another email attachment and absorb the bottom line. Less than a quarter of our retirement savings remain. White dots crowd my vision, and there’s a weird feathery feeling in my skull. “This can’t be right. More than $320,000 is missing.” I’m almost whispering.

Michele says softly, “He withdrew amounts of less than ten thousand, spaced a week apart so they wouldn’t set off alarm bells in the system.”

“Michele, I want to think about what to do, how to handle this. Now that you know he conned me, can you freeze the accounts, keep him from withdrawing any more cash?”

“Sure can,” she says. “I’ll send you a document. Just sign, scan, and email it back.”

“He hasn’t cashed out our life insurance, has he?”

“He tried. I told him I’d be informing you, and he dropped it.” As I hang up the phone, she says, “I’m sorry.”

So much hard work to accumulate some savings, to live carefully and diligently. Now, what am I going to do? Another disaster and another betrayal. I thought I was all cried out, but suddenly I can’t hold back. Rage, hate, disgust, frustration. My god, there aren’t enough names for the painful emotions from this devastation. I have two days before Austin will be back. I need to do something, but what?

Austin swindled our savings. Over the last thirty-six hours, I haven't been able to eat or sleep, and I can no longer cry. My anger has boiled my tears, along with every possible emotion, to nothing. I sip wine and wonder for the millionth time where I go from here. Sick of rerunning the scenarios, I turn on TV news, which is showing raging fires threatening the homes of movie stars. Sleep finally takes me, and I'm in a dream.

Before me, a movie is running. Austin and Salem are on the beach riding galloping palomino horses. They dismount and run hand in hand into their stunning house filled with antiques and treasures. They lounge in a huge bathtub, splashing and playing in suds, then dry each other with fluffy white towels. They leisurely feast at a huge table, gorging on every imaginable exotic food. Of course, she never gains an ounce because of all their running through daisy-filled meadows and white-sand beaches, and all their marathon, porn-star-worthy screwing.

Then things change. I'm in the movie, standing in their opulent mirrored foyer. In my reflection, I'm sultry, wearing my kimono that has slid off my right shoulder, almost a Victoria's Secret model moment. Yeah, baby. I glide smoothly across marble tile into the living room.

Ocean air smelling of saltwater and moonflowers—for once not Salem's perfume—comes through open twelve-foot, floor-to-ceiling French doors. Layers of gauzy curtains lift on the breeze as if reaching for me.

A lit torch appears in my hand, and without hesitation, I touch the flame to the sheers, and the blaze scales the fabric. Burning pieces break free and drift onto the lacquered and waxed surfaces of furniture and hardwood. Catching and flaring flames dash across the floor, igniting carpet and upholstery, then up walls to boil and billow across the ceiling. The blaze forms an open path for me, and unafraid, with flames and black smoke closing behind me, I move through the tunnel of fire to their bedroom. I'm invincible.

Salem is naked, her wrists and ankles lashed to the posts of a Rococo, wooden four-poster, as I was tied to the target in my dream. Austin tickles her with a feather until she screams; then, he takes one of many ornate bottles of aromatic oil from the bedside table. As he opens the lid, some of the contents splash across the sheets and pillows, then he pours the rest over her breasts, and kneads them like bread dough, which I recognize as the way he treats me; part of our normal.

We make eye contact. "You have five minutes to leave, or you'll roast like the pigs you are."

Austin laughs. Again, he underestimates me. The bedroom is an arsonist's dream. A spark from the torch leaps to the mosquito netting draping their bed, flashing high. Embers fall onto the bed linens igniting the spilled oil and the fire races across their sheets.

As I approach the bedroom door, the vials and flacons explode like a bomb blast in a perfume factory, and the sweet smells mix with the smoke. Creaking and groaning, gnawing and devouring furniture, art, and rugs, the inferno is deafening. Wood splits and sizzles; flame gyrates across the floor.

Outside on the beach, I turn and watch the conflagration. Underlying the smoke and cologne is the stench of burning flesh and hair. Waves lap peacefully behind me in contrast to the roar and heat of the fire, and the house detonates, blowing out windows. Walls implode as the roof collapses. Sparks and flame light up the night. I smile and think, So much water in the sea, and none can help you. And the structure collapses into ash.

Chapter Fifteen

Apparently, I slept half the night and most of the day until five in the afternoon. Unheard of. And wow, happy hour when you wake up. I chuckle, pour a large glass of chardonnay, and contemplate my dream, which fortunately occurred without sleepwalking, as I might have burned down the house.

The dreams have changed. Now I have the power of fire, and I can end everything—their trysts, their frills, their very lives. And as smug as Austin was in this dream, he was weak, and he died. I murdered them both, or did I? I warned them, but I hadn't untied Salem or attempted to drag them from the bedroom. I'd calmly incinerated them. Do I want them dead? Not exactly. I want them gone.

Austin and Salem. I've never experienced such intense hate.

I was calm in the dream, but now there's taut hot rage. My fury nudges me into Austin's bedroom closet, which smells of *Incredible Me*, no doubt the perfume in the dream, pollution that has become part of my atmosphere, and at one time threatened to displace my scent, my identity. But I'm not that meek girl, not anymore.

Opening the lid of his wicker laundry hamper and the bin for the dry cleaner releases plumes of the gaseous fumes. I pull out a shirt and see tan makeup on the collar. Another shirt has pink lipstick smears. So cliché. Even in the face of our supposed attempts at reconciliation, Austin hasn't tried to hide the evidence.

I tamp down his laundry and dump in his dry cleaning, then pull out drawers and empty them into the hamper: underwear, socks, T-shirts. I yank business wear off the hangers: shirts and suits. In go clothes chosen by Salem: the gigolo jeans, jackets, and shiny tight shirts, new ties in migraine-inducing prints and colors, his baby-shit-brown suit. I drag the bin to the patio and tip the contents into the fire pit, then go back for another load. Soon, his closet is ransacked, with empty drawers stacked haphazardly on the floor and bare hangers rattling on the rods.

Back outside and breathless, I stand a moment, admiring the color and texture of his clothes in the fire pit, in solids and patterns; the undulations, accentuated by highlights and sheen. Gorgeous. I take a photo for a painting.

Back in the house, I top up my chardonnay and grab Austin's prize bottle of the Balvenie 21 single-malt Scotch, about a thousand bucks a bottle. From his bathroom, I take the musky aftershave I loathe.

I pour the liquor and aftershave over the billows of fabric, deepening colors and tinting Austin's white shirts amber as they collapse with the weight of the liquid. I light and toss a match, and there is a satisfying *whoosh*! Flames volley high. Alcohol, an efficient, dependable combustible, whether for tableside crêpe suzette or torching a philandering, thieving dick-head's belongings. The fire warms my face, cleansing me of guilt or shame. The inferno dances as spirals of smoke rise. I take more photos. As I feed more clothes into the flames, I consider my unapologetically deliberate act. There is no reversal, no misunderstanding my intent, and serenity invades me as if by osmosis, slipping through my skin, gliding like the fine oil in my dream around cells and molecules, penetrating to my center.

I leisurely add clothes until the laundry basket sits empty, but I don't dare burn the wicker hamper as errant sparks could set fire to the neighborhood. I heave the hamper into the pool to bob on the surface and slowly sink.

An hour after I first lit the fire, the flames begin to recede. In the house and the lanai, the smell of lightly scorched cotton, like my mother's freshly ironed laundry when I was a child, has displaced Salem's perfume. I open windows in the bedroom to air out the noxious pong of Salem's unwelcome presence.

Having finished the chardonnay, I open a bottle of Riesling and collapse on a chaise to think. Is this how people become alcoholics? No, I decide, this is situational, and I'll cut back soon. In the murky glow of the yard's lighting, an armadillo roots in the garden, and silhouettes of bats spiral against the deep-blue night sky as they scoop bugs. Ah, to be one of those ugly little creatures of the night, hanging tightly together to sleep, taking wing at dusk, a lot like my kids' nocturnal lives. I have another glass of wine, then head to bed, and to my relief, I fall instantly asleep.

I wake late morning; thankful I don't have a hangover. In Austin's closet, I shove mismatching clothes hangers, any leftover underwear and T-shirts that escaped the bonfire, along with his shoes, into a garbage bag, and put it on the guestroom bed.

I'm tidying the kitchen when the twins enter, dressed, and ready to go out. I glance at the clock, "It's only three-thirty. You're going out now?"

Sarah laughs self-consciously. "I know, crazy-early, right? We're going bowling first; then later, we'll go to the Armor-Dildo concert."

"Armor-Dildo?"

Bryan laughs. "Yeah, armadillo, get it? They're local."

"Sounds like fun," I say to their backs as they head to the door.

"We'll be super late or might be out all night," he calls over his shoulder.

I've been googling articles on divorce for a couple of hours when Austin arrives late afternoon. I trot to the kitchen window to watch him. He sniffs the air, scans the yard, and saunters to the fire pit where fragments of fabric and a few smoking embers languish. He has a lightbulb moment and almost seems to spin his wheels like Wile E. Coyote, then gets up to speed, and storms into the kitchen.

Blustering, he shrieks, "Fuck! You burned my clothes?" He runs down the hall to the master bedroom. I picture him surveying his empty closet as he slams drawers. He returns and yells, "You fucking bitch. You're going to pay for this. I'm going to call the cops!"

I lean with my back against the kitchen counter, my arms crossed, and mimic his strident tone and volume, shouting, "Be sure to tell them you stole my life savings!" I watch as he registers that the game is up. His shoulders hunch making his neck shorter like he's a turtle pulling his head in to protect himself. I add, "I will never forgive you. I want you out of my sight right now and forever. Pack your stuff and leave, or I'll burn a whole lot more of your shit."

"Fuck you," he says, "there's nothing left to burn."

"True. Burn might not be the operative word for what might happen to your car, which could contain," I count items off on my fingers," your computer, firearms, files, passport, wallet, phone, and whatever else. Drown might be a more appropriate word if your vehicle somehow runs off the driveway into the pool."

I leave him sputtering in the kitchen and work on a new illustration job of packaging for coconut water. When I look up, the clock shows eight o'clock. Austin appears at my studio door with hands in pockets. He rocks back on his heels. "Clayton's coming over to trade guns."

I exhale. "Absolutely not. I don't want Clayton or you in my house. Got it?" Is saying *got it?* the same as saying *okay?* I decide, *got it?* is more forceful.

"In case you've forgotten, this is my house too." He crosses his arms.

"That's not true since you swindled more than your share of this place."

"Bullshit."

"Don't bring Clayton here, Austin. For all our sakes. With your porn circulating, he might be aware you're making whoopee with Salem."

He shakes his head, "Overreacting, as usual."

"You're screwing his wife, and you don't see the danger? Surely you can't be this dumb. Or…wait a second." I put a finger to my cheek, pretending deep thought. "Is he a participant in the sex? Does he watch you fuck his wife, or do you both fuck her, double penetration? Does he screw you, or do you suck his dick? Is the anal sex you have with him mind-blowing? So many possibilities."

"Go fuck yourself, Julia," he says as red creeps up his neck.

"Hmm, apparently I struck a nerve. Have you packed anything yet?"

"I'm staying in this house as long as I damn well please, so get over it." He strolls away.

Bristling with rage, my hands shaking, I yell at his back, "Don't test me." Could I get a restraining order? Probably not. Although he's armed to the teeth and courting disaster with Clayton, other than the wall punch, he hasn't been violent.

The divorce articles I've been reading online all instruct against leaving, citing the possibility of losing points in the court's eyes, but I'm aching to get away from him. I'm so pissed and given my fantasies and my dreams lately, maybe

I'm the one who should be declared violent.

If only I could get a restraining order against myself, so I'd have to leave. Now there's an interesting concept, a self-restraining law that wouldn't be about punitively restricting someone. Instead, it would be elective, a promise to stay away from a volatile situation. The new edict could be called a Self-Compelling Order. Unlike the stigma of a restraining-order, filing a Self-Compelling Order would be considered a mature, intelligent step to take and be viewed sympathetically by the courts. The idea tickles me.

The doorbell rings, and Clayton's white van is parked at the curb. The poor schmuck, the cuckold. He stands on the porch, a bulky figure with rifle cases slung over his shoulder, almost a silhouette. The porch light catches the gang insignia on his jacket, art designed to be fearsome, emblems made to warn of danger, as clearly as a weapon in his hand.

Austin answers the doorbell and leads Clayton to his office. Their conversation is muffled, but there's occasional laughter. I go to the lanai and paint for a while. Around eleven o'clock, there's still the murmur of their dialogue, but the tone has become more heated, with Clayton vigorously asserting something. I edge closer to Austin's office.

"Dude, I'm tellin' you, they fired us without cause," Austin says in a wheedling tone. "Salem's a good salesperson. It's unfair."

"No shit," Clayton says, baritone and gravelly. "They fuckin' gave'r that pricey watch for her amazing sales record, then turn around and fire'r? And them pricks took the fuckin' watch back. The corporate world is fucked up, man."

I can't help but roll my eyes.

"Yep. It's not fair. Salem's lucky she's got you. Maybe you could mess with them some, 'specially that fat cow, Marcy." Austin is laying his crap on thick, revealing the oleaginous, mealy-mouthed conman he truly is.

"I was gonna go there and tear someone a new one, maybe slash tires, rough some a them up, but she said it'd just make things worse. She knows I got a fucking temper, coulda put someone in the hospital, or in the ground."

For now, Salem is keeping him clear of the office. A good idea, since Marcy wouldn't exactly tell Clayton, but she'd lead him to the damning evidence somehow, as she did with me at the fateful party.

Austin says he needs to finish writing his resume, and Clayton wishes him good luck in his job hunt. I duck into my studio and watch from the doorway as Austin's office door opens. Clayton emerges, turns away from me, lumbers down the hall, and leaves the house. In his wake lingers the smell of the same aftershave Austin wears. Ah… Salem, in a fit of self-preservation, bought that scent for Austin. How astute of her to ensure both men smell the same, so Clayton doesn't smell a rat—in more ways than one. But evidently, matching my perfume was not a consideration for her, or she would have been using my brand, *Kai*, instead of sending Austin home drenched in *Incredible Me*.

I put away my paints and brushes and take the paintings—of Lucy, the jack-in-the-box, two depicting the knife thrower dream, and a nearly-completed canvas of the fire dream—to the living room and place them on the fireplace mantle and a bookshelf. Out of the workroom, they take on a different character. I study my compositions, palette, and brushwork, and decide they are both proficient and daring, and I'm gratified they aren't a sequence. Each can stand alone.

Heading to bed, as I pass Austin's door, his voice is low, probably on the phone with Salem. As I lock the front door, I look through the tall narrow side-window. Clayton's van is still parked down the street, his bald head silhouetted by a streetlight. Universally, love triangles are emotional hothouses, cultivating all manner of poison. Is Austin unafraid because lying makes him feel smarter than Clayton? Meanwhile, I'm trembling, terrified of Clayton. After all, if Clayton wants to kill Austin, he will assume he's sleeping in the master bedroom with me.

I text the kids, and they respond they might be home very late, or out all night. Perfect. They're out of harm's way. With the bedroom door and all windows locked, curtains closed, and doorstop installed, in bed, there's no relief from my anger, and I'm sinking once again into hate and frustration. His refusal to leave has created a chasm within me that's filling with festering emotional lava, like a boil painful and hot to the touch, that needs to erupt but can't. Finally, mercifully, waves of sleep pull me under.

Chapter Sixteen

I wake and silently sit up. There's a presence. My eyes adjust, and I can see the doorknob is turning slowly, almost imperceptibly. There's no light visible beneath the door. The door gives a little at the top as if a shoulder is pushing, which means someone picked the lock, but the doorstop is holding its ground. The knob is slowly released, then turned, and the door pushed again. I quietly open my bedside table, but feeling around inside the drawer, I realize that either Clayton or Austin have confiscated my .357—probably Austin.

If Clayton is at the door, he wants Austin, not me. I change tactics and say boldly, "Clayton, Austin is in the guest room. Down the hall, second on the left."

After a pause, Austin answers, "It's me, Julia. You ratted me out! Thanks a lot for your loyalty."

He is trying to engage me. That he still thinks he can shame or manipulate me is humorous, but it also makes me fearful of his motive. Austin-the-salesman will say anything to get what he wants. Instead of being drawn in and distracted by his bull, I need to consider what he's really up to, the equivalent of ignoring the magician's hand performing the trick to concentrate on the other hand.

I tune him out to assess the situation. He could never resist lecturing me on his newfound self-defense and stealth tactics, learned at survivalist-camps. No light shining beneath the door means he came silently and slowly along the hallway in darkness, so when the door opened, he would avoid creating a target in silhouette—in case I had a weapon or gun stashed other than my missing .357. Now I'm sure he took my revolver earlier today, while I was working, which means he planned whatever he's up to, with malice intent.

"You want me to leave tomorrow, so I'm packing my stuff, and I want to get any clothes you didn't burn." I recognize the inveigling tone he uses when he's unreasonable. "Let me in. I just want my things, and I'll go."

If that were true, he would have knocked instead of being sneaky. He sounds agitated, most likely provoked by my silence. I picture him in the dark hallway. He's armed and wearing night-vision goggles, which only work in the dark; in the light, they are blinding. Phone in hand, I silently slip out of bed and turn on every fixture, lighting the room like a stadium.

He rattles the door handle. My resistance is getting to him. I say sternly, "Go away, or I'll call nine-one-one."

"And tell them what? That I want to get my things, and you won't let me? You're ridiculous."

"No. I'll tell them you're distraught because you've ruined your life. You got caught screwing a biker's wife, and your intelligent, hardworking, caring wife—that's me, by the way—is divorcing you, and you're ashamed because you turned out to be nothing more than a thief who stole our savings, and your sex tape made the rounds and cost you your job. And now you took my gun, and you're trying to break into my bedroom, and you're threatening me. How am I doing so far?"

He's silent a moment; then, there are receding

footsteps. I turn the lights off again so he can't see my silhouette through curtains or track me by peering under the door. I lock the door and wrestle the recliner into his empty walk-in closet and sit tilted back, terrified.

Only one scenario makes sense: a staged suicide. Austin planned to overpower me and shoot me with my own gun in my hand so I would have gunshot residue on me. Then he would shower, pretend he slept all night in the guest room where he didn't hear anything, and supposedly discover my lifeless body in the morning.

If my suicide had gone according to his plan, Austin's story would be credible. Outsiders would accept my sadness over his affair, our plundered savings, and our impending divorce.

It's a scenario he could pull off. He might come off as the world's biggest jerk, but if he played his hand well, he could be pitied as a victim. He'd get away with murder, and he would inherit the house, what's left of our savings, and the life insurance, which has no forfeiture clause for suicide. If I were able to fight hard enough, scratching and biting, to at least implicate him, he might go to prison, but I'd still be dead.

I thought my bonfire of Austin's clothes had burned away my rage, but the anger has flared up twofold. Austin's transgressions—his disparaging comments, infidelity, thievery, invasion of privacy, baseless denigrations, emotional and physical cruelty, mind games, rejection, and humiliation—roll through my mind like a train. I leave the recliner and get back into bed, but the thoughts continue to unfurl on and on, like counting sheep until a flickering, disturbed sleep visits, and I'm plunged into a nightmare.

Thousands of stinking bats are in my bedroom. They're tightly crowded, hanging from the ceiling and walls, the furniture and drapes, dropping their awful guano along with something else like putrid molasses, as if they are melting.

I'm seething with fury and frustration at the ludicrous and unfair turns my life has taken, and now, what is this fresh hell?

I'm wearing a white-lace, long, clingy negligee and high-heeled gold sandals. Everything else in the room, including Austin's side of the bed, is fouled, but somehow I'm perfectly clean. I remove the doorstop and run into the hallway where more squeaking bats are swooping and flapping. One brushes by, leathery wings and hairy body slipping across my neck and cheek, and nausea grips me. I pause to let my stomach settle, and my eyes adjust to the dark. The fetid bat tar coats the floor and walls, but I am still immaculate.

Passing the living room, I notice Austin's phone sitting on a side table. I pick it up and stroll into the kitchen. Beaver sashays in and jumps high, catching a screeching and flailing bat in his teeth. I whisper, "Beav, I want to be like you and land on my feet and hurt Austin like you'll torture that bat. Austin should suffer physical pain equal to the emotional agony he's inflicted on me."

As I warm to the payback, Beaver's eyes turn a soft red like smoldering coals, and he sinks his claws into the bat's body. "That prick, Austin, I'll strangle him. I'll choke him till he turns blue and begs me to stop, and then I'll squeeze harder." My fury builds, and the cat's eyes become brighter—crimson—as he rips apart the bat's wings with his teeth.

The prospect of inflicting physical pain is exhilarating, and my voice is rising. "No. On second thought, I won't strangle him. That's too bloodless. I'll be the new knife thrower and throw knives at him." I lay his phone on the counter and take a carving knife and a butcher knife from the countertop. "I will eviscerate him. Retaliation for all the times that knife thrower cut me down." The bat shrieks as my anger becomes more heated, and the cat's eyes, in sync with my wrath, glow a more intense red.

Austin comes into the kitchen. He's shirtless, wearing

only jeans. He says, "Put the knives down and go to bed. You're sleepwalking."

"Where's my gun? Admit it. You're planning to kill me."

He turns slightly to show my revolver tucked into the back of his waistband and snorts derisive laughter. "You're right. For once, you're not imagining things." The bat in Beav's grip cries out, and Austin observes the cat. He casually puts his hands in his pockets, and I step closer to him, expecting him to back away, but he stands his ground unafraid and smug as always, which further infuriates me. The room darkens as more bats crowd above us. He says, "I'd love to beat you to death, but I have to be careful not to leave any marks other than a single shot to the right temple since you are right-handed."

I heft the weight of the knives in my hands. "You better be careful," I snicker. "Things could get dicey." He's puzzled by the word, and I chuckle.

He starts to pull his right hand from his pocket. Going for the gun I suspect, and in a flash, I strike. The large knife extends my reach, and I slash through skin and fat into the muscle of his bicep, then again on his forearm and wrist. Stunned, he appraises the blood running down his arm and trailing from his fingers. "Great," he says, examining his wounds. "Self-defense now."

"Actually, I can say the same."

He frowns, baffled again, and in his moment of distraction, I react, lunging for his gut. The blades breach his skin and sink to the hilt. Nose to nose, I watch his eyes go startled, then afraid, angry, bewildered.

Profound release blossoms in my chest and radiates into my limbs. Austin staggers back two steps, pulling away, leaving the bloody knives in my hands. Regaining his footing, he's silent a second, then touches his wounds incredulously and shouts, "You stupid fucking bitch!"

The cat's eyes are now neon red, and I smile. "Well, well. Look, Beav. The knife thrower isn't immune to his blades."

"Call an ambulance!"

I shake my head, and he shouts, "Where the fuck is my phone?"

I pluck the phone from the countertop and smile as I wiggle it at him. "Come and take it." I laugh at my wit, using that old Texas slogan.

He slowly reaches behind him and finds my weapon, but his arm is useless—I must have cut some ligaments—and the gun slips from his grip. I quickly grab the handle, release the barrel, and empty all the bullets onto the floor. I place the firearm next to his phone on the counter. I lunge again, striking higher, through ribs. Metal scrapes bone. His knees give out, and flailing, grasping at the countertop and cabinet handles, he falls, smearing blood as he crumples onto his back on the floor. His strength is drained by punctures spouting blood, a sucking wound in his chest, shock, and disbelief.

There's a roaring in my ears and in a sticky, stinking burst, the bats swarm over us, crashing together and rustling, their gristly wings and bristling bodies brushing my face, shoulders, and arms. Under cover of oily darkness, as Austin struggles to stand, I place my foot on his chest and push him down. He has no strength to resist. Straddling him, I drop to my knees and plunge the knives into his chest, neck, and gut. There is so much blood—spurting, spraying in arcs, flying from the tips of the blades, spattering walls, floor, and cabinets.

I watch his eyes go vacant as his vitality oozes away, and with his heart stopped, the blood runs passively from his wounds. "Don't bring a gun to a knife fight." I laugh softly, then realize tears are streaming down my cheeks and dripping from my chin.

I place the knives on the counter with his gun and phone as headlights pierce the dark. A vehicle pulls into the driveway. Breathless from exertion and crying, I straighten and watch as a clown, a very fat Ronald McDonald, trudges from the driver's side of the van. Fat Ronald shambles into the kitchen and screams, "Holy shit, lady! What the fuck did you do?"

What the clown says is funny. He is a clown after all, and I laugh long and hard and say, "Don't point the finger at me, fatso. I killed one person, but you're responsible for the obesity epidemic that's killed millions. That's why it's called morbid obesity, tubby. Hell, you used to be thin, but now look at you. You're a disgrace." I'm mystified why I'm so judgmental. "Besides, you're a fool, a big fat joke. I can't take a clown seriously."

Fat Ronald shakes his head and rushes toward his van, moving very quickly for his size, but more headlights appear, and two cars block his escape like a TV show about cops and robbers. A stranger carrying a handgun, and my mother, who has been dead for ten years, get out of the cars. They argue with Fat Ronald and march him back to the kitchen at gunpoint.

My mother puts her arm around me and says, "Don't worry. I'll clean this up." And she leads me to the shower. My eyes fill with tears at her kindness and her presence, and I hold her so tightly she squirms to get free. She smiles as she says, "Now, now, don't you worry."

Without undressing, I step into the shower in the dark. I remove and wring out the lace gown and scrub with my loofah, watching the blood on the white tile swirl into the drain. I towel off, and my mother hands me my robe. Weeping, I make my way to bed. The bats are gone, and the room is clean. I let my kimono fall from my shoulders to the floor, and I slip between fresh, smooth sheets.

Waking naked, covered by a sheet and duvet, the clock glows 2:20, snippets of the nightmare surface, and I scan the room to ensure the bats are gone. Sleep tugs at me. There's muffled conversation—maybe Austin on the phone, or the kids are home. Somewhere in the house a door closes, the voices disappear, and I sink back into sleep.

It's after eight when I open my eyes to my bedroom in its usual state, and as has been happening lately, I remember the entire dream. The nightmare is by far the most violent and realistic so far. Has Austin been murdered by my hand while I sleepwalked? As a child, I was accused of killing a little dog. Can I do in my sleep, what is unthinkable while awake? If there's a mutilated body in the kitchen, I'll need a credible story.

What a disturbing night, starting with Austin trying to get into the bedroom. His threat must have triggered the dream. The doorstop and my robe are in the middle of the floor, a bad sign. But in the bathroom, the lace peignoir isn't hanging on the shower door. Good. And in the shower stall, there's no blood on the grout.

Breathing deeply, fighting anxiety, I put one foot in front of the other and tentatively make my way fearfully along the hallway. My palms are damp and gooseflesh forms on my arms and the back of my neck. I brace myself for Austin's mutilated body lying in coagulated blood, rigor mortis setting in, his face contorted by surprise and pain. Or worse, what if I injured him and left him there to die slowly, in agony? I turn the corner into the kitchen and find…emptiness.

There's no corpse on the floor, no pools of blood, or spatter on the walls. No bats. Sun streams through the east-facing windows, casting near-white rectangles on the travertine-tile floor. Black-granite countertops gleam and appliances sparkle. Beaver is eating at his kibble tower. I've been holding my breath. Dizzy, I sit on a stool, put my face to my knees, and breathe slowly.

I go to Austin's office. His furniture is intact, but his gun safe, which is the size of a fridge and full of weapons and ammo, is missing. How did he move a thousand-pound object in the night? There are no shoe prints but there are the faint wheel marks of an appliance dolly.

In the guest room, the bed is unmade, and on the

nightstand, there are two bags of new jeans and shirts with tags still attached. I check rooms and closets. Outside, his car is gone, and when I phone him, my call goes to voicemail. So, he complied with my demands and left, taking his guns and his car. But why nothing else?

Then, in my new Austin-free incarnation, I say, "Who cares? Not my problem." And I stand straighter and swipe my hands together as if dusting off dirt. Now I'll simply wait until he informs me where he wants his belongings shipped, down the block, or to Timbuktu.

Chapter Seventeen

I pay bills, answer email, and daydream about my new single life, of being free of the house, spending more time painting, the children becoming independent. I inform them Austin has moved out, and they stare at me wide-eyed but don't ask questions, which is either a disinterested reaction or they're stoned.

Every so often, the dream of murdering Austin surfaces—the disgusting, stinking, fluttering bats, the blood spatter. And I shudder but can't help visualizing a painting of the dream.

A job to illustrate a children's book, *The Selfish Shellfish*, arrives by email, along with an ad campaign for a teen fashion line called Emo-Boho. I'll need the money. The client has supplied samples of the style of art they want, showing girls with spiky hair, tiny mouths and noses, lots of swoopy eyeliner, and bodies like pencils. For an instant, I'm concerned about contributing to teen girls' angst and their body dysmorphia, but saving the world isn't on my to-do list today…maybe next week. There is also a request for several more sketches for the furniture store. I'm swamped.

At dinnertime, I half expect Austin to arrive and expect to be fed, but to my relief he doesn't show up. The kids are still out. With a thrown-together meal of salad, baguette, and cheese, I eat in the living room and study my paintings. They appear more significant and polished in a room setting. I start working on a storyboard of thumbnail sketches for the children's book, replete with humorously animated greedy crustaceans. Time sails by, and well past midnight, I'm tired enough to sleep.

For nearly two weeks, there is no communication from Austin. The kids keep to themselves, continuing their nighttime forays. I'm working twelve-hour days, seven days a week, and while it helps keep my mind off everything relating to Austin, I'm worried if my divorce doesn't get settled soon, I won't be able to support the house and kids on my income alone. I phone the divorce lawyer and set an appointment.

However, while keeping my career intact is essential, I'm getting burned out, and starting to have trouble concentrating on work. I'm not *Julia Green, the art machine*, as Austin liked to call me, and I need to give myself a break. I phone Trix. "Hon, I'm going stir-crazy, and I desperately need to get out of here. I have a meeting with my divorce lawyer at the end of the day in Houston. Are you free this evening for a low-key dinner?"

"You bet, girlfriend. Get your butt to Houston. There's a grungy house party tonight. It doesn't get rolling until about eleven, so before, we'll go to the Big Easy for live blues. The music starts at ten. Come to my place after your meeting. We'll hang out here, then grab margaritas and a bite to eat."

Grungy party, live blues? Sure, why not live a little. "Uh…sounds like fun."

"You can stay the night. Dress casual-sexy," she says

and hangs up.

Hmmm, casual-sexy? Using my cell phone's flashlight, I tiptoe into Sarah's room. She's snoring, her exhalations whistling like a teakettle. Closer, her breath has a rancid edge. I gently shake her and say, "Hey, I'm going to borrow your top with the sequins, skinny jeans, and blue cowboy boots."

She's wearing an *I ♥ TX* oversized T-shirt, which has crept up to her armpits and displays a new tattoo of a happy-face emoji on her outie belly button, with the nub incorporated into the face as a nose. My laugh disturbs her, and she grunts and flops over onto her stomach.

With Sarah's clothes, my undies, makeup, and a bottle of Malbec in my overnight bag, I change into a business suit and set out for Houston. To evict Austin from my thoughts, I turn up the middle-of-the-road station loud and shout along.

The attorney's office is in a sleek downtown high-rise, and the elevator whisks me eleven floors to Ms. William's office. She is exactly what I'd hoped for—articulate, well dressed, and direct. She listens patiently to the full story of Austin's disappearance and says, "You have absolutely no idea where he might have gone?"

"I'm starting to believe he left everything behind to make a new start."

She says, "Or not. You need to give Austin time to resurface. Keep Googling him. Access his bank account and monitor his activity if possible, especially his credit cards. Try to think of what he would use as an alias and where he might go."

"Okay, but I can't afford to live in that house waiting for him to show up. I want to sell and move."

She waves a finger side to side. "Oh, no. You're not moving anywhere until all the financial business has been nailed down."

"As far as I'm concerned, he's stolen the half he was entitled to. Living there is killing me emotionally and financially."

She sits back and observes me a moment. "Give me the prices of what comparable houses in the neighborhood are selling for, what you had saved, and what Austin took from your savings, and I'll see if a judge will examine the situation."

"Okay. I'll get that paperwork together." I write a check for her retainer and pick up the forms. She stands, and I follow suit and leave.

In the car, I consider how, in the way my dreams have given the power over to me, I'm finally in control of my destiny. And how the lawyer's advice and strategy; for the sale of the house, our finances, bank accounts, and credit cards is technical and dry, like maneuvers for a chess game, or war. As for selling the house, our local realtors will turn up their noses at our dated furniture, room colors, and the kids' teen décor. The place needs an overhaul and staging.

At Trix's loft, she immediately uncorks the Malbec, and after a large swig, I say, "It's possible he took off, drove to Mexico. Maybe he'll never turn up, and I'll be in marriage purgatory forever."

Trix shakes her head. "I saw a show where a guy disappeared, and his wife had him declared dead."

"Wishful thinking." I catch her eye, and we chuckle. "I wonder how long it takes."

"A question for your attorney."

"Or for Google."

The poppies painting is gone, and there's a new arrangement, a slate-blue background with a blue-and-white Oriental vase of pink-tinged creamy roses in full bloom, some past their prime, their heads tipped, the petals flabby. "Those are gorgeous," I comment.

She smirks. "They were prettier when they were fresh and new."

"But now they have character."

"Like us. Goodbye perkiness, hello charisma."

"And experience."

"Personality," she adds.

I grin. "Wisdom. Definitely smarts." I pause. "A commission?"

"Yes." She nods. "Five by eight feet. I'll be on my ladder for a couple of months."

"Wow. That's why you get the big bucks."

"Of course." She laughs and says she wants to grab a nap. I agree, occupying the sofa while she goes to the bedroom. I wake to Trix singing in the shower. Reality rushes back in. Now I'm waking into a nightmare instead of falling asleep into one.

Trix emerges from the bathroom, wrapped in a towel, and smoking a cigarette. "Chop, chop. Get dressed."

I dress in Sarah's clothes, which fit me better than I had anticipated, add some smoky eye makeup, and gel my hair for volume. Trix enters from the bedroom wearing her customary all-black, but tighter, with more leg and cleavage exposed, and heels instead of her usual ballerina flats. She has applied a very pale foundation, smudged on black eyeliner, added creamy cerise lipstick, and her orange hair is spiky.

As I finish my makeup, Trix comes up behind me, and I ask her reflection, "Want me to drive?"

"No, we're gonna Uber; all the better for drinking. And, by the way, no cock-blocking."

"Of course. I remember. But I can't say I'm ready for a hookup. Hell, I still feel married." On campus, there had been straitlaced cliques of girls advocating *chicks before dicks*, meaning no member of their posse could defect for sex. Our mandate was different; to have fun drinking and partying together, and possibly some sexual hijinks independently. Back then, Trix was far better at casual intimacy than me, and now, having been with Austin for so long, the notion of a no-strings-attached boink is a brutally foreign concept. Aside from Earl, there have been other come-ons from men over my married years—PTA dads, guys in the supermarket, and more than one married neighbor—but despite several stretches of sexual drought, my wedding vows were enough for me. I kept my monogamy intact. What will dating be like, to meet someone new, assess them as a sex partner or a new mate, touch or kiss for the first time?

"Oh, please!" she chides. "Austin has been getting his jollies elsewhere for years. He broke the covenant, so in my book, you're unmarried. Remember, revenge sex is cleansing. What you need is a great temporary lover."

I shake my head, chuckling. "Don't know about that."

Trix summons a car that deposits us at Hugo's. This upscale Mexican restaurant eschews sombreros, mariachi bands, and machine-dispensed margaritas for an ambiance that is Cabo (tile, leather, wrought iron) meets Manhattan (tall windows, waitstaff in black and white, margaritas from a shaker). We sip the salty, tart-sweet drinks and share appetizers. An ample seating of revelers and many tables of couples celebrating milestones takes me back to how the kudzu-like obligations of housework, kids, and work smothered our married life; how frivolity seemed, well, frivolous, compared to the supposedly important things. We fell into a rut, a featureless ditch without turnoffs for fun.

Trix is staring at me. "Stop thinking about him." she admonishes.

I blush. "Busted. You're right."

After ten, we leave the restaurant for *The Big Easy Social and Pleasure Club*, an unapologetic dive. The crowd is a mix of regulars, hipsters, suburbanites, and moneyed classes from gated Houston enclaves who crave a night out of careless slumming, hearing damage, and an impending, raging hangover. The club has a timeworn biker-bunker personality and no curb appeal. Pigs will fly before bric-a-brac, or potted plants decorate this place; no tiara on this swine of a building; no appeasing nearby homeowners' associations, those champions of conformity. The patrons of the Big Easy (affectionately known locally as the Big Sleazy) like to roll in the mud with this particular piggy.

Inside, the owner is in sunglasses, as always, and collecting the cover charge. There's beat-up seating, a long bar, a few pool tables, and the murky pong of sweat and stale booze. The place is packed and thrumming with Alan Haynes' live, virtuoso guitar.

At the bar, we observe the scene. The younger male patrons favor facial scruff, shaggy hair, loose clothing, and dance styles that run from noncommittal disinterest to simulated sex. Meanwhile, men of my generation and older, wear classic Texan: buttoned-up long-sleeved shirts tucked into high-waisted Lee Wrangler jeans and big silver buckles on leather belts, western boots, a close shave, and fresh haircuts. They shuffle and twirl their women around the dance floor to a prescribed sequence of steps. Their routines display discipline and detachment as if passion has been replaced by orderliness. Have their marriages gone the same route? Maybe, but those couples are still together, still dancing, touching, holding each other, however routine their style. Probably Austin and I should have danced more.

Trix is staring again. "Okay!" I laugh. "I'll stop thinking about him."

Slouching up to the bar and idling near us are a few young men. They're somewhat older than the twins but wearing the same style; quasi-unkempt-appearing clothing, but their grooming is meticulous. In tune with their spotless shabbiness, their poses are aggressively laid-back, making the entire presentation oxymoronic. One of them winks at me. He is about fifteen years my junior, and handsome in a bad-boy way, all dark-hair, cognac-colored eyes, and dimples. He makes eye contact, smiles, sidles closer, and says, "What're you drinkin', darlin'?" with confidence, as if we have an understanding.

It's apparent he's the alpha of the group. He places his hand over mine, and a slight shock travels between us. He orders drinks and nods to a couple down the bar, then breaks away to talk to them.

Trix approaches and says, "I know these dudes. Eric,

the one you're talking to is cool. He's a good guy. Have fun. Text me if you need anything." And she saunters off.

He reminds me of the cool, older guys I met in college, the ones who smoked a lot of pot and had sex with a lot of girls. He returns as our drinks arrive, and his friends converge, including me in their group. Two barstools over, Trix is in conversation with a blue-haired, tattooed, and stapled man-boy.

My guy says, "Hey, I'm Eric." We shake hands, and he doesn't let go, pulling me closer to him.

A woman in red stiletto-heeled cowboy boots and short skirt, makeup applied with a paintball gun, and platinum rats'-nest hair, shouts, "Hey, dawg!" She runs up and jumps on Eric, hooking her legs around his waist. Her miniskirt rides up, exposing a bright purple thong bisecting her butt. She attaches her lips to his like a leech and pulls her phone from her bra for a selfie. He laughs and pries her off. She smooches him again, then leaves, staggering to the loo. She's what I imagine Marcy would look like if I were on LSD (not that I've ever done LSD). Strangely, her antics, rather than being offensive, are merely humorous.

Eric says, "Don't mind her; she's the resident bargoyle."

"Bargoyle? Like a gargoyle?"

He says, "Yeah. A bar-girl, a drunk old chick who hangs around a bar. Every bar has one, right?"

Unease stings me. Could I become a bargoyle? If the good men are taken, will dating at my age be a series of unhappy hookups, of hoping for the unattainable? Will the local bar substitute for a family, a home, and I'll be a hunched crone getting sloshed to pass the hours, looking for validation or love at the bottom of a bottle?

I have an almost overwhelming urge to flee and run home to safety. But I don't. Maybe I should cut down on the booze. The idea of getting pigeonholed as a bargoyle, or any sad stereotype is scary. Oh well, whatever my destiny, there's no going back. I venture, "What's a male bargoyle called?"

"A grampire; an old codger that sucks the life outta young people." We stand hip to hip at the bar, and he runs his hand up my arm. I give in to his gaze and allow myself to absorb the possibility that I'm wanted, desired. And if I desire physical closeness, there won't be any begging or pleading. An emotional tectonic shift is taking place, with new plates—of choices and freedom—moving over my ingrained connection to Austin. Am I a cougar in his eyes, or maybe the new face, and he's after first dibs? Perhaps I can admit he likes my looks.

One of his friends leans over smiling sardonically, and says, "I'm scoring some weed, you want in?"

"Nah, I'm good, Blitz," Eric says.

"Later, gator," Blitz says.

"In a while, pedophile," Eric replies, and they laugh a little. I'm uneasy with the casual, even humorous use of the word *pedophile*. It's irresponsible, reckless, and dangerous, equivalent to saying *bomb* at the airport. Am I showing my age, or is some humor simply wrong? These cautious reactions of mine are what prompts Austin to say I'm uptight, a drama queen. Now I recognize his name-calling as manipulation through shaming, to condition me to be obedient and complacent.

Blitz shambles away, and Eric catches my expression and says, "Hey, hey. It's okay. Blitz knows I'm just messing with him."

The band starts on "Stormy Monday," slow and gritty. Eric takes the drink from my hand, places it on the bar, and leads me to the dance floor. Planting his feet, he pulls me into full-frontal contact, his leg between mine. Dirty dancing; Austin would consider us vulgar. Dancing with Eric is different and exciting. His taut muscles flex against me, my cheek on his jawline. Austin and I danced like the older couples I observed earlier, our familiarity and dance steps predictable, and like most of our routines, whether home chores or dancing, we barely needed to be present, and eventually—physically, emotionally, intimately—we weren't.

The powerful rhythm of the music hurtling over us is dazzling. Slowly, thin strand by thin strand, hidden ropes linking me to my former life are breaking. And I melt into my dance partner and go where his body takes me. Sex with him, a new position or two, lust, someone with desires to be explored, could inoculate me against Austin's memories—amnesia by injection.

When the tune shifts to something fast-paced, we stroll back to the bar. I spot Trix, and she tosses me a wink. Eric glances away, but stands close, and runs his hand down my spine, stops in the arch of my lower back and pulls me close.

The bargoyle is back and stands fists on hips. "Honey," she addresses Blitz, "you always promise to sleep with me, then you disappear."

He smiles. "You're too much woman for me."

She hoots, "We should test that theory…" and staggers away. Resident bargoyle. Her age is indeterminate, either a rough forty or average sixty.

Trix and her blue-haired boy approach, "We're heading to the party. Want to bring your guy?"

I nod, then lean into Eric and tell him about the party. He says, "Yeah, I know the guys throwing the party." Houston, a small town, after all. I resist checking my watch as I would in my mommy persona, no doubt an effect of the alcohol. We thread through the dancers out into fresh air, and take an Uber, me between two men in the back, Trix in front.

CHAPTER EIGHTEEN

The party house is the only lit-up house on the street, an old clapboard bungalow with peeling paint exposing rotten wood. The yard is weedy and half-bald, edged by chain-link. Faded crêpe paper is threaded through the fence, and clumps of dog shit and dirty plastic toys litter the yard, a disturbing indication children are visiting or live here. Weepiness almost overcomes me. Who are these children, and how can I rescue them?

A heavy bass beat vibrates the porch. The interior continues the exterior's decrepitude with dumpster-diver furniture and surfaces littered with plastic cups and drug paraphernalia. In a corner is a highchair piled with colorful plastic toys and a sippy cup. Again, I have the impulse to rescue the kids. To give them what? Immunizations, clean clothes, healthy food, take them to an area of lush lawns and maid service, and seemingly no crime? Would they be better off in my burb, coddled, protected, and convinced they're somehow superior? Superficial confidence is no armor for the beatings meted out beyond those idealistic doors. A quick visual search determines no children are present.

The crowd is diverse with men in T-shirts and jackets, hipsters with topknots, scene-making slick types, and women as Barbie cuties, retro rockabilly girls, and a few hippies. I suspect by day these guests are engineers, teachers, middle-management salaried paper pushers, or lawyers. Tattoos and piercings are prevalent, and for a fleeting instant, I wonder if Sarah might be in the crowd.

The bargoyle arrives noisily trailed by sycophants, her makeup clownish, and red boots glittering. She swills Don Julio from a bottle then jumps on Eric again, and laughing, he peels her off. She offers me her bottle, and I shake my head. I ask, "What's your name?"

She guzzles tequila, gasps, and says, "I'm Euphoria." She notices a male acquaintance across the room, and runs, shrieking, launching herself onto him.

Huge 80s vintage speakers are blasting a song I like; maybe I'm not as uncool as I thought. Wherever there is open floor space, dancers lean on each other, swaying lazily as if their batteries are dying, given the music's high energy and pounding rhythm. Smoke hangs above us, and one bare bulb backlights figures in unbalanced compositions, reminiscent of noir pulp fiction or graphic-novel illustrations. A time machine has flung me back to my early twenties, with random strangers to meet, screw, and shed—what we called *fucking and chucking*, or *humping and dumping*. The air is heavy with the acrid smell of cigarettes, pot, alcohol, and musky body odor, overlaying a tinge of mold.

Eric points to a pair of dancing, kissing men, and says, "Those two, Prince Jack and Princess Donald, are trust fund oilfield trash, and the proud owners of..." He makes a wide arc with his arm and laughs caustically. "...this meth-den shithole."

He takes my hand, and we weave our way through the crush of bodies to the kitchen where the faucet drips, and

Texas-size inch long roaches scurry across the worn linoleum floor. I crush two of them—a puny start on a heavy infestation.

While Eric sifts through detritus on a table to find bottles of rum and coke, I wander until my nose detects the monkey-cage aroma of the bathroom. The door is a curtain, and there's no toilet seat. The toilet paper roll mercifully has two squares left, and given the dirty towel and sink, I rinse my hands and dry them on my jeans.

Trix is waiting when I leave the bathroom, and she hands me three condoms. I laugh, "Three?" She smiles knowingly and strolls away. Back in the kitchen, Eric gives me a drink in a plastic cup, then leads me to a hallway off the living room, and we lean against the wall where he lights a joint, hands it to me, and says, "Moderation in all things—including moderation." I inhale.

The music has switched to Stevie Ray Vaughan's *Texas Flood.* Eric takes hold of my hair and turns my mouth to his. The sensation of a stranger's soft, insistent lips is so different from Austin, who was never much for kissing. Lately, Austin's kisses have been tightly puckered pecks—what I once heard termed *like kissing an asshole*—which, in a sense, is accurate.

Eric shuffles closer, pinning me against decaying wallpaper, his free hand edging my breast, testing, and I don't pull away. As our pheromones collide, I enter a portal of primitive want. And the anonymity and my deprived libido conspire with the pounding beat and intoxicants, and I'm vibrating with a hungry yearning. Still kissing, he hands off the joint to another partier, cups his hands under my butt, and my feet clear the floor. I hook a leg around his hip, and his erection, now up against a sensitive spot, produces a heavenly sensation one notch beneath orgasm. I want him.

He carries me along the hall into a back bedroom, where he knees the door shut, muffling the music's volume to a tolerable decibel range. I hope the party crowd recognizes the closed door as the universal symbol of *go away.* On the bedside table is a vintage lamp with a china base shaped like a cowboy. There's no lampshade and one of four bulbs works, illuminating an unmade bed with a sagging mattress, and stained linens and pillows draped partway on the floor. Eric drops me onto the mattress, and somehow I resist the fear of bedbugs and of comparing the tainted sheets to my six-hundred thread count, coordinated, Egyptian-cotton bedding at home. Evidently, I'm extravagantly bombed.

We are both chuckling as he yanks off my boots and pulls down my jeans, their tight fit presenting a struggle, then he theatrically twirls and tosses them over his shoulder, ride-'em-cowboy style, which elevates my snickering to helpless laughter. He straddles me, unbuckling his belt and unzipping his fly. He tears open and removes a condom. Suddenly I'm not ready, and I plead, "Wait…wait," pushing him away. "Stop. I can't do this. I want to, but…"

He tosses the condom toward a beat-up trash can printed with a retro picture of Dale Evans. The prophylactic hits her square in the eye and falls to the floor, and we are gasping with laughter. He stays straddling me and lights a cigarette while I lie in a booze and weed-induced, peculiar rapture. "I'm wasted."

He smiles. "Wonderful."

He balances his smoke on the bedside table's edge, bends forward, and pushes up my top and bra. He palms my breasts, then rubs his lips and whiskers on my nipples, turning them into ball bearings. I lift his T-shirt. He resumes smoking as I examine him.

To my stoned artist's eyes, angels have designed his ideally proportioned youthful body with supple and tight flesh, but a prickle of concern surfaces at the spectacle of his shoulders, chest, and back, inked with tattoos. Over time they will fade, the art becoming outdated, the designs distorted as his flesh sags, or becomes fat, or ropey. Oh screw it. I'm not his mom.

The window frames him, and he is backlit by weak outdoor lighting and a slim crescent moon like a sickle's blade. His silhouette is like a black paper cutout, tattoo-free and featureless, an anonymous everyman. I notice there's a rhythm, a motion, and for a second, I believe the shaking is an earthquake, then holy crap! With a startled gasp, I realize he is masturbating. His actions quicken, and as he nears climax, a memory, slender and sharp as the moon, superimposes Austin onto Eric; youthful and in the same position, his head tipped back in abandonment.

He pauses, gasps a shuddering breath as he orgasms on my naked torso, then collapses his full weight on me, mingling his sweat and sperm, his body hot, heart pounding, breathing labored. For a while, he stays like that, and I'm happy to let him. We are still, becalmed. Damn, I'm high.

Eric rolls off me onto his back and is immediately asleep. The drugs in my system start their slide to sobriety. Maybe the bargoyle, Euphoria, lives the lifestyle of this house. Is euphoria defined as an unapologetic absence of discipline? Is paradise defined as smoking cigarettes and weed, drinking to excess daily, staying up all night, and snoozing the day away? Would it be ideal to skip the bathing and oral hygiene whenever one can't be bothered, goof off at work, or not show up and blindly trust that someone else will take care of things? Ultimately, that has the ring of a vacation, or maybe childhood, not real, adult life. My sober self would say, *That's how you end up living on the street.* Even in my inebriated state, I'm aware doing the minimum isn't my strong suit.

I use the sheet to wipe off his sperm, then get dressed, take the lit cigarette from Eric's fingers and extinguish it in the overflowing ashtray. In the hall outside the bedroom door, Euphoria is on her back, passed out, her blond, backcombed hair in disarray, her makeup smeared, the empty tequila bottle still in her hand. Her skirt is bunched at her waist, her purple thong around her knees. I arrange her clothes to cover her. She doesn't stir.

In the living room, guests are passed out or still imbibing. Outside, the night air is bracing. As if on cue, Trix emerges, straightening her outfit. We hug, dial a car, then wait quietly. The sun is beginning to rise, casting a thin light, glimmering on the roofs of houses.

At Trix's loft, I nod off on her sofa. We both wake near noon. I ask, "Are you hungover?"

"Nope, you?"

"Not really. Just tired."

"Did you have fun?"

"Definitely. Just what I needed." We make toast and coffee in silence, then sit at the bistro table on her balcony, looking out over the city. After breakfast, I thank her for having me. We hug and I leave.

Back home, the garage door is standing open, which is a Homeowner's Association 'no-no.' I stroll over to close it and can't believe my eyes. It's nearly empty. I run into the house and do a quick tally, but electronics are intact, and nothing appears to be missing. I call Lucy. "Did you notice any unusual activity over here in the last 24 hours? I spent last night at Trix's place, and my garage has been cleaned out."

"There were a couple of guys with a truck there early this morning, like around five or six o'clock. I figured you hired them to get rid of some stuff."

"Nope. There was nothing of value, which just makes it all the weirder." I pause a second. "I wonder if Austin paid them to collect some of his stuff. He had some old power tools and car parts, and there was a mower. I'm not sure if I should even report it to the cops. Even if the police found the stuff, I don't want it back."

Lucy laughs. "I wish some robbers would clean out my garage."

"They did me a favor." We laugh and hang up.

I wander back outside, glancing into the greenhouse as I pass, and I'm drawn up short, again. It is also empty. My garden hoses, watering cans, plant pots, gardening tools, broom, bags of plant food, and bug spray, have been cleared out. What the hell? I call the gate guard and ask if somebody driving a truck gave my address to enter and collect some stuff. He says no, but they could have come when the guard was on break.

There are three reasons not to call law enforcement. It was possible Austin took the stuff, the value of the stolen goods wouldn't meet our insurance deductible, and the robbers didn't come into the house. *Weird.*

CHAPTER NINETEEN

Online, I begin filling in the necessary paperwork to file for divorce. Austin's signature will be needed, so I must find him. He should have contacted me by now to get his few remaining things, although maybe he only wanted his guns and whatever was in the garage, and he doesn't care about whatever he left behind. My phone calls go straight to his voicemail, which is now full, and Marcy hasn't heard from him. On Facebook, Salem has postings, but none of them tag Austin.

Something is wrong. Near noon I call Trix and fill her in on the empty garage and greenhouse. She says, "I've read how construction contractors' tools get ripped-off all the time, so they've started installing cameras and security systems on their jobs. It sounds similar."

"Yep, tools. Austin's absence is weird. He took his gun safe and his car, but his laptop is here. I'm hacking his email now."

Trix asks, "Anything of interest?"

"Loads of emails from Salem. She demands to know why he isn't emailing or calling her. Something's not right. Being unemployed, they should be all over each other."

"Maybe it's not fun because they're not sneaking around anymore."

"Maybe, but his last email was to Salem the night he vanished, telling her I was kicking him out. He blames her Facebook posts."

Trix says, "Even though there's truth in that—that's our Austin—nothing's ever his fault."

"In her next email, Salem begs him not to dump her. And she says he can discipline her when they get together."

"Ugh," Trix grunts. "They've got some dominant-submissive stuff going on, which is in keeping with how he pushed you around."

"I should have left long ago, but…well, I can't justify hanging in so long."

"Maybe Salem's right for him. Maybe he needs a punching bag, and she's some kind of masochist."

I snort. "A match made in hell. Anyway, his last email was when Clayton left the house after trading guns. Since then, nothing. It's suspicious."

"Especially considering he was messing with a big bad biker."

"I guess I better report him missing. I need him to sign divorce paperwork."

"Yep. People do weird shit when they're in a tight spot. Maybe he's lying low someplace in Houston."

"I'm going to put in a missing person report."

"Good luck. And hey, send me some photos of your paintings. You've told me a lot about them, but I need the visual." A buzzer sounds in the background. "Some friends just arrived. We're going for lunch. Gotta go. Call me later, or tomorrow?"

"Okay." We hang up.

Why didn't he take his laptop? I scroll back through his email, but nothing catches my eye. What else did he leave? I dial his phone, and there's a faint vibration. The middle desk drawer is locked. I search the side drawers and find a key on a hook. In the middle drawer is his cellphone with the ringer turned off, his wallet, passport, and a flash drive. Jesus.

The battery is in the red zone, and I plug it in to charge. The factory code for phones is often 9999. I log in. Ha! Austin is a creature of habit regarding passwords. I touch *Recent Calls*. He has plenty of incoming calls, mainly from Salem and work. There are a few that are unrecognizable, and one to the Westin Hotel a week ago, but no outgoing activity since Clayton's visit. His texts have been deleted. Leaving his phone behind is very fishy.

The twins are in Bryan's room, reclining, angled across his bed, concentrating on their phones. "Do you know where your dad is staying?" Both shrug. Without Austin around preventing a discussion with them, I'll address their unemployment and drug use soon. "Please tell me when you hear from him. In the meantime, I'm going to declare him missing." They both shrug again.

Gathering his phone, laptop, and wallet, I drive to the nearest police station. A female officer types information into her computer and asks the expected questions of when he was last seen and the circumstances surrounding his leaving. She downloads a photo of him from Salem's Facebook timeline, and checks his cell phone, but gives it back to me. Good. I want to monitor his calls. She says she'll put out a BOLO, which she explains is *Be on the lookout*.

"Are you worried something's happened to him?" she asks, her fingers hovering over her keyboard.

"No. Austin is a guy who's been to a hundred survivalist camps; however, he is involved in a love triangle, so..." The officer nods knowingly.

In the car, Austin's phone rings with Salem's ID and her ringtone, which is the tune *Do Ya Think I'm Sexy?* Oh, brother. Judging from her correspondence, she hasn't heard from him, but I want to listen to what she has to say. I accept the call, and before I can speak, she launches a tirade, mistaking me for Austin.

She half shouts and half whines in her baby doll voice, "Finally! Why haven't you been answering my calls?"

"Salem—"

"We were supposed to stay at the Westin for the last three days, in case you forgot, asshole. I drove there, but there was construction on the parking lot's ramp, and I couldn't go in. I had to park at the mall, and I was late. When I got to the hotel, the bitch on the desk said you never checked in.

"Salem—"

"Was the bitch lying? Why would she say that? Man, I never expected you'd just fuckin' leave 'cause I'm late. I tried to call you like about a hundred fucking times, and you wouldn't pick up, damn you."

"Salem—"

"I'm still pissed! I should dump your sorry ass!"

"Salem—"

"Wait! What? Who is this?"

"Salem, this is Julia, y'know, Austin's *wife*. Austin is missing. I haven't seen him in four days, and I just—"

She cuts me off. "This is bullshit. You're trying to keep us apart—"

I shout, "Shut the fuck up." She inhales sharply, and I add, "I'd love to torture you longer, let you think he's ignoring you, but he's not. I filed a missing person report with the police."

"But—"

"No. Shut up. I'm not discussing anything with you. If you want information, check with the cops, but I doubt they'll share info with you. And don't call this number again."

I hang up, and Salem calls back. I let it ring. The ringtone strikes me as funny, and I start laughing. In Salem's phone call, she seemed genuinely distressed. That he was supposed to meet her at the Westin but didn't show up is significant. I phone the cop who made the missing person report. The call goes to voicemail, and I leave a message suggesting they check the hotel's garage.

I spend the evening painting, quitting near midnight, but I'm sleepless and watch a TV show which profiles honeymoon murders. One man collected two big insurance payouts a few years apart by pushing his new brides off cliffs. There's a woman who hired a hitman, and a groom whose new wife died while diving off the coast of Australia. The last one is inconclusive. As a non-swimmer, I fear water. If I were an animal, I'd probably be a cat, so the underwater reenactment of her struggle for air kindles anxiety, and the small, anxious wavering memory I've had about water lately, nudges me again.

After the TV show, in bed, as I slip into sleep, the memory playing at the edge of my consciousness barrels in, full force as a dream.

Waves are cresting over my face. I'm swallowing water, and I'm tired. Austin is making headway, and he's coming closer. I continue trying to swim, but my arms ache, my legs are like lead. I stop a moment to tread water, and I lose any progress I've made. Still, there is no one on the beach to rescue me, and now I'm scared of drowning, of jellyfish, stingrays, and sharks. I try to calm myself by remembering the rhythm my dad taught me for treading water. When I straighten up to begin, to my surprise, my toe touches bottom. A sandbar—and the water is chest-deep. As afraid as I was before, the relief is fantastic, and I can't stop laughing.

Suddenly, I'm awake and sitting upright. When we were on vacation I got caught in a riptide. The memory had been anxiously teasing me, but the TV show brought the full experience back. I relive the memory until I fall asleep.

In the morning, I'm making thumbnail sketches of ideas for more paintings when Trix calls, "I opened the email with the images of your paintings. I like the mix. You've got dreamscapes and statement pieces, like the one of Lucy, that are narratives about the suburbs."

"I have to admit, the process is satisfying, although I'm afraid of being derivative. Everything has been done."

"No derivation that I can see. You've captured eerie and nightmarish dreams, as well as loneliness and middle-class angst, in a wonderfully unique style."

"I've got more subject matter. I just had a memory from our trip to Nassau."

"I remember your trip. You and Austin went a few years ago, but you never talked about it when you got back. I figured you must have been at odds with Austin during the vacation."

"Right. I had a problem on that trip I was trying to ignore. Anyway, a piece of memory kept poking at me, and I've started remembering things. We were hanging out on a beach crowded with tourists. There was an obnoxious group of drunk, very tanned, older Germans. The women had tree-trunk bodies, and the fat men were wearing Speedos; you know the type."

"Ugh, sausage slings," she laughs.

"Banana hammocks."

Trix chuckles, "Ever notice how swimwear has the pretense of modesty but actually draws attention to the naughty bits it covers up?"

"I never thought of that, but it's true."

"Sorry, didn't mean to interrupt. Go on."

"So, we watched the Germans until a local guy selling drugs arrived—and I don't care if you're in a back alley in Houston or on a gorgeous Nassau beach—those handshakes are obvious dope deals. I noticed the police were coming, patrolling the beach, and Austin said there was going to be trouble, and we should go."

"Good idea."

"Indeed. We strolled to a deserted inlet with a beach shaded by sea-grape trees. In the cove, the water was smooth while farther out there were whitecaps. Austin waded in and threw himself on the water and started swimming. He always does that. I was shell picking and wading."

"Sounds glorious."

"Totally. Austin was swimming straight out to sea. I was bobbing. The water was nice and warm, and the saltwater was, of course, buoyant. Austin was quite far out."

"Were you worried about him?"

"No. He's a strong swimmer, but I laughed and called to him. *Are you swimming to Belize?* He turned around and started back. The distant waves had gotten bigger, and they were rolling like they were chasing each other, crashing, and the inlet had become choppy."

She inhales audibly. "Oh, crap. This doesn't sound good."

"Yes. I was alarmed because I'd drifted out into water, twenty, maybe a hundred feet deep. And however hard I swam; I was losing ground. I flipped over because I'm a somewhat stronger swimmer on my back, but I still made no headway.

Then my toes touched something. A sandbar. A stroke of luck."

"Where was Austin?"

"He swam to me, and I told him we should stay, but he didn't want to because we were so far from the hotel, he thought no one would show up. I told him we were caught in a rip current, but he didn't believe me."

"Did he agree to stay put?"

"Yes. We waited a while, but no one came, and again Austin said we should swim for shore. I was frightened and told him to go if he wanted, but I wouldn't make it. He started pulling my wrist. I tried to pry his fingers loose, but he held tight and kicked away, pulling me off the sandbar, and I was in trouble again."

"That fucker," she says quietly.

"I was afloat, but inevitably, I was going to drown." I pause.

"Then what happened?"

"Two men came along the shore, and I screamed for help. They stripped off their shirts and were instantly in the water. After what seemed like an eternity, they reached me, and not a moment too soon because I was sinking; the water was over my lips, right at my nose. They got to me and managed to shove me along into the cove, then they moved sideways, and the current died in the shallows."

"That was a close call."

"I've never given the incident a second thought. To me, it was purely an accident, but now that I believe Austin would have killed me the other night, I don't know. In the first place, there was absolutely no reason for Austin to pull me from the safety of the sandbar into the riptide."

Trix says, "No kidding. Plus, if you had died, no one would have realized what he'd done, or suspected foul play."

"Exactly. Austin could have said he fell asleep on the beach, and when he woke, I was gone. Anyone would assume I went for a dip and got pulled out to sea. Just another casualty."

Trix says, "Okay, not to defend Austin, but can everything in the past be reevaluated and given evil intent? Did he know there was a riptide?"

"The next morning, a woman told me she had warned him when we checked in. I didn't hear her because I was getting info from the concierge. So yeah, he knew. Anyway, I've got a drowning-woman painting to work on."

"Love your attitude. At least he's not there to scare the living hell out of you. You should change the locks."

"I will, but I sense Austin's gone, that he took off for someplace tropical and remote. If he's still in Houston, now that he is officially missing, the cops will probably find him." We make small talk and sign off.

CHAPTER TWENTY

The flash drive from Austin's desk might shed some light on where he went. Maybe there's info about a little casita he bought in a tropical locale with the cash he stole. I plug in the flash drive, and a video appears. The camera pans a tastefully decorated hotel room with textured wall coverings, a king bed, pure white linens, and a view of downtown Houston through enormous, seamless windows. Apparently, not a casita in the BVIs.

Salem's chipmunk-y voice asks, "Are you taping?"

"Yes. Something to turn my crank whenever we're apart."

"No one can keep us apart, not even your bitch wife. Now come over here and fuck me."

Oh crap. Every five minutes, there's some issue with Austin and Salem's sex life. This is probably the tape that circulated in the office and got Austin fired. I consider hitting stop but decide to watch. The camera focuses on Salem wearing expensive business attire: black skirt, pink blouse, red-soled high-heels, and gold jewelry, no doubt purchased with my money.

Austin approaches the camera to check the picture. Close-up, his face is disturbingly three dimensional and life-sized, and I cringe. Salem begins undressing. He sidles away from the camera, and they kiss as he unbuttons her blouse.

"You shouldn't have our video on your laptop in case Bitchy finds it and emails it to Clayton. He'll kill me."

"If only," I say aloud.

"Don't worry. Bitchy and Goofy won't see it." Austin says. "I'll download it to a flash drive and hide it."

Austin unzips her skirt, letting it fall onto Salem's shoes. She sits on the bed and kicks the skirt away as she removes bra and thong. Down to lace-topped stockings and shoes, she stands and unbuttons Austin's shirt, then unbuckles his belt. "Where will you hide the video?"

He laughs. "In my desk, a drawer that locks."

They start necking in earnest, tugging his clothes off until he is naked except for his socks. I'm about to hit stop when mercifully, he shoves Salem onto the bed, which flips a pillow over, blocking the camera. Phew, no visual, only sound.

There's a loud slap. "Ooow, that stung," Salem whines. There's girlish laughter, more scuffling, and another slap. She gasps and giggles.

There are grunts and oohs and heavy breathing. Austin's sex noises make me nauseous. I remove the flash drive and toss it into the box of odds and ends on my desk. Not sure why he kept this tape locked up, considering there are merely noises, and I doubt this is the video that got them fired because, according to Marcy, that clip contained graphic pornographic visuals.

Deadlines are looming, and I force myself to work. Another illustration of a chest of drawers for the furniture store entitled *Hold Everything!* is in my email and labeled a rush job. I quickly sketch the piece and send the drawing by courier to the client. Strangely, I'm not lonely, or perhaps with Austin's absences, I became used to being alone. Small godsends.

Dinner time, I heat soup and take it to my studio. Then with my iPod tuned to blues, I start working on full-sized rough sketches for the kids' book, quitting at ten, as the twins leave the house. I watch a late-night talk show and go to bed.

For the better part of a week, my current heavy workload means no distractions allowed, which I don't mind as it helps keep my mind off divorce and Austin. Household chores, gardening, and painting at my easel have fallen by the wayside, but I'm not sad because the thought of revisiting the dreams—deciphering their meanings and pain—brings queasiness.

I deliver a job in Houston and meet Trix outdoors at La Guadalupana, an authentic Mexican bakery-café for cinnamon-infused coffee. Trix says, "I've been thinking about the drowning incident. Do you still think it was deliberate?"

"No, and yes. Maybe a crime of opportunity, but possibly, when he was warned about the riptide, he started fantasizing about his payout and his freedom if I died." I sip my coffee. "Austin would have gotten our savings and the insurance, plus the house. Plenty of husbands have killed their wives for less."

"He'd also get his freedom."

"Austin could have drowned too. What a meathead."

"But he knew I wouldn't go into the ocean if he didn't, so he had to go swimming."

"He swam quite far. He would have been smarter to wade in the shallows."

"I doubt he thought the scenario through. He saw himself as a super-strong swimmer—invincible."

"Yep, sounds like the arrogant Austin we know. And with the riptide, he didn't need to lay a finger on you."

"Everyone knows I can't swim worth a shit. But finding

the sandbar—"

"Not a good turn of events for him." She sips coffee.

"Exactly. But we weren't the only ones in danger. The guys who rescued me could have drowned too."

"Fucking selfish of him. What was he like after?"

"He got drunk. I thought out of guilt and regret, but maybe it was frustration over his plan being ruined by the pure chance of those men saving me." I pause a moment. "The real question is why didn't he try again? We have a pool right in our backyard."

Trix inhales and blows a plume of smoke into the parking lot next to our table. "Maybe he didn't need to. You were his live-in gardener, maid, pool-girl, nanny, cook, and shopper, who also funded his lifestyle." We both nod our heads. Trix sighs. "You buried the near-drowning incident. Why? Or maybe the question is, *how?* How do you wipe that memory from your mind? Obliterating a traumatic event is way beyond simple denial. I wonder what else you've got buried."

Tears sting. "You're right. I've been thinking that lately, my subconscious isn't allowing me to turn a blind eye anymore. It's trying to wake me up, with nightmares, if that makes sense."

"There was nothing wrong with hiding things from yourself in the past. Just don't do it anymore."

I say brightly, "Working on it," and we laugh.

We exchange hugs. Trix says, "I sent my gallery owner your paintings. Expect a call."

I chuckle and shake my head. As I drive out of Houston, I contemplate my previously lovely tidy life, now demolished and raggedy. Sick of analyzing, I turn on the radio and sing along to 90s hits.

At home, I try to concentrate on drawing flowers for a tissue box design, but after a few hours, exhaustion drives me to a chaise in the lanai for a quick nap, and I run headlong into a dream.

The dreamscape is shaded flower beds, and I'm weeding with a hoe. Our yard has been transformed into the London Botanic Gardens we visited nearly ten years ago. There are formal plantings, mazes, terraces, and sweeping lawns. Pulling weeds is futile as more sprout and mature instantly in their place. I say, "Why are they growing so fast? This place is huge. I'll never get finished at this rate."

Austin appears from behind a statue and says, "I'll help." He pulls one dandelion and holds the weed aloft. Lucy calls out in fake encouragement as she would to a child, "Good job, Austin! Look what a wonderful, handsome husband and gardener you are." She dances into his arms, and he waltzes her along the walkways, her beautiful hair rippling in the breeze and her gauzy dress billowing.

Exasperated, I say, "Hey, can you get busy? There are a lot more where that one came from, and they aren't going to pull themselves." I point to a bushel basket I have nearly filled while he's been dancing.

He comes close. "I can't do any more weeding because I'm in my custom-tailored suit, but you're wearing your usual work crap, and it's your fault there are weeds, so get crack-a-lackin', bitch."

As he turns to leave, movement catches my eye. A cottonmouth is coiled on the mulch less than a yard from my feet, brown on brown, perfectly camouflaged. The reptile hisses. I whisper fearfully, "There's a huge snake!"

From under his jacket, Austin pulls an enormous firearm, a cross between a bazooka and an AK-47, and says, "I'll save you. Look out!" He pulls the trigger, and a flag printed with BANG! pops out. "Oops," he says, "I guess you're gonna die."

Shaking my head. "Shit. You are useless." The snake begins to uncoil, head pulling back, getting into striking position. An adrenaline high kicks in, and gooseflesh lifts my hair on end. I swing the hoe, and the sharp edge slices cleanly through the snake, behind its head.

Everything goes soft and quiet, then rushes back louder, my heart rattling in my chest, and my breathing ragged. Austin begins to cry, and I want to comfort him, but I can't, because doing so would bring attention to his failure to dispatch the snake, and to him as a big crybaby.

I wake up standing in the garden with the hoe in my hands, but it's not Austin crying, it's Sarah. I take her hand and ask, "What's the matter? Why are you upset?"

She tries to talk, but she's choked up. After a moment, she says in a faint voice, "You chopped the head off that monster snake." With the back of her hand, she swipes at tears coursing down her cheeks in rivulets of black eye makeup.

I follow her gaze to the snake, which is as I'd dreamed, it's head severed from the writhing body. I turn my attention back to Sarah. I can't remember the last time I saw her cry. "Why are you upset? What happened?"

"You killed the snake."

"Sarah, did killing the snake upset you? Tell me what's wrong. Your dad was here. He tried to help."

Bryan is on the deck, eating yogurt from a plastic tub. He says, "Sarah—"

She interrupts him. "No, Mom. Remember? Dad's gone, he—"

Cutting her off, Bryan says quickly, "Sarah. Come here. I want to talk to you about the thing in Fort Worth."

Sarah obeys, trotting into the house, wiping her tears. He says to her back, "I'll be there in a minute. Chill, okay?" Focused on his yogurt, Bryan saunters to me and says, "Hey, Mom, can we have gas and hotel money to go to a tech convention in Fort Worth this weekend?" He stops and stares at the snake, then tiptoes closer, going pale in fascination and revulsion. "So, Mom, you were sleepwalking. You were pretty funny until you found the snake."

He takes out his phone and shows me a video. On the little screen, I march into the backyard from the lanai and to the pool deck, babbling as if conversing with someone, then I back away from the pool and point at various plants as if conducting a tour. I lead invisible people along the paths in the garden. I excuse myself, retrieve the hoe and weed in earnest. The foolishness of my actions makes me giggle. In the video, I suddenly freeze, point, and wait. Finally, I act, the hoe whipping through the air, decapitating the serpent.

Between the fire dream, the murder nightmare, and this one, the power has been passed to me. This time I have a sharp weapon, and Austin was inept, but the dreams are becoming invasive, merging with my waking life. The snake, long and thick, still twists in violent death throes, and even though it's as good as dead, I recoil.

Bryan says, "Yo, dude… I hope that's not a kingsnake."

Shaking my head, "No. They look a lot alike, but that's a cottonmouth. I wouldn't kill a kingsnake. They're beneficial."

"Yeah," he says. "Kingsnakes kill rodents."

"I also sprayed a wasps' nest under the eaves yesterday, and there may still be some around, so watch out." I turn to him. "Is Sarah okay? Why is she crying? Is she upset I killed the snake?"

He laughs dismissively, "Naw. She got a break-up text from this guy she was seeing."

"Who?"

He shakes his head in disgust. "A real douchebag. Runs a titty bar on the highway. He's totally gross. Good riddance."

Worried, I implore him, "Please tell me Sarah wasn't dancing there."

"The dude wanted her to, but I put a stop to it."

"Thanks, Bryan."

Bryan slides the flat metal of the hoe under the snake's head and carries it to the compost pile, then makes a second trip for the body. When he's back, he asks with an obviously fake grin, "Now, can we have some money to go to Fort Worth?"

"Smooth, Bryan… I'll think about it." Indoors I splash cold water on my face. I pour a glass of iced tea and head to my studio. My drafting table is clear, and when I check email, there is spam, but no jobs. Not having a pressing deadline feels odd.

CHAPTER TWENTY-ONE

My cell rings. A husky female voice with a Brooklyn accent says, "Hi Julia. Trix's gallery owner here. They call me Gallerina. Trix sent me some of your snapshots. Where do you currently show your work?"

"Um…hi, Gallerina. I don't have gallery representation. I'm a commercial illustrator, and the paintings are something recent, aside from my usual work. I'm not sure anyone will ever see them outside of my friends."

"That's the best kind of art. What's the subject matter?"

"They're scenes from some odd dreams I've been having."

"Dreams? Really? Well, I like them."

"Thank you." Although I had already resigned myself to never showing my paintings, I'm relieved. At that moment, I welcomed the flattery, particularly from an art broker with Gallerina's reputation.

She snorts, "Email me some good quality images, and

let's see about getting together." She hangs up before I can explain that the paintings are not finished enough to show.

In the kitchen, the twins are rummaging for more snacks. I assume Bryan gave Sarah a pep talk because she's no longer teary-eyed. She's cut her bangs very short, and she's wearing a rockabilly 50s-style dress and high-heeled Mary Janes with shorty socks. Bryan is in his standard jeans and a rock-concert T-shirt. He says, "We're going out in a minute. First, we're going to a comic-con thing, and then tonight the Freaky Lizards are playing at the Mucky Duck." They take bags of potato chips from the pantry and head out the door.

Using my Nikon, I shoot high-resolution photos of the paintings, crop, color-correct them, and email them to Gallerina. The sketchpad and Conté are on the coffee table in the living room, and a quick critique convinces me my last drawing of murdering Austin is missing some necessary tension. I start again; this time, he is on the floor as I straddle him.

When the doorbell rings, the drawing is finally taking form, and I'm irritated by the interruption. Canvassers don't usually get past the gatekeeper, especially during the dinner hour, and I'm not expecting anyone. I prop the sketchpad against the side of the chair and go to investigate. The door's window reveals two men on the porch, but these guys don't look like planet-saving do-gooders or shameless proselytizers. Both wear brown, dated, off-the-rack suits, one standard-issue with a cream shirt and knit necktie, the other with Western accessories: boots, bolo tie, and cowboy hat. They notice my approach and hold up badges. Behind them are two of our burb's finest, in uniform, looking much too young to be cops and already going soft. Tension creeps over me. Either the twins got busted, or Austin has had a wreck. I open the door.

The tall and rangy older cop removes his hat. "Ma'am," he clears his throat. "Are you Julia Green?"

"Yes."

"I'm Detective Wilson, and this is Detective Reeves. May we come in?" His voice is baritone, and his drawl is straight out of Central Casting for the Old West.

I gesture them into the foyer, leaving the beat cops to loiter outside, sweating in the early evening heat. "Please tell me my kids are okay. Nothing's happened to my kids."

"No, it's not about your children."

"Did something happen to Austin?" I demand more impatiently than intended.

He clears his throat again. "I'm sorry to tell y'all this, but your husband…he's deceased, ma'am. His body was found."

A hundred questions crash in, and the magnitude, the weight of them, collapses my knees folding me up, and the younger detective catches me. They lead me to the living room and place me, weak, deaf, and mute, in a chair. They are talking, their faces mouthing silent words, their blurry figures swimming in and out of my vision. Then the cops aren't where they were standing. I've lost some time. Things are out of focus, out of sync and silent, until the drone of the air conditioner and refrigerator rise again, but too loud, as if someone turned up the volume, then the hum settles to normal.

Austin is *dead*. Unexpectedly, I'm crying. A deluge of tears that drip off my chin, but I make no sound.

The older cop, Wilson, asks, "Ma'am, can I call someone, a neighbor, a relative, to come be with you?" And I nod consent, still silently weeping. I hit Lucy's number on speed dial and hand my phone to Reeves. My tears continue, and I watch the drops make dark dots on my jeans and T-shirt. Reeves murmurs into the phone. I catch a few words: death, Austin, his car, Westin, as Wilson wanders to the window and gazes out over the yard. "Real nice spot you've got here," he says.

The detectives can't hide their investigative curiosity, their suspicion, scanning the room and sweeping over me, perhaps searching for CSI goodies: wounds or scratches, blood, gunshot residue. The young one, Reeves, hands me a tissue from the box on the coffee table, and I dab. He leaves the room, the fridge door clunks, and he returns and hands me a bottle of water. His hair is thick and black, his eyes alert. He is attractive but unsophisticated, with his cheap suit and chunky knit tie, polyester shirt, and the crisp part in his hair. He scrutinizes me, and despite my innocence relating to Austin's death, the demeanor of the detectives with their quietly jaded and businesslike distrust provokes guilt about my dream. Reeves sits in a chair facing me and takes out his notepad while Wilson stands, examining the bookshelf.

My voice returns. "What happened? How did Austin die?"

Wilson says, "Our preliminary examination indicates he was stabbed, ma'am. He was found in his car at the Westin hotel."

He watches me closely, and after my shock passes, I console myself that shock is the proper, normal reaction of a grieving wife to the brutal murder of her husband.

Lucy arrives and rushes to hug me, squishing the side of my face into her bosom, then she sits protectively on the arm of my chair. I pat her hand.

I take a deep breath. "Who found Austin?"

He says, "A coworker."

"Who?"

"Salem Kingston."

"Coworker…that's a stretch. Did Salem explain why they were meeting at the Westin? They were having an affair, and he hired her to work at his firm so they could see each other?"

"Yes, she did," Reeves says.

"And they were both fired from their jobs? You should talk to Marcy at Austin's office."

Reeves murmurs, "I'm sorry," and makes a note.

"How did Salem find him?"

He reads from his notes. "Salem claims they were supposed to meet a week ago at the Westin. They usually met on the fourth level in the parking garage, but there was a problem, and they didn't connect. Today, she walked the parking garage and found his body in his car."

"What?" My anger is noticeable, but I don't care about niceties. "I called the officer who filled out the missing-person report and reported Salem was supposed to meet him there. Are you telling me no one called the hotel or searched the hotel's garage? And that bitch, Salem, had to find him? This is unbelievable."

Reeves flips through his paperwork, and says, "There's nothing here says you mentioned that."

"I left a voicemail."

"Sorry, ma'am." Reeves shakes his head. "Looks like your call fell through the cracks."

Wilson shapes his cowboy hat as he asks, "Miss Julia, where were you last Sunday night?"

"I was here working in my studio. Then I went to bed." I'm aware don't have an alibi.

"When did you last see your husband?"

"It's in the missing person report I filed. The last time I saw him was the night that, Clayton, Salem's husband, came here to trade guns with Austin." The detectives glance at each other. "That's right, Austin was immensely proud of duping Clayton, pretending they were friends. Then, after Clayton left and I went to bed, Austin woke me. He was at my bedroom door, saying he was packing his stuff and wanted to get things, but I was afraid of him, and I didn't let him in. In the morning, he was gone."

"Did you wonder where Austin was?"

"Not at first. I'd told him to leave. He said he would, so I assumed he'd simply left. I'd already hired a lawyer to divorce him."

Lucy is openly staring at me. I glance at her, and her expression is concerned, most of this being news to her.

Reeves jots a note, and Wilson asks, "When did you last see Clayton, Salem's husband?"

"The night Clayton came here. He left around eleven, I

think, but when I went to bed, he was in his van, parked down the street. The next morning Austin, his gun safe presumably full of weapons, and his car were gone."

Wilson is studying my paintings, seemingly captivated, and I'm as uneasy and self-conscious, as if he's a voyeur, and I'm exposed in a private moment. What does he make of my depictions of women who can torch a house, bake cookies, and be lacerated by a knife thrower? Hopefully, nothing, since artists are expected to be wacky. Wilson turns from the artwork and says to Lucy, "A very curious portrait of you, ma'am."

Lucy hops up and studies her image, which she hasn't seen before. "Wow! I love it!" she says, then returns, a little flushed.

Wilson sits opposite Lucy and me, and says, "Can you think of anyone who might have wanted to harm your husband?"

I nod as I wipe my eyes. "You're talking about a guy who pretended to be a biker's friend while he was screwing the guy's wife. Businesswise, I can't even guess at who might have had a grudge against him."

Wilson says, "If either of you happens to think of anything, please call us." He places two business cards on the coffee table.

I ask, "Do I have to do anything, um, official, like identify his body?" Lucy places a hand on my arm.

"He was identified at the scene. The woman who found him identified him."

"Well, that figures." I bark mirthless laughter. "She interfered in our lives, and she's all wrapped up in his death, too."

Wilson says, "Sorry, Miss Julia, but I have to ask you this question. Did you kill Austin?"

I regard him sharply. "I was upset, but the plan was divorce. As I said, I'd already hired a divorce lawyer."

"Okay," Wilson says, "But we need to look around." He takes folded paper from his jacket pocket. "Ma'am, this is a search-and-seizure warrant for this property. Our techs will execute."

"If you tell me what you're searching for, I could probably help."

"No need. We want Austin's computer and possibly some paperwork, copies of checks, things like that."

I scan the warrant, but the words blur together and make no sense. I nod. Two techs wearing latex gloves enter and head to Austin's office. Wilson and Reeves start inspecting each room for clues and evidence. Wilson points to a faint stain on the carpet near the living room's French doors, and Reeves goes to find a tech. The tech and Reeves return with a spray bottle and a portable black light. They close the drapes and spray the stain. I've watched enough CSI shows to deduce the chemical is Luminol, used to detect human fluids, including blood.

I announce, "That's red wine. And the one near the door in Austin's office is cat barf. Beav has a sensitive stomach."

They all turn toward me, and when the spray doesn't illuminate, the tech goes back to Austin's office. Wilson and Reeves leave the room, and Lucy and I sit quietly, listening. Closet doors open and close in the master bedroom. I tap Lucy's hand and put a finger to my lips. She nods, and I go silently upstairs and find Sarah's, then Bryan's stash of weed in small baggies, and their paraphernalia of two pipes and a bong.

Marijuana is illegal in Texas. I flush the weed down the toilet and shove the pipes into the toes of a pair of over-the-knee boots in Sarah's closet, and fold them over. Hopefully, the pungent smell will be disguised or at least trapped. I put the bong and some items I can't identify, on the fitted sheet of Sarah's bed and cover the paraphernalia with her comforter, and a heap of plush toys and throw pillows.

There are footsteps on the stairs, and the cops arrive at Sarah's bedroom, where I'm now sitting on the bed, gazing at a large framed photo of Austin with Sarah and Bryan. Wilson is wearing his hat again. He observes me suspiciously, then with disgust, he uses a ballpoint pen to lift and move articles and sniffs audibly at the sight of a fast-food box.

Still staring at the photo, I say to his back, "There were plenty of good times. I want to remember him like this photo with the kids. And now I'm glad Salem found his body, not me."

"My eighteen-year-old daughter was fixin' t'paint her room dark purple like this, but the color got nixed, along with drinking, partying, and so forth."

"Let me guess. Your daughter's room got painted pink." He swings his gaze on me, giving me the stink-eye. I say pointedly, "Well, being a cop, I'm sure you have very rigid rules and boundaries."

"In my job, I've seen enough acting out by teens to last five lifetimes. Kids need rules. After all, once you're grown, it's hard to *rise above yer raisin'*." Oh brother. He frowns and digs into dresser drawers and Sarah's closet, where he shifts her shoes around. He jostles her boots, and my hands become damp.

He examines some piles of junk on the floor and asks, "Two kids?"

"Yes, twins."

"How old?"

"Twenty-five."

"Still living at home, are they?" accompanied by a smirk.

What an asshole. I spout the party line, "Yes. They're inventing software. The process is expensive, so we're helping out," and I embellish, "but their app is about to be submitted for a patent." I just lied to a cop. Shit.

He turns away, maybe to hide his astonishment that such overindulged brats could be industrious geniuses. "Where are your kids?"

"They're at a friend's place. I'll phone them in a minute." The thought of telling the kids their father is dead brings more tears but has the benefit of driving Wilson from the room. After a while, I head back to the big chair in the living room. Sounds indicate the techs are examining my studio.

Lucy approaches, and I tell her in a whisper what I did with the twins' drug paraphernalia. There are sounds of her rooting in the kitchen, then after a while, the oven pings, and she heads upstairs. Presently she reappears wearing oven mitts and carrying my white porcelain lasagna pan covered in foil, grins at me briefly and leaves. I hear one of the technicians open the back door for her. "Careful," she says. "It's hot."

The techs carry objects in paper bags to their van, and after nearly three hours, they drive away into the night. The detectives continue scrutinizing until they finally come to the living room. Wilson fingers the brim of his hat as he says, "Just a couple more questions—"

I cut him off. "No, sir. I'm exhausted and done answering questions. I'm hiring an attorney."

"Ma'am, we'll probably want to question you further."

Lucy says, "Gentlemen?" She stands, knocking my sketchpad over. Reeves and Wilson glance toward the sketch of Austin lying on the floor with me straddling him, knives in my hands. Lucy swiftly picks up the pad and places the drawing facedown on the coffee table. I can't tell if they registered the subject matter or not, but they appear oblivious as Lucy again says, "Gentlemen?" and drags them in her wake, to the door.

Wilson says to Lucy, "Ma'am, we'd like to talk to you a moment."

When I phone Bryan and Sarah, both calls go to voicemail. I text, *Family emergency. Call me!!!!!* and picture the twins' dismissive chortles as they ignore my texts. I don't want them to hear of their father's murder through strangers or the news media. Lucy is back from seeing the detectives out, and I put my finger to my lips and lead her on tiptoe through the studio into the lanai, near where Wilson and Reeves have stopped on the driveway, in the dark, lighting cigarettes.

Reeves says, “Man, it’s so frickin’ hot, even after sundown.” He pauses a moment. “What do you think about her lawyering up?”

Wilson dons his hat and tugs the brim. “You ’spectin’ her to be yer new best friend, boy?” He chuckles. “She ain’t gonna drop her gun to hug no grizzly.”

Reeves scratches his head, and a cowlick pops up. They saunter down the driveway, throw their cigarette butts onto the lawn, get into their unmarked car, and drive away.

Lucy says, “Come and sit. What can I get you?”

“A stiff drink, please.”

She says, “No problem.” Then after a pause, she says, “Those detectives asked if you have any reason to want Austin dead.”

I lock a goggle-eyed gaze on her, and she says, “I know, I know.” She waves dismissively. “They know it’s one of those questions where yes is a bad answer, and no is a lie. I told them anyone married for more than about five minutes has plenty of reasons to want their spouse dead at one time or another, but you’d never do anything to harm anyone.”

“Thanks, Lucy.”

“It’s the truth.” She smiles sadly. “So… What happened?”

“As I mentioned the other day, Austin was having an affair. The husband of his bimbo came to see him one night, and Austin vanished. They found his body today.”

“My God. This is terrible.” She shakes her head and goes to the kitchen to mix martinis.

Alone for a moment, I sit waiting for this latest bombshell to sink in. I’d wanted Austin gone, couldn’t stand him anymore, felt threatened by him, but dead? Does dreaming him dead mean I want him dead? Only in the same way I might tell him to *drop dead*, but not literally. And the scary part is, I’ve watched enough police-procedural shows to know they always look at the spouse first. I’m a suspect, and maybe I should be if I’ve done more than dream his murder. I call my family lawyer's emergency number, and he promises to have a criminal defense attorney call to advise me.

Throughout the evening, Lucy and I sip martinis, and I call the twins until their mailboxes are full. I consider mentioning my murderous dream to Lucy but decide not to. Trix, who is a more abstract thinker and open-minded, is a better confidant than Lucy-the-literalist for whom my tragedy will be valuable social currency in our burb. I've heard Lucy called *the mouth of the South,* and I'm aware Lucy and Earl will dine out on the heartbreak-next-door for months.

Chapter Twenty-Two

Lucy reluctantly leaves after midnight, assuring me I must call her anytime, day or night if I need anything.

Room by room, gray fingerprint powder coats surfaces, and as expected, Austin's laptop and some files, his wallet, passport, and phone are gone. They took my computer's hard drive, which only makes sense if they suspect me, and for a moment, I'm anxious. What did I search on the internet? Seed catalogs, air conditioning, and pool services, recipes. Not exactly stuff that should lead to my indictment.

Trix's phone goes to voicemail. No doubt, she's out on the town, unaware. I want to be unaware too, to turn the clock back to before Salem, before misery, before divorce and death, or shift into the future, past this crushing, suffocating quicksand of grief and betrayal, to start anew.

In the lanai, I recline on a chaise. The heat and humidity are sauna-like. I could use some cool, dry air, but summer's not a time for newness; that would have been spring, energetic and fresh, a sweet young virgin, not the sweaty and sluggish whore of summer with her stink of rot masked by cloying dime-store magnolia perfume.

Sorting through thoughts, assessing my grief, keeps sleep at bay, with my mind thrashing between long-ago glowing memories of Austin, recent depressing events, and the killing-dream that was so realistic. I spend the dark hours reclining and weeping, my tears, sweat, and my recollections a watershed of melancholy. Cry me a river. No shit.

A smiling crescent moon is cleanly etched against a star-salted sky. The bats swoop, but tonight they're like strange fairytale night birds that will peck the breadcrumb stars out of the firmament, rip apart and devour the buttery croissant moon, consuming the light and rendering the world impenetrably dark forever. And as if my thoughts are commands, opaque clouds congregate, obscuring any glimmer, and the density of the darkness shrouds me in fear: fear of what happened to Austin, of his pain at the end, of murderers on the loose, fear for my future.

My hands grip the armrests of the chaise as if letting go will release me to float away into the endless black sky. I consciously release my grasp, then find I'm holding tight again. There's a murderer at large. I should go inside to safety, latch every window and door. But I don't. If the killer comes for me, I'll be awake and waiting.

Finally, a faint edge of light creeps in, gilding the landscape, withering the night blooms and opening day flowers, hushing nocturnal creatures to bring on the birds and the buzz-saw whine of cicadas. I'm still in the lanai, dripping sweat as the scorching sun breaks the horizon, its white-hot glare burning me through the screen, even at a low angle. I have a crushing headache, maybe a hangover, or dehydration, or shock. Mourning doves coo their dreary four-note call. In the time of Bubonic plague, it was believed the doves were saying *bring out your dead.*

The heat penetrates my bones. I've lived in this seductive and oppressive climate my whole life, and I know it can lure and kill the weak. And weak is what I am now, feeble, frail, puny. I'm inert, paralyzed, and content to stay and become desiccated, shrunken, and sunbaked. My headache pounds to the thump of my heart. The heat is a warning to go indoors, crank the AC. Be smart. Better water everything twice today, including myself, or die.

Finally, dizzy and disoriented, I peel myself off the chaise and go to the kitchen. Two large glasses of water and painkillers should hopefully soon anesthetize my skull. Muted voices draw me to a window. A man carrying a microphone and notepad strolls into the front yard. What the hell? Following him is a stocky man shouldering a boxy camera with a TV station's logo on the side. I back out of their sightline. The reporter paces in front of the garden and says, "Christ, still early, and I'm already sweating."

The cameraman says, "Back up. I want to get some color."

The announcer takes three steps back into the flowerbed, crushing daylilies and petunias. I call out, "Hey, you're trespassing! And you better be careful. There are snakes and fire ants in there."

"Shit!" he splutters, dashing onto the lawn, stamping his feet. I quickly shut and lock the window and close the drapes as the camera swings toward me.

The first phone call is from Trix. She says, "My God, Julia. I'm so, so, so unbelievably sorry. How are you holding up?"

"I can't absorb what's happened. And there are reporters in my yard. Everything is weird."

"I'm coming to you right now, and I'm bringing Frankie."

"Thank God."

As I hang up the phone, the back door opens, and Lucy calls, "Hellooo." Frazzled, she marches straight to me and holds me long and hard. My tears start again, which starts her bawling, and we make our way to the living room. She says, "There are two media trucks outside and two reporters with camera guys. I told them to leave, but they won't."

"One of them walked in my flowerbed."

"They probably can't stay too long. They have generators running AC in their vehicles, and presumably, they'll run out of gas or propane soon." A news chopper arrives, buzzing the treetops, then hovers above the roof. Lucy shouts, "Holy shit, that noise puts the *hell* in helicopter." She takes Detective Wilson's card from the coffee table, pulls out her phone, and leaves the room. Soon after, she's back and says, "Wilson said he has no control over the media, and at some point, more techs will go through the whole house again. Oh, and the autopsy is underway this morning and will be filed today unless there are more tests to do, such as tox-screens."

Austin, on a cold table and cut from neck to groin, comes to mind, and I close my eyes briefly. Lucy pats my arm, then leaves to harass the media. I try reaching my kids again without luck. Trix and Frankie arrive in Trix's Fiat. They dodge the reporters and enter through the back door.

Their presence is so welcome, trustworthy, calming; I shed tears. "Good God, you took that puddle jumper on the highway?"

Frankie bear hugs me and lifts me off the floor, carries me to a chair, plonks me down, and covers me with a throw. "You poor little peanut. I've been freaking out since I saw the news. Don't move. We are at your beck and call. Your wish is our command." He bows theatrically. "First order of the day, booze, the magic coping elixir, and food to keep your strength up. And the Trix pharmacopeia for the relief of pain and insomnia."

In the kitchen, Frankie commences cooking, and Lucy joins him. I sit quietly, and Trix squeezes into the chair with me. "Stupid question… Are you okay?"

"Yes. No. Yes. Sort of. It hasn't quite hit me. I almost need to see Austin dead to accept he's gone, but Salem identified him, and of course, I don't actually want to see him. I couldn't bear to see him. I guess there's a disconnect. I'm numb, in shock. By the way, a bunch of techs are coming to search the house."

Trix stands and surveys the room. "I watch a lot of CSI, so I'm going to take a quick look around," and she leaves the room.

Two technicians arrive, hand me a warrant, and commence spraying, dusting, and photographing throughout every room, inspecting my paintings and artwork, going through drawers and cabinets. Yesterday's efforts seem superficial compared to this thorough search. Hopefully, the twins don't have any other drugs in their rooms.

"I wonder why they're tearing your house apart," Trix says. "Do they think he was killed here?"

"I don't know. The detectives haven't told me anything." I shrug. "He could have been killed anywhere, then driven to the hotel parking lot."

The detectives arrive and loiter in the foyer, then go outside to chat with reporters. During the search of the house, we sit quietly waiting until the techs and the detectives finally leave.

Trix says, "We were at a function last night with phones turned off, which is why we missed your call, and we got in late, then this morning we finally saw the news."

"For the love of God, what else can possibly happen?" I scowl, "On second thought, don't answer that."

Again, I call the twins and get the same recording saying their voicemail is full. I text, and then email them. My phone rings, and I recognize the name of a reporter, so I don't pick up, and it begins ringing again. I turn the ringer off.

I sit in my usual dining chair, then shift to another seat so I won't be facing Austin's place. Trix sits in Austin's spot, and Frankie brings us omelets and Bloody Marys as Lucy heads home.

My cell rings. Call display shows Bryan, and I'm adamant, "Something has happened. You and Sarah need to come home right now."

"We're way up in Magnolia. It'll take more than two

hours to get home. We already know about Dad."

"I'm so sorry. What a terrible thing. Are you okay?"

He says despondently, "It's horrible, but we're all right."

"When did you find out?"

"Just now."

"I want to see you and Sarah in person."

"Yeah. We'll leave soon." He hangs up.

"Damn."

Trix nibbles her omelet, and reaches across and lays her hand over mine. "After Frankie called me, I saw some coverage on this morning's news, but only a brief mention."

Frankie eats with enthusiasm. He pats his lips with his napkin, takes out his phone, and says, "Wow, the attention has expanded, with pictures of Austin, Salem with her husband Clayton, your illustrations, and your headshot from your website. They're getting pretty worked up."

I cover my face with my hands. "I don't get why. You'd think Austin was a celebrity."

"The story's got all the juicy elements: sex, murder, intrigue," Trix says, nodding. "Perfect for TV and internet news."

"Yes. Plus, Austin wasn't some inner-city two-bit gangbanger who got bumped off in a drive-by," Frankie agrees. "Those are a dime a dozen."

"I'm the last person you'd think would be headline news."

"That's why it's news," Frankie asserts. "The media likes to throw a case out to the public to see if it resonates. If it does, they run with it. The people involved in the crime don't have to be royalty, or famous, or even attractive."

"Exactly," Trix adds. "Like that woman, Jodi Arias, who killed her boyfriend. She was very ordinary, in fact, mousey. But the case was riveting."

Frankie nods his head. "Then there was Laci Peterson. According to the media, her husband didn't act the way a bereaved husband should. He wasn't passionate enough or grieving the right way when she vanished. Man, they crucified him. And of course, his wife was pregnant, so she acquired sainthood."

"Yep," Trix says. "Again, just an ordinary middle-class couple, but now they're known around the world."

I sit back in my chair. "An interesting viewpoint—the unexpected, or maybe the story is hitting too close to home."

"It's like a cautionary tale; cliché midlife-crisis-guy, Austin, meets the dark side," Trix says as she sits back in her chair.

"The dark side being Salem, who is tied to biker-guy Clayton." I eat a small forkful of egg.

"Jesus." Trix pretend-shudders. "Messing with a dude like that, Austin was even more arrogant than I thought."

"Deception rears its ugly head, and things get violent," Frankie says.

While I nibble my food, I relate the dream of stabbing Austin. "The dream was so real; I was afraid I'd find his body in the morning."

"Do the detectives know about your dream?" Trix appears concerned.

"No. But they saw my sketch, although they didn't seem too interested." I realize I'm practically whispering.

Frankie inspects my paintings. "They're terrific. Where's the sketch of the stabbing?"

I point, and he retrieves the sketchpad and holds up the drawing. He says, "Maybe you should burn this."

I sigh. "It was only a dream. Besides, there's no way I could have killed him. I couldn't move his body or clean up blood, all while I was sleepwalking. I also couldn't move his gun safe and firearms."

They stare at me quizzically. Trix asks, "His gun safe is missing? With all the guns?"

I nod. "Yes. I thought I told you."

Frankie places the sketch pad on the coffee table. "Wow. All the dots connect to the skankster's husband. He finds out about the affair, kills Austin, and steals the guns.

Then, as her punishment, he sits and waits for Salem to find Austin's body. She has to see Austin's corpse, know she caused his death, and her husband is the killer."

"Salem found the body. Maybe *she* killed him." Trix pauses and sips her mimosa. "I've seen lots of crime shows where the killer acts like a grieving friend, and even helps search for the body."

"But what's her motive?" I put my fork down and ease back in my chair. "Salem is morally bankrupt and capable of murder, but like me, she would have needed help with the logistics of moving his body and so forth."

Frankie says, "I know…they worked together. Clayton found out about the affair and told Salem he'd kill her unless she helped him rip off the guns, then shit went sideways, and one of them killed Austin."

I nod. "Maybe. But why stab Austin if they're stealing a ton of firearms? Why not shoot him?"

"According to every detective documentary, stabbing is a crime of passion, up-close and personal, which fits Salem or Clayton. Besides, guns are noisy and leave gunshot residue, bullet casings, and so forth." Trix says and sips her bloody Mary.

"I agree, but Austin was adamant Clayton knew nothing of the affair," I interject.

"Maybe Austin was wrong. Austin thought he was smarter than everyone, and that's when people screw up." Frankie pauses then says excitedly, "What if Austin had another chick on the side who was jealous of him seeing Salem, and *she* killed him?"

"Crazy. Anything is possible." Trix tops up our water glasses.

I shake my head. "It's hard to believe Salem was involved because she called Austin's phone and genuinely seemed to think she was talking to him and yelled at him for standing her up."

"Maybe someone loyal to you killed him," Trix says. "Someone who knew about the affair and hated him for putting you through the wringer."

Frankie chuckles. "Like us?"

Trix says, "Not us. We're too far away, but Lucy and her husband, how about them?"

"Doubtful." I shake my head. "The cops probably think I'm the guilty party. I'm the cheated-on spouse, and I've got motive and opportunity. But I lacked the means to get rid of the body."

Frankie says solemnly, "You need a lawyer."

I nod and sigh. "I'm going to consult a criminal defense attorney."

"Not the skydiving Otis Boudreaux guy," Trix says, laughing. I grimace and mouth the words, *no way*.

Frankie takes a call and says, "For crap's sake, I have an event to manage tonight, and apparently in all of Houston, only I can find baby zucchini." He calls a ride and promises to return with reinforcements, anytime.

Trix says, "I'll stay a few nights. You'll need someone to get food, maybe deal with your kids and whatever else."

I sigh. "My kids should be here soon. What a nightmare. I'm dazed."

"Try to rest."

"I'm too wound up." We scan the street. "There are more news vans now."

Trix sets up her laptop on the breakfast bar and begins surfing. She says, "They took your computer. Why?"

"Covering all their bases, I guess. Fortunately, I have off-site backup. I'll download whatever I need to my old clunker laptop." I go to my studio, take out my laptop, and boot it up. A job is in email for the furniture store—a drawing of a poufy chair studded with buttons. The tagline is *Tuft Love*. I reluctantly turn the job down, and email apologies to my clients for my impending downtime. I pace the studio, then roam the house in a fog of disbelief and exhaustion.

CHAPTER TWENTY-THREE

My new attorney, Stan Leibovitz, calls. He introduces himself, and I tell him about yesterday's visit by the detectives. Call-waiting beeps, and I flash to Detective Wilson, who says they are on their way over with information I need to see. I object and demand my lawyer be present, and I'm waiting for my kids.

Wilson says, "You can remain silent if you like, but we have info you need to hear."

I go back to Leibovitz's call and explain, and he says, "Who are the detectives?"

"Reeves and Wilson."

Leibovitz says, "I've run into Wilson before. Yee-Haw Wilson is what he's called, but not to his face. Don't let his *howdy-ma'am* act fool you. He's sharp. Reeves must be new."

"Probably. He's young." To my amazement, Leibovitz says he'll be right over. Twenty minutes later, Trix answers the door, introduces herself, greets Wilson and Reeves, and shows them to the living room.

"As soon as my lawyer gets here, we can start," I inform them. Wilson nods, while Reeves appears to wilt. I wait with Trix in the kitchen, and after a few minutes, the doorbell rings again. My attorney is forty-something, attractive, but not intimidating. We enter the living room, the men shake hands, and we take seats on the oversized chairs and sofa. Leibovitz's expensive custom-tailored dark gray suit and professionally-laundered white shirt with French cuffs, contrasts sharply with both detectives' rather appallingly rumpled appearance, wearing what appears to be the same clothes as yesterday.

Wilson says, "Ma'am, we don't have the autopsy results yet, but a preliminary visual check indicates Austin was stabbed multiple times."

Trix asks, "What was he stabbed with?"

Wilson says, "Sorry, we can't disclose that information."

"Why not?" I hear my frustration.

He clears his throat and ignores my question. "Do y'all have life insurance on your husband?"

"I bet you already know the answer to that." I'm aware my insolence is showing, but he better not confuse me with women in his life he condescends to, or intimidates.

Wilson says, "Ma'am? Please answer the question."

I glance at Leibovitz, and he nods. "Yes," I state, "we have a policy for a half-million. Whoever dies first, the other is the beneficiary." Reeves, the note-taker, jots something in his pad. His cowlick springs up, and I notice Trix hold back a smile.

"How about savings—stocks, bonds, things like that? Wilson says, "Y'all got those?"

"Yes. We *had* about five-hundred thousand in retirement savings until my husband cashed out most of it, without my knowledge, to squander on hotels, gifts, and meals with his mistress."

Wilson says, "Y'all are divorcing. What are the

circumstances leadin' up to that particular event?" He pronounces particular, *par-tickler*.

"You already know. I explained the circumstances yesterday, and I'd rather not relive it again."

Reeves peers up from his notes, seemingly bewildered by my irritation. Wilson says with exaggerated patience, "We'd like to hear your recollection again."

I suspect this is a test to see if my story has changed or is word-for-word the same and overly rehearsed. I turn to Leibovitz, and he nods again. "My husband took up with that woman, Salem, at least two, maybe three, years ago, after they met at a motorcycle show. Then he hired her so they could see a lot of each other. Even if he wasn't cheating, our marriage was over. He was absent, both physically and emotionally. Plus, in retrospect, I'd say he was abusive."

Wilson says, "Abusive, how?"

"At the beginning of our marriage, he was physically abusive, but it stopped because I wouldn't take the bait when he was instigating a fight. Lately, his abuse was emotional. He criticized me, lied to me, cheated on me, said I was imagining things when I wasn't...and he withheld affection and sex."

Reeves shifts in his seat, the straight-arrow cop, uncomfortable with the older lady saying I wanted sex, but couldn't get laid. Or maybe his sensibilities are offended by my marriage's immoral mess, or he is uncomfortable with my pain. Trix notices him squirm, and she smiles almost imperceptibly.

Wilson says, "Miss Julia, we contacted your financial planner..."

Reeves flips a page in his notes.

"Michele Andrews," I inform him, ever helpful. The thought of Austin's extravagant spending clenches my gut.

Wilson meets my eyes. "Right. Miss Michele says he withdrew most of your savings. I want to ask you, ma'am, was his taking the retirement money and having an affair enough reason for you to kill him?"

"No!" I declare emphatically. "I was going to divorce him."

"We're done, gentlemen," Leibovitz says curtly.

Wilson says, "That's all we have for the moment, ma'am," and they stand to leave.

"Hold on," I demand. "I have some questions." Wilson and Reeves wait, their impatience showing. "Have you questioned Salem's husband? He was here at our house the night Austin disappeared."

"Yes, we questioned him," Wilson says. "Clayton Kingston admits stealin' the firearms and the gun safe, but he ain't 'fessin' to nothin' in regards to Austin's murder, swears nine ways to Sunday he didn't touch Austin."

I inhale. "Clayton admits stealing the guns?"

Wilson shifts from foot to foot. "Yes ma'am, but so far we have no forensic evidence tying him to Austin's murder."

"You're buying this even with loads of circumstantial evidence? After all, he was here and the last person to see Austin alive. Austin was having an affair with Clayton's wife. He's strong enough to have dumped Austin's body, and he's a biker, so probably no stranger to violence, and he may have friends who would help him."

"Circumstantial evidence ain't enough." Wilson puts his hat on. "We need forensics or a confession. And he ain't confessin'."

I cross my arms. "And by the way, aren't those firearms mine now? Where are they?"

"The guns are safe. They are still possible evidence in a homicide."

Leibovitz says, "Detectives, I'd like an inventory."

Wilson says, "Yessir." Then, indicating the paintings, he asks, "Are you the artist, ma'am?" I nod, and he continues, "What are these paintin's about?"

Leibovitz shakes his head and says, "Detectives, anything else?"

I ask, "Who are your suspects?"

"Ma'am, with all due respect, this ain't our first rodeo."

Reeves says, "We'll catch the guy who did it."

"So, a guy did it?" Trix asks.

Reeves is puzzled. "What?"

"You said you'll *catch the guy who did it*."

Reeves blushes and says, "It's a figure of speech."

"I'm sure Salem's husband, Clayton, killed Austin. Please question him again, do a lie-detector test on him, test DNA, whatever you need to do to prove he's the killer. He's at large, and I'm afraid of him." I can hear pleading in my tone.

"We'll be very thorough," Reeves says. "I promise we'll catch the killer."

Trix sees them out, and I excuse myself to eavesdrop. They pause again in the driveway, lighting their cigarettes. Wilson says, "Promisin' to solve the case is squattin' with yer spurs on, son. Don't go writin' checks with your mouth that your ass can't cash."

Reeves frowns. "Right. Sorry." He stares at the ground, ashamed, and I can see the schoolboy inside the man.

I return to the living room, and Leibovitz says, "I have to run, but I'll need to interview you about the night your husband disappeared."

"Thank you for coming on such short notice."

Leibovitz nods and says, "No problem. I made a call to the coroner this morning. I should have the autopsy results today or tomorrow. I'm sorry. This is tough. The cops are in the investigation stage, and as the spouse, they'll focus on you. You can bet the media coverage is putting a lot of pressure on the police. And while I know it's difficult, you need to follow the news to see which way the media is leaning."

Leibovitz leaves as my reeling thoughts are interrupted by Bryan and Sarah's loud voices outside. Bryan yells, "Get the hell away from my house!"

Not to be outdone, Sarah adds, "Bunch of vultures!"

My eyes are squeezed shut, dreading what the cameras captured. A uniformed cop ushers the kids inside. I stand as they come to me and hold them both tight.

Sarah wails, "Why did he *diiiiieee*? It's not *faaaaiirrr*!"

"C'mon," Bryan says as he pulls her away.

Later, I go upstairs and knock on Bryan's door. The room is in its usual twilight state with blinds closed against both afternoon sun and reporters. Sarah is zoned out on the bed while Bryan is on his back on the floor. In the dim, their faces are fish-belly pale and shocked.

I sit on the edge of the bed. "I'm so sorry, guys. Is there anything you want to know? Anything I can tell you that will help?"

Sarah says, "It's so fucking horrible," and she starts to cry. I gather her up and pull her partway onto my lap.

Bryan glances over and says, "You're like the mom in the book you used to read us, holding the big, grown-up kid on her lap and singing the song."

The mention of the book brings tears to my eyes. Sarah says, "OMG, we used to make you read it to see you cry. Now you just think about it, and you turn into a puddle."

Bryan stares at Sarah's tear-streaked, puffy and blotchy face. "Look who's talking."

I wipe my eyes. "This next while is going to be extremely hard. Let's be kind to each other and support and love each other, and we'll make it through." My leg has pins and needles, and I shift Sarah back onto the bed. She heads to her room. I go to Bryan and kneel to hold him tight and whisper, "There are lots more hugs where this came from."

"It's okay, Mom," he says. "We'll be okay. The worst is over."

"It's terrible you heard it on the news. I wanted us to sit and help each other come to grips together."

"Maybe it's better we found out from the TV. The news gave us the lowdown on what he was doing on the down-low; stuff that would be hard to discuss with you."

"It saddens me you had to see that side of him because even though we went through some rocky times in our relationship, there were good times you spent with him as a dad; all those sporting events, boy scouts, school plays, Christmases, and birthdays. I'd like you to remember him that way."

"It's okay, Mom. I'm just so mad at him. I think, *why did he have to be such a dick?* Then I feel bad for being pissed."

Tears run past his ears, and I put my cheek and temple against his. I say, "I'm sorry to bring this up, but on a practical note, the police have been here twice. I dumped your weed and paraphernalia, but they could be back at any time with another search warrant, so the house needs to be drug-free."

"Yeah, I know," he allows unhappily.

Seeing the two of them so restrained and serious is strange. I want the twins to be more responsible and down to earth, but under normal circumstances. I back out of the room, close the door and collapse on the sofa next to Trix.

Trix shakes her head. "You're going to be okay. Hang in until things settle. We'll figure it out."

I sigh. "I guess…"

"Good thing you have a career and can support yourself. A lot of people would be ruined. What he did is so freakin' unfair."

"The shock and anger of his betrayal, his death is awful, but somehow I'll be okay. Right now I'm just rattled."

"I'd be more worried about you if you weren't rattled."

We are quiet for a while. I shift to the end of the sofa and put my feet up. "What did you think of the detectives?"

"Reeves is cute, in fact, quite hot, but it'll take a tractor to pull the toothpick out of his ass. He needs a good shagging. I might make it my mission."

"Seriously?" I smile doubtfully.

"Seriously. Reeves is my type…occasionally." She grins. "But those cheap suits. Ugh. I bet they come with an extra pair of pants. I have a feeling some specialized Trix therapy, and a makeover could cure what ails him."

"Reeves wasn't wearing a ring," I say, recalling how

the detectives studied Trix. "Probably through their eyes, you're the beautiful, edgy downtowner, the sophisticated bad girl. I bet they're scared you're smarter than both of them put together, unpredictable, everything they don't want in their wives or daughters."

She laughs. "Call me the Mother Teresa of sex. If you don't want details, I won't kiss and tell… And what about Wilson, dressed like he's headed for the rodeo? He's all gee-golly-willickers. I can't decide if he's acting."

"Leibovitz says he lays it on, but he's smart. He reminds me of the old detective show, *Columbo*. He wants to be underestimated." I add in a bumpkin's voice and Wilson's drawl, "I'm just a simple, country yokel, ma'am."

She pauses. "I'll do a little research on Reeves. Hey, mind if we sit outside so I can smoke?"

We go to the lanai, and I turn on overhead fans. "Summer in Texas, phew."

Trix says, "The lawyer has a point about the media. A killer who murdered a suburban dad in a gated community is at large, and Middle-class America is shaking in its boots. The cops are probably under more pressure than a Sumo wrestler wearing size-small Spanx."

"Now, that brings a funny picture to mind." I sip water and add, "I'm confident Clayton is the killer. Who else could it logically be?"

"Are you worried he'll return?"

"To finish the job and get rid of me, too? No. I don't consider Clayton a threat to me because I don't see a motive. His beef was with Austin. But here's a question, if Clayton isn't the murderer, who is?"

Trix exhales, and the fans carry the smoke away. "You might want to have a weapon handy."

"First, Austin took my gun, and now the cops took it. And first, Austin treated me like a mushroom, and now the detectives are keeping me in the dark and feeding me shit."

She says, "It's a weird parallel, isn't it? By the way, for protection at my place, I have a can of wasp killer near the bed. The spray can hit a target at thirty feet, and you know that shit's gotta sting like crazy. Go for the eyes, but keep on spraying."

"I'll get the spray from the garage, and I'll keep using the doorstop." I pause. "Sometimes it sinks in that Austin has been murdered, and I start shaking. It's like a magician said *Presto-change-o*, and out of the blue, I'm a widow, a suspect, and a victim."

"All in the blink of an eye."

"Plus, with the newshounds outside, the whole world knows. And while they are free to speculate, I can't defend myself."

Chapter Twenty-Four

"Leibovitz said to watch the news. Ugh."

I'll watch it with you." Trix said. "We'll get a sense of what kind of story they are putting together."

We spend the afternoon riveted to the television, analyzing and criticizing the reports. A collection of self-styled authorities on crime and murder, clamor to be more in-the-know. They speculate whether the murderer is Clayton, Salem, or me, and hazard guesses about our lifestyles, motives, and everybody's sex life.

Concentrating on Salem, they allege she was an escort when she was younger, attributing the claim to an anonymous source, and show a website with what might be her escort profile and a slow-motion close-up of what might be needle-marks on her arm.

"This is biased," I remark. "Nothing more than innuendo. Does calling her a hooker have anything to do with Austin's murder?"

"They're pointing out character flaws and saying any

type of shady behavior can lead to becoming a murderer." Trix says, "By the way, when did the words *hooker* and *prostitute* get changed to *escort*?"

"Right around the time, *unfriend* became a word, and the word *remove* got changed to *uninstall*." We smile.

Unflattering pictures of Salem are aired. They appear edited to emphasize imperfections. Some photos are from her social media pages, of her in bikinis, posing on beaches, kissing men who aren't her husband.

Trix chuckles sadly and says, "I bet Salem would love being a celebrity if they showed even one attractive shot of her."

"I'm afraid of how they'll tar-and-feather me."

"Julia, there's nothing negative to report about you. Besides, Austin wasn't the only victim. You're also a victim."

Angry women defend me, saying Austin got what he deserved. "Those ladies aren't helping my cause by saying it was a justifiable homicide."

Marcy calls. I put her on speaker. She yells, "Oh my fucking God! Julia, this is so crazy! There were plenty of times I wanted him dead, would have killed him myself, but holy shit! Darlin', you've got my number. Call me if you need anything. Anything!"

"Thanks, Marcy," and she is gone.

"Amazing. Marcy can say out loud she wanted him dead, and she's not offensive." Trix shakes her head. "Maybe Marcy should be a suspect."

The commercials end, and the announcer portrays Salem as a home-wrecker extraordinaire. I shake my head. "Not to defend Salem, but she couldn't entice Austin if he weren't open to the idea. If not her, he would've found someone else. Even I realize there was something huge missing in our relationship. After all, we were at odds on all levels."

The next clip features anonymous interviews with other married men she has supposedly slept with, including one who claims she threatened him with a knife.

"Whoa!" Trix says. "Talk about pooping in the jury pool."

"I wonder why these guys came forward…and notice how the married men are anonymous, filmed in silhouette, and so forth. That's not fair." The footage is forcing me to recognize my habit of wishful thinking. I'd clung to, believed-in, my perfect life and perfect love, even after it had been run into the ditch.

Replayed ad tedium is another unbecoming clip of Salem racing from her car to her house, which is cement blocks and industrial metal. With some care, the structure could have been cool-contemporary, but instead, it's bunker-like.

Additional clips show someone egged Clayton and Salem's house. Trix says, "The press acts as if the vandalism happened spontaneously, yet they're the ones who are vilifying her and showing her house, which is pretty distinctive. Not that I care one iota about Salem's sensibilities, but…just sayin'."

"Also, me, Austin, Clayton, and Salem can't defend ourselves. The media are the equivalent of a kangaroo court." Footage shows Clayton, bald and beefy, shouting at the reporters to get off his property. A helicopter shot shows a sturdy dog leaping against the backyard fence and barking. "Looks like an equal number of reporters are at both our houses." I lean forward to scrutinize the screen. "I saw Clayton the night he was here. He's huge."

I wince at the next clip showing the twins screaming at the press to leave. Next is Lucy as she unloads groceries, and she says, "The police need to concentrate on Austin's mistress and her biker husband. Common sense, fellas."

The reportage begins again. Trix turns off the TV, and we go to the kitchen. A pan of chicken crêpes is in the fridge. I say with wonderment, "Who is the casserole fairy?"

"Lucy brought it this morning. I'm sure there will be more." Trix smiles weakly. "Nothing says *bad shit happened* like neighbors bearing casseroles."

When I lift the lid, the creamy smell produces a squeeze of nausea. "Oh well, at least the kids will be fed."

"Oh, no, you don't." She puts the crêpes in the oven. "Call your kids to come and eat."

The twins take plates to their bedrooms, and Trix and I eat at the breakfast bar. The evening wears on; darkness falls, and the media vans drift away.

"I'm so thankful for your company, Trix. There are too many hours…" and I fight tears. She hugs me. We pour chardonnay, go into the humid heat of the lanai, stretch out on chaises, and observe the moonlit night.

Trix lights a cigarette and says, "Christ, look at all the freakin' bats. It's like a vampire movie. No wonder they're in your dreams."

"I don't mind the bats. They eat their weight in mosquitoes every night."

"In that case, too bad they don't weigh ten pounds each."

I pretend-grimace. "Ha. Bats the size of cats; now that would be a nightmare."

We sit for a while in the sultry stillness and finally make our way inside. She produces sleep meds from her bag that I gratefully consume and go to bed in the master bedroom while Trix hits the sheets in the guest room. As I lie in what used to be our bed, I detect Austin's scent. I force myself not to visualize the condition of his body after being in the heat for days. I'm more played out than I thought humanly possible, and finally, I sleep as unmoving and dreamlessly as a road hump.

It's been ten days since the discovery of Austin's body. I wake in the wee hours and drag myself into the shower, which has become my crying closet, and let loose, sobbing. After, in robe and panties, I place witch hazel pads, then eye cream, on my swollen red orbs. My weary limbs can barely haul my carcass around the house. How do emotional events of enormity siphon one's physical strength in this way? I start a drawing of Clayton, sketching his bald head on a pit-bull that's wearing a do-rag and straddling a Harley.

I sketch until the sun comes up, then with the household still asleep, I take coffee over ice to the lanai. The muggy heat is intense, penetrating skin, muscle, into the bone. Who the hell needs a sauna in Houston? I run Austin's murder scenarios through my mind and keep coming back to Clayton. What is he like? Can a guy sporting gang insignia be a sweet-natured gentle giant? More likely, he's a bruiser engaged in all manner of illegal activity, a bully with size on his side.

In the yard heat mirages shimmer above the lawn like gasoline vapor. I picture Clayton with his posse; their menacing and intimidating presence, their motorcycles revving aggressively, the ether of fuel and heat rising as the men sweat malodorously into their leathers and bandanas. There's no helmet law in Texas, so they wear do-rags to soak up the sweat and keep it out of their eyes. Their *bitches* are women like Salem, who buy into the biker image. They ride behind their man, wearing shorts and skimpy tops, trusting their guy won't get them mangled, pinned and burned under the engine, skinned alive as they slide across the pavement, heads cracked like eggs, blood spilled, organs and limbs crushed, pain and screaming, messed up for life, or killed.

Do the detectives believe Clayton simply because he insists he's innocent? Surely, they can't be that gullible. He's using a strategy I've seen my kids use; admit a little to deny a lot, something along the lines of *I took five dollars*—see how honest I am—now believe me when I say this, *but I didn't take the missing twenty-dollar bill.*

If the detectives are right and he isn't the killer, the murderer is still at large.

Trix comes to the lanai carrying her coffee and reclines on a chaise. I relate my thoughts about Clayton, and she says, "Unfortunately, Austin brought his misfortune on himself."

She lights up. "I got a call to do a big commission, so I have to head home and meet the client." She promises to return on a moment's notice if I need anything.

"I'm amazed you stayed here as long as you did, and I appreciate so much that you took the time to help me through this mess." Trix packs up her clothes and hugs me goodbye. I enjoyed her company, but I also need to be alone without distractions, to find my new normal.

Leibovitz calls and says the detectives want the twins and me at the police station for more questioning. I shower and dress, summon my kids, and check the street for news vans. The press has thinned to one trailer. Others show up occasionally, but their coverage has become sporadic.

We leave the house by the back way. While the kids and I dash to Lucy's garage, where she stashed our cars, Trix's Fiat is the decoy, attracting the reporters' attention while we escape.

First, we meet with Leibovitz at his office. He says, "I have the coroner's written report, but no diagrams. According to the report, Austin was killed the first night he disappeared."

At the thought of his body rotting in his hot car for a week, blood leaves my head and dizziness forces my eyes closed a moment. Leibovitz notices and fetches me water. He briefs us on the protocol. "The detectives will Mirandize you. I'm sure you know the drill from cop shows."

Sarah says, "You have the right to remain silent, yada yada. I thought they only do that when they arrest you."

"They'll probably Mirandize upfront to ensure everything is admissible in court. Either another lawyer from my firm or I will always be with you. If you are concerned about any of the questions, either defer to your lawyer or don't answer."

"This is dumb," Bryan says. "We weren't around the night he went missing, period."

"Then your interview should be pretty short," Leibovitz says. "Where were you?"

"We went bowling, then hung out with friends and went to a concert; then we went to Dylan's place, where we stayed all night and the next day."

"Which band did you see?"

"Armor-Dildo." He shifts in his seat and places his forearms on the table, relaxing.

"Was the concert good?"

"Hell, yeah."

Leibovitz smiles. "What was their first song?"

"It was *I'll Do You.*"

Sarah chimes in, "No, it was *Let Me Have It.*"

Leibovitz says, "See what just happened? That sounded like a regular conversation, right? The detectives might be conversational like I was, and you may not realize your contradiction raised a red flag. Whatever they ask, they'll probably already know the answer, or they'll Google the info later."

Bryan says, "Got it."

"If there are factual gaps, the cops won't give you the benefit of the doubt for forgetfulness or making a mistake. But I don't want you to prepare. A rehearsed statement tends to come off as bad acting. Just be thoughtful and accurate. If you've forgotten something, no problem. It's okay to say so; don't make stuff up."

"Okay," they say in stereo.

Leibovitz's phone rings. He takes the call, then says to me, "Wilson wants you to take a polygraph. Are you all right with that?"

"Yes. I'm innocent," I say, "but I should tell you, I dreamed I killed Austin, and I'm worried whether my dream will affect the outcome." Bryan and Sarah exchange glances, and I say, "Don't worry, kiddos. I know dreams aren't real."

Leibovitz says, "You should be fine."

At the police station, ushered to separate rooms, the cops' questions are a rerun of many already asked and answered. The kids are gone when I finish, and the detectives take me to another room for my polygraph, where "Did you kill your husband?" is asked in three different ways tucked at random among innocuous questions.

Back home, the news vans are back, lining the street. Our precinct visit has rejuvenated their interest, and on the news channel, there are clips of us entering the police station. The talking-heads exchange comments on my lawyer and debate our interrogation. After running the same footage to the point of irritation, they switch to previous clips of Clayton and Salem.

Upstairs in Bryan's room, he and Sarah are in their previous prone positions. I ask, "How did it go with the detectives?"

Bryan says, "Easy. There's nothing to tell."

Sarah props herself on her elbows. "We made a decision."

"Yeah." Bryan stops texting and says, "With cops coming around and news guys watching the house, and all that crap, we're gonna move out."

"I doubt the police will be coming around anymore. Besides, the cops are more interested in me than you."

Bryan says, "Yeah, well…reporters have been stalking us. Somehow, they got our cell numbers, and they were tracking us by the GPS in our phones, so we turned it off. But they still keep showing up and taking pictures."

"It turns out the paparazzi hacked our friends' Facebook postings. They find the GPS location in the photos' properties, and they show up hoping to find us out of control—which, hello, we are," Sarah says with disgust. "Our dad was just killed!"

I step into the room. "Were the pictures incriminating?"

"Nope, but like you said, the cops might bring a search warrant, so we can't hang out here with friends, in case we all get busted."

"Or, you could stop smoking dope."

"Mom," Bryan says in mock-disbelief, "it's your big chance to get rid of us. Don't blow it."

I smile. "Where will you go?"

"For now, we'll stay with our friends, Darren and Dylan," Sarah says.

My phone rings. Leibovitz reports that I passed the polygraph, and all my answers are cleared as *No indication of deception.* We hang up, and I head to the kitchen to assess the casserole situation. One is a ground beef dish that looks awful but smells appetizing. I scoop some onto a plate and set the microwave's timer.

My phone rings again—Detective Wilson. "Howdy, ma'am." He sounds like he is also eating. I picture tacos, brisket, or crawdads. "All of the forensics have been processed, and we're releasing your husband's body to the funeral home today."

"All right." I push my plate away. Austin wanted to buy gravesites for the two of us, but we never got around to it. Instead of his imaginary sumptuous twenty-grand sendoff, a small fraction of that will get me his ashes in a cardboard box to toss to the wind—a disposable husband. I ask, "Do I have to do something? Sign some papers?"

"No, ma'am." There is some sympathy in his tone. "They'll take care of everything." He pauses. "How are you and your kids holding up?"

"About as well as can be expected, I guess."

The conversation stalls until he says, "I'm truly sorry for your loss, ma'am."

He sounds sincere, and I'm touched. "Yes, so much loss in so many ways," I say. "My kids are packing up to go and stay with friends. The reporters have been hounding them." I pause. "It's weird how the media has latched onto Austin's murder."

"Not really. The press needs material day in and day out to feed the beast. The more sensational, the better. Believe me; nobody wishes they'd back off more than me."

I don't believe him. The police seem to have a reciprocal relationship with the media. "Is it possible to get a restraining order to keep them away from me and my kids?"

"Getting a restraining order on the media would be like tryin' to shoo away cats by throwin' fish at them."

The image makes me laugh, "Right, of course, it would be counterproductive. They'd be arguing their right to freedom of speech and so forth, on the air." I pause. "Please let me know if there is a break in the case."

"Of course." He says goodbye and hangs up.

I go to the garage where the kids are loading their cars out of sight of the reporters. We hug. "Your dad is being cremated in the next couple of days. Do you want to get together to scatter his ashes?"

Sarah says, "Can you get the ashes and keep them for now?"

Bryan nods, and I agree. "Good plan."

They leave, flipping off the photographers that dog them, and I can't help but smile.

Chapter Twenty-Five

It has been three months since Austin's murder. Recently, a pair of self-proclaimed cold-case experts appeared on a national news program and discussed Austin's case. Their appearance coincided with the release of an episode of the show *Murder Mysteries* featuring Austin's murder. As a result, the media have descended again.

I find the show and tune in. A banner proclaims *Ripped from the Headlines*, and photos rotate of Austin and me, interspersed with screenshots of partial files and paperwork, the detectives, Salem, and Clayton, and the police and media vans on our street. The episode is a collage of old news clips, and interviews with the detectives. The show offers nothing new, but I still find their creation of a storyline fascinating. I record the show to examine it again, later.

My curtains are my moat, protection from the media, and stalkers. The doorbell rings for the fourth time today, and the camera I installed on the porch beams my visitor's image to my laptop. It is not a reporter, but one of the schadenfreude-tourists that follow tragic news like stink trails a garbage truck.

What character defect compels these news groupies to stalk and harass complete strangers? I bet they started as neighborhood busybodies who, over time, whether from loneliness or lack of mental acuity, became obsessive predators of the salacious.

But really, they're merely mimicking the behavior of the multi-billion-dollar business of tabloids, paparazzi, gossip TV, and reality shows—an industry that panders to our prurient appetites, and sanctions the pursuit and collection of juicy details, at any cost.

Someone posted the gatekeeper's hours on social media, and when he's on break, the gawkers slither in to prowl the neighborhood until they find the news vans. They deliver greeting cards, teddy bears, cups of coffee, store-bought desserts, either as atonement for the aggravation they cause, or as lube to penetrate my life.

Whenever the doorbell rings, I text Lucy, who acts as the gator or piranha in my moat, and she pounces, separates the giver from their goods, and delivers the item to my back door. Lucy's interception irritates some of them, and results in raised voices and scuffles, resulting in squished cupcakes, dented boxes, spilled coffee.

Time creeps. I shave off hours in segments assigned by television. When my image appears on the screen, I don't recognize that person as a two-dimensional me. She could be anyone. I reside on the crumbling edge of my existence, disengaged, a witness to my life replicated in soul-sucking sound bites and videos.

Slumped on the sofa, nibbling a piece of cake left by the latest misery-junkie, hoping the confection isn't poisoned—since it appears to be homemade and has *R.I.P. Austin* written in black icing on top—I tune to the news channel. The news anchor says, "This just in!"

A five-year-old film fills the screen showing me at one of Austin's coworkers' backyard parties. Uh oh. Now what?

In the clip, I'm facing the camera wearing capris and a turquoise top, chatting with several women. My appearance is pulled-together and healthy. The announcer says, "Stay with us to see what else this video reveals." Commercials unspool, then the news anchor says, "Our techs have enhanced this clip to clarify what we are about to show you."

The camera zooms past me, magnifying the background. Bushes partially hide two figures, but as the focus tightens, they are identifiable as Austin and a young woman who, even though they've blurred her face, is recognizable to me as an intern who once worked at his firm. She grasps the back of Austin's neck, pulls herself onto tiptoes and kisses him on the mouth. He returns the kiss, then realizes his transgression. He removes her hands, glances around, and turns his back, but not before a bulge in his pants is evident. The young woman giggles.

The announcer says, "Now, viewers, let us know what you think. Here's Julia Green, oblivious to what her husband is cooking up, and there's Austin, doing his thing."

The clip runs again. Evidently, I was a mushroom longer than I thought. The intern was about five years older than our kids and came to our house several times. Her kiss attests to her youthful recklessness, but what about him? He's risking his job and marriage to canoodle in the shrubbery in my presence at a company barbecue. Marcy must have filmed the video back then. She would have noticed what was happening, literally behind my back. This new revelation is another slap to Austin's reputation. However, the media, who are desperately trying to identify the murderer, will probably view more cheating as adding to my motive. My mood slips from lousy to downright shitty.

Lucy calls and says, "I saw the news. Unbelievable."

"What's unbelievable is I never figured it out. He certainly was prolific."

"My god, Julia, all the pussy he attracted, Austin's package must have been made of catnip!"

I almost smile. "That's funny. Hey Lucy, I've

concluded I need some solitary. I appreciate everything you've done. Truly. You've been a godsend, but for the time being, I need some alone time to grasp everything that's happened."

"No problem, hon, just let me know if there's anything you need. I'm here for you." While she's got the sentiment down in words, there's a shade of hurt in her tone, but my emotional suitcase is packed full with no space for pity or empathy. We sign off.

Doors locked and maid service canceled, I wander the house considering the dead. So many were taken by tragedy, unexpectedly and too soon: in car wrecks, by coronary or stroke, by suicide, virus, cancer, some by drug overdose. Each fresh loss was a gap like a pulled tooth, with the painful, pulpy emptiness impossible to resist probing.

Austin's void is as if his form has been cut from the atmosphere in a thousand places, and the surrounding air hasn't filled the vacant space yet. There's the scent of him, a blend of aftershave, leather, cigars, man-musk that still rises from soft furnishings when they're touched. I pace and sleep and roam the house. I drink but don't eat much. I order my groceries because the whispers of strangers or neighbors in the supermarket, glances at a restaurant or the gas pump, will flay or scald me.

Mysteriously, my paintbrushes each weigh five hundred pounds. I stand before the canvas for hours, immobile, uninspired, limp, then wander back to the television. My creativity and drive have vanished.

The sofa has developed a vacuum quality, like some type of supergravity that holds me down, and I adore its insistence, and location close to the TV, bathroom, and kitchen, and seemingly a hundred miles from the bed we shared that seethes with Austin's essence. Over and over, I watch the *Murder Mysteries* episode about Austin's murder, hoping for some tiny fragment of a clue, something said or concealed in the background of a photo, but there's nothing.

The television. Daytime-television-shows appear to be

corporate America's revenge for malingerers who skip work. The shows feature mumbling rednecks, rude and crude so-called housewives; weight-loss and plastic surgery drama; all manner of sports; and home renovation struggles. Each is like a blob of mental mucous, scraped from the brains of studio execs, and spit into our living rooms. The shows relentlessly feature America's lowest common denominator; however, as vapid and intellectually impoverished the dreck may be, it passes the time in chunky, orderly segments. I alternate the pointless distraction of television with reluctant and fitful sleep.

I'm aware I am depressed. This sadness is an ogre that wants to wear me down and win me over. In this abyss, I believe the worst of myself, and I lie rotting on the sofa for what seems like years but is less than a month.

Then there's a night when a wave of disgust and self-recrimination at my indolence crashes over me, prying me from my cocoon. Joints aching from immobility, my cotton gown stiff with dried sweat and dirt, I totter to the liquor cabinet and retrieve the skull-shaped bottle of tequila. In the dark, I sink into the overstuffed chair. The first swallow traces a fiery route between my throat and stomach, inflaming my heart as it rushes past.

Thumbing through my music, I click on Leonard Cohen's *Famous Blue Raincoat*, moody, dark, perfectly ominous. I turn it up loud, take the tequila outside leaving the French doors wide open, and sit in the grainy darkness near the pool, away from the cloying embrace of the house. Clouds block the moon, and in the murk, the shapes of objects are formless, their shadows absorbed.

There's been rain, and the damp chill permeating my nightgown is an intoxicating shock that sends goosebumps along my arms. Beaver chirps to get my attention, then flows from the fence onto a planter and to the patio slinking to me all sinuous and needy, swirling his tail around my legs. I scratch his head, and he purrs. Something about his undaunted and natural self, his indifference to my abject hopelessness, his refusal to tolerate deviation from his norm, tickles me. His simple reaction causes some hidden inner wires within me to touch and connect, and a circuit is completed, bringing me to life.

There's the fragrance of night blooms, damp earth, grass, faint wood smoke from somewhere. Night creatures rustle in the undergrowth, and the cat, warm and vibrating on my lap, hooks his claws through my nightgown and into my thighs, the pain a reminder I still want to feel every raw, cutting emotion from all of the knives that have and will continue to visit me. Life has given and will keep giving me scars of all kinds, proof I'm living because the dead don't heal.

Moths, drawn to the porch light, flap haphazardly until they fall. The clouds part, and in the deep blue sky, the glowing-wafer of a full moon silhouettes the landscape, casting shadows. Droplets fall from black foliage, plinking on stone. Freight trains grumble and moan in the distance, and a siren wails, perhaps for a victim, like Austin, or possibly an imminent birth. New life.

When light shimmers under the clouds, the bats head for their daytime roost, and pigeons and doves start their repetitive cooing as the sun breaks above the horizon, flooding the land with honeyed light. I wipe my face on my damp gown. The cat hops down, and belly to the ground, he slinks after a sound on the far side of the garden.

I stand, and the glass skull takes on the persona of Austin, his rictus grin mocking my feebleness. I heft the crystalline, cold weight in my hand, wind up, and throw. The bottle makes a slow-motion arc, turning and righting itself, glares at me with glistening, vacant eyes, and smashes into the corner of the house, exploding, shards and fragments catching the light.

Inside, the music finishes playing Cohen's *Closing Time* and stops. I open windows, take a long shower, and don clean clothes, put out the garbage, wipe down countertops, empty the dishwasher, change sheets, and load laundry, resuming my former life of satisfying small accomplishments.

Over the next days, I wash many trailing thoughts of Austin and his betrayals away with a flood of tears. I slowly and deliberately pick up the shattered pieces and reassemble my inner life. And I repair my outer life as well, restocking the fridge, contacting everyone who has tried to connect, except the reporters. I finish the neighbors' casseroles, and open and respond to mail that Lucy has compiled: cards, letters, postcards, an outpouring of support and heartfelt condolences.

The days stagger by, and the paintbrushes lose their intimidation. I work on the stabbing painting. I resume my coffee dates with Lucy and daily phone calls with Trix as well as staying connected to the twins, to whom I send articles and clips of uplifting or informative messages, and they respond in kind. I assume they are hunkered down, tending, and healing their wounds.

My strength is returning. I'm not so wilted, not so weak, and I force myself to take care of the sort of unpleasant tasks that tempt procrastination: paying bills, picking up Austin's ashes, and taking another polygraph, as requested by Wilson. He phones the next day. I debate answering since Leibovitz isn't present, but I touch the green dot. He says, "Ma'am, I want you to know your polygraph indicated no deception."

"No surprise there. Are there new leads?" I ask glibly, "How about Clayton, remember him, Salem's husband?" Passing my second polygraph entitles me to snippiness. I want to lash out at someone, and Wilson is handy. "Is there any forensic stuff like maybe a bloody knife belonging to Clayton?"

"Ma'am," he says, "if we caught Clayton with the murder weapon, that'd be like findin' a bird's nest on the ground. You need to understand—Clayton was a guest in your home. Austin traveled with him and spent time socializin'. Clayton's prints are meaningless unless they're in Austin's blood. Besides, he has an alibi."

I sigh. "It's frustrating. Have you searched Clayton's property?"

"Ma'am, we're doing everything we can."

Wilson's exaggerated twang and his pacifying manner irritate me, and I say, "Someone murdered Austin more than four months ago, and the killer is still at large, while you guys sit with your heads up your—"

He cuts me off, saying, "Y'all have a nice day," and hangs up. Good-old boys like Wilson dig their heels in when a woman pushes them. From long ago, my mother whispers, *You'll catch more flies with honey than vinegar.*

Early evening after a light dinner, I return to my drawing of the near-drowning. Diagonally, across a large piece of parchment paper, in my pencil sketch, Austin's muscular hand grips my wrist. I picture the gleam of his wedding band against his tanned skin. I study my sketch and judge the composition all wrong. There's not enough terror.

I put the paper aside, place a fresh canvas on the easel, and sketch a new drawing in charcoal, an underwater scene of the soon-to-be-drowned victim. To create this scene, I need to remain impartial and visualize her as a stranger, not as myself. Sunlight dapples her body. Her face is above the surface, making her anonymous. Austin's hand pulls her outstretched arm, which shows flexed muscle, resistance. She has bent knees, tensely pulling back. A mist of disturbed sand is below her feet, and beyond is the menacing immensity of the deep. I step back to evaluate. Yes.

Cerulean blue, then burnt sienna, mixed directly, and the painting begins to come to life as if my touch is liberating the image from the canvas.

My phone rings with call-display indicating Bryan. He says, "Yo."

"Yo, to you, too."

"We want to come visit you, like now."

"Sure."

They arrive in twenty minutes. After hugs, Sarah gets Cokes from the fridge. Surprisingly, she pours me red wine. As she hands the glass to me, my hand slips and I slosh wine onto the floor. "Shit!"

"Mom, language!" Sarah says, and the twins both laugh ironically. She hops up and says, "Don't worry. I'll clean up," and she returns with paper towels.

In mock fear, I ask, "Who are you, and what did you do with my daughter?"

She abruptly laughs, her reaction a departure from the old prickly Sarah. They exchange glances, and Bryan says, "We have stuff to tell you."

"Okay," I say. "Not more bad news, I hope."

Bryan says, "There's good news and bad news. Here's the dealio. We kinda took advantage of Dad for a couple of months when we found out he was cheating." Two pink spots develop on his cheeks.

Sarah smiles and says, "That's why Dad gave us anything we wanted." No blushing for her.

"You've got to be kidding. So there was no app in the works?"

Bryan leans forward, elbows on knees, indicating thoughtfulness, and clarifies, "At first there was, but after doing some research, we realized our idea sucked. So, no app. Anyway, we hacked dad's email and his bank account. Then we saw he was taking money from your retirement fund and wiring the cash to a separate account in Atlanta. We found a check for the Atlanta account hidden in the hollowed-out book we gave him for Christmas."

In contrast to Bryan's tense posture, Sarah lounges. She says, "That check gave us the transfer code and account number, and he'd written the password and username on the back. Like duh. What a friggin' amateur."

Bryan says, "When we realized he was blowing big bucks on his bimbo, we started taking out, like, a few grand at a time, wiring the money into a new account we set up for you. Dad didn't notice. Then we decided what he was doing was off the chain, and we cleaned him out. According to emails he sent to Salem, he couldn't figure out what happened, and she didn't believe him. So funny."

Sarah says, "They spent a lot of the money, but there's close to a hundred fifty grand we diverted."

I'm reeling, shaking my head in astonishment. "I don't know what to say. Thanks. It'll be a real godsend." I hesitate. "I appreciate your help." There's apology in their expressions.

I want to lecture, to say *you shouldn't have.* To remind the twins of the plaque we had when they were little kids, which read, *Character—it's what you do when no one's looking.* If they had divulged this earlier, would Austin's murder have been prevented? Maybe, and for that reason, I can't say it and lay guilt at their feet.

Sarah stands and says, "I gotta go back to work. I'm on the evening shift."

"Yeah, me too," Bryan says.

I put down my wineglass carefully, not wanting to spill wine again. "What? You have jobs?"

They grin at each other. "Yeah," says Sarah. "Bryan's working for Gig.com, the job-finding website, and I'm with BuildABook.com, the self-publishing company."

We exchange congratulations and hugs, and they go, leaving me dazed. But while I'm happy for some cash, what kind of people did I raise? Maybe one day we'll speak of this again, but for now, I must let it rest.

I access my new bank account courtesy of the twins and wire the money into my personal account. Hallelujah. I text the kids, thanking them again. For dinner, I defrost and start on the last casserole.

Chapter Twenty-Six

The phone breaks my train of thought. It's Lucy. "I know it's late, but I've got dessert." She arrives with brownies and says, "Wow. You look great."

"Thanks Lucy. I chalk it up to being on the misery diet, but I'll take any compliments I can get."

"How are you doing, now that the media has vamoosed?"

"It's hard to fill the hours, and I'm not used to being alone."

"You're lonely."

"Maybe, but I *wanted* to split with Austin."

"Of course you're lonely," she says, "Hell, anyone can be lonely, even people who are in a relationship, and that's the loneliest lonely of all." She sings a few bars of Roy Orbison's "Only the Lonely."

"Impressive."

"Karaoke. I've been practicing."

I break off a chunk of brownie and push the plate

toward Lucy. "I've decided to sell the house. This place is too big, too expensive, and too much work for one person. Plus, there are too many memories."

There's a dazed aspect to her. "Can I come live with you? Let's get a place together. I've had enough of this burb, and I'm sick of Earl and my kids. Seriously! We'll be like Thelma and Louise and have a blast." The idea is so farfetched my jaw unhinges. She catches my expression, says, "Kidding!" and laughs, but too loudly.

I say slowly, "Yeah, sounds like fun, but Thelma and Louise came to a bad end."

"I said I was just kidding," she barks, and then becomes lost in thought. I attempt to engage her in conversation twice, but she is silent as she finishes her brownie, gives me a thin-lipped smile, and heads home. Halfway across the lawn, she stops and turns, and I see something in her face I've never seen before; it's a fierce expression, almost like hatred. Fear bristles my arms and spine, making chill bumps. She notices me watching, and I wave, but she solemnly turns away.

I've known Lucy for a long time, and I understand she'll never see my situation from my perspective, but I'm gob-smacked she'd think this life of mine is desirable. Austin's murder, suddenly unencumbering me, is nothing like choosing one's freedom.

Maybe no one will ever understand. Should I start a support group called Widows of Murdered Philandering Spouses: WOMPS? We could sit around honking into soggy hankies, exchanging stories of how we were duped, giving tips on dealing with the media, telling how friends let us down, the agony of our children's grief. No. Now that my misery and Austin are banished, a group griefathon would be a step backward.

Not surprisingly, there's nothing relatable on TV for a peri-menopausal, widowed, starting-over female such as myself. I tune to the movie *Fatal Attraction.* Austin and I watched it together, but obviously, the cautionary tale didn't affect his faithfulness. I've finally accepted that Austin was a real Don Juan, or in modern parlance, a sex addict. No doubt, the promiscuity I'm aware of is just the tip of the iceberg. He was the hottest husband in the subdivision, so maybe he was screwing all the horny wives in our neighborhood. Lucy talked about her and Earl's open marriage, and I'm suddenly sure Austin had sex with Lucy. Earl is pleasant but bland, and in comparison, Austin was a movie star.

In bed in the dark, the creaks and groans of the house are magnified. Did Lucy and Earl murder Austin? Despite their declared open marriage, maybe Earl was okay with Lucy having sex with a random cable guy but not neighbors or friends. Did he catch them in the act and kill him? One's spouse screwing someone else is one thing when it's a concept, but watching them have sex could be something else entirely. Everyone has boundaries that mustn't be crossed.

But, since I'm usually home, how did Austin and Lucy get together? At a hotel out of the neighborhood? Unlikely since Lucy is usually home. Did they have sex in my house? Not during the day, so the most likely scenario is that they met at night for one of Austin's rough quickies after their spouses were asleep; in the garage, up against a wall, on a countertop.

I visualize the scene. Austin sneaks into Lucy's garage or her garden shed. Lucy's there wearing lingerie—a sexy lace teddy—and Austin is in his boxers. He pulls her top down to rub her abundant breasts and twiddle big dark-brown nipples. She unsnaps the crotch of her teddy and hooks a big leg on his hip to open up and allow him to do his usual, fast and furious rut, like a dog in heat. Am I imagining things now, Austin?

Could Lucy be so two-faced she'd have coffee in my kitchen several times a week while cheating with my husband? Until Austin cheated on me and befriended Clayton, I could never conceive of such a scenario, but now I believe anything is possible.

Another possibility is that Lucy and Earl hated what Austin did to me. Lucy and Trix were the only people who saw me after Austin beat me up. Lucy drove me to the hospital. The police came, and like legions of battered women, I refused to press charges. Nowadays, in many places, it's not up to the abused spouse. The state pursues charges if the evidence warrants them.

Austin was angry the police had been summoned, even though Lucy said Austin had the cops eating out of his hand, acting all buddy-buddy. He'd explained how clumsy I was, how I fell down the stairs. We wives have such precarious balance, always tripping, falling, bumping into god-knows-what and getting bruises and black eyes.

I'm the closest thing Lucy has to a real friend, and I'm planning to leave. If she—and Earl at her behest—killed Austin to help me, will she judge me for moving away, see me as ungrateful, and kill me too? Her face had shown rage and sorrow. I guess only one thing's certain; I no longer trust anyone.

But this is all speculation. The police insist the murderer isn't Clayton, and if it isn't Salem, me, Lucy and Earl, Marcy, or my kids, then who? Gang friends of Clayton? Someone violent is still lurking. Fear seeps into my bones. I get up and check all doors and windows are locked, drapes closed, and I put the doorstop in place. Finally, I sleep restlessly, waking before five.

Thoughts of murderers at large prompt me to sift through Austin's computer files, hoping to see something, a clue, or an email everyone else has missed. I call a locksmith. He arrives, and while he re-keys locks, I check email. A new client proposes drawings for a graphic novel. A magazine enquires about a series of Houston street scenes. Inspiration floods me, a soaring excitement at the possibilities ahead, and I'm energized.

Trix calls. "Have you done any new paintings?"

I groan. "I'm kind of blocked. I'm concentrating on jobs that pay instead."

"Here's an idea," she says. "Approach each painting as an illustration job."

"I know you're joking Trix, but that's a great idea. I'll view them as book illustrations and do a series of layout sketches of the type I get from my art directors."

"Glad to help," she says, and we hang up, chuckling.

Placing a call to a real estate agent who specializes in my neighborhood results in a bubbly brunette, Sandy Morgan, ringing my doorbell. After a tour of the house, she says, "The area is terrific, very high demand—"

I jump in. "I know the house needs tweaking. Give me a couple of weeks, and you can put your sign on the lawn. Got a recommendation for a painter?" She can't hide her relief, and we both laugh.

I watch a few decorating and house-flipping shows, then remind myself it's not rocket science and head to the hardware store to choose pale neutral paint colors. I remove old curtains, rods, valances, and framed art, and repair the drywall. Decluttering, stripping the place of our personalities to make way for the new owners' imprint, is a given. I sort and pack personal belongings for donation, disposal, or to move. The only room I skip is my studio because I'm still working, although I tidy and clean, hiding away my art and supplies. The master bedroom is the last to be cleared. Memories lurk here of the love we made, the pillow talk. There are dresses and shoes bought for special occasions, a few of Austin's things that escaped my bonfire; his cufflinks, humidor, and baseball caps.

The Salvation Army hauls away boxes of clothes, odds and ends, souvenirs, and our old worn bedroom and living room furnishings, leaving just the essentials. Then comes the crew of painters who push the furniture to the center of each room and cover the piles with drop sheets. The crew is a flurry of brushes and paint cans and tape, as they roll fresh off-white over the living room's gloomy taupe, the murky cigar-brown of Austin's office, and the black and deep purple of Sarah's and Bryan's rooms. And soon, glossy white enamel gleams on doors, molding, and trim.

I stage the house with carefully chosen contemporary accessories and paint a splashy, black-and-white, three-by-five-foot, Motherwell-style abstract—the most impersonal genre I can think of—and hang it in the living room. Online, I order white linen slipcovers for the sofa and chairs, and fresh sheets for the beds. I text my kids to come and collect their last few possessions. The purge is cathartic, and the entire house is lighter. Not only the wall color; even the air seems fresher, crisper, and thinner.

The twins arrive and load their cars, and we wander through the house, a goodbye ceremony. Sarah scans the rooms and raises her eyebrows. "Holy crap, Mom. This doesn't look like the same place."

"Yeah," Bryan adds. "It's like a model home, where no one actually lives."

"According to every show on flipping houses, that's the idea. Neutral and generic, generic, generic," I inform them.

"I like it." Sarah admits, smiling. I hug her, and she laughs.

Outdoors, away from activity and paint fumes, I ask, "How are you holding up?"

Bryan says, "Things are fine. Hey, did you get Dad's ashes?"

"Yes, they're in a box in my car. I didn't want them to get thrown out or something weird to happen in all the sprucing-up commotion."

Sarah says, "Let's scatter them in the backyard while we're here. This place was his home."

I return with the ashes, and we go to the bottom of the yard. Bryan and Sarah take turns, shaking the ashes onto the grass. None of us cries. As if on cue, a small, dark cloud drifts over us and begins a sun shower.

Sarah exclaims, "Shut the fuck up! If this were a movie, I'd say it was so fake."

We turn our faces skyward, and the raindrops anoint us. Bryan folds his hands over his heart and says, "Good one,

Dad. We loved you."

We ramble around the yard. The kids drive away as Juan pulls into the driveway. I ask him to sweep and wash the empty garage's floor. He's happy for a change from cutting grass. Using my extendable pole and squeegee, I clean the greenhouse roof of dirt, a dead bat, and guano, possibly for the last time. This house and its yard smack of the ties that bind—things you believe you own, but they end up owning you.

The real estate agent arrives laden with flyers and snacks. She checks each room, turns on lights, sticks her Open House sign into the front lawn, and attaches balloons. I leave to find my new abode in the arts district.

How will leaving the neighborhood feel? Will I get homesick? Maybe one day when I'm driving on autopilot, I'll find myself halfway to the old place.

After three hours of touring open houses, I arrive home. Sandy reports she had traffic, and I have an offer. Negotiations take several days, but one week later, the house is in escrow.

I juggle work with packing and purchasing a new home in the city with my must-haves—two bedrooms, a high-ceilinged studio, and a courtyard with a small garden. Moving day arrives in a blur of men with dollies, boxes, and plastic-wrapped furniture. The kids stop by for one last look, and we load artwork and Beaver in his carrier, into my car.

I lock up and driving away, a sharp realization strikes—it's been almost a year to the day since Austin's murder—and I'm not sad. Trix said recently that the opposite of love isn't hate, it's indifference. How true. I say aloud, "I'm so over you!" and laugh. Disconnecting from that millstone-chunk of real estate, Austin, and my former life, liberation as light and bright as sunshine flounces into the atmosphere and overlays my spirit. I drive away without looking back. At the title company, the deal is closed, and I surrender the key.

Late in the day, after the movers leave, amid stacks of boxes, Trix, Frankie, and I sit on folding chairs, eating pizza and sipping champagne from plastic cups. Trix says, "Here's to a new start, new chapter, new life."

"Goodbye, burbs and hello, city," Frankie adds, "You're downtown and free."

I laugh. "I am, and now that it's a reality, I need to figure out what to do with my life."

Trix says, "That's easy. You need to have your gallery show, and we'll get you set up with an online dating profile.

"I'm sure you're right," I say. I shift in my chair and cross my legs. "I could start dating, but can you imagine what it'll be like explaining Austin's killing?" I put on a perky persona. "Nice to meet you. By the way, my husband was murdered, stabbed to death. And the new guy will say," I adopt a male voice, "Great! I'll lock up the knives. Let's have sex." Trix and Frankie laugh loudly, and I add, "For the moment, I'm simply happy to be here, finally."

"No shit!" Trix says. "Twenty-five years is a life sentence. You've done more than your time, and are officially released."

Throughout the week, I unpack the last boxes and deflect well-meaning invitations from friends and acquaintances to meet single men.

Trix calls and asks, "How goes the settling in?"

"Fine. Now I'm fine-tuning with IKEA, and my place is full of flat-pack cardboard, little plastic hardware bags, and leaflets of instructions."

"I have such a love-hate relationship with that store," she says. "I decided that translated, IKEA means *out of stock.*"

"I thought it meant Swedish meatballs."

Trix laughs. "My pet peeve is the product names. Just try to figure out what's on your receipt. Is the bookcase Malm or Hemnes? No, the bookcase is a Billy. Sheesh."

I groan my agreement. "My gripe is the silly wheels on the carts that all swivel. The two back wheels should be stationary. My cart dragged me halfway across the parking lot."

"Wish I could've seen that." We sign off laughing, and every time I see the humor in a situation, I'm startled, amazed I can find joy, that I'm okay. I fold and dump the cartons in the recycling bin. My hands ache from powering the drill for several days.

Upstairs in my studio, I unroll a seven-foot-high by ten-foot-wide expanse of primed linen, tack it to the wall and stand back to assess the size and scope of this painting. I say aloud, "Get to work, girl. It's not going to paint itself."

Using indigo blue and alizarin crimson, I compose a montage. Memories transport me back, and once again, I've been force-fed anger, inflamed with black passion, carried by rage, viciously applying paint, building texture, attacking the canvas like the surface is a living and wild thing to be tamed. There is a dense, anthracite sky at the top that breaks apart into bats. Beaver with his glowing eyes hunkers nearby with the bat in his teeth, its wings torn. There is an ogre representing sadness and pain, there is the severed snake, and fragments of light from a full moon casting my shadow over Austin's prone body.

But when I try to draw Austin's face, a peculiar thing happens. I can recall his nose, an ear, or an eyebrow, but the pieces don't add up to him. In the way a police sketch can come off as clinical or disjointed; the parts may hold a certain likeness, but don't capture the subtly distinctive character and proportion that makes a good portrait, one that seizes and portrays the person's unique spirit. How did I lose Austin's image? He should be etched permanently on my memory, but I can't bring him into focus. I replace his face with a large, thick, black X. For annihilated? For X-rated? For exiled?

Exiled… Austin on a remote island, with a long beard and wearing raggedy pants, standing on a mound with one palm tree, surrounded by an endless ocean. The water is certainly fitting. Try swimming back now, Austin.

The phone rings. The sudden sound startles, breaking my trance, and I drop my brush, splattering black paint across the hardwood. Breathless, I snatch up the receiver without checking caller-ID.

Gallerina tells me, "I had lunch with Trix." Her voice fades a moment as she says something to someone nearby, then she returns full-volume. "It's been super busy, and I lost your last email. Given your backstory and Trix's endorsement, email me your images again."

"All right," I say, to get her off my back.

"I need them within the next hour, for our gallery meeting." And she is gone.

Damn. And what's this… *My backstory*? Should I be offended her call was because of Austin's murder and its attendant publicity, and Trix's involvement? Screw it. This time, the end justifies the means. "You owe me, Austin," I whisper.

I pick up my brush, tear off some paper towels, and wipe up some of the dropped paint. Beav steps in the residue and walks black paw prints through the room. I scoop him up, wiping his toes, and scold, "You are *such* a cat."

I photograph paintings I've completed since the last email, except for the one I'm working on, which is still too raw and embryonic, and email them to Gallerina, then resume working on the large piece.

Two weeks pass quickly, my time absorbed by the massive canvas. Gallerina's caller ID appears on my phone. I take a deep breath and answer. "I've reviewed your work, and I'd like to represent you," she says briskly.

Previously, I'd assured myself my paintings were personal, and I didn't care if I ever got signed to a gallery. However, a surge of accomplishment washes over me, and I don't care if my tone is calm or professional. I say ecstatically, "Oh. That's great news. Wow! Thank you."

"Come in tomorrow and sign our contract, and we'll discuss dates for a solo show."

We hang up, and I slowly exhale, then break into a happy dance that carries me, punching the air and whooping, around the living room, and up and down the stairs.

I catch my breath and call Trix. She says succinctly, "Let's celebrate."

Chapter Twenty-Seven

We meet at the bar in Fleming's Steakhouse, an upscale businessmen's hangout, with lots of dark wood and shiny bottles, happy hour specialties, and low lighting. Frankie joins us. We're sharing appetizers, and the bartender is pouring champagne when a familiar voice shrieks, "Julia! Julia!"

I cringe, then turn to see Marcy and her boyfriend, Gage. She is sporting an advanced baby bump, the rest of her rounder than ever. She barrels up and grabs me in a suffocating hug, then shouts, "Git!" as she shoves Frankie off his barstool and wiggles onto it, leaving Gage and Frankie standing. I make introductions. Gage makes eye contact, and a current of attraction finds my center.

Marcy dispatches Gage to get them a table, and she leans against me. "Can't sit at the bar. It's way too tempting to drink. See what we sacrifice for our children even before they're born?" She shrieks laughter then abruptly goes solemn and quiet. "So sorry for you, going through the

Austin horrors." She glances around conspiratorially. "Not to speak ill of the dead, but it couldn't have happened to a more deserving asshole! Ha!" She indicates her supposed sorrow with a dramatic pout. "How have you been since that bastard croaked?"

"Fine. I've moved out of the old house, got a new life. But check you out—pregnant! Congratulations to you and Gage."

"Ha-ha!" she howls. "It's not Gage's kid! I'm flyin' solo. This kid's daddy is Mr. Sperm Bank. One divorce was way *too* much, and one man *isn't* enough!" Her piercing laughter or possibly the subject of conversation attracts frowns from nearby patrons. Trix and Frankie stifle giggles.

Bewildered, I say, "But you introduced Gage to me as *your man*."

Flipping her hand, dismissively, "I always say he's my man, just for fun." She wraps Frankie in an embrace and rests her head against his chest. "Here's my new man…" She laughs again. "See how easy that is?"

Frankie has a mock-fearful expression. Marcy winks at Trix and lets him go. "He's all yours, hon." She turns back to me with a smirky smile, "Gage likes you."

"So if Gage isn't your boyfriend—"

She guffaws, "He's single! Divorced a few years now." Suddenly serious, she asks, "You interested?" She gives me an exaggerated wink. "What's goin' on with you, sugar? You hangin' in okay?"

"I recently got gallery representation, and I'll be having an art show soon. I'll put you on the invitation list."

She pats her belly, "My attendance will depend on whether little booger here, Jeeves, is behaving." She laughs boisterously. "That's what I'm going to name it."

Trix asks dryly, "You're going to name your baby, *Little Booger*?"

"Ha, that'd be amazing! But no, silly. I'm naming it Jeeves."

Frankie says, "Oh, it's a boy."

"Don't know yet." She blasts us with hyena laughter.

Gage returns, and Marcy snakes a pudgy arm around his waist and leans into him. He grins at me, and I reciprocate. Marcy says, "This lovely lady is going to have a big art show of her paintings."

Gage tips his head slightly. "I thought you did commercial work."

"I do, but I'm branching out." I say confidently.

In a surprisingly agile move, Marcy hops down from the barstool and waddles speedily away with her non-boyfriend.

Trix says with surprise, "Talk about being blunt. Holy shit. She hated Austin. I wonder if the cops consider her a suspect. By the way, *Jeeves*? Seriously?"

Frankie says facetiously, "It's what you name your kid if you want them to be a butler when they grow up."

"Knowing Marcy, she will name her kid Jeeves, especially if it's a girl."

Trix sips champagne. "Maybe she'll start a trend. So, Gage, from the awful party, who *isn't* her boyfriend. Hubba hubba, girl."

"Oh yeah, a real dreamboat."

"What's his story?" Frankie asks, getting back onto his stool.

"He's a reporter. Aside from that, I don't know much about him."

"A reporter." Frankie makes a one-eyebrow half-frown. "At least he had enough class to stay away during the Austin debacle and not try to take advantage of his connection."

"Yes, classy," Trix says, and I nod.

Frankie holds up his glass. "The winds have changed, Julia. You're in your element. Congrats."

We clink glasses and fall quiet. "Thanks," I say, sipping. "Well, I guess I better get some paintings finished."

"Amen," Trix says, and we leave the restaurant.

At home, I give the enormous painting a rest and study a medium-sized piece I had barely started at the old house, then abandoned. The subject is a view of Austin lying dead on the floor, wearing only jeans, stab wounds visible on his torso neck, and arms. I'd been dissatisfied and put it aside because the composition is static and lacking finesse. He's in the center of the canvas, so there's no tension, and again I'm unhappy with his face; his likeness isn't true. However, the basic drawing, executed by brush in burnt umber, is salvageable.

I paint sidewalk-gray loosely around the figure, leaving a white border against his form, a metaphorical chalk line. Next, I take transparent alizarin crimson and X out his face, letting the paint run, as I did on the massive painting, and I paint small Xs all over the crotch of his jeans. I'm tempted to fling red paint across the canvas, but decide it would be a too-obvious play on blood spatter. His X-rated pants are enough symbolism. Instead, I pour blue and green paint thinned with mineral spirits, along the top edge of the canvas to drip and run over the figure, then flick small random dots of red into the wet thinner to bloom. I set the painting aside to dry and go to bed with visions of my solo art show dancing in my head.

I'm agitated waiting till my appointed midafternoon time to meet with Gallerina, and I pass the time assessing the paintings one by one until finally, I walk to the gallery. As I approach, I have a whoosh of excitement and pride. This is my brass ring, right here, right now.

I recognize Gallerina from other visits to her gallery with Trix. She is in her sixties, slim and flamboyant, in a bright purple business suit, orange satin blouse, and coral lipstick, black hair up in an exaggerated 50s-style beehive, talking into her cell phone. She hangs up and turns to me, laying paperwork on her desk. We shake hands, and she says, "Welcome to A-Space, Houston's best gallery."

"Happy to be here." I smile.

She pulls a calendar from under the papers and flips

forward a couple of months. "This artist took a full-time teaching job in Paris, so his show has been canceled. If you can be ready in two months, that show can be yours."

Nodding vigorously, I'm practically vibrating with excitement. "Yes. I can be ready."

She studies me with a grain of skepticism. "You're sure? Most people don't realize how much thought and hard work goes into a show. Once you commit, there's no going back."

"I'm used to deadlines. I deal with them every day. Besides, I have fifteen finished paintings ready to be varnished, and one large one to finish. I'm also framing ten charcoal and pencil drawings."

Gallerina takes me paragraph by paragraph through the contract. We both sign and date the document, and I take a copy. Back home, I take time out for some daydreaming about my show.

Two weeks to go until my opening, I've framed the drawings, and I lay the paintings flat to sign and date them, then apply low-luster varnish to enrich color, even out dull versus glossy areas of finish, and protect the paint. I've adopted Trix's implicit declaration, that varnish means the piece is finished.

The only unfinished painting is the centerpiece of the show, nearly as big as the wall to which it's pinned. Various scenes appear to have been released from the depiction of Austin's murder as if ejected from a cyclone. Whenever I work on the canvas, my anger surfaces, and I plow into the piece with feverish desire and commitment.

Day by day, I vigorously apply layers—paint thinned and glazed, straight from the tube, brushed with large, small, stiff and soft brushes, palette knives, paint daubed in error, then wiped or scraped down in frustration, paint reapplied. Sleep is fitful. There are late-night calls to and from Trix, bottles of wine, and carafes of coffee. As I work, something takes over, and I give in. The painting is a living thing materializing under my brushes, rags, gloved and bare hands.

Standing on a short ladder, as I scumble highlights onto the depiction of shards from the smashed, skull-shaped bottle of tequila, the phone rings. The number is unfamiliar, but the voice is recognizable—Gage. He says, "Your opening is a week from Saturday, so I'm assuming you're very busy."

His voice has a peculiar effect: something sweet and warm, honey poured into my ear to travel along my spine. Oh my God, he's going to ask me out. "Yes, I'm in the final stretch, and there is still a lot to do, including hanging the show."

He pauses a moment, "I'm looking forward to your opening, but I'm also calling to ask if I could interview you for an article in the *Chronicle*."

Oh. Not asking me out after all. I regroup, recalling what Frankie said about Gage taking advantage of his connection, and I ask, "What would the interview cover?"

"Your paintings..."

"Is this about my husband's homicide?"

"If the paintings are tied to the murder, his death would be an element."

"Um… I'm not sure." The unpleasantness before and since Austin's death gushes back in: his betrayals, the relentless invasion of the press, the harassment, the scrutiny on television, the prying strangers dissecting my life, my searing embarrassment at their off-hand and off-base opinions.

He waits in silence and finally says, as if he read my mind, "I know the press has plagued you. I promise I'll be fair and restrained."

I still hesitate. "Gage, can I get back to you?"

"I need to turn this article in very soon. I've got a tight deadline." He waits again.

Am I misjudging this? He is doing his job, and I need

people to show up at my opening. Why not turn the tables, make use of the paparazzi and the press for a change? I say quickly, "Wait. I don't need to call you back. Yes. When?"

"This afternoon? I can be there in an hour."

I hesitate. "Can you make it two hours? I've got my gallery owner stopping by. Oh, and I'll need to work while we talk."

"No problem, but I have one condition." There's a smile in his voice.

"Okay. What is the condition?"

"That I buy you dinner."

He's asking me out after all. I laugh. "You're on. I'd love to get out of here for a while. I'm afraid I'm becoming conjoined with this painting I'm working on." We hang up, and a Cheshire-cat grin overtakes me. I wash up, do a quick touch-up on my face, and pull on a clean T-shirt.

The doorbell rings. Gallerina is a vision in chartreuse, complemented with purple stilettos and eyeshadow, and red chopsticks in her black hair. "Are you ready for your show?" she asks.

"Finishing the final piece."

"The photos and info you sent me indicate you have a good group of medium-sized canvases and smaller drawings, which is fine since most pieces need to be of a size to fit someone's home or office easily. However, it's good to have a large statement piece—something commanding, attention-getting—even if the painting doesn't sell. The gallery is huge, which can dwarf the work."

We climb the stairs to my studio, and Gallerina goes slack-jawed, staring at the canvas pinned to the wall. "Holy mother of invention! It's fantastic. Terrible and beautiful and wonderful all at the same time. That, my dear, is an amazing piece." After a few minutes, she turns her attention to the other paintings, taking her time scanning the canvases leaning against the walls.

I shake my head. "I'm not sure about the painting with the stab wounds. It's pretty graphic. I might lose my nerve and hold it back."

She holds the painting up at arm's length, then puts it down, backs away, and says, "That would be a shame. Your layering of color is interesting, especially the blues and greens. And I love the Xs. But, your call." She turns to me and says, "I've seen enough. You're going to have a phenomenal show."

"A reporter is coming over to do an article on my show. I hope that's okay. I probably should have run it by you before I agreed, but he just called, and he's on a tight deadline."

"Fantastic. You don't need to get approval for publicity. Just make sure your reporter gets the name of the gallery spelled right." She winks, laughs, and heads toward the stairs. At the front door, she grabs me tight and kisses my cheeks. Her cell phone rings, and she dashes out the door with it pressed to her ear, leaving me in a drift of Chanel No 5.

I sit on the sofa and bask in her first reaction to the large painting—her stunned expression and her praise, what any artist hopes for from anyone, let alone someone who has seen, dealt in, handled, and sold the best. Then there's the dead-Austin painting that she's in favor of including in the show, but I'm still not sure, and until I decide, I don't want Gage to include it in his interview. I go to my studio and shut the painting in the closet. The doorbell rings.

Gage. I take a deep breath, clench and unclench my fists, shake them out, then square my shoulders. My composure intact, I open the door. The impact, the pleasurable jolt of seeing him is undiminished, and we stand a second beaming at each other.

Agitation warms my cheeks, and I say, "Come in, please." He steps inside and puts out his hand. As we shake, he holds on a beat longer than necessary as he takes in my house. My gaze follows his. I wish I could see the place through his filter. Is the style comfortable modern, or too stark, fresh and light-filled, or under-furnished? Does it speak to who I am? But comprehension comes, that he can like it, or not—this is me, mine, whatever the décor conveys—and I shut down my analysis.

"How is Marcy? Has she given birth yet?"

He smiles. "She's got less than a month until her due date. She's the same old Marcy. Taking the pregnancy in stride."

"Does she know the gender?"

"Yes, but she won't tell. Although having the honor of assembling her nursery furniture, I can tell you there's a lot of pink in the room."

We both chuckle, and I offer, "Can I get you something—iced tea, water, vino?"

"No, thank you, I'm fine."

I'll say you're fine. I think, then, immediately hope I didn't say it aloud.

Gage surveys the main floor and says, "I don't see any evidence of your work. Maybe hanging your work in your home is like the saying '*a busman's holiday*?'"

I admit, "Yes, like the parable about the cobbler's son's shoes. My work is upstairs, this way," and I start for the stairs. I could do an impersonation of Mae West saying *Come upstairs and see my etchings*, but if the joke falls flat, I might not recover my dignity. Hopefully, everything I say to Gage won't have some flustered, unintentional sexual connotation.

CHAPTER TWENTY-EIGHT

As I lead Gage upstairs to my studio, uncomfortable thoughts crowd in: why do I trust him? Maybe because we met through Marcy, I assume he is a known quantity, but he might be as bad as the overwrought speculators on TV.

Or maybe my needy, lonely ego is fooling me into believing he's attracted to me, even if he's not. Am I giving a wolf in sheep's clothing access to my work, my environment, my reputation, and possibly my emotional wellbeing? Is he using me?

In my studio, I shake off my negativity and watch as he views the big canvas with a reaction similar to Gallerina, and I explain, "It's a montage of the dreams and experiences that had me sleepwalking."

I point out the elements—Austin as a knife thrower, the fire, the snake, the jack-in-the-box, bats, the knives and daggers, the tequila bottle, Beaver, the rip-tide, translucent blood spatter over areas, my revolver, dollar bills floating and vanishing.

I show him some of the smaller paintings and drawings. He comments on some and takes notes. Then, as if he's reading my mind, he says, "Is this all of them?"

I hesitate, but a perception hovers in my mind's periphery like smoke. I tease the concept closer until it solidifies and is identifiable as full disclosure. "There's a piece I was thinking of excluding, but I've decided it should be in the show," and I take the painting from the closet and relate the dream of killing Austin, the violence, the blood in the kitchen, the bats. "It's the dream the others were leading me to. This one was so vivid I briefly thought I'd actually done it."

Gage's expression is unreadable. He gestures to the suite of paintings. "They're a story."

"Yes, a kind of narrative."

"The dreams, the infidelity, the murder of your husband… How did you get through it?"

"It wasn't easy." I pull out sketches and the canvas of the ogre I call Sadness. "This wasn't exactly a nightmare. I was shattered. There are still some difficult days, but they get farther and farther apart, and hopefully will eventually disappear."

He steps closer to the large piece. "The tension in this painting is gripping."

"I owe my sanity, even my life, to my friends…and don't laugh, my cat. They never gave up, and their presence was, is, a reminder there will be a new day, and I'm not alone—a reminder to put one foot in front of the other and keep going. If I go through the motions of normality long enough, they'll blend into, and eventually become, my reality."

We fall quiet for a while.

Gage stares at his notes as he asks, "Do you miss him?"

"At first, I missed him. I didn't think I would after all the betrayal, but we'd been together a long time, and sometimes he still seemed present. Now, his absence is more like those amputees who still feel the phantom pain of their missing limbs. Intellectually, logically, I've accepted his absence."

"Do you still have dreams?"

"Dreams, yes, but not nightmares. They've stopped. And I no longer have the weird little waking fantasies I used to have, like the jack-in-the-box. Maybe the source of my sleep disturbance is gone."

Gage makes notes, takes photos of some of the paintings, and announces, "I've got what I need. Let's go and eat."

"I'll change clothes."

"Absolutely not. You're gorgeous in what you're wearing."

I look down at my jeans with holes that weren't ripped at the factory, and the color on my right thigh where I sometimes wipe paint from my brush, and my casual T-shirt, and laugh. "Flattery wins, let's grab a burger or something else easy."

He valet-parks at Brenner's, a place far too upscale for my work clothes, and I smile, shaking my head. "Are you sure about this? I might ruin your dashing, bachelor-about-town reputation."

He smiles. "You're funny."

Over dinner, we talk about our backgrounds and cultures, and the Houston art scene, which is Gage's beat. Fortunately, he's talkative since I'm only half-listening while I replay the interview. I still assume his article will be positive. Am I naïve? My story is controversial, perhaps infamous, given the press coverage. Could he be out to skewer the hack-artist? To pan my work, and report I'm a manipulative phony, fabricating grief to exploit Austin's brutal murder for profit, or worse, for attention?

He drives me home and reaches across me to open the door, and his nearness threatens to break out a feral desire that immediately fades as my earlier thoughts and reticence crowd in again. "Thank you for dinner," I say as I step out of the car. "I look forward to your article."

He nods. "It will be out a couple of days before your opening."

I call Trix and tell her about the interview and dinner. She comments, "Awesome. These days an artist's story is as important as their work."

"But there's more. I told Gage about the dream of killing Austin and showed him the painting of dead Austin with puncture wounds all over him. I hope I did the right thing."

"If the painting will be in the show, you did the right thing." She says, "Get ready. The news-locusts might be a plague at your door again."

"Fortunately, the press won't know about the show until his article is published a couple of days before the opening, so I have some breathing room till then. Besides, you never know, they might not care anymore."

Trix snorts, "Doubtful. Just in case, pick up some Paparazzi-B-Gone spray."

I laugh. "We should invent that. I wish I'd done a painting of it, like the Andy Warhol soup can."

"Now, get back to work!" she says.

Two days before the show's opening, I head to the gallery to assess the hanging space. The moment I'm through the door, Gallerina, in a chrome-yellow suit, knee-high magenta boots, yellow and pink dangly earrings, and hair in a bun, motors over, waving a newspaper. Her aroma is a blend of coffee breath and Chanel No 5. As she skids to a stop beside me and snaps the paper open, she says, "Have you seen *The Chronicle*? Look!"

"Oh, my God. Is the article in today?"

One of her staff waves the phone at her. "It's been ringing all morning." She says, "Your opening will be packed. Here." She slaps the paper into my hands and heads to the phone.

The title on Gage's piece is *The Knife Thrower's Wife* with his byline and a photo of me working on the large painting. I'd been unaware of him shooting it as we talked.

Damn. I concede the art looks good, and what the hell, so do I.

Trix arrives wearing black jeans and a motorcycle jacket. She points at the paper. "Look! You scooped the entire front page of the entertainment section. I should be jealous. In fact, I am jealous!" She punches my bicep, and I rub the spot, feigning pain.

I read the intro silently, then skip ahead, aloud: "'The artist, who has been touched by tragedy, blasts the viewer out of complacency with vivid depictions of her struggles. Woven through her art are her husband's infidelity, deception, and murder, and her depression and mourning. These images visited her in nightmares, and viewers will have to decide—is this series art imitating dreams, or dreams imitating life?' Holy crap," I grimace. "Is this good or bad?"

"It's amazing. Keep reading."

"'Her husband's notorious and tawdry homicide was a murder that gripped the media for weeks, a murder as yet unsolved, a case that has gone cold. The show includes a painting of a scene from a nightmare the artist had of committing the murder, waking to find him gone without a trace—no blood, no weapons.'"

"You're like a deer in the you-know-whatsits."

"No kidding. I can't figure out if Gage is pointing the finger at me or not."

"Julia, no one in their right mind believes you killed him."

"I'm not so sure Detective Wilson agrees with you. Shit, he included a photo of my least favorite painting that ironically everyone else likes." I point to a photo of the dead-Austin painting.

"I love that painting," she says, laughing. "What's the title?"

"X."

"Perfect title. Look, Gage did his job. Sure, he got the scoop of the year, but he also did you a huge favor. You've got a full page of ink here, more coverage than any artist I've ever known. Let's grab lunch."

On the patio at La Griglia, my phone rings. Bryan says, "You're on speaker. We saw the article on your show. We're coming to the opening."

Sarah laughs. "You don't know this, but we peeked at your paintings sometimes when you were asleep. Pretty crazy and creepy stuff, Mom."

"Brats!" I chuckle. "I should have known. I look forward to seeing you there."

After lunch, I spend the remainder of the day framing and wrapping the canvases in glassine paper for delivery. As night falls, I immerse myself in the tub, then, dried off, I lie on fresh sheets, watching Naples-yellow light from my neighbor's outdoor lamp splay leaf patterns across the ceiling. I run through the paintings in my mind, over and over, until resignation allows mercifully dreamless sleep.

The day before the opening, we hang the show, and the next day, there is nothing for me to do but show up and *be*. My phone rings early. Trix says, "There's something you need to know… I got together with Detective Reeves. Fortunately, as suspected, he's single since I don't do married."

"You slept with him?"

"No, it didn't go that far."

"So, sort of a date…how did you manage that feat?"

Trix laughs. "It was one of those *I chased him till he caught me* deals. I happened, haha, to run into him at the grocery store, and accused him, jokingly, of stalking me. I said my car was in the shop, and *of course,* he offered me a ride, and *of course,* I offered him a drink at my place. Straight-arrow guys like him, the artist's loft makes them feel adventurous like they're livin' on the edge. I kept the booze flowing, got him telling me his problems. Anyway, he said he and Wilson will be at the opening tonight. I debated telling you this because I don't want you to worry, but they think there's incriminating evidence in your paintings."

"What evidence?"

"He clammed up when he realized what he'd said. I tried to get it out of him, but no dice. I'm good, but apparently, I'm not that good." She lights a cigarette and inhales. "So, great clandestine hijinks, consorting with the enemy, and all that."

"You're like some kind of international spy or something. Thanks for the heads-up."

"See you tonight." We hang up.

I tidy and clean my studio, which looks barren without the paintings, but I can't shut down thoughts of what Reeves told Trix. Until finally, I say aloud, "Fuck it," and cast Reeves and Wilson out of my mind. I dress in specially chosen, artful layers of gray.

At the gallery, the big painting is visible from the front door. At a distance, the piece is a spectacle, and I'm suddenly viewing it objectively, as if it were painted by someone else. The energetic, almost manic application of paint establishes authority and power. The composition leads the viewer through the scenes, the dense black exploding into movement and color. I'm tickled by panicky excitement. Well, well, backstory or not, I can in all good conscience claim to be a painter, after all.

In the chill of the gallery, the staff wear black and set up the cheese and alcoholic inducements to loosen inhibitions and, consequently, purse strings. As I inspect the placement of paintings and their scale in the open and soaring space, Gallerina, in a teal blue suit and red stilettoes, approaches, air-kisses, then hands me a catalog with prices. She says, "Our former starving-artist prices have skyrocketed. Check it out."

The phone is being waved at her again, and she goes to answer. My notoriety and Gage's article have conspired to triple and quadruple the prices. From across the room, Gallerina winks at me.

One minute I'm pacing, surfing my phone, and examining the wine selection, checking the paintings are straight, killing time, and seemingly the next minute I'm in a crowd. There are friends, old neighbors, and strangers. Lucy smothers me in a hug, and the next time I see her, she is holding court with a flock of suburbanites. I thought the attention of the press had immunized me against embarrassment, but my cheeks go hot, and I turn away.

These paintings were private for a time and going public with my emotional revelations is difficult. Gallerina introduces me to interested buyers. The evening is everything an artist hopes for as I'm prodded for the meanings and symbolism of my work. Green "hold" and red "sold" stickers appear beside paintings, and the media arrive. The ever-full glass of wine in my hand speaks to the constant crush of conversation.

Trix arrives wearing what appears to be spiderwebs over a black satin slip. Her hair fluoresces under the spotlights, and her chunky silver jewelry gleams. She goes lips-to-ears with the downtowners, the glitterati, sharing, and extracting information. Frankie struts through the gallery basking in his insider knowledge, with hopeful lemmings in tow. Sarah and Bryan are suddenly present with friends who emanate a frisson of wonderment and approval, quiet and implicit. The press of bodies and smells of cologne, alcohol, and humanity mingle with conversation and blasts of laughter.

Then my nose is struck by a familiar scent with a locker room undertone like cologne over nervous sweat. Silence spreads with the smell. I turn to find Salem and Clayton.

Frankie is at my elbow, and he whispers loudly, "Oh my Jezebel! Gurl, what is she doing here?"

The twins are on my other side. Sarah cranes her neck to stare directly into my face and says, "Seriously?"

Seeing Salem before me is alarming. She had become flimsy and two-dimensional in my mind, but like the dry sponges resembling potato chips that swell into animal forms, she's suddenly 3-D. Is she here to confront me, intimidate me? Or maybe she's attention-seeking, her last hurrah. She's wearing a tight white dress and vertiginous stilettos. She no longer possesses the power she wielded at the company party. Tonight, she's just a woman who had big plans that backfired, and by showing up, she is again courting disaster. Brazenness is risky business, and risk either rewards or penalizes, no halfway. I suspect she'd like me to make a scene, but I play possum, quiet and still.

I turn toward Sarah beside me. She whispers through a smile, "Let's chat like she's not here. Don't look at her. Smile at me." Still grinning, she says, "That bitch, coming here tonight. She's pathetic."

"I guess she saw my write-up." We both laugh. I let my gaze linger on Sarah's determinedly happy face, return her smile, and say, "Thanks for coming this evening. I hope you're having fun."

She laughs. "Wouldn't have missed this for the world. Never a dull friggin' moment, Mom."

Undeterred, Salem hurries to us. Clayton is off to the side, staring at the floor. I again turn away as Lucy and several others intervene, forcing Salem to back off. Salem shouts, "I just want to talk." Reporters, sensing drama, draw near. Frankie approaches with a security guard, and Salem puts up resistance as she's led to the door.

Two familiar figures trundle past the window—the detectives. Wilson is in his usual discount suit with western accessories, but Reeves has traded his dung-brown suit in for black-and-tailored over a dark gray shirt with the top two buttons open. He exudes confidence, with better posture and a swagger in his step. His hair is grease-free in a more up-to-date cut. Trix may have understated what happened between her and Reeves last night. I nudge Trix, and she winks at me. As the detectives inspect each painting, the crowd resumes their previous din. My peripheral vision catches a flash of Salem's white dress through the gallery's floor-to-ceiling glass. She trips the uniformed security guard, and they fall together on the sidewalk, her tanned legs scissoring skyward, the commotion is like viewing a silent movie.

As I observe Salem, a squeal reaches through the din.

Marcy and Gage. His good looks dovetail with my lust, and he outdoes my previous impressions—a finger of lightning races through my chest. We hug in a way good friends might, but it isn't casual in the least. I haven't seen Marcy in a couple of months, and she's dangerously close to her due date. She deliberately crushes me against her belly, then laughs uproariously, and she and Gage go to view the art.

Familiar voices distract me from Salem's turmoil. The detectives are waving a piece of paper at Gallerina as they push past her. They are accompanied by uniformed cops, one of which carries a telescoping cardboard box. A photographer notices the police and leaves Salem to run to the new action. The rest of the press trails. The officers push back the crowd as the framed painting of Austin's lifeless body is removed from the wall and slid into the box. Suddenly the detectives are snapping handcuffs on my wrists. "You must be joking. Handcuffs?" I ask with disgust, "What's the charge, painting in the first degree? Being an artist in a public place?"

Wilson smirks, "Very funny, ma'am."

Chapter Twenty-Nine

Gallerina races to the vacant wall space with a huge sharpie and dramatically scrawls on the wall, *painting seized by Houston PD* as the paparazzi lap up the spectacle.

I call to Trix, "Phone Leibovitz!" She nods as Wilson and Reeves take hold of my upper arms and lead me to a waiting cruiser—the legendary perp-walk. Like every cop show, Wilson guides me into the backseat with his hand on my head. The driver is a uniformed officer, and the detectives leave for their car. The flashing cameras, up against the cruiser's windows, are blinding. Art patrons watch from inside the gallery, and Frankie, Bryan, and Gallerina emerge onto the sidewalk. Trix dials her cell, one arm hugging Sarah.

At the precinct, I'm Mirandized and taken to an interrogation room with a gray table and chairs and the expected camera high on the wall. The framed painting has been removed from the packing and is propped on a chair in a corner. Wilson, Reeves, and Leibovitz enter, and Wilson places a copy of the entertainment section of the *Chronicle* on the table. Lines of type are highlighted.

Leibovitz says with distaste, "Officers, the show is over. Remove the handcuffs."

Wilson complies, appearing not at all chagrined, as Reeves displays his newfound confidence leaning against the wall in an affected slouch. His transformation from choirboy to sex symbol is impressive. I wonder if he told Wilson about his visit with Trix. Probably not, since getting drunk with, and possibly bedding witnesses and potential suspects, even peripheral ones like Trix, is undoubtedly an abuse of power and a firing offense. I stare at him unblinking until he returns my gaze, and his ears turn pink. Did her loyalty to me just occur to him? Besties like us tell each other everything—but he needn't worry—not yet. His indiscretion may be more useful as leverage later.

Wilson says, "Ma'am, why didn't you mention any dreams of murdering your husband?"

I avoid the question. "You knew from the newspaper article that I dreamt of Austin's death, and I've been painting my dreams, but you didn't arrest me days ago when the article came out. Instead, you waited until you had an audience." Over the last months, I've traded my soft side for toughness, confidence, or maybe what's viewed as sophistication. Am I jaded or cynical? I don't want to lose my tenderness, but I won't be vulnerable and beaten down. Not anymore.

Wilson adopts a crooked smile of strained tolerance. "You're pretty cocky for a woman who is about to be charged with murderin' her husband. Not producin' this artwork of the murder scene is withholding evidence."

"So, are you claiming you murdered Austin while you were asleep?" Reeves wades in. "While you were sleepwalking?"

"No!" I nearly shout. "I didn't kill him, *waking or sleeping*!"

Leibovitz asks, "Evidence? In what way is the painting

evidence?"

"We'll get to that, counselor," Wilson says. His belligerent control of the interview reminds me that the perp-walk will exist on the internet in perpetuity, and people who don't associate handcuffs with guilt are mighty rare. Most believe cops have a compelling reason to arrest someone. The walk of shame is merely one drop of the pollution they can use to poison the minds of my potential jury pool. They can frame me, and when it comes to evidence, they can plant it, lose it, or withhold it, falsify paperwork, threaten or bribe witnesses, and influence the media.

Leibovitz interjects, "Detectives, she passed your polygraph—twice."

Wilson half-smiles again. "As you know, counselor, polygraphs aren't admissible."

"I get it," I hear acid in my voice. "Polygraphs are only acceptable if they suit your agenda."

Reeves' color has subsided, "Ma'am, did you at any time ever see your husband's dead body?"

"No, thank god."

"You didn't see him at the scene where his body was found?"

"No."

"You didn't see him at the morgue?"

"No."

"You didn't see him at the funeral home?"

"No."

Wilson says, "There's some mighty interestin' things in that paintin' of yours." He takes a printed sheet of paper—a copy of the coroner's report—and holds it up next to the painting. "This is the diagram of Austin Green's stab wounds. Note the patterns—three small punctures close together, and nearby, another single and wide one. That pattern repeats on his chest, neck, arms, and abdomen. He was stabbed quite a few times, forty-four punctures by the forensic examiner's count. Now, let's inspect your paintin'. You painted most of the wounds exactly right." He leisurely points out each wound on the painting and the corresponding mark on the diagram. "So, Miss Julia, please enlighten us. How could you do that if you never saw him dead?"

A trap door opens in my neck, and the blood falls out of my head. The room blurs for a moment. Compared to the coroner's diagram, the stab wounds in the painting are accurate. But how? I painted fast, not considering the locations or appearance of the punctures, so how did I know where to place the wounds on his body? Also, the injuries don't match my dream. In the nightmare, I stabbed him with long knives. If I killed him, what implement did I use to make those wounds? I mentally inventory my kitchen implements—meat thermometer, scissors, steak knives, carving fork, pizza cutter, ice pick—nothing fits. I can't fully recall the dream anymore. Had I held three knives in one hand and one in the other?

"What's your theory?" Leibovitz asks.

"Simple. The painting proves Julia Green killed her husband," Reeves answers. "She never saw the body, so to know the location of the wounds, she obviously inflicted them."

Leibovitz barks derisive laughter. "Any other evidence, detectives? Even you must realize how flimsy your evidence is."

"We're working on that," Reeves says, relaxed and confident.

Wilson adds, "Since y'all's painting depicts the murder in the kitchen, we're fixin' t'go back over the area, see if there's evidence we missed."

"I don't live there anymore. New people moved in," I inform them, and consider mentioning that the house was painted before I moved out, but they may accuse me of trying to cover up evidence. No wonder lawyers tell their clients to keep quiet. Anything can be incriminating.

"We reviewed our forensics. A tech took this photo." Wilson slides a photo across the table. It shows my former kitchen's travertine floor tiles. There are pale, barely-noticeable, brownish stains in a regular formation across the floor, becoming lighter the farther they progress into the kitchen. Wilson rocks back in his chair, clearly enjoying feeding the information to us in increments. He says, "Those are bloody footprints someone tried to clean up."

"They're small and not in the shape of feet." I declare. "My cat has been known to jump onto my palette, then run through the house. Those look like paw prints in burnt sienna oil paint."

Wilson falters and exchanges a glance with Reeves. I expect him to lay out scientific forensic expertise to justify his claim. Instead, he says, "We also have video from the Westin Hotel showing Miss Julia driving her husband's vehicle into the parking garage with his body in the back seat."

"What?" I exclaim. "I've *never* been to that hotel."

"I want to see the evidence," Leibovitz says.

With a thin-lipped smile, Wilson nods, "We'll get it to you."

"Unless my client is under arrest, we'll be going." Leibovitz stands, pats his pockets, and picks up his briefcase.

Wilson says, "Miss Julia needs to stay within the greater Houston area. Take that as an order."

Back home, I stretch out on my bed and stare at the ceiling, pondering, worried the detectives will construct a convincing scenario with circumstantial evidence, and I'll be put down like a vicious dog. But if they are correct, and I killed Austin in my sleep with no recollection, they should protect society from me. However, if I killed him, I'm back to my same old questions—why wasn't there massive blood spatter? In my dream, I'd watched blood pooling around him and spraying from the wounds. And according to my nightmare, the painting, and the coroner's diagram, he was stabbed a lot.

Arraignment day, Leibovitz picks me up. "Judge Judy time,"

he says. We park under a high-rise modern courthouse building, take an elevator to a wood-paneled courtroom, and sit at a table. The detectives are seated behind us on benches. Leibovitz indicates a table ten feet away, and says softly, "The man in the olive-green suit is Jake Forrest, the district attorney, and the woman is Mary Maddow, assistant district attorney. The DA's presence means your case is high-priority."

We stand as the judge, Judy Harrington, arrives and takes her place. She looks the part—no-nonsense, tiny, and stern. Leibovitz is on his feet, saying, "Your Honor, I respectfully demand Houston PD and the DA's office drop their showboating for the press, and release my client. They don't have a shred of solid evidence linking Julia Green to her husband's murder; no fingerprints, blood spatter, DNA, not even the weapon. Also noteworthy is Ms. Green's passing of *two* polygraph tests administered by Houston PD."

Judge Judy swings her gaze onto the DA. "What's your case?"

Forrest stands, a spindly ectomorph unfolding, bringing to mind a praying mantis, his green suit adding to the effect. He is balding with friar-fringe hair, a protuberant nose and ears, and a bobbing Adam's apple. Forrest and the ADA take my painting and the diagram of the stab wounds to the bench for the judge's scrutiny. She flicks her gaze toward me, then back at the image.

Forrest says, "Judge, the defendant recently had an art show with many artworks depicting her stabbing and killing her husband, Austin Green. Also, despite claiming to have never seen her husband's dead body, this piece of art by Julia Green shows stab wounds that match the coroner's wound-pattern diagram." He adds meaningfully, "She didn't ID his body when he was found, never went to the morgue, and didn't see the body at the mortuary, but she painted this painting, proving she committed the murder."

The prosecutor lets the judge absorb the evidence and

continues. "As you can see from the painting, the killing took place in the kitchen. There were partial footprints on the kitchen floor we believe were in Austin Green's blood. And we have determined two weapons killed Austin Green." He holds up two pictures. "One was most likely a three-pronged ice pick or carving fork like these, and the other was a butcher knife."

I whisper, "Those aren't mine. My ice pick is the old-fashioned kind like a pointed hammer, and my carving fork has two prongs, not three."

Leibovitz stands. "Judge, with all due respect, the police don't have the actual weapons, and they are guessing at what the weapons might be. Those pictures are from the internet, not from my client's kitchen drawer. Also, there is no DNA linking my client to those footprints, if indeed they are human footprints because my client believes they were made by her cat stepping in paint. The detectives went back after more than a year to test the stains and struck out, so they are speculating."

Forrest says peevishly, "The police have been thorough."

Leibovitz chuckles dismissively. "Your Honor, the detectives' case is entirely circumstantial. They have focused exclusively on my client and ignored other prime suspects with equal, if not more, motive, means, and opportunity, including Austin Green's mistress, the husband of the mistress, and the victim's enemies among his work associates. Their case amounts to nothing more than wishful thinking, or in this instance, dreaming."

Forrest leans forward, hands on the table, and states, "Mrs. Green is the murderer of her husband. We request she be held without bail."

"My client is innocent," Leibovitz says, exasperated. "The police have no basis for charging her, let alone pursue a trial on these charges."

The judge pauses a moment then says, "The wounds depicted in the painting are a match for the coroner's drawing." She addresses Forrest. "You're certain she never saw her husband's dead body, or the coroner's notes and diagrams?"

"Absolutely certain." Forrest asserts. "Only the police and the coroner had copies."

She says, "That's good enough for me. We'll see what happens at trial."

"Judge, my client has no criminal record, and she has ties to the community. She is not a flight risk." Leibovitz says, "There is no reason to incarcerate her."

Judge Judy says, "Anything else?" No one answers, and she states matter-of-factly, "Julia Green, you're remanded for trial. Until that time, you're under house arrest."

Terms of my house arrest are: I can have internet, cable TV, and phone, but no interviews with the press, no media or book deals, I must surrender my passport and my firearm (if I still had one) and I must not consort with criminals.

I'm stunned. Noises, time, and activity slow, and Leibovitz stares at me. He places my purse in my hand and steers me out of the courtroom. As we leave the courthouse, mobbed by the press, Leibovitz says close to my ear, "Just hold it together. We'll turn this around."

Outside, dark clouds threaten. The networks are out in full force, and my attorney addresses them on the front steps of the building. He says, "Houston PD and the DA's office will eventually come to realize and admit that my client is innocent."

A reporter shouts, "What about the painting she did, the one of killing him? We got a tip that the wounds in the painting match the coroner's findings." Huge raindrops start slanting onto the stone steps. I'm faint, and like a bobble-head doll can't keep my head still on my neck.

"She painted a dream. If you dream you've won the lottery, do you wake up rich?" Leibovitz answers, skirting the question. The reporters laugh in appreciation at his clever sound bite.

Wilson, Reeves, and Forrest stand nearby, giving their

own interview. Wilson is a down-home, simple-country cop, and the reporters are eating it up. He's getting the trial and publicity he craves. A reporter asks him if the case is solid, and he answers, "She ought to be scared as a cat at the dog pound." I resist rolling my eyes.

A reporter shouts, "Are you going for the death penalty?"

"That's the plan," Forrest asserts.

The rain starts in earnest, and the reporters hurry away. A uniformed cop drives me home in a squad car, straps an electronic monitor to my ankle, and leaves with my passport.

Chapter Thirty

Trix arrives bearing white wine. "I just caught a bit of a newscast, and the police have released the info of how Austin's stab wounds match your painting."

"That's interesting, considering how we can't get any information from the police, such as Clayton's involvement, but they'll leak info to the media."

"The way they're focused on you, they've got tunnel vision, for sure."

"This is surreal. I didn't believe my situation could get worse. But the DA, Forrest, says he'll go for the death penalty. There must be an explanation for how I knew where to show the wounds in the painting."

"I'll do whatever I can to help."

"I know, and I appreciate your support. Hell, you already went the distance with Reeves." We glance at each other, and I raise my eyebrows. "However, even if he told you what their plan was, it wouldn't have made any difference because Gage had a photo of the painting in his article. Oh, well."

"I have another date with Reeves."

"You're a trooper."

"Not entirely. I kinda like him."

"Thanks to you, Reeves is all Mr. Sexy-pants."

She giggles, "Hey, I'd do Wilson if it'd help your case. D'you think he'd keep his hat and boots on?"

"Oh man, that's a funky thought." We sit a while quietly until I say slowly, "Forrest asked for the death penalty. It's a public-relations tactic to warp public perception, make them believe I'm guilty for sure, and the only decision is whether I get life or lethal-injection. Now, to the public, life in prison looks like I'm getting off easy."

"Shit. Hey, I taped the news footage of your opening." She downloads the recording from her phone to my laptop. "Look."

The female newscaster's voice-over utters, "…and this is the scene at A-Space Gallery where Julia Green's show opened…" The camera tours the paintings, the crowd, the atmosphere. Then the picture cuts to Salem, standing before me until I'm swallowed by the gathering.

The next cut shows her expulsion from the gallery. The security guard hugs her, his chest tight to her back, her arms trapped, as he marches her forward. She repeatedly tries to reach up or behind to grab or scratch him, without luck. Then she hooks her feet around his ankles. He struggles to maintain his balance, which causes her dress to slip up. "How awful," I whisper.

Trix says, "Karma comes knocking and finds… Salem!"

The guard staggers forward, lurches back several steps, teeters in an off-kilter pirouette, and they both go down hard. She tries to stand but falls, landing a face-plant on the sidewalk, and as Clayton tries to help her up and arrange her dress, she shouts and slaps at him as her nose gushes blood into her cleavage.

Trix laughs. "It's like slapstick comedy."

"I almost feel sorry for her…almost."

The camera zooms in on Salem's hair extensions ripped off in the struggle. The hairpiece is attached to an elastic loop, and in the gutter it brings to mind scruffy roadkill.

I shake my head. "I always thought Austin had class."

"Guys get tired of gourmet meals. Sometimes they crave fast food. You're chateaubriand. She's a burger."

I grin. "You're hilarious. Judging by recent reports, he liked junk food a lot."

"Austin may have been a narcissistic sociopath, or whatever, but he was handsome and charming, and an alpha male, all the ingredients needed to attract a woman who was tempted to stray."

"And rich, since he had hundreds of thousands of bucks to throw around," I add, frowning.

"Check this out." Trix hands me a piece of paper from her purse.

Printed on it is "*A Narcissist's Prayer:*

That didn't happen.
And if it did, it wasn't that bad.
And if it was, that's not a big deal.
And if it is, it is not my fault.
And if it was, I didn't mean it.
And if I did.
You deserved it."

"Wow. That sums things up. At one time or another, Austin said exactly these words to me."

After midnight, Trix heads home. I start a self-portrait from my reflection in a window opposite my chair, wearing a bra, panties, and ankle monitor. Maybe this will be my next art show: as a prisoner, possibly a death-row prisoner. How do those dime store caged budgies and canaries keep on singing? In the sketch, I add canary-yellow wings to my back with a highlighter. This jailbird needs to somehow free herself.

Despite the bulky, uncomfortable ankle monitor, I sleep for nearly two solid days and nights, waking only for necessities. Day three, I wake midday with the sun streaming in through a gap in the curtains and hitting me in the eye, a karmic wakeup call I interpret as *get up or things could get worse*. The thing about house arrest is not only the isolation, but filling the hours. I shower and putter, thoroughly and systematically clean the house, and polish off any busy work I can find.

Trix calls and says, "Remember when Austin was first found dead, and all those techs came through the house? Before they arrived, I did a little reconnaissance and pocketed things from your desk that I thought might be sensitive, or that you wouldn't want deleted by a police techie with fat fingers. I want to give them back to you. Plus, I have some news."

Fifteen minutes later, Trix is standing in my living room. She produces three camera cards and the flash drive I found in Austin's desk. I turn the cards in my hand. "One of these has pictures of my garden that I took the day before Austin disappeared. One is an archive of illustrations, and the other has shots of the kids, just candid stuff."

"This flash drive has AG inked on the side, which I figured stands for Austin Green."

"Yeah, I already watched the video." I make an ugh-face. "Austin accidentally blocked the picture, but the audio was recorded. I'm glad there was no visual because the content was some sort of sex thing, and it sounded like he spanked Salem. Revolting." I shudder.

"Yeah, but did you listen to the end?"

"No, I couldn't stand the sex noises."

She plugs the drive into the laptop, fast forwards and hits *play*. There's the sound of static and some movement. Suddenly, Salem's little-girl voice says, "This was all supposed to be over by now. Bitchy should be wearing wings and playing a fucking harp." She sighs. "Too bad she didn't drown in the undertow."

I inhale sharply and gawk bug-eyed at Trix. She nods vigorously. Austin's voice follows. "That was so close and so easy; no weapons, no blood, just pull her off the sandbar. It woulda been perfect if those two assholes didn't show up. I was hoping all three of 'em; her and the dudes would drown. It woulda been even better, a major accident. It's what got me looking for a similar thing, an accident."

Salem: "Yeah. The pills woulda been like that, no blood, no weapons, but you fucked up and didn't give her enough. It wasn't easy to get those propranolol pills. Took nearly two years to collect them all. We're lucky my ma didn't notice her prescription was always low, and then you go and only use half."

I gasp, and Trix nods again, eyebrows raised knowingly.

Austin: "Any more pills in that wine, and it woulda tasted bad. She woulda noticed. At least when I did it, I was out of town so it wouldn't be connected to me. I need to find another riptide."

Salem: "Maybe at Galveston."

Austin: "Galveston, there's too many people on the beach. Someone would notice her struggling."

Salem: "Yeah, I guess. And you totally wimped out on the other one."

Austin: "The other one; you mean the pillow? She woke up. I woulda had scratches and shit, because believe me, she woulda fought hard."

Salem: "You're chicken. You either don't have the balls, or you just don't want to anymore. I bet you're still having sex with her." There's a slap and Salem gasps, then sniffles. "I told you not to hit my face. If there's a mark, Clayton will ask questions."

"Watch your mouth, or there'll be more where that came from." Austin mutters something unintelligible in an exasperated tone, then says, "You should be thanking me. If I'd actually killed her with one of your lame plans, I never coulda got away with it. I woulda got caught, which means you'd've got caught too."

Salem: "At least I came up with some plans. You're just coasting." She says with finality, "Well, you need to *off* her soon."

Austin: "Easy for you to say. You're not trying to *off* Clayton."

Salem: "I *am.* I'm gonna fry him with a toaster bath." She laughs. "I'll have to run an extension cord from another room because he put those safety outlets in the bathroom. Maybe I can do it somewhere else, like in his footbath-thingy, or somethin'."

Austin: "Yeah, rig that thing, so it malfunctions and fries him. I got a friend who's an electrician. He'll help with that for some cash."

Salem: "Then I'll blame the manufacturer and get millions in a lawsuit. A two-fer! I'll figure it out, but Bitchy is the priority right now. Try the pillow thing again."

Austin: "No. She might've told someone about waking up and seeing me there. In the meantime, she better not catch us together. If she does, she'll file for divorce, and there'll be no way I'll be able to do it. No matter how perfect I'd pull it off, I'd be in prison forever, for sure."

Salem: "Everyone at work already knows we're fuckin', so what's the big deal if she finds out?"

Austin: "The difference is that screwin' around is no biggie, but if I bump her off during a divorce, it'll be way more suspicious. Anyway, divorce or no divorce, I have a plan."

Salem: "What's your plan?"

Austin: "The less you know, the safer for you. I'll just say this. She's been real depressed lately, talking about not wanting to live." They both laugh.

The sound quits, and I've got a fist to my lips, my shoulders are hunched, and I'm trembling. I stare at Trix in disbelief. "I was married to a psycho. He…they…were planning to murder me."

"If I hadn't heard the recording, I would find it very

hard to believe. I bet when you were sick, and you had the wild knife-thrower dream, it was because they poisoned you. The dream was like a warning."

"The riptide. That was Austin's first attempt. Then, on the night he disappeared, I was sure he was trying to stage my suicide. The doorstop you gave me saved my life. But here's a question. The cops should have the incriminating soundtrack because the video was on Austin's hard-drive. So why didn't they arrest Salem ages ago?"

She shrugs, "There are about five minutes of sex sounds and ten minutes of indistinct chat before Austin and Salem talk about killing you. I'd say that, like you, once there was no visual, they turned it off." Trix pauses a moment and says, "Or… Austin may have deleted the video from his hard drive figuring the flash drive was the best method of saving and hiding the video."

"I'm stunned. They were going to kill me. It's surreal."

"I wonder why Austin kept the recording of the incriminating conversation?"

I shake my head. "Maybe he wanted something to hold over Salem in case she tried to blackmail him, or something similar."

"Makes sense. By the way, I probably should have run this by you first, but I leaked the recording to the press. Austin and Salem's murder plots should balance out the matching-stab-wounds leak. The average person can assess what he did to you—the affair, the stealing, the plots to kill you, and if they agree with the cops that the matching stab wounds mean you killed him, they'll hopefully view it as self-defense."

I shake my head in disbelief again, and Trix unmutes the TV. The female talking-head says, "Caught on tape. This clip was received from an anonymous source. Listen to what Austin Green and his mistress, Salem Kingston, had to say when they thought they weren't being recorded."

The announcer shuffles papers, and the screen turns dark gray. As Austin and Salem talk, their dialogue scrolls up the monitor, with expletives blacked out. Then it segues to a video of Salem being rousted from her bed and doing her own perp-walk, in a chemise and sandals, makeup-smudged, raccoon-eyed, and messy-haired, to the waiting cop car. Next, the skydiving attorney is interviewed. Salem has retained him, maintaining her innocence on charges of conspiracy to commit murder.

"Otis certainly has a tough case on his hands," Trix declares. "If he can find reasonable doubt for her, he's a freakin' magician."

"I thought I couldn't be shocked. But this...this is shocking."

"Hell yeah," Trix agrees.

"Austin's murder…there's so much I can't figure out. Wilson said they have me on camera driving into the Westin parking garage with Austin's body in the car, and Wilson is also concentrating on some bloody footprints in the kitchen. My mother was in my dream and said she'd clean up the blood. Nothing makes sense. They have no clue what weapon was used to kill him, plus he's been dead more than a year. Memories fade. Evidence gets lost or goes stale."

My phone rings, and caller-ID reads Leibovitz. "I just saw the news."

"This latest development, of Salem's murder conspiracy, does it change anything for my case?"

"No," he states. "First off, even if you had killed him, you didn't know he was plotting to kill you, so her plots are useless as a self-defense argument. Second, you're innocent, so stick with that. We plead not guilty and work to establish reasonable doubt."

"I had suspicions he wanted to kill me, but..."

"No evidence, though. As for your trial, the leak of the recording helps make you sympathetic, but the prosecution is still hanging their hat on the wounds in the painting being a match for the coroner's report. We must concentrate on that. For us, everything else is window dressing to build your credibility and develop reasonable doubt. My assistant will email you two videos. One is from the Westin Hotel's garage, and the other is from the gatehouse of your former subdivision." He adds, "Sorry, but Austin is visible in the parking lot clip, in the backseat of the car."

"Trix is here. We'll watch the videos right away."

"The cops don't have a clear picture of the driver, whoever she is, leaving the parking garage because there are no cameras on the exits. And she's not on the hotel lobby cameras. She either walked out, or someone else drove her out in a different car. Let me know if you have any interpretations or ah-ha moments."

Leibovitz's email arrives, and I play the Westin's garage tape. The picture is jerky. I say, "Good grief, black and white. The quality is awful."

Trix says, "It's like an old-time movie. I expect Charlie Chaplin to come around the corner twirling his cane, doing his wiggle walk."

The timestamp reads 3:47 a.m. as Austin's dark SUV pulls up. The driver leans out to take a ticket, and is unrecognizable, wearing an oversized man's blazer, leather gloves, black cowboy hat, and a scarf pulled across the driver's face and tucked under huge sunglasses. The traffic arm rises, and the car drives into the garage. The top of Austin's head is visible in the backseat, the rest of him covered by a plain-colored blanket.

Trix says, "I'd say the driver is a woman."

"Leibovitz thinks she walked out of the garage exit after she parked his car, but you'd expect the hotel to have a camera on the exit to make sure everyone pays."

Trix shakes her head, "No. I've parked there. The exit is blocked by a heavy-duty gate until you pay, but a pedestrian could duck around and get out." She adds, "Leaving through the hotel wouldn't work because presumably, the hotel has cameras all over the interior which would have filmed and identified her."

"Makes sense." I peer at the screen. "Everything the driver is wearing is generic men's wear. Dressing in men's clothes and driving to the Westin Hotel wasn't in my dream. I'm not getting any sense of déjà vu. That's not me at the wheel."

"Where does Wilson get off saying the driver is you, anyway? She's totally incognito."

"He's bluffing."

We run the gatehouse video, which is also low-resolution and grainy. Clayton pulls up in his white van, leaving the subdivision. The timestamp is 2:10 a.m.

"After meeting with Austin, Clayton left my house around midnight, but I saw him parked on our street. Wonder what he was he doing in the subdivision for over two hours? It's a long time to sit."

Trix sips wine and says, "Clayton left your subdivision about an hour and a half *before* Austin was delivered to the parking lot."

"But he's huge, definitely not the driver of Austin's car to the hotel garage."

On the screen, the night guard steps out of the gatehouse and talks through the driver's window. Clayton gets out of his van, follows the guard to the back, and opens the van's back doors. There's the shadowy dark rectangle of the gun safe and what are most likely firearms stacked on the floor. The guard peers inside, and the men bump fists. They spend a minute or so in what appears to be friendly conversation, and Clayton drives away.

Trix says, "Not much weird there."

"Except the guard doesn't usually stop people who are leaving, but I guess Clayton's looks and the van made him suspicious." I call Leibovitz and put him on speaker. "How Wilson can claim I'm the hotel parking lot driver is beyond comprehension."

"I agree," he says. "The only similarity is the driver appears to be female, but could also be a small male."

"Something else," I add. "While I couldn't have done it because I would have needed helpers, Clayton would too. Even if he's big and strong enough to have moved Austin and the gun safe, he couldn't drive both his van and Austin's SUV at the same time. If he killed Austin, I'd say Salem was the one driving into the garage. Another thing, the cops say he was killed in my kitchen, but I think they have decided that based on my painting. He could have been killed anywhere."

Leibovitz grunts. "Good point. I will definitely bring that up at trial. This happens all too often. Something is suggested and after that no one questions its veracity."

"The gatehouse tape is odd, but I'm not sure why," Trix says,

Leibovitz adds, "Our investigator just called. He said what's *not* on the tape is important. The investigator watched more footage than we sent you, and Austin's car never passed through the gatehouse to leave the subdivision that night. If Austin was killed outside the subdivision, how did his vehicle leave the subdivision from your place to wherever he was killed. Or, if the murder was at your house, how did his car leave your place to get to the Westin Hotel's parking garage?"

"The gatehouse is the only entrance and exit," I say.

"Wow," Trix adds. "So the cops aren't questioning how he left the subdivision or where he was killed, and I bet there's a lot more. I think Wilson desperately wants to be the one who solves the case and, in his eagerness, he has come up with a scenario and then he's made everything fit his storyline. He's got monomania, and Reeves, being impressionable and inexperienced trusts and believes him, and now they're feeding off each other."

"I agree. I saw the police interrogation of the gatekeeper," Leibovitz says. "According to the guard, nothing unusual occurred. However, they didn't ask him anything specific, or about Austin's car."

"Can you please send all the footage?"

"Sending right now." We hang up.

Trix says, "Maybe the gatehouse guy turned off his camera."

"Under threat from Clayton?"

She shrugs. "Threat? Bribery? A few free guns, maybe."

We sit awhile quietly, and I say, "I'm pissed. The cops must have confiscated the videos right after they found Austin's body, and they never shared them with the news media to see if anyone saw anything suspicious in the garage or at the gate."

I lean back and say to the ceiling, "I think you're right. The cops are fixated on me. And now it turns out Austin nearly murdered me. All the standard crime-show methods: drowning, poison, suffocation, staging my suicide."

CHAPTER THIRTY-ONE

Gage texts me exclaiming shock at Salem's arrest and an apology for the fallout his article caused. He hopes we can get together soon. I write back, *Not your fault. Nothing to forgive. Yes, I'd like to see you too, but you are a member of the media, with whom I'm not allowed to hang out. So under the circumstances, it'll have to be after the trial.*

Reviews of my show are breathlessly positive, some gushingly so. Gallerina's response was to increase the prices once again, and the show still sold out. She wants the painting back from the cops ASAP. I say a small thank you to the finance gods for the cash infusion because I'm sure I'll need every penny for Leibovitz's fees.

My gallery show is certainly a sales success. Time will tell whether the work is important enough to hold its value. The art world is one screwy planet, where suspicion of murder bolsters star power. Are there other painters who murdered? Caravaggio comes to mind, although I've read differing accounts of his life and crimes.

I sit back, weary. "My show sold out. Not sure I can follow up with another blockbuster."

Trix smiles wryly. "Don't worry. You'll do something great."

"I better start dreaming again." We exchange pretend-grimaces.

The morning dawns with a phone call from Leibovitz. He informs me my trial date is set to start in ten months. He says time is advantageous, to let lousy press and speculation fade from the jury pool's memory. While I wish the trial were only a week away, the ten-month timeframe makes it at least finite.

The ankle monitor's punishment is sensory deprivation. This gadget is an electronic chaperone, a modern-day dunce cap on the sit-in-the-corner offender; the adults' version of time-out, of the mommy-state ordering, *go to your room and think about what you did.* I'm benched, a dog on a short leash, and isolated by the media's invasion, which calls for drawn blinds, imposing a dusk-like dim. And I recognize this imposed status as similar to when the ogre I've named Sadness visited.

I fill time with TV, books, phone calls, and thumbnails for more paintings. My thoughts meander. I need to solve my mystery, but how do you figure things out if you can't go searching? The cops have not only shut down their investigation since they are certain I'm the murderer, they also aren't sharing their findings.

I can only venture as far as my small courtyard. As fall turns to winter and then spring, Trix brings seedlings for my planters, and as we head into summer, I mark time by their growth. Once the heat has descended, and the outdoors no longer beckons, the days pass in stiflingly similar succession. Finally, bored with sketching and reading, I give in to the urge to stretch out on the sofa and catch up on the grotesqueries of network TV. Again, the TV shows strike me as modern-day versions of old-time circus freakshows; all watched from the comfortable privacy of our living rooms where our vulgar fascination won't be judged.

Leibovitz calls and announces, "We have the list of witnesses the DA will be calling to testify. There's Clayton, of course, Salem, Lucy, Marcy, Trix." He runs through the list. "And what about this person, James Ward?"

Shit. "Jimmy Ward. When I was a kid, a neighbor's dog was killed. I was sleepwalking outside that night and woke up next to the dog, which had been disemboweled. Some kids said I did it; however, Jimmy and some of his friends were out carousing that night, and those boys had a history of trouble. I was blamed, but I'm sure I didn't kill the puppy. I loved that little dog." I hope I haven't lost credibility.

Leibovitz says, "Not good. But he's last on their list so he might get bumped."

"The detectives asked if we were going to use a sleepwalking defense. I saw a show on TV recently where a guy killed his in-laws while he was sleepwalking, and he got off."

"Absolutely not," Leibovitz states firmly. "There's no evidence you killed Austin, and there's no evidence you were sleepwalking."

"Right. Who do you have on our witness list?"

"Not too many since we will be cross-examining most of the major players when the prosecution calls them. The big question is whether you want to take the stand."

I say carefully, "Whenever I see a defendant not testifying, they seem cowardly or guilty."

"Give it some thought. There's time." He says, and we hang up.

The phone call haunts me. What will Jimmy say about that little dog and me? The cross-examination of Clayton will no doubt be heated. Maybe fifty bikers will storm the courtroom, guns blazing like an old-time western, mowing down Wilson, Reeves, and the bailiff, as the lawyers duck under tables. Then there's the question of me testifying—if

I do, will I win them over or fuck up big time?

Finally, the trial date is imminent, and Leibovitz is phoning daily. He unsuccessfully argues for a change of venue, claiming I won't get a fair trial in Houston. His motion is denied. Secretly, I am relieved. I prefer to be on my home turf, and given the sordid events, not subjected to the prejudices of small-townies. Then there is jury selection, which, on Leibovitz's advice, I don't attend.

Contact with reporters, including Gage, is still forbidden. With Trix's help, I study TV courtroom footage of other cases, researching what makes a female defendant unlikeable. The unlikeables' demeanors are brittle and remote, with rigid posture, severe suits, dark matte lipstick, powdered faces, stiffly styled hair, a pinched expression. I hope my softer approach to fashion and deportment works in my favor. I'm not kidding myself; this is a popularity contest outstripping any encountered in high school.

The jury is impaneled and sequestered, their autonomy curtailed, stuck until the trial ends, cut off from family, friends, the internet and television.

Day one of my trial, there are considerable advantages to not being incarcerated. I can have a familiar breakfast, and my wardrobe is available. I choose a powder-blue cotton shirt, navy pants, and white jacket; pumps; small earrings; hair down, shoulder-length and shiny; short natural nails; spare makeup. I hope I'm every-woman: approachable, confident, feminine, albeit with a deprogrammed ankle monitor, and a chauffeur courtesy Houston PD. In total, I've been cooped up for more than a year.

The hot and steamy wet towel of summer has been wrung dry and snapped taught. It's fall, crisp and bright. The wood-lined courtroom has a back entrance, and I join Leibovitz and a younger male associate, Andrew Smith, who is a preppy complement to my older, custom-tailored attorney. An easel and a large flat-screen TV with electronic boxes attached stand waiting to display evidence. *In God, We Trust* is in gold lettering with the Texas seal above the judge's bench.

The DA, Forrest, is turned away, talking to his middle-aged female co-counsel. The jury takes their places. I pick out some jurors I believe are Leibovitz's selections, the ones who would dislike Austin's character. I count a gray-haired church lady with her glasses on a beaded chain, a young hippie-ish woman I see as an idealist, and three women in business attire who might identify with my life.

No doubt, the prosecution favored the four fifty-something men. They are all wearing golf shirts and Dockers. I attribute every midlife crisis cliché to these good-ole-boys of Austin's generation. I characterize them as card-carrying Republicans and NRA members who will identify with Austin's he-man interests. I assume they married their high school sweethearts who are no longer interested in sex, they watch lots of porn, and they've cheated on their wives.

There is a young man who looks nerdy, and a woman I suspect is a lesbian—the wildcards. No doubt, there were people of color, and they were eliminated by the prosecution. I'd love a no-nonsense, sick-of-cheaters, outspoken black woman, and a reserved, tough, tiny Asian gal who is fed up with being underestimated.

Behind me, there's standing room only. The bailiff demands cell phones be powered off, and cameras are banned. There are sketch artists and reporters, including Gage two rows back. My children, the cops, and other witnesses are kept out in the hallway, untainted by testimony, waiting to be called. The jurors stare at me, assessing, and I make brief and hopefully unchallenging eye contact. I'm trembling, and attempt to appear pleasant and unafraid, but not cocky, and I look away to let them evaluate me at their leisure.

I know some of the jurors have already decided I'm guilty. Their judgment is in the squint of their eyes, their frowns, or their crossed arms, and I'm confident they lied during voir dire when they denied their bias, denied viewing news reports. Perhaps in daily life, they are ignored or marginalized, but now they have real power to get me fried by Old Sparky, as *the electric chair* was once called. I wonder if some are the news-groupies who stalked my house.

But they don't know that I, and my attorneys, will sway them subtly and thoroughly. Later, much later, they will try to pinpoint the pivotal item that caused reasonable doubt. But it won't be one thing, it will be hundreds, a gesture, a sympathetic glance, a witness's single word, a tear falling, that together, piled atop each other, will cause their certainty to sag, then collapse. All of that is what I tell myself as I sense them assessing me. Sit up straight but don't be stiff, be neutral but alert. Make notes. Be present. Stay engaged.

All stand. The judge arrives—not Judge Judy this time—she is sixtyish with a dark-brown home dye job leaning toward maroon, reading glasses, not much makeup. Be seated. Court is in session. The prosecuting attorney, Forrest, stands to deliver his opening statement. Three long-legged steps take him halfway to the jury box where he stops, straightens his posture, and pauses.

"Judge, ladies, and gentlemen of the jury, I am Jake Forrest, district attorney for Harris County." He stops, turns, and points to me. "That woman, Julia Green, is a killer. She killed her husband, Austin Green." He rests his hands on the wooden rail and leans forward, a mistake, as it causes several jurists who had appeared eager to back away. He scans the jurors' faces lingering on them one by one.

He continues, "And just who was Austin Green, besides the victim of a vicious attack and murder?" He steeples his fingers, forefingers on his bottom lip, then in an attitude of resignation, drops his hands. "Austin Green was a family man, a hardworking and caring man, the breadwinner for his family." I resist rolling my eyes. "He was a dedicated man who worked the same career path at the same firm for more than two decades."

Forrest pauses, then continues. "He was a sportsman who loved the outdoors, a man who appreciated the simple things in life. Not a perfect man by any means, but a good friend to many, a doting, generous father to his children, a man whose life was cut short by his wife, the person he trusted most in the entire world." He is humanizing Austin, and other than the headlines, which they may have forgotten by now, the jurors have no reason to doubt him.

"I know what you're thinking. Sure, the defendant appears to be harmless." He extends an arm in my direction, and the jury inspects me again. "And why not? After all, she was a wife, mother, and an artist, living a charmed life with all the trappings of the American dream." He spreads his arms wide, signifying the bounty of my lifestyle.

"The defendant had it all: two healthy and well-educated children, a beautiful house with gardens and a swimming pool, maids and gardeners, and an employed and loving husband." Clever, leading the jury to visualize a gold-plated mansion swarming with help, me a spoiled dilettante indulging in my hobby.

My frustration at his characterization of Austin, the inability to counter his statements, to have to sit tight and allow his portrayals, raises anger, and I force myself to appear unruffled. The jurors study me as I watch Forrest with what I hope is an expression of calm concern.

"...and on top of all that, she possesses a God-given *artistic talent*. Julia Green is a successful *artist*." His tone is outraged, as if I pigged out, leaving no talent for anyone else. He continues, "If you see artwork in a magazine or newspaper, or on packages of products, those drawings may well be her illustrations."

Forrest pauses, then shakes his head. "But—and this is important—she is not successful enough to be self-supporting in the style she desires, and so, despite all her good fortune, she killed her husband. Why? For money and revenge. We will show she has the three necessary ingredients for her husband's murder: motive, means, and opportunity. Her motive is twofold. First, she discovered her husband was engaged in a long-term affair with a married woman. Yes, as I mentioned, Austin Green wasn't perfect. He was flawed. He did stray."

I glance at the jury. Church-lady's lips are pursed. Forrest goes on. "But please, before you judge the murder *victim* for his infidelity, you must keep in mind that having an affair is not punishable by death. No. At most, it's punishable by divorce."

He slowly saunters the length of the jury box, running his fingers along the wooden rail. "Indeed, Austin and his mistress were very good at keeping their love affair a secret from Austin Green's wife, Julia, but she finally found out." He steps back slightly.

"You may ask, why didn't she simply divorce him? That sounds logical, but if they divorced, everything would be split fifty-fifty, and they hadn't been the most rigorous savers or investors, so she would be forced to become self-supporting."

I sit mute in the face of what can only be described as an unfair, biased, insulting attack. I'm aware, from studying courtroom drama movies and reality shows, that a defendant comes off as desperate if they nod or shake their head, trying to tacitly influence the judge or jury.

Forrest continues, "The next component to this murder is *means*. The victim was stabbed to death. We will show the defendant created many paintings featuring knives, stabbing, and blood, but most damning of all, the stab wounds in one painting match the wounds marked on the coroner's diagram. The defendant never saw her husband's dead body, yet she has accurately depicted how he died."

He pauses for emphasis. "And finally, there is *opportunity*. The defendant had ample opportunity to murder her husband. After all, she lived with the victim. And in an act of vengeance, she then led Austin's girlfriend to discover his mutilated and decomposing body. In the end, you will arrive at the only logical conclusion." He straightens and points at me. "Julia Green killed her husband for monetary gain and revenge."

Forrest sits down and shuffles papers. The judge declares lunchtime, and I'm ushered to a separate room with a guard at the door, and a ham sandwich, Diet Coke, chocolate-chip cookie, and an apple on a table. I eat the ham with its yellow mustard and the apple. Then back to court, the jury takes their seats, and Leibovitz is up.

He stands, neatens some papers, and closes a jacket button as he steps before the jury, allowing them to absorb his looks: medium height and solid, with enough imperfection to appear approachable. He clasps his hands before him, and there's tranquility in his expression that won't alienate my twelve peers.

Unlike the DA, he stays back from the rail and speaks in a modulated manner. Jurors stop fidgeting and lean forward to hear. He says, "This is a sad case. A man is dead, and his children, his wife, and friends are in mourning. There is no winner in this tragedy, just heartache."

Leibovitz glances over at the DA, indicating who he is about to discuss, and the jury does the same. He says, "The prosecution, District Attorney Forrest, wants you to believe the victim's wife has committed a calculated and cold-blooded act that benefits her, which is patently false. We will show how charging Julia Green with murder is lazy and inept detective work; that she is a convenient scapegoat for the prosecution and the detectives. Meanwhile, due to their obsession with charging Julia, Austin's Green's killer is loose in our city, free to kill again."

He clears his throat and continues, "The prosecution presented Austin Green as a hardworking, honest man. That portrayal of Austin is fiction. Austin Green cheated on his wife many times; he stole her hard-earned retirement savings to spend on his mistress, and he infiltrated his mistress's family, playing his mistress's husband for an ignorant patsy and pathetic cuckold. Austin Green was a liar, a thief, and a philanderer."

He steps closer to the jury and places his hands on the rail. "The prosecution wants to portray Julia as coddled and spoiled, living on a huge estate, where her every whim is indulged, and she needn't lift a finger. The truth is, like the rest of us, she gets up every morning and works all day, often seven days a week, running her own business as well as taking care of their children and home. Julia has always been more than an equal contributor to their household."

He pauses a moment. "The police charged Julia, even though they have no witnesses, no murder weapon, no DNA, no fingerprints, fibers, or hairs; in fact, no physical evidence whatsoever connecting her to the killing. Plus, not only do the police not know *where* Austin was killed, they don't know for certain *what* killed him. Their entire case is based on a dream Julia had, and a painting she subsequently painted of her dream."

He scans the jurors' faces. "We all dream. If we dream of eating chocolate cake, have we eaten chocolate cake? No. If we dream of flying, do we wake up with wings? No. If we dream of a crime, have we committed a crime? Of course not. Yet despite this, the police have overlooked other obvious suspects, including Austin Green's mistress's husband and the mistress herself. One can only ask *why. Why?*"

He crosses then uncrosses his arms. "Julia is innocent and stands accused of a crime she did not commit, and the prosecution's case is riddled with inconsistencies and is a case study in reasonable doubt. Julia is innocent. Exonerate her and send a message to the police and the prosecution to do their job, to do it effectively, and to not railroad an innocent person."

Leibovitz returns to his seat, and I watch the jurors. They're astonished, confused, miffed. Leibovitz contradicted virtually every point the prosecution made. Who will they believe? The judge adjourns the court. I'm shepherded through a back entrance, chauffeured home in a squad car, the ankle-monitor reprogrammed.

The phone rings. Leibovitz says, "There's a plea offer on the table of eight years with five years parole."

"No, thank you."

"Good."

"By the way, you were terrific."

"Thanks, Julia. I read *Lawyering for Dummies* last night. Sleep well. Tomorrow, the prosecution calls their witnesses."

CHAPTER THIRTY-TWO

My hope for a good night's sleep falls by the wayside. The Sandman stays away as I run through every nuance of the day. I wish for a transcript of the opening arguments. I sleep, but at 6:30 a.m., the alarm sounds, and it's as if I haven't slept at all. My reflection shows me puffy and exhausted, and I take five minutes to lay cucumber slices on my steamer-trunk eye baggage. I dress in a gray suit with silver jewelry, offsetting the cool tones with a coral blouse. A cop arrives, deprograms the ankle monitor, and drives me to court. The jury files in and is seated.

The judge swishes to the bench, and the DA calls Lucy as his first witness. Earl is in the courtroom as an observer. Lucy has toned down her style by adding a jacket to her flowing dress and tying up her hair. She is sworn in, and the ADA, Mary Maddow, takes over. Maddow strikes me as a fifty-year-old hardworking woman with little time, money, or patience for grooming and fashion. She has home-cut bangs, runaway eyebrows, and as her jacket shifts, there's the silver gleam of a safety pin at her skirt's too-snug waistband.

She runs through the preamble of Lucy as my neighbor.

Maddow: "Did Julia Green tell you her husband, Austin, was cheating?"

"Yes. Julia found out Austin was cheating with a woman from his office."

Maddow: "Why did she confide in you?"

"We're friends. Plus, she knew about my open relationship with my husband." A murmur swells through the courtroom, the onlookers hoping for open-marriage salacious details, and I'm thankful she edited out Earl's physical attraction to me.

Maddow steers the questioning back to my case: "What was Julia's reaction to his philandering?"

"She was unhappy."

Maddow: "Unhappy or angry?"

"Well, as you'd expect, both. But Julia wasn't freaking out. She was thoughtful."

Maddow: "What revenge did Julia take against Austin?"

"She only took revenge when he kept cheating after he promised he'd stopped."

Maddow: "Answer the question. What was her revenge?"

Lucy can't suppress a small smile. "She burned his clothes because she was sick of smelling the other woman's perfume." There's a murmur of laughter, and the judge bangs her gavel.

Maddow: "Did she take any other revenge or punishment against Austin?"

"None I'm aware of. Just the usual…made Austin sleep in the guest room." Maddow appears frustrated. If they were hoping my revenge would make me seem heartless and violent, it's backfiring. She takes her seat.

Leibovitz stands, shuffles some papers, and approaches Lucy. "Lucy, in your opinion, knowing Julia as you have for the last two-plus decades, do you believe Julia killed her husband, Austin Green?"

"Absolutely not. If anything, Julia was too nice. There's not a mean bone in her body. She loved Austin and hung in way longer than anyone else would have."

Leibovitz: "Now, Lucy, our DA, has talked about the huge house and cushy lifestyle Julia supposedly enjoyed. How many maids and gardeners did Julia employ?"

"She had the same maid service as me, once every second week, and she had a guy to cut grass. That's all. Even though she was working, she never even had a nanny for their twins."

Leibovitz: "Did she do things around the house herself?"

"Oh, yes. She did the pool and all the gardening and landscaping on their huge yard. She also did DIY stuff, too, like painting, fixing things and so forth. She was the household handywoman. She's one of those rare women who can be fixing the toilet at four o'clock then look like a million bucks, dressed up and ready to go to dinner at the mayor's home at six."

Leibovitz thanks her and takes his seat. Lucy blows me a kiss as she leaves the courtroom.

The judge orders a short break. Waiting for me in the anteroom is a doughnut and coffee. A uniformed officer remains outside chatting with random people who must spend a good part of their lives in those hallways. Fifteen minutes later, everyone files back in.

The bailiff brings Salem into the courtroom through a side entrance. Prison has given her four-inch black roots against her platinum blonde, but interestingly, her natural face has an attractive vulnerability that was lost under her usual heavy makeup. She's dressed in black pants, a bright pink blouse, and pumps. I surmise that the DA, to replace Salem's prejudicial orange prison jumpsuit, selected the clothes from her closet. However, while each article of clothing on a coat hanger would appear suitable for court, on

Salem, the outfit is very snug and sexy, with too many buttons open on the blouse, showing cleavage.

She is chewing gum like a horse, and the bailiff holds a trashcan up for her to spit it out. She inhales, then blows the wad past her lips like a missile. The thunk in the garbage can is audible, and someone in the spectator seating guffaws. Not exactly a demure moment.

She is sworn in. Maddow stands and smiles, and Salem reciprocates. Maddow says, "Mrs. Kingston, please tell us why you are currently incarcerated."

"I'm charged with conspiracy to commit murder." Salem's cutesy, breathless inflection brings a murmur from the spectators. "But I haven't had a trial yet, and my lawyer's gonna get me off." Interesting. She doesn't protest her innocence.

"Who were you allegedly conspiring to kill?"

Salem lifts her chin in my direction. "Her. Julia Green."

"Thank you. Did you have a two-year affair with Julia Green's husband, Austin Green?" Maddow is smart, getting the bad behavior out there, upfront.

"Yeah, like, more than two years, closer to three."

"Were the two of you in love?"

"Yeah."

"What was your time together like?"

"It was awesome. We went everywhere and did everything together. And we told each other everything, too."

Maddow says, "Do you know any reason Austin's wife would have killed him?"

"Yeah." Salem eyeballs the jury. "Our affair, of course. She was real mad."

"What did Austin's wife do in her anger?"

"She burned Austin's clothes, and when we were out of town, she emptied his bank accounts, cut off his credit cards and his phone, and she had his car repo'd." She dabs at her eyes. Chuckles and surprise ripple through the courtroom at this additional facet of the comeuppance of which Lucy hadn't spoken. "Poor Austin. It was so horrible."

Not as horrible as having you mess up my life, I think. Is the ADA successfully characterizing me as violent and unpredictable, unforgiving, and vengeful? Even so, the flip side is that Salem's presence—her looks, her voice, her attitude—is eroding sympathy for Austin.

Salem ads with a whine, "And then Austin was murdered. And I found his dead body!" Maddow thanks her for her testimony and returns to her table.

Leibovitz approaches Salem and says without preamble, "Why did Julia do those things to Austin's stuff?"

"Because we still saw each other after he told her we broke up." Every cheated-on woman in the room, no doubt, thoroughly related to me in that moment.

Leibovitz: "He promised Julia he'd break up with you, but you and Austin were still having sex and spending Julia's money, correct? The money he stole from their savings?"

Salem pouts, "It was his money too." A low *oooh* sound skims the spectators, and the prosecution slumps slightly.

"When you were conspiring to murder Julia, were you also conspiring to murder your husband?"

"No. I said I would, but I wasn't going to."

Leibovitz: "Ah. So, you lied. Why did you say that if it wasn't true?"

"Because I wanted Austin to kill his wife." A collective gasp.

Leibovitz: "So, you were manipulating him?"

"Yeah. I mean, no. Now you're getting me mixed up."

Leibovitz: "Did he buy you expensive gifts, take you to five-star hotels?

"Yeah." Smiling now.

"He even got you hired where he worked, didn't he?"

"Yeah."

I have a moment of rage so intense I'm scared it will show.

I pull out a tote I'd stashed. The stink wafting from the bag makes me gag, but undaunted, I stick my hand into a slimy mass and lift out rotten eggs and tomatoes. I stand and throw handful after handful at Salem. The eggs break open, the reeking black yolk and foul, moldy tomatoes sliding over her hair, her face, and neck, into her cleavage, soaking her blouse, the stench making her shriek and retch... There, much better. I haven't had one of those quick fantasies for a while. They are certainly liberating.

Leibovitz: "Why did Austin take up with you?"

She turns her gaze on me and says, "Because his wife was a major bitch." I give her a level stare, calm and blank.

Leibovitz: "Unlike you. You aren't bitchy, are you, Salem? You're fun and sexy, right?"

"Yeah."

Leibovitz: "Did you have a friendship with Austin's wife?"

"No."

Leibovitz: "So what you know about Julia's bitchiness and so forth are strictly what Austin told you?"

"Yeah. We nicknamed her *Bitchy.*"

Leibovitz: "Salem, what if he was lying to get you to have sex with him?"

"They weren't lies."

Leibovitz: "How do you know?"

She tips her head to one side. "I just know."

Leibovitz: "But didn't he break up with you?"

"He said I had to leave my family." She drops her chin and studies her lap a minute.

Leibovitz: "Why?"

"I don't know."

Leibovitz: "Come on, Salem, you know why."

She looks up again and glances at the jury. "Austin said sneaking around with a married woman with kids was dumb if he's single. It wasn't fair."

Leibovitz: "Because you would lose the cash, the gifts, the trips, and probably even your job. Being dumped made you really angry. Right, Salem?"

"Yeah."

Leibovitz: "So, you and Austin had a violent fight?"

"Okay, so we fought." She stares into the middle distance.

Leibovitz: "It was a bad fight, wasn't it?"

"Yeah, pretty bad. So what?"

Leibovitz: "Do you remember Marcy, from work? Marcy said you hit and scratched Austin. You broke his computer and a framed photo of Julia and his kids. She said the police were called."

"You make it sound worse than it was." She gazes over the jurors' heads.

Leibovitz: "Okay, Salem, stay with me here…" She returns her stare to him. "So, Austin was breaking up with you, and you fought. Were you outraged?"

Salem shrugs. "Yeah, sure. I was super pissed."

Leibovitz: "Want to know what I think?" She stares at him as he continues, "You killed Austin in a rage because he was dumping you, didn't you, Salem? And your husband helped you move his body, and he stole Austin's firearms. That's what really happened, isn't it?"

"No—" she starts, but he cuts her off.

"The prosecution has a film clip of a woman, driving Austin's car with him dead in the backseat. She's driving into the Westin Hotel's parking garage. You were driving, weren't you, Salem? Then, because nobody found his body for days, you finally had to pretend you found him." The spectators hold their collective breath hoping for a Perry Mason moment.

"No! I never drove him anywhere. I didn't kill him. I loved Austin!" She sobs, but there are no tears. "That's not me. I'm being framed."

"Framed?" Leibovitz shakes his head derisively. "That's all for this witness."

Both prosecutors slowly sink in their seats like inflatables that have sprung leaks.

Reporters rush from the room, phones out, and dialing.

Chapter Thirty-Three

The judge calls a recess. In the breakroom, Leibovitz says, "Prosecution just added a witness to the list. His name is Mr. Whitmeyer. I gave permission." He raises his eyebrows, imploring information.

"I have no idea who he is. The name doesn't ring a bell."

After the break, the jury takes their seats, and the prosecution calls Mr. Whitmeyer. A young, groomed, and attractive man enters. He is thirty-something and wearing gray Armani over a black T-shirt, buffed leather shoes, silver-buckled belt. Who is he? And then it dawns. *Oh, my effing God...* Eric. The change in appearance from rough-around-the-edges to handsome-polished is remarkable. How did the detectives find him, and why?

Leibovitz regards me pointedly, questioningly. I whisper in his ear, "Trix and I went to a blues club, where I met him, then we went to a house party. We kind-of fooled around, then I never saw him again. We were pretty drunk and stoned, and he looked different, way more casual. I'm sorry to blindside you." I hope I'm not losing credibility in Leibovitz's eyes.

Leibovitz whispers, "No problem." He stands and says, "Judge, I'd like to bring to the court's attention that this witness was only added this morning."

The judge looks over her glasses. "Do you object to this witness?"

"No, Judge, but I'd like to reserve the right to redirect at a future time if necessary."

She says, "Granted."

He sits down and whispers, "Did your friend Trix know this guy?"

I cast my mind back to that night. "Yes. They move in the same circles," I say, cautious not to overstate.

Eric is sworn in. Forrest stands, staying behind his table, appearing irritated, maybe still smarting from the Salem debacle. He asks, "What line of work are you in, Eric?"

"Some modeling, acting, personal training, a little guitar playing, and singing. Whatever gig comes up."

"Do you know the defendant, Julia Green?" Forrest's delivery is clipped.

Eric observes me with a small smile. "I only met her once at the Big Easy—it's a blues bar."

"When you met her, were you dressed as you are now?"

"Nope. I wear jeans to a place like the Big Easy. It's kind of a dive, but with good live music."

Leibovitz whispers, "They coached him. Something's off, but I'm not sure what."

Forrest says, "I see. Eric, could you please remove your jacket?" Eric does as requested, revealing his snug T-shirt. There's a current of appreciation through the women. "Would you also be so kind as to remove your shirt?" Eric seems confused, and the judge asks Leibovitz if he objects.

Leibovitz says, "If the witness agrees, it's all right with

us." He sits and whispers, "I'm pretty sure they asked him to dress the same as when you met him, and he ignored the request. They want to portray you as going with any grubby jerk, but he showed up looking great."

Eric shrugs, and reaching behind his neck, the way cool guys do in movies, pulls off his T-shirt, exposing his wall-to-wall tattoos. I resist assessing the jury. The DA, sounding optimistic, says, "Thank you. You can get dressed. Oh, and Eric, is there anything else different about your appearance?"

"Maybe I wasn't shaved." Eric smiles at the jury. "Hey, I dress for the occasion. Today, I'm in court, so I wear this suit—"

Forrest cuts him off, "Please relate how you met Mrs. Green."

"Julia and me, we had a couple drinks and danced." His smile has expanded, and he focuses his gaze on me. Trying not to respond is difficult, so I scribble notes.

"Then what happened?"

"We went to a house party, got pretty wasted, and had sex." Something, energy or electricity zips through the room. I hope I'm not about to lose Gage. "Well," he corrected, "I should say I had sex, but Julia didn't."

"What does that mean, Eric?"

"It means Julia wasn't up for sex, so I gave myself a handjob. She didn't know what I was doing until I was nearly finished." I blush, and there's nowhere to hide.

"Did you know she was married?"

"I didn't care."

"That's not what I asked. Did you know Julia Green was married?"

"Yes. She was wearing a wedding ring, not hidin' it. And y'know, she *looks* married, healthy and clean, like she takes care of herself. No skank in that gal. I like that."

The prosecutor says, "That's all for this witness." Appearing satisfied, he heads back to his table.

Leibovitz stands and strides to Eric. He says, "Eric—

can I call you Eric?"

"Sure."

"Eric, when you met Julia at the Big Easy and had drinks and danced, was she there by herself?"

"No, she was with Trix."

Leibovitz: "Let the record reflect that *Trix* is Beatrix Donohue, a longtime female friend of the defendant." Leibovitz pauses a moment. "Eric, did you already know Julia's friend, Trix?"

"Sure. I've seen Trix around plenty, and we've hung out together before. I've been to her parties and whatnot."

Leibovitz: "So, Julia wasn't out by herself, trolling for sex."

Forrest: "Objection, leading the witness."

The judge responds, "Sustained."

Leibovitz: "I'll rephrase. In your opinion, was Julia out on the town by herself that night trolling for sex?"

Forrest: "Objection. Calls for speculation."

The judge sighs, "I'm allowing the question. Sit down, counselor." Forrest sits and doodles in his notepad, his Adam's apple bobbing a few times, undoubtedly anxious the jury might not judge me a slut.

Leibovitz: "I'll repeat the question. In your opinion, was Julia out by herself that night trolling for sex?"

"No. It was just a girls' night out."

Leibovitz: "Did Trix go with you and Julia to the house party after the Big Easy?"

"Yes. There's no way Julia would've gone without a girlfriend." Forrest gets partway out of his seat, then changes his mind and sits down.

Leibovitz: "Was it a good party? You said you got somewhat wasted."

"It was fun. Especially since Julia and me, we almost hooked up."

Leibovitz: "You said you knew she was married?"

"When Julia went to the restroom, Trix said Julia's husband was a jerk who was screwing around, and they were getting divorced."

Forrest jumps up. "Objection, hearsay."

The judge says, "Overruled. I'll allow it."

Leibovitz: "Eric, when the news stories about Julia's husband's murder came out, did you follow the case in the media?" Leibovitz turns away from Eric, observing the courtroom.

"Totally. Who *didn't* follow it? Besides, I felt like I knew Julia."

Leibovitz: "Why did the prosecution call you as a witness?"

Forrest is on his feet. "Objection, speculation."

The judge sounding irritated, says, "Counselor, you brought this witness. I'll allow it."

Leibovitz repeats the question, and Eric says, "Um…for character assassination?"

Leibovitz: "And whose character are you supposed to assassinate?"

Eric glances at me, nodding. "Julia's character."

Leibovitz: "How did the prosecution find you, Eric?"

"Yeah. Seriously random, right? There's this gal, calls herself Euphoria. She's this old, crazy punk chick, and small world, she's one of Salem's five billion friends on Facebook. Cops can access your Facebook no matter how private you make it. The detectives searched the Facebook friends' pages of Salem and found Euphoria. She posted a selfie from that night at the Big Easy. Euphoria does this thing where she jumps on a guy and takes a selfie. She had jumped on me. Julia was in the background of her selfie, and we got tagged. The detectives got in touch with Euphoria, then found me, and here I am."

Damn social media. Damn phone cameras. The cops were probably hunting for dirt on Salem or her husband by searching her Facebook friends, and they found my one dubious evening out, the only person who could besmirch my character, my reputation as a faithful, hardworking wife. Eric is excused and winks at me as he leaves the witness stand, avoiding eye contact with the DA. I close my eyes and inhale, and my shoulders unknot. While we didn't exactly score a victory, I'm aware it could have been much worse.

After some shuffling of papers and whispered collaboration at the DA's table, Bryan is called, and my shoulders and neck bunch painfully again. I say to Leibovitz, "Why on earth are they calling Bryan?"

"Bryan admitted under questioning by the police that he hacked Austin's computer, and anything personal about you they want to ferret out, he's the most likely to know."

"Are they going to call Sarah?"

"No. Bryan knows more about hacking than Sarah."

All eyes are on the door, and I sigh with relief at Bryan's appropriate attire: black jeans, a white shirt with a buttoned-down collar, skinny black tie, leather shoes. Maddow has Bryan introduce and identify himself as my son, and she approaches the witness stand.

Maddow: "Bryan, did you ever see your mom kill anything?"

"My mom isn't any good at killing stuff, not even palmetto bugs, or spiders, or fire ants." I notice he left out the snake, and I say a silent thank you.

Maddow: "Thank you. Did your mom have anything to do with your dad's murder?"

"No. She didn't do it."

Maddow: "How can you be so sure?"

"I know my mom."

Maddow closes in on the witness stand, trying to be chummy. "Bryan, I understand you are trained as an IT specialist, which means you can hack computers. Is that true?"

"Yes," Bryan says.

Maddow: "Did you ever hack your mother's or father's computers?"

"I only hacked Mom's a couple of times, pretty boring stuff. All YouTube cats and art stuff. Dad's was more fun. I checked his email, saw what porn he's into, stuff like that."

The audience chuckles. My eyebrows rise.

Maddow: "Bryan, did you see anything on your mother's computer to suggest she might have had something to do with your dad's disappearance and murder?"

Bryan says emphatically, "No. I told you; she didn't do it."

Maddow: "What did you find on your father's computer?"

"There were hotel bookings, airfare, for him and his girlfriend."

Maddow: "So, Bryan, did you ever confront your dad?"

"Yeah. And he gave us anything we wanted as hush money." He pauses, looks my way, and says, "Sorry, Mom." His attention back on the ADA, he says, "Then we started seeing things on his computer that were totally jacked."

Maddow: "What was he doing?"

"Dad and that chick were into swinging, and they'd hook up with creeps from the personals."

Optimism emanates from the prosecution. While Bryan is discrediting Austin, he is adding to my motive. My hands become clammy.

Bryan continues, "Plus, they belonged to a swingers' club that had, like, orgies at expensive hotels, not only in Houston, but Vegas, New York, and Miami. They made a bunch of sex vids with other people, not to mention *lots* of themselves, and they even downloaded them to the website, *Porn Dog*."

Austin saw himself as a porn star? If I'd found this out when I realized he'd been cheating, Salem could have had him. We would have been *finito*.

Maddow radiates confidence. She says, "Did your mom know of Austin and Salem's swinging and so forth?"

"Not the swinging, but right near the end, she found out he was cheating."

"How did your mom react, Bryan?"

"She wanted to save their marriage, but if he kept cheating, she wanted a divorce."

Maddow falters. She ambles to her table and pretends to consult notes, but she's unnerved.

Leibovitz whispers, "Lawyering 101: Don't ask a question if you don't know the answer. What Bryan said weakened your motive."

"Was that in the *Lawyering for Dummies* book?" I whisper, and he smirks.

Maddow regroups. "How do you know she had no knowledge of his swinging and so forth?" Her voice holds a flicker of desperation.

"Easy. By reading his email. The day my mom figured out he was cheating, my dad emailed his girlfriend telling her what happened, and they even met up again on the same night he promised my mom he'd never see her again."

Maddow: "How did your dad describe your mom finding out?"

"He said my mom found an expensive ladies' watch he'd bought, and she thought it was for her. Then she saw that woman wearing it at his company party."

Maddow: "Did it make your mom angry?"

"It made her upset. Anger issues were my dad's specialty."

Maddow: "Yes. Betrayal would make anyone upset. Thank you, Bryan. That's all for this witness." She turns and begins to walk to her seat.

Bryan says loudly and defiantly, "You guys have the wrong person! My mom is innocent." Maddow freezes, cringing as if a rock had been thrown at her back.

Leibovitz waits until the courtroom settles. He says, "Bryan, I'm sure this is difficult for you. I'm sorry for the loss of your dad." Bryan sighs, and Leibovitz says, "I only have a few questions. Did you hack Salem's or her husband Clayton's computer?"

"Yes." The prosecution table sits up, surprised, and taking notice.

Leibovitz: "What did you find?"

"I checked their email and browsing history, stuff like

that."

Leibovitz: "What was on Salem's computer, Bryan?"

"I found some interesting stuff, but probably nothing the cops don't already know since they've got techs who've had months to dig around in their hard drives."

Leibovitz: "Such as?"

"Salem surfed how to kill people." Excitement washes through the courtroom. "But as I said, the cops probably already know that."

Leibovitz: "What about Clayton's computer?"

"Getting into his computer took a while, but I found out he watched Salem and my dad's home-baked porn on the Porn Dog website." The prosecution whisper and shuffle paper.

Leibovitz: "When did Clayton watch their videos?"

Bryan says, "He watched them off and on, but he binge-watched them the same afternoon he came over to our house, the night my dad disappeared. I told my dad to be careful, but he..." Bryan stops. Tears emerge, and he wipes his eyes. Leibovitz thanks Bryan and sits down.

Forrest stands. "Re-cross, Judge?"

She nods. "Yes."

Forrest talks from behind his table. "Bryan, why didn't you tell the police you hacked Clayton Kingston's computer?

Bryan says, "No one asked."

Forrest: "Why didn't you inform the police Clayton had seen the porn of his wife with Austin Green, *just hours before* he met with Austin, and Austin disappeared?"

"I just told you. No one asked."

Forrest: "But why didn't you volunteer the information? Withholding evidence is a crime."

Bryan snickers, "The cops had Clayton's computer and a bunch of techs to hack it, so they should've had this info. Besides, you're acting like we were a team with the detectives. The cops weren't sharing; we had to find out everything by ourselves."

Deflated, Forrest takes his seat. Bryan is excused. He waves to me as he leaves the courtroom. My head is reeling. Clayton knew? The courtroom is awash in excitement as reporters push through the exit doors. The judge calls a break for lunch.

I ask Leibovitz, "With this evidence, are they arresting Clayton?"

Leibovitz phones Detective Wilson. When he hangs up, he says, "They're sticking with the theory you killed him. He said Clayton has an alibi."

"My God, they're ridiculous."

Back in the anteroom with the muted TV still running crime shows, a turkey-cheese-white-bread sandwich in a plastic clamshell is delivered, and I have an hour to think about the morning's testimony. There was Salem with her twisted logic, then the oh-my-god moment of Eric's appearance and how Forrest had him disrobe, and Bryan and his hacking.

I sit back in my chair, and the bloody footprints in the kitchen come to mind. I'm surprised the ADA didn't ask Bryan about them. Maybe they were tested and found it wasn't blood after all. Then there was Bryan's big revelation—Clayton knew of Salem and Austin's affair.

I pause. Or did he? Wilson claims Clayton has an alibi. If that's true, did Bryan lie, planting reasonable doubt, knowing he could deliver the best news tidbit of the day and the prosecution wouldn't be able to recover? Bryan has told some nose-stretchers before. I wouldn't put it past the twins to cook up one perfect lie to fit the line of questioning about hacking computers, then drop the bomb and let the explosion happen as it may.

Can Bryan be charged with perjury? On the other hand, Clayton came to visit, and Austin died, so maybe what he said is true. If so, when did he find this info? If he hacked Clayton's computer's search history months ago surely he would have told me, although he may have only done this recently since even deleting one's search history doesn't get rid of it. I still wonder how Austin's murder went down, and who Clayton's helper was.

Chapter Thirty-Four

After pondering Bryan's testimony, I nibble the turkey and cheese sandwich which tastes like refrigerator, as I flip through a magazine with endless shots of people on the red carpet. The television shows a banner proclaiming *Ripped from the Headlines*, and photos rotate of our whole cast of characters, including the detectives. I recorded this show and watched it time and again when I was depressed. It makes sense that they would run this episode while my trial is in progress. However, it does seem weird to have it on in the courthouse, but since it's not in view of the jury, I suppose they aren't being influenced.

In the fridge, there's leftover morning coffee. I pour a cup and add half-and-half, sit and flip through more magazines with photos of celebrities with their new babies, weddings, plastic surgery, bikini bodies. Then there are several shots of women who have disproportionately large rear ends. I close the magazine.

I sip the iced coffee and watch the intro to the show. The dated headshot from my website is shown, pictures of my illustrations roll by dissolving into photos of bloody knives, and a dog-eared folder opens to reveal crime scene paperwork, and then Austin's smiling face.

The remote is on the table, and I unmute the volume as a male voice-over says ominously, *In the sleepy outskirts of Houston, Texas, a man is stabbed to death...* There are photos of our street, the large houses, groomed yards, and children getting on school buses. The voiceover continues: *In this bucolic outcropping of a booming oil town, murder is a rarity, but Austin Green had a secret, a secret he would die for.*

The intro and the interview with Reeves haven't changed since I watched the show long ago. The questions the reporter asks Reeves are more like statements in disguise. Reeves sits at a table with an open file in front of him. As he is interviewed, he's nervous and hesitant answering each loaded question that insinuates a lack of professionalism by the police. But when the subject turns to my guilt, Reeves is transformed; with posture squared, facial expression predatory, suddenly he has all the answers.

At the advertising break, the same introduction runs. I dump my remaining coffee, rinse and toss the cup into the recycling bin. There's a half-ring stain where I'd put my cup on the magazine, and I wipe it guiltily. On TV Reeves is placing his mug on the documents, and I almost laugh, *Hope that's not coffee, Mr. Know-it-all.*

More footage has been added to the original show, including my art opening and arrest, and a police interview with Salem in jail after she was charged with conspiracy to commit murder. There's footage of Salem and Clayton's house with Clayton racking and aiming a shotgun at a fleeing reporter. Gunplay wasn't a strategy I'd considered for dealing with the media, but I can't help but grin. The bailiff interrupts the episode, calling me into court.

In the courtroom, the coroner's template with Austin's stab wounds is on the flat-screen monitor enlarged to the same size as my painting, which is on an easel next to the screen. How I matched the stab wounds is disturbing and mystifying.

The jury takes their seats. The judge arrives, and the next witness is called.

Leibovitz leans over and says, "It's Hudson, the medical examiner. In our county, he acts as coroner."

Hudson resembles a Wild Thing from the kids' book: barrel-shaped, bushy-around-the-edges, thin comb-over; goggle-eyed glasses that magnify; and a stained, very short tie, a clip-on that appears to have been borrowed from a child. Hudson has a small, dismissive constant smile, which gives the impression he's about to impart some gallows-humor.

Forrest introduces Hudson and asks him to describe his job. He says, "An autopsy seeks information in three key areas, what I call the three M's. There's the medical cause of death, what ended the person's life—disease, medical error, or violence. There's the mechanism, the weapon that caused the death—a gun, a knife, or poison. And the manner of death, namely suicide, homicide, or an accident. Most diseases and natural causes don't require an autopsy."

"Mr. Hudson, what was the medical cause of death in the case of Austin Green?" the DA asks.

"Mr. Green died from being stabbed multiple times, resulting in organ failure, blood loss, and shock." He goes on to discuss rigor mortis and liver mortis, heart, carotid, lung, and diaphragm punctures.

Forrest uses a pointer to indicate the similar stab wounds on the coroner's diagram and in my painting, and asks, "For someone to depict so many wounds accurately would they need to see the body?"

Hudson says, "It defies logic that someone could imagine puncture wounds that match the stab wounds on the body, especially so many. This type of depiction requires seeing them firsthand."

I watch Forrest's pointer linger on each wound, making his argument of how vicious the attack was. Hudson's diagram—the outline of a man's back and front, marked with his injuries—is familiar, but maybe that's because we see these diagrams all the time on TV crime shows. I tune out Forrest and concentrate on Hudson's diagram. There's a small smear on a knife-wound mark as if wet ink was disturbed.

With a self-assured bearing, Forrest thanks Hudson and goes back to his table. For a while, I was marginally ahead in this race, but now the jury has the blankly dazed expressions of dolls. Their wide-open, glassy eyes of hate and disappointment roam over the blood and vulnerability, violence, and despair in my painting. *I'm so fucked if Leibovitz can't pull this off.*

Leibovitz approaches the stand. "Mr. Hudson."

"That's what they call me." Hudson chuckles, eliciting smiles from the jury. Now he is a gruff-but-lovable grandpa. He pulls out a large handkerchief and wipes his forehead, then nods in acknowledgment.

Leibovitz continues. "Let me get this straight. You look for the medical, the mechanism, and manner of death."

"Yessir, I'm the M&Ms of murder." Hudson laughs, drawing a titter from the spectators.

Leibovitz: "You have explained what the medical cause of death is for Austin Green and that the manner of death is homicide, but you haven't told us what mechanism—what implement—his killer used to stab him."

Hudson says through his smirk, "The weapon has not been determined. However, I believe there were two weapons; a butcher knife and some type of fork implement such as a carving fork."

Leibovitz: "Is that a guess?"

Hudson wipes his face again. "In my line of work, I don't guess."

Leibovitz: "But you *did* guess that for Julia Green to have depicted the stab marks in the painting, she must have seen them on her husband's corpse, in person. Correct?"

I can't stop staring at the diagram and notice that aside

from the smudged ink, there is a small portion of brownish stain in the margin. The rest of the stain is cut off by the edge of the monitor's screen. Am I confusing this mark with the stain I made on the magazine, less than an hour ago? My thoughts turn to Reeves, and how he may have put a coffee ring on his papers.

Hudson says brusquely, "That's a deduction, not a guess. You know the difference, don't you?" A chubby hand shoots out to smooth his comb-over.

Leibovitz strides closer to the jury and turns back to Hudson. "As a matter of fact, I believe everyone present knows the difference." He pivots to address the courtroom. "Is there anyone here who wants the doctor to explain the difference between a guess and a deduction?" Hudson's condescension is exposed, and his crusty-yet-cute act has just slipped in popularity. Leibovitz continues, "Dr. Hudson, can you tell me where the murder took place?"

"That hasn't been determined as yet."

Leibovitz: "No *deductions*?"

"That's the detectives' job. I only do the bodies."

Leibovitz says, "Ah, so you and the detectives have separate jobs in the investigation. Surely, there must be someone who puts all the pieces together."

"The detectives put all their findings together with my report and try to solve the crime."

Leibovitz: "Since we're using Julia Green's paintings as a guide, enlighten me. The defendant's other paintings show Austin in a kitchen full of bats. Were there any dead bats or guano on Austin's body?"

"No. No bat guano."

I try to detach from my surroundings—the coffee-ring I made on the magazine—Reeves may have stained his documents. I coax the thought forward, closing my eyes, letting obstacles fall away, willing myself into a fugue-state, like hypnosis. Leibovitz's voice softens. Hudson's speech buzzes in the distance, far away.

I'm transported to my sofa in the old house. The place

is dim, and melancholy fills me as I watch television. The show about Austin's murder is on TV. Reeves is talking about the stab wounds, then the same montage of photos I'd seen at lunch dissolve into each other. I force myself to go deeper and disengage, making room for the concept to surface and solidify. I rewind the television and slow the images. After the photos, the dog-eared folder opens and reveals the coroner's diagram. It is brief, lasting perhaps a second, but it's there. The realization startles me so out of my trance, and I jump like I've been slapped.

My second-chair lawyer is staring at me in alarm. I lean over and whisper, "I just realized, I've seen the coroner's diagram on TV many, many times before I did the painting. It's at the start and finish of the show about Austin's murder, and in the advertisement that they run at nearly every commercial break."

Hudson is still on the stand, sounding flummoxed as he asserts, "Things aren't *that* compartmentalized. Conclusions can be drawn."

My second-chair lawyer asks, "Why didn't you tell us this before?"

"The show was playing on the lunchroom TV. I didn't figure it out until now."

He inhales, nearly a gasp. "Wow. What is the show called?"

"*Murder Mystery*, or something like that."

He takes out his phone. "*Murder Mysteries*. Got it." He streams the show, running fast-forward until the coroner's paperwork shows up. He watches a moment, and I say, "Pause at the diagram. See the stain in the margin that's almost cropped out, and the smeared ink on the stab wound? They're the same as the diagram on the monitor. They match."

He mouths the words, *holy crap.* I add, "I've watched that show at least thirty times, probably more. Whenever they do a rerun, they update it with news clips and interviews, and I taped every new version." He watches a while longer, smiles, and puts the phone away, then catches Leibovitz's eye. The young lawyer explains the situation to Leibovitz and leaves the courtroom. Leibovitz requests a short recess.

Twenty minutes later, we are back in court, with Hudson back on the stand. Leibovitz says, "Mr. Hudson, have you ever heard of subliminal seduction?"

"Of course. It's when visuals buried in film influence the audience's subconscious."

Leibovitz: "Do you believe subliminal seduction works?"

Hudson appears wary. He pauses, then gives in and says, "I'm no shrink, and subliminal seduction is controversial, but yes. I'm a believer."

Leibovitz: "Julia Green is a visual person. In her commercial artwork, she must be meticulous, getting every detail of a product correct. Do you think if Julia Green had seen your diagrams for only a few seconds, but hundreds of times, she could have known where Austin's stab wounds were on his body?"

"Ahhh…" Hudson wipes his face again. "Sorry, chief, I run hot." He smiles, stalling, and chuckles. No one joins his laughter, and he turns serious. "The problem with your theory is she couldn't have seen the diagrams. The paperwork on this case only went to the police and the district attorney's office, so she couldn't have seen the file."

"What would you say if I told you your diagrams are being shown repeatedly on the TV show *Murder Mysteries?*"

Forrest stands. "Objection. Where is this going?"

"Overruled. I'll allow it, but get to the point, counselor."

The coroner's smirk is gone. He says, "That's not possible."

Leibovitz says, "Judge, may I access the court's flat-screen?"

She nods, "Yes."

The stabbing diagram is reduced to show the full page, and Leibovitz points to the crescent-shaped coffee stain and asks the jury to take note. Then Leibovitz streams the show, and as the photos rotate in sequence, he runs through the intro in slow motion, then scrolls back and pauses at the diagram. Leibovitz turns to the jury. "Please watch this again." They lean forward in their seats as he repeats the exercise.

Leibovitz says to Hudson, "Sir, look at the screen, and tell me whether that is your diagram."

Hudson is a strange shade of reddish-mauve. I picture the headline: *Coroner Has Coronary!*

"Yes," he says. "That is my diagram, or I should say, a *copy* of my diagram."

"Were you aware it was shown at the beginning and closing of this show, at every commercial break, and in the advertisements for this episode?"

"Of course not!"

Co-counsel rushes in and hands a slip of paper to Leibovitz, who asks, "Mr. Hudson, how did your files of Austin's autopsy get on this show?"

"They aren't my files," Hudson splutters. "My files are locked up. They had to be copies leaked by the police or someone in the DA's office."

"This is from the producer of *Murder Mysteries*." Leibovitz holds up the note and reads, "In thirty days, before each airing of the episode, the promo ad aired a hundred and thirty-five times."

Forrest stood. "Objection! The defense is testifying."

"Overruled."

Hudson says, "I did not leak the file."

Leibovitz says heatedly, "If the defendant saw these ads and the TV show multiple times, would you say she could accurately place the wound pattern on her painting?"

Hudson wipes his face again. "I suppose…"

Chapter Thirty-Five

Forrest stands. “Judge, may we approach?” The judge nods, and all four lawyers crowd the bench. Leibovitz is talking, but I seem to catch only every second word; the DA offers a year’s probation, but Leibovitz heatedly demands an acquittal.

The DA capitulates but wants a mistrial. A mistrial would allow a new trial, but an acquittal engages double jeopardy. Leibovitz again demands an acquittal, guarding against an attempt by the prosecution to reopen the case.

The judge waves the attorneys away. She strikes her gavel, then says, “This trial is concluded. The defendant is acquitted. Thank you, jurors, for your service. You may go.”

We all stand, and after the judge leaves the bench, the jury files out. I turn and see Reeves, his complexion ashen as he lurches from the courtroom. Obviously, he had the paperwork for the television interview. But how did it get on the air? If I give him the benefit of the doubt, I could suppose he took a bathroom break, and a TV station employee or producer photocopied or scanned the diagram. Even so, at best, he was appallingly careless, and at worst, he orchestrated the document's leak.

The spectators leave. I'm free and liberated of the ankle monitor. In the hallway, I'm mobbed by friends and my kids, and behind all of them, I see the familiar form of a man I'd known as a kid; Jimmy, the friend of the boy who said I killed a small dog. With his ginger hair, chubby body, little eyes, and freckles, he's the same but bigger. He stands unmoving as we approach en masse, and I stop, facing him. "Why are you here, Jimmy? To crucify me?"

He says, "Sorry, but I was subpoenaed. I had t'come."

My group leads me past him. Outside, the press and paparazzi surround us with another group swarming the detectives and DA. A reporter asks Wilson, "Wasn't it you who said, 'She ought to be nervous as a cat at the dog pound?'"

A light rain sends the mob scattering. Trix and I get into her car and drive to Trix's loft to celebrate my freedom from ankle-monitor tyranny, the media, and the threat of lethal injection. I text the twins, and they arrive with wine, beer, and a giant bag of Doritos.

Trix says, "Hey, you guys haven't been here since you were rug rats."

Sarah stands before Trix's latest huge painting and exclaims, "Wow. This is awesome." Bryan joins her, equally mesmerized.

Trix says, "If only I could get the same look on my critics' faces." She turns on the local news. Jerky footage shot from a helicopter shows Salem and Clayton's cinder-block house. Squad cars and unmarked cruisers line the street. Their dog barks incessantly, throwing itself against the chain-link. A cop shouts and gesticulates, and Clayton hands his shotgun over. Animal Control pulls up as the police produce handcuffs.

Clayton reluctantly backs off and enters the dog run,

where he takes the animal by its collar and shuts it in a small outbuilding, allowing police techs to enter the yard and the garage. The point of view changes to ground level, showing techs emerging with paper bags. A conservatively dressed woman arrives and takes two children from the house.

A female news anchor stares solemnly into the camera and ad-libs a voice-over. "This is the scene earlier today at the home of Clayton and Salem Kingston when Child Protective Services came to remove their children. Salem Kingston is currently incarcerated on conspiracy-to-commit-murder charges. Police raided the property, ostensibly in search of the murder weapon used to kill Austin Green. The police tried to search the premises before, but their request for a warrant was turned down by a judge who decided there wasn't probable cause."

"Well, well," I say sadly, "it wasn't the cops stonewalling. It was a judge. No wonder they focused on me. I'm all they had."

Trix says, "Our fallible, messy justice system at work."

The reporter, Clark, appears, in front of a police cruiser. "Right, Sharon. The detectives say Clayton Kingston has an alibi, which justified their focus on the victim's wife, Julia Green. In any case, Sharon, Houston PD received an anonymous tip that the weapon used in the homicide would be found on this property. This follows hard on the heels of the acquittal today of the victim's wife."

"Thanks, Clark. That footage showed the husband, Clayton Kingston, in a very agitated state."

"Yes, Sharon. Things could have gotten violent today, with Clayton Kingston refusing to isolate his attack dog and threatening the police, but cooler heads prevailed. Sharon, here is Clayton Kingston now, in handcuffs, being taken into custody."

"Yes, Clark, we can see that."

Bryan says, "If they call each other by their names one more time, I'll scream."

"Imagine if everyone did that." Sarah imitates the

strident tone of the announcer. "Well, Bryan, screaming would be justifiable."

"I agree, Sarah."

"Are you hungry, Bryan?"

"Sarah, I do believe I am."

"I'll order Chinese, Bryan."

Sarah orders online, while on TV, the video shrinks and runs in the corner of the screen. The announcer reappears and says, "Let's go live to the police station where Clayton Kingston is being held. Raymond?"

Raymond stands before a bland low-rise building, and says, "Here comes the police chief for a briefing." He steps into a crowd of reporters and holds out his microphone. The video shifts to the chief, and the cameraman adjusts focus.

The chief states, "Thanks to a Crime Stoppers tip, we believe we have located the weapons used in the murder of Austin Green."

"We are confident forensics will verify that DNA collected from the weapons will incriminate either or both Salem and Clayton Kingston."

Raymond calls out, "Chief, are the weapons knives?"

The chief answers, "We're not divulging that at this time."

Raymond asks, "Your detectives said early on that Clayton Kingston has an alibi. Has that changed?" The chief ignores him, says thank you to everyone, and shuts down the press conference. Gage and Frankie arrive at the loft, followed by Chinese food delivery.

"This calls for champagne," Trix says and pulls a bottle of Veuve Clicquot from the fridge.

"Ah," I say, "the widow Clicquot's favorite and mine as well. Thanks, Trix."

She says, "Widows unite."

We toast my acquittal and Clayton and Salem's arrests. Trix says, "I wonder which of them did it."

On TV, the news anchor, Sharon, says, "We have breaking news from Raymond at police headquarters."

Raymond appears on split-screen and says solemnly, "Sharon, the Kingstons were questioned for hours regarding the murder weapons allegedly used to kill Austin Green. We have received word that Clayton Kingston has implicated his wife, Salem, in the murder."

Sharon continues, "Raymond, can you tell us how this came about?"

"Sharon, according to Clayton Kingston, he had nothing to do with Austin Green's murder. Clayton Kingston admits he stole Austin's guns, and there is speculation he may have moved Austin Green's body, but he maintains his innocence in the murder."

Frustrated, I say, "More of the same. First, Clayton says he *just* stole the guns, and now he *just* got rid of the body."

Bryan says disparagingly, "Clayton is *just* getting rid of his lyin', cheatin' wife. He can send her to jail forever, on his say-so."

The news anchor says, "Well, Raymond, this case has more twists than a bag of pretzels." Then she turns serious. "What do the police make of the husband having a much stronger motive to kill Austin Green than his wife?"

"He certainly has a strong motive, Sharon, but today his alibi is equally persuasive."

"Raymond, have the police finally released his alibi?"

"Yes, Sharon. At the time of Austin Green's murder, Clayton Kingston was unloading the guns he stole from the victim at a shooting range, and he has proof on security camera footage."

"That's certainly compelling, Raymond."

Sarah mimics, "That's certainly *convenient*, Raymond."

Sharon continues, "Let's take a look at the surveillance-camera evidence, Raymond." Grainy and jerky black-and-white footage shows a large man taking firearms from a van into a cinder-block building. The timestamp shows 2:40 a.m.

"That's half an hour after he left your subdivision," Trix declares. "And an hour before Austin was driven into the parking garage."

I pause the TV and squint at the screen. "The camera is up high and far away from him. I don't see anything that identifies the guy as Clayton."

Trix says, "It's about as definitive as the garage video where Wilson claimed the driver was Julia."

Gage laughs. "The license plate isn't visible, and his face is hidden by the bill of his cap. And if he has any identifying tattoos, they're covered by the shirt. You'd see a dozen guys like him at any biker bar."

I nod. "Evidently, Clayton is a world-class manipulator of cops. And why didn't we get to see this surveillance video before?"

Trix says, "Maybe they just got their hands on it, courtesy of Clayton."

The newscast cuts to a commercial for the skydiving lawyer. He free-falls, his canopy opening as he shouts, "I'm Otis Boudreaux, and if you hire me for your DUI, I'll guarantee a soft landing!"

Sarah chuckles, "That Boudreaux guy is Salem's lawyer."

Gage says, "Even a crap lawyer like Otis should be able to create reasonable doubt by pointing the finger at Clayton, and maybe get her off."

"I'm pretty sure that was Leibovitz's plan for my defense."

"She's still got the conspiracy-to-commit-murder charges," Trix says. "She won't get away with that."

Bryan stands and stretches, and Sarah follows suit. "We got a shindig to attend."

Trix pauses the TV while we say our goodbyes.

When Gage and I arrive at my house near midnight, the street is silent, and my place is without network vans. I no longer need to keep the shades drawn against prying reporters, and without the ankle monitor, the house isn't a cage, it's a refuge. Freedom, like water, air, love, goes unnoticed until it's lacking.

I tune my iPod to jazz. Then Gage pulls me in to straddle his lap. His hands go into my hair, and we close the distance to kiss. Every glance, touch, conversation, has been a long and graceful seduction. Gage's hands on the back of my neck and the small of my back, maneuver me to recline. We continue kissing, his breath, heat, scent, stubble, releasing a torrent of ecstasy. He opens buttons on my shirt and traces the lace edge of my bra with a fingertip, moving under the strap, slipping it from my shoulder as he trails the tip of his tongue along my collarbone, then onto my breast. I unbutton and remove his shirt and run my hands over his torso, smooth skin undulating over muscle and dipping into his spine, exploring shoulders and biceps, neck, and jaw.

Every movement is exquisitely rendered, a tender touch, a carefully choreographed dance. I can practically smell and taste romance as we kiss, and I take his cues of heat and sweat, our fingers entwined, my eyes on him, watching him become ever more aroused.

After, we are on our sides front to front, my nose against his chin, panting, smiling, until Beaver jumps onto my hip, loses his balance, and slips into the indentation of our waists, where he panics and scrambles to get out. I shriek at the sensation of fluff and claws as he struggles, and I grab him up and drop him on the floor. Laughing, we adjourn to the bedroom.

We resume our lovemaking and end up lying in muddled sheets until his breathing changes, signaling sleep, and I lie still, thinking, smiling.

The morning arrives with a serenity I'd forgotten existed. Gage leaves for meetings. A courier delivers my painting, my hard drive, and passport that Leibovitz retrieved from the police. The safe full of firearms is going to a dealer. I set up my computer on the dining table in the TV's sightline. The news isn't finished parsing Austin's murder, and the footage of Clayton is running again.

I hit the television's Record button and turn my attention to email. My inbox contains several thousand congratulatory emails, but it's short work to delete most of them and peruse the remainder. There is an illustration job for the furniture store. The ad is for brightly colored furniture with the tagline: "Stuck in Neutral?"

Not stuck anymore, I think. A note with the job reads, *Glad everything has worked out in your favor. We're behind you 100 percent.* I'm touched to realize my clients mean more to me, and I to them, than just business. A commercial job is so familiar and welcome, tears threaten.

My phone sounds, and I answer tentatively. An unfamiliar male voice says, "Hi, Julia, this's Jimmy Ward."

Surprised, I say, "Oh. Jimmy. Hi."

"Julia, I tole 'em, I don't know who killed the dog, but them lawyers din't care. They were lookin' to bring it up in the trial. Julia… I can't say you didn't do it, but I can't say you did, either. I woulda tole the truth."

"Okay, Jimmy. I wish you could have told them for sure I didn't do it, but…"

"Yeah. Well, sorry. Bye." He hangs up.

The TV's news anchor, Sharon and reporters Clark and Raymond, are reciting yesterday's stories. The case is stagnant, but with hours to fill, they are updating every few minutes between weather, a shooting on the west side, and traffic reports. I sip coffee and watch for a while, then turn my attention back to my computer.

There is an email from Lucy with congratulations on my acquittal and notifying me I'll see her soon for coffee. She has attached a photo of my former backyard with a pool party in full swing: kids in the pool, foam noodles littering the surface, men holding beer bottles and grilling meat, women wearing shorts or summer dresses.

Something is different. Lucy's message gossips about other neighbors who have moved away and the newcomers who now occupy their houses, how the flood and windstorm insurance has increased, updates about her kids and Earl.

Then she writes, *Guess we're lucky! The new people, the Andersons, who bought your place, are great neighbors. They love the house and the yard, and they've kept everything the same except for your greenhouse. Their kid put a baseball through the glass TWICE!!! So they tore it down.*

The greenhouse. Lucy's mention reminds me I have more photos of my former garden in its glory; photos I'd taken just before Austin died. Where are those pictures? Trix brought the camera card back when I was under house arrest, but I never downloaded them. I get the card from the box of odds and ends on my desk, plug it into my hard drive, and watch TV as the images download.

On television, old footage of Salem's embarrassing tumble is rerun. Muted, it's like a metaphor for her fall from grace from her former life and freedom. Now she's incarcerated in the Harris County Jail, but soon, if found guilty of Austin's murder, or the conspiracy-to-commit-murder charges, she'll be sent to the high-security jail for women, the Mountain View Unit. I Google it, and see no mountains to view, and judging by the photos of featureless buildings, razor-wire-topped fences, and barren surroundings; it might have been named by the same guy who called a hunk of ice-covered dirt, Greenland.

I turn back to the computer's monitor filled with rows of thumbnail photos, close-ups of flowers alongside distant shots of the gardens. Clicking the slideshow button fills the monitor with the first high-resolution picture. It pauses several seconds, then dissolves into the next. One by one, there are garden-magazine-worthy pictures of Louisiana iris, clematis, plumbago, canna lilies.

Something new on TV catches my eye. I unmute the sound. The news anchor says, "The Kingstons hid the weapons by burying them in the dog pen." They show footage of the sturdy animal throwing itself against the chain-link. Sharon says, "Clark, that's a good hiding spot."

"I wouldn't want to go in there, Sharon."

A photo of the sparkling clean greenhouse fills my computer monitor, then fades, and the next shot emerges. There is a reflection in the greenhouse-glass of the garden and my image holding my camera

Chapter Thirty-Six

On TV, Sharon catches my full attention as she says, "The police have released a photo of the *actual* murder weapons." The screen shows a photo of a gardener's hand-fork next to a rusty butcher knife.

Clark says, "This just in, Sharon. The police have reported their forensics team found traces of blood on both the knife and the garden fork; blood they believe will match Austin Green's DNA."

I inhale sharply. I know those garden implements. I pause the television. Then, practically hyperventilating, I click through the photos on my computer until I find a photo showing the greenhouse interior. My gardening tools are lined up on the worn wooden countertop of the repurposed kitchen cabinets. Among them is my hand-fork with its blue-painted wooden handle and three flat-metal tines. There's also the butcher knife I used for all manner of miscellaneous chores—weeding, slicing garden cloth, and opening bags of soil. Those two implements, if used in concert, match the stab wounds the coroner transcribed from Austin's body.

I zoom in. My tools match what is on TV: a nick in the butcher knife's blade and a crack in its handle, blue paint chipped and worn in places on the fork's handle.

Tears scald my eyes, and I'm shaking. Austin was killed with my gardening tools. I've used those tools and handled them hundreds of times. The garage and greenhouse had been emptied soon after Austin disappeared, when I'd spent the night at Trix's. Salem hadn't found his body yet. This doesn't make sense.

The most straightforward explanation for the weapons being at Clayton's house is that he killed Austin with my tools. If Clayton and Salem murdered Austin, maybe they were in a rush or killing him was unintentional and disorganized. It makes sense that if they accidentally left the weapons behind, they came back for them, using the theft of the contents of the garage and greenhouse as a cover.

Where did they kill him? Why keep the weapons? Something bilious is creeping into my mind, an acidic blob, a realization, but it's stuck, and I need a mental Heimlich maneuver.

I close my eyes and visualize them as weapons in my hands, and try to make them fit a slice of my dream, of me plunging them into Austin's gut under a ceiling full of deafening squeaking bats. The scenario doesn't bring back any memories. Besides, if I killed him, there had to be at least one other person involved.

Something isn't adding up. I go back to the living room and watch the gatehouse surveillance from the night Austin vanished, to determine when his car left the subdivision. I start at three in the afternoon and speed up the video. The twins drive out at three-thirty, earlier than usual to go bowling before attending the concert. Austin's SUV arrives at four. Neighbors come home after work and are waved through, and visitors get quizzed. The rush hour ends, and people leave the subdivision for an evening out. Then there is a long lull with only an occasional car.

At nine o'clock, the night guard gets into a small car parked behind the gatehouse and goes on his break. Five minutes later Clayton drives through the open gate, coming to visit Austin. The guard returns soon after, carrying a sack from Whataburger.

Only two cars in the next hour, then residents arrive home and those visiting the subdivision exit. After the flurry of activity, it's dead until teenagers start coming back near midnight, a popular curfew.

At 2:10 a.m., Clayton stops on his way out, opens the rear doors of the van for the guard, chats, and leaves. The rest of the night is quiet until close to five when the early birds leave to get a jump on rush hour, and as the sun rises, residents leave for work. I stop the video at 10:21 a.m. Supposedly Austin's SUV didn't leave all night, but Austin's car was gone in the morning. How did he leave? Something else is wrong with the tape, but I don't know what, and I pause it.

The photo of the greenhouse again fills the monitor. Staring at the photo that shows the interior of the greenhouse. The day I took the picture was a day of spreading mulch and cleaning. With my extendable pole and mop, I'd cleaned the greenhouse glass of dirt and bat guano from the colony hanging above. Then I'd showered outdoors.

The bats. The dream took place in the kitchen—or did it? Could it have been in the greenhouse? And in the nightmare, knives are in my hands, but they could have easily been other weapons. The dream was so vivid that I'd accepted the specifics very literally, but what if I was wrong about the location? I had stuck to details of my dream the way the detectives had clung to their supposition about my painting. But dreams are open to interpretation.

I open a photo of the large painting that was shot by the gallery photographer. The image features kitchen cabinets and counters, which could be our kitchen, but they could also be the old cabinets I installed in the greenhouse. My fingers stray to my lips, and I go dizzy. I've been holding my breath, inhale deeply, and became dizzy again.

If. If. If… If I killed Austin. How was his six-foot-two, two-hundred-twenty-pound body moved? How did the blood get cleaned up? That was my alibi all along. *I couldn't have done it because…*

And then, with absolute certainty, I know what happened. I was sleepwalking, and I killed Austin.

My ten-years-dead mother was in the dream, saying she would clean up. But it was Sarah. The same words and voice as when she said she'd clean up my spilled wine. Trix said I often overlook the obvious, and here was more proof, because I've never noticed Sarah had my mom's voice.

Bryan said they'd gone to the concert and stayed with a friend in Magnolia overnight. Right. As if Bryan never lies. A memory surfaces, of faint conversation in the house after the killing-dream, when I woke in the small hours.

Another piece of the dream presents itself. The fat clown tried to leave, but a stranger pulled a gun and forced him to return. Austin didn't keep all his firearms in the safe. Some were hidden in the house. Bryan knew where they were, and for all I know, Bryan has a loaded pistol in his car. The clown was Clayton, and he was in the process of loading the gun safe, full of weapons, into his van when he found me standing over murdered Austin. The gun toting stranger in the dream was Bryan. And my mother's voice was Sarah.

The problem with the gatehouse video isn't only that Austin's car—with his body inside—is never shown leaving. If my theory of what happened is correct, the kids came home and then exited again. But after their midafternoon exit, the twins' vehicles neither enter nor leave. It's crazy.

Leibovitz noticed the absence of Austin's car but not the kids' cars, which fit, because they claimed they were out all night. And the detectives never noticed anything out of the ordinary, which is human nature. When one watches for something to happen, we don't notice what didn't happen.

I killed him. The formless sickness in my mind has

slipped to my throat. Gagging, dazed, and faint, I sit so I won't fall. The light-headedness and revulsion pass, but the queasiness lingers.

That night, Austin and Clayton seemed friendly. But at trial Bryan said Clayton had already seen their porn on the Porn Dog website, and knew Salem was cheating. I thought Bryan was lying, but now I believe he was truthful.

Meanwhile, the cops believed Clayton when he said he had an alibi. Maybe I only heard a small part of Clayton and Austin's conversation, and I hadn't heard Clayton making threats. I sensed Clayton's anger and had one of my crazy little fantasies of hiding in the storage closet while Clayton shot up the house and killed Austin. Then he'd seemed to leave, but he hadn't, not really, because I'd seen him parked down the street.

Why did Clayton visit Austin that night? To see if Austin would shine him on, and to study Austin's behavior? Yes. He was in Austin's office, getting angrier and angrier with the two-faced, smug bastard who feigned friendship while diddling his wife. He left but sat in his van, fuming, planning what to do next.

The night of the killing dream, in bed, contemplating all the physical and emotional wounds Austin had inflicted, I was in an overwhelming rage. Austin had snuck to the bedroom door to murder me and make it look like a suicide, but he was thwarted by the doorstop. Then I dreamt I was in the kitchen, but in fact, I went to the greenhouse a short distance away, where Austin found me with the garden fork and the butcher knife in my hands. He showed me he had my gun tucked in his waistband.

I told him I knew he tried to kill me, and when he attempted to get his weapon, I cut his arm. He said shooting me would be self-defense. Did I feel threatened? Would he have shot me? I don't know for sure, but stabbing him at that moment could logically be viewed as self-defense.

Then Clayton, murderously angry, came back to the house, maybe to beat up Austin, or kill him and steal his guns. He backed his van into the driveway out of sight of the street and loaded the safe, which was full of firearms, into his vehicle. Presumably he didn't have the combination and was planning to deal with opening it, later. Then maybe he heard me moving around or caught a glimpse of me in the greenhouse, came to investigate, and found Austin, dead.

Clayton is featured in my dream as a fat clown, a fool. How fitting. When he saw Austin's body, he wanted to get the hell out of there and tried to escape, but the twins arrived and caught him fleeing. The kids blocked his vehicle in the driveway. Bryan held him at gunpoint, and probably threatened to call the cops to have him arrested for the theft *and* the murder. Clayton, having opportunity, motive, and means, knew he'd be blamed. It would be his word against the twins, who would say they caught him in the act.

But after Bryan forced him back to the scene, what was Clayton's part? Something is off. In the gatehouse video, the guns are loose in the back of Clayton's van next to the safe. Bryan knew the combination and he must have opened the safe for Clayton. But then in Clayton's alibi video, he is shown wheeling the safe, presumably full of Austin's firearms, since there were no loose guns being carried out of his van. Why? When he took the guns from Austin's office, why didn't he simply keep the weapons in the safe?

Because, of course, Austin's body was in the safe. Clayton is telling the truth. He didn't kill Austin because I did. He *just* stole the guns and *just* moved the body. Maybe he convinced the detectives because he passed multiple polygraphs, as I had.

The futility of the scene, everything too far gone, Austin was already dead. There was nothing left to do but damage control. The kids wanted to protect me, but they must have been panicked, tortured by guilt, bereaved. Austin was their dad, after all, killed by their mother. And they may have felt culpable, since taking hush money from Austin prolonged the affair, which in turn inflamed emotions, setting the stage for murder.

They may have been unaware of what they set in motion, because like a lot of offspring their age, the twins were wrapped up in their own little world. Young adults see their parents through a lens; a lens that blurs or eliminates aspects of our lives; our sex life, our relationship difficulties, our vulnerability. In this case, our troubles and the twins' youthful insensitivity, allowed them to extract the cash and creature comforts they desired.

Once Clayton was implicated, he had to help. He and the twins placed Austin's body in the safe to get him past the gatekeeper and loaded the safe into Clayton's van. They piled the guns on the van's floor. Taking Austin's corpse out of the neighborhood in the trunk or backseat of a car would have been risky, even late at night. They could have been stopped for a minor infraction, such as the classic burned-out taillight. In the wee hours, cops take notice of random drivers and pull them over *just because*.

Clayton drove his van out of the subdivision. Then Sarah drove Austin's SUV, and Bryan drove his car because they needed one of their vehicles to return after dropping off Austin in his SUV at the Westin. It's strange that their vehicles aren't on the gate's video leaving or returning.

They met Clayton at the cinder-block building. Then, out of range of the security camera, they removed Austin's body from the safe and loaded him into his car to take him to the Westin's parking garage. I assume Clayton bleached and power-washed his van and the gun safe inside and out to get rid of DNA. But again, how did the kids get out of the subdivision and return without being caught on camera? If they'd all been on the tape, the detectives would have quickly put two and two together. Could Bryan and Sarah have hacked the camera? I laugh. Of course they could, and they did.

To check my theory, I Google *Can surveillance cameras be hacked?* The answer is yes. The twins accessed the camera's system and paused the camera every time one of their cars drove through. I rerun the video, this time watching only the timestamp. Watching the numbers scroll, advancing through the night, is hypnotic. I run the video much faster than normal time and force my eyes not to glaze over.

Soon after Clayton left the gatehouse, the guard took another break, and during his time away, there are two forty-second jumps in the time. One time-gap would have been for Austin's SUV and the other for Bryan's car. Then they went to meet Clayton, took Austin's body from the gun safe and put him in his vehicle, and Sarah delivered Austin's SUV to the Westin Hotel's parking garage. She wore the oversized men's clothing to be unrecognizable, and to be sure no tattoos would peek out of a sleeve or neckline. Bryan must have parked nearby and picked up Sarah when she left.

Three hours later, after they have unloaded the firearms and driven Austin to the parking garage, there is another jump in the time. Bryan and Sarah came back home. Why? To get their other car, but no doubt also because of the blood.

Leibovitz pointed out the voluminous blood spatter in my painting and challenged the prosecution to find the corresponding blood in my kitchen. But the blood wasn't in the kitchen, it was in the greenhouse, where cleanup was simple with a jug of bleach and a hose to clean the glass, the cabinets, and flood the dirt floor, then sprinkle around the highly-scented cedar mulch to disguise the blood-stink of iron and death.

When the police techs came to the house, they hadn't set foot in the greenhouse, the cabana, or the outdoor shower. They also hadn't brought in cadaver-sniffing dogs, no doubt because Austin had already been found, so they weren't searching for a body, but a dog would have surely alerted to the smell in the greenhouse. Instead, they'd done a quick, cursory search of the garage but concentrated on the interior of the house, including testing the kitchen sink, the bathrooms and master-bathroom drains and p-traps for blood residue.

Sarah directed me into the shower, sounding exactly

like my mother. In my dream, I showered in the master bathroom, but if the murder took place in the greenhouse, the logical place to clean up was the outdoor shower.

Just before I moved, when I used the shower, the faucet was dripping, and the stall smelled strongly of pool-chlorine, which I would never use as a cleaner. However, Sarah needed to clean up the blood in the shower fast, and undoubtedly as far as she was concerned, the chlorine was handy and did the job, and she was unaware the faucet dripped and needed to be turned off tightly.

The next day, my bloody white-lace outfit was gone, probably tossed by the twins into a dumpster or burned at a friend's place, wherever they'd ended up after that awful night.

Wilson was correct about the bloody footprints. Sarah cleaned the shower stall and the kitchen's travertine tile, where I tracked in Austin's blood, but she couldn't completely eliminate the bloodstains from the porous stone tiles. I'm not sure why the police didn't determine the blood was Austin's. Maybe they simply couldn't get a decent sample, or the evidence wasn't strong enough to use. After all, Austin lived there. A few small traces of blood can be explained away; a paper cut, a broken glass, a nick while chopping vegetables. The same logic will extend to the murder weapons. My DNA will be on them, but since they were my implements that Clayton took from my house, my DNA won't count.

The cops got a tip that the weapons were at Clayton's house. From whom? When Clayton was arrested, he pinned the murder on Salem to save himself. Strange that Clayton kept the murder weapons at his home in the first place, although burying them in the dog run of a fierce pit bull is pretty cunning. Maybe he intended to burn or dispose of them, maybe toss them into a bayou, but being under scrutiny by the media and police, he procrastinated. Or he simply messed up. As always, God is in the details.

Finally, the time scroll shows a two-minute jump. That

pause has to be the twins leaving, going to their friends' place in both of their vehicles, to cook up their alibi. The guard is absent before and after the time gap. Bryan was thorough, hacking and removing their comings and goings from the footage but also timing the gaps, so the guard was away on break. No witnesses.

Then Salem found Austin's body. I wonder why the hotel staff didn't locate his corpse, but in the nine-level garage, they undoubtedly have plenty of long-term guests, and a car sitting for days might not be any reason for concern.

I'm sure Salem is innocent of the murder because of her reaction when I answered Austin's phone. However, with the affair, her refusal to back off, her various plots to murder me, she set the chain of events in motion. The twins and Clayton could have put in an anonymous call to the hotel or Crime Stoppers, but they opted to let Salem find his body, which by then, in Houston's August heat, had to be stinking to high heaven. Even so, I have no empathy or pity for her.

Maybe the twins thought if Salem found Austin's corpse, she would come to the attention of law enforcement, while Clayton's strategy was revenge. Bryan knew from their emails they were to meet in the Westin Hotel's parking garage, so that's where they left him. Salem should have found him the day after he was killed, but she was delayed.

Then, as time passed, someone, probably Sarah, realized that soon I would notice my gardening fork and the knife were missing. Fortunately, after Austin left, I'd been swamped with work and hadn't done any gardening, because when Austin was finally found, I could have mentioned the tools' absence to the detectives. And if I had, the police would have put two and two together based on his wounds. As a cover, the twins and Clayton must have staged the robbery of the tools and junk in the garage and greenhouse, and bet correctly, that I wouldn't call the police.

It must have been torture for the twins to wait for Salem to discover his body. Sarah had cried after I sleepwalked and killed the snake. She had said something like, *No, Mom. Remember? Dad's gone,* and Bryan ordered her into the house, which was out of character for him. Sarah is the boss of the two. Then he told me she was crying because some guy had dumped her, but now I believe she was emotional about everything that had happened and frustrated with Salem not finding the body. Plus, seeing me once again kill something in my sleep must have been very upsetting.

After all that, Clayton and the twins simply kept quiet and let me beat the rap in my unique way, by believing strongly enough in my innocence. After all, I passed two polygraphs. I have to applaud my kids—despite their character flaws they have nerves of steel, never once breaking their silence to confess to me. Naturally, I regret this new burden imposed on them, which will tie them to each other for life, although they have been linked since birth, and always will be.

What is the right thing to do? Incriminate me, Clayton, my children? Keep quiet and allow Salem to take a dive, as her skydiving lawyer's billboards warn against? I can't be tried for Austin's murder because I've been acquitted, but Clayton and my kids could go to prison.

And with that reality resonating, I will do nothing. The incriminating details will never be spoken of, ever. To anyone.

Several weeks pass before the TV news breathlessly announces Salem's plea agreement of ten years in prison plus five years parole for plotting my murder. Her trial for Austin's murder is imminent. I suspect with only Clayton's word against Salem's, her lawyer will create enough reasonable doubt for a mistrial, a hung jury, or a reduced charge; certainly, no death penalty.

Clayton got parole for moving Austin's body. And sometimes I wonder how strong Salem and Clayton's bond is, and whether he'll take her back when she gets out, and whether she'll want him. Does that make me an incurable romantic? Maybe.

Chapter Thirty-Seven

My life isn't wrapped up all neat and tidy with a bow, like a Hollywood happy ending with swelling and crashing strains of music, but there are many positives. As for painting, I'm supposed to start a new series, but I don't yet have subject matter or a title.

When I complained to Trix about being blocked, she said, "Artists don't die. When we lose our angst, we fade away like watercolors in the sun." Her statement brought another revelation— I have genuinely lost my angst—I'm happy.

The gallery currently has a sold-out show of Trix's large floral paintings, plus she has enough commissions to keep her busy for the next year. One of her commissions was for a wealthy widowed oilman who she is dating exclusively. She confided he proposed marriage, but she turned him down. Trix said she likes falling in love but has a hard time sustaining a relationship. Time will tell.

A small notice in the news reported that Reeves is on

unpaid leave for his clumsy leak of the coroner's drawing. He is also accused of other leaks to the media, and of having sex with several suspects and many witnesses, although not Trix, because she never turned him in, and sees herself as the instigator.

Following Trix's show is a retrospective of my illustration work. Funny how things can come full circle. Painting is an important, personal side of my working life. I consider myself fortunate. My commercial work gave me the time to find myself and hone my message and, dare I say, my talent before I laid my heart on the canvas for all to see. There will be more paintings when I have something for those *thousand words* to express.

Austin. If we had downsized and moved into the city, he would have had the same itchy discontent I had in the burbs. We were incompatible. Do I regret the years I spent in our union? No. I loved him for a long time, cared for him, was invested in him, but there is no love any longer, and perhaps the love we had was never completely real or realized. I hadn't accessed the deepest parts of Austin's inner self if there was an inner self of his to discover, and he didn't access mine. All of our former life, the time spent birthing and raising children, of marriage, and of finding a narrow way to accomplish our goals, is over, and I have evolved and changed for the better.

I saw Marcy and her baby girl, Jeeves, the other day at Whole Foods. The baby is her doppelganger and nearly as bubbly and loud.

Frankie was recently catering a wedding for two men when one of them called it off at the last moment. Frankie and the jilted groom have been an item ever since, and there is talk of their own wedding.

Then there is Gage. We are on the verge of forming something profound: an attachment rooted in our history. I have a warm regard for the man, his intelligence, and his life that came before and what will come later.

And I am pleased to report on my dreams. I haven't

sleepwalked lately, but I still have dreams. Dreams, not nightmares, in my sleep and for my life, of good work, good relationships, and a good life.

And these days, my heart often takes flight with a purity of delight, airy happiness, maybe even glee, and finally…

Finally, I don't need to examine my love, question my trust, or try to will, tame, or cage anything—not the knives, or the hurt, not my scars, or my happiness. My only secret of pain and homicide is untouched by guilt or shame. Instead, I embrace my life, my work, my children and friends, my love, and my one and only, *now*.

CPSIA information can be obtained
at www.ICGtesting.com
Printed in the USA
LVHW041518290920
667401LV00001B/202